PRAISE FOR CAROLYN MILLER

"Carolyn Miller's ability to pull you into a story is outstanding! ...a brilliant story of romance, exhilarating sporting excitement and devastating disappointment of hurdles to be overcome... I never thought I would give 5 stars to a book about ice hockey and speed skating!" ~ *KAYE'S REVIEWS & NEWS*

"*Love on Ice* by Carolyn Miller is the second book in the Original Six Hockey series, and a fantastic page turner!" ~ *BECKY'S BOOKSHELVES*

"Adrenaline, chemistry, romance, and lots of wooing!...You do not have to be a fan of sports or even knowledgeable in hockey and short track to appreciate the love story." ~ *GOODREADS review*

"Carolyn Miller scores another win with *Love on Ice*, the second book in her Original Six Hockey series. I absolutely loved the faith thread in this story. It's message that success does not lie on what we do, but who we are is powerful." ~ *GOODREADS review*

"Sporty? Tick. Faith-filled? Double tick. Romantic? Triple Tick. Take it from me - *The Breakup Project* has all the feels and then some!" ~ *ANDREA GRIGG, author of All Is Bright*

"*The Breakup Project* is a fun, charming, and faith-filled contemporary romance with adorable characters set in the competitive North American ice hockey world. Highly recommended." ~ *NARELLE ATKINS, Author of Solo Tu & Her Tycoon Hero*

LOVE ON ICE

CAROLYN MILLER

CHAPTER 1

Toronto, Canada
June

Not bad for a sports-and-science-focused tomboy, Holly Travers thought, eyeing the intricate paper rose she'd just fashioned, her lips lifted in satisfaction.

"That's beautiful!" Bree Karlsson peered closer, her long dark hair gleaming as the sun poured through the lounge window. "I swear, Holly Travers, you're full of hidden talents. How did you learn to do origami?"

"I saw it at a banquet earlier this year in Japan. It was good to focus on something other than this." Holly pointed to the pale scar on her upper arm that her T-shirt couldn't hide. Her stomach tensed. Ten stitches in a Tokyo hospital hadn't been fun. But it could've been worse. Thank God the other skater had shifted in time, otherwise Holly's face would be wearing a permanent reminder of the debacle that was Japan.

Her best friend shuddered. "I'll never understand why you do short track. It's so dangerous."

"What can I say? I have a need for speed." And she *loved* the sport. Mostly. "Now, do you want me to teach you how to fold the roses into place cards? I thought they'd be great for the tables at the reception. But it gets a little tricky, so you must be patient..."

Bree's laughter was as joyous as her vivacious personality. "It's so funny to hear you, the speed queen, go on about patience."

Holly grinned. Bree's perpetual bubbly smile was even bigger now that the family was counting down to Bree's wedding in seven days. "I brought some beautiful paper with me. I'll go get it."

Holly raced up the stairs to the guestroom of the Karlsson's family home. The room was painted white with apricot accents now, but the old oak tree in the backyard still spread welcoming arms. She smoothed her boring light-brown hair into its usual high ponytail, then retrieved the expensive mauve-flecked handmade paper from her suitcase. A car door slammed outside.

As she made her way down the hall, she studied the pictures on the walls. Cute baby photos, vacations, high school and college graduations, hockey photos. The only constants were the glossy dark hair and blue-gray eyes the Karlsson family shared. She smiled. Her time here in Toronto as an exchange student seven years ago had been the best year of her life.

As Holly headed down the stairs, she caught the vague murmur of voices. She paused at the sound of Bree's voice coming from the kitchen. "But Holly—"

"Holly?" There was a snort. "Bree, I'm over you and Mom trying to fix me up with one of your good little girl friends. I get enough offers as it is. Drop it, okay?"

Holly stilled. Little? So she wasn't a giant like the rest of the

Karlsson clan. And anyway, what was so bad about being good? So she didn't have a past you'd ever read about in *People* magazine. Where were the guys who could appreciate that? Not that she was here to find a man.

She bit her lip, uncertainty keeping her rooted to the step. Arrogance always made her prickly and defensive. Should she go in guns blazing or smile and just pretend she hadn't heard? Eavesdroppers never heard good about themselves, did they? She closed her eyes for a few seconds and drew in a deep breath. One of Coach Chan's mottos floated into memory: *Put on brave face; don't let fear win.*

She lifted her chin and headed into the sunny modern kitchen, pasting on a smile as three faces swung her way. "Hi!" Aim for bright and perky. "Mike, how are you?" She stepped forward to give Bree's burly hockey-playing fiancé a quick hug.

"Holly. Good to see you again." He eyed her with good humor. "Bree was telling us you got off the plane this morning and went straight into bridesmaid mode. The wonder from Down Under, eh?"

"Ha. Not that wonderful. But it's nice to know I've got some long-distance fans."

Her smile faded as she turned to the other man. Brent. Breanna Karlsson's twin. Bree's emailed photos of her family hadn't done him justice. Muscled, probably a foot taller than Holly, dark hair and blue eyes holding hints of gray and green—he'd grown even better looking than the guy she recalled from her time here on exchange. Back then, he'd lived away, playing junior hockey in Sault Ste. Marie. But on his few visits home, he'd made an impression.

Holly's hand strayed to the tiny scar on her forehead. Brent had made an impression, all right. His skating lessons—reluctantly given—might've left her with this scar, but they'd ultimately set the direction for her life. And his popularity with girls had further strengthened her resolve to never, *ever* throw herself at a guy or settle for cheering from the sidelines. Nope. She'd much rather be the one who actually did something worth cheering about, and between her skating and her university studies, she was going to do it. According to Bree's emails over the years, many girls continued to be charmed by that physique and those unusual eyes. Not that looks mattered if his attitude stank. "Hello, Brent."

He swallowed. Hopefully it was some pride. "Hey, Holly. How's it going?"

She pasted on a big smile. "Great!" Okay, maybe tone down the perkiness a tad. "Congratulations on your Cup win."

"Thanks." He still eyed her warily.

"How are you?"

He shrugged. "Can't complain."

Holly snickered. No, with his recent NHL championship win and multi-million dollar contract with Detroit, she bet he had little to complain about.

He stared at her blankly. "What?"

Holly gave her sweetest smile. "I imagine the only thing you have to complain about is all the girls throwing themselves at you."

He blinked. Bull's-eye. What was it with women and pro athletes? Her stomach twisted. Girls could be so stupid. She shook her head as she carefully placed the package of special Ogura lace paper down on the marble counter top. "But you don't need to worry about me. You're not my type."

The room filled with Mike's laughter. "So, what is your type, Holly?"

Not arrogant, for starters. Brent might share the same genetic pool as Bree, but he seemed the polar opposite of Holly's warm-hearted, generous friend. Brent leaned back against the marble counter, watching them, eyes narrowed, arms folded across his broad chest.

"I like guys who are short, blond, and plump, who aren't

obsessed by sport and can show their feelings." She smiled, thinking of the little boys at church, their chubby arms that wrapped tightly around her whenever she was in town and able to help lead their Sunday school class. Yep, they definitely knew how to help her feel the love.

Bree chuckled. They'd emailed about Holly's "guys" before. "Now, before we start on the place cards, are you hungry? Mom said to make yourself at home, eat whatever. She was so sorry not to be here for your arrival. She had to take Grandma Violet to a doctor's appointment."

"No worries." Holly watched Bree hunt through a cupboard. "I hope everything's okay?"

"Granny V wants her blood pressure checked. She's a little excited about next weekend." Bree produced a container. "Ta da! Muffins. Mom said she tried to make them healthy for you."

Holly sighed, even as her saliva glands kicked into overdrive. "Your mum's such a good cook. But I need to be careful while I'm here. I can't afford to put on any weight."

Brent snorted as she grabbed an apple. "You one of these girls who's always on a diet?"

Bree laughed again, tossing her hair over a shoulder. "Just look at her, Brent. She's the only one of us who didn't need to diet before the wedding."

Holly stifled the sigh. She sometimes wished she weren't so lightly framed and had Bree's more voluptuous curves. It might help her feel more feminine. She'd never been a girly girl, too busy trying to keep up with her sporty brother and his mates, trailing after them on the bike or running, getting pretty good at the disciplines even before training started demanding it of her.

Oh well. Wishing never changed anything.

She eyed Brent. "I've a week off on the proviso I eat well, train, and visit the gym as much as possible. Competition season starts again soon, and my coach wants me ready."

His eyebrows shot up. "Your coach?"

Mike wrapped an arm around Bree. "Come on, man. Even I know she's the best short track skater in Australia." His blue eyes twinkled. "And going to compete at the Games in a couple of years."

Holly forced a smile. Crashing out in Japan had raised serious doubts about whether she should even be part of the skating program, let alone dream of competing in Vancouver. And yet this passion to prove herself burned inside and wouldn't be denied.

Brent shrugged. "Oh. I forgot what you do."

His indifference felt like a slap. Obviously she didn't rate too highly on Brent's radar. She bit into her apple, wiped juice from her chin.

"Maybe Brent can take you to the gym. He's always training and watching what he eats." Bree's smile widened. "He's like you, even if he's not exactly your *type*."

Holly slid a look at Brent, who seemed unimpressed. No way was she going to force her company on him. She shrugged. "It's fine. I'm sure I can walk or bike there."

Mike's lips twitched. "He's gonna need a new training partner now that I'm too busy."

Bree turned to her twin, her purple-hued eyes wide. "You don't mind, do you, Brent?"

The siblings engaged in a stare-off before Brent sighed, shook his head, and finally turned to Holly. "I like to go pretty early in the morning. Six thirty okay?"

She smothered the smile. Six thirty was an hour later than her usual training started. "That'll be fine. Thank you." She threw the apple core in the bin and carefully wiped her fingers, then turned to her best friend. "So, Bree, are you ready to start on those place cards now?"

. . .

HOLLY GLANCED up from her muesli at the kitchen's new arrival. "Good morning."

Brent nodded, grabbed a bowl, poured in cereal and milk, and started eating silently.

O-kay. Obviously not a morning person. She refocused on her breakfast. Last night Brent had looked at her askance more than once as she happily answered questions from Bree's parents about her recent travels. Perhaps God's gift to women thought she was here to find a man—namely him. Her lips curled up on one side. As if he'd ever meet her boyfriend criteria.

Top of the list was someone whose actions and attitudes demonstrated his love for God. Second was someone who could cope with the demands her sport placed on her, like no time for a social life and constant jetting off for competitions around the planet. Hello? What guy could cope with that? Those two qualifiers always filtered out any prospective candidates. Handsome had certainly never needed to be factored in. Not that she could afford to be interested, even if Mr. Right should miraculously appear. Coach Chan said it best: *Firsts need focus, not distraction.*

Brent grabbed two bananas and nodded to the door. "Ready?"

Holly quickly scooped up the last mouthful. "Yep." After rinsing her bowl, she grabbed her gym bag and followed him to the Jeep outside. A few fat raindrops splattered against the windshield as they drove through Toronto's busy suburban streets.

As they waited for the red light to change, she tried out a tentative smile. He was Bree's brother, after all. "So, Bree mentioned you bought a house in Detroit last year."

"Yeah." His face grew animated for the first time that morning. "After staying in hotels and rooming with others for so long, it's great to have my own space."

"It would be." She nodded. "People think the travel for

competitions is glamorous, but staying in crowded dorms and long bus rides with all that gear isn't always easy."

"I had some of that growing up." He flicked a look at her. "It's easier now, of course."

Oh. Right. Of course. Mr. Millionaire, who flew with his team on private planes, stayed in five-star hotels, and had bought his first house at the ripe old age of twenty-five. Holly glanced out the window and sighed inwardly. She'd always had to trust God with finances. There wasn't much money to be made in short track, or much financial support, especially in Australia. Most skaters had to have a full-time job to help supplement the basic scholarship from the Australian Institute of Sport. She'd always had to work hard, save harder, and budget well to make ends meet.

Enough of the pity party. "So, how will you cope with being on your own? Will you get lonely?" Her cheeks heated. For goodness' sake—she sounded like a desperate groupie! "I mean, when you live by yourself, that'll be different..." She glanced over, noticing a twitch in his jaw as he pulled sharply into the gym parking lot and quit the engine.

He reached into the back to collect his gym bag. "I haven't thought about it much, to be honest."

So much for chit chat. She grabbed her gear. "Uh, thanks for doing this."

"No problem." He led the way in, holding the gym's front door open for her.

Maybe he was nice, and she'd misread the ego. "Um, sorry about yesterday."

He turned to study her steadily for a beat before shrugging. "Sorry for liking short blond guys?" A grin flickered. "Don't be. No skin off my nose."

She took a deep breath and lifted her chin. Ignore him. Act like a grown up. Usually she was pretty good at the ice maiden persona. Not for nothing did she train on ice.

He signed them in, and she followed silently as he gave a quick tour of the bright, spacious facility with its gleaming equipment. She swallowed a chuckle at the blatant ogling he got from some women working out. If only they knew. She stowed her bag in the locker, grabbed her towel, phone, earbuds, and water bottle, and headed back to the cardio room.

Brent was there, already warming up on an exercise bike. He glanced over. "So, should we be on the lookout?"

She moved to the treadmill, pulling her ponytail tight. "What for?"

He mimed short and plump before smirking.

Holly nodded toward the big-haired, big-busted woman in the far corner. Seriously, who wore that much makeup to exercise? She kept her voice low. "Funny. I thought you'd prefer a Barbie clone."

He looked over. The woman smiled a *hi there*. Brent nodded before turning back to Holly with a scowl. "Yeah, you sure got me pegged."

She gave him a tight smile and jammed in her earbuds, flicking her phone to her favorite workout playlist. Honestly, what was wrong with her? She wasn't normally so snarky. Maybe working up a sweat would help her heart and brain function normally. This was ridiculous.

BRENT STOOD at the front of his family's church, watching as Mike rocked gently on his toes, his eyes on the big double doors at the other end of the aisle. "How're you doing?"

"I can't wait to see her." Mike grinned. "This'll be you too one day, my friend."

Brent rolled his eyes. Not for a very long time. Miss Right had to appear first.

He caught the smiles of his older brother Dean and his

sister-in-law Laura, balancing their six-month-old son on her lap, then nodded to Jai Mullins, Beau Nash, and Dan Walton, fellow hockey Bible study friends, here for Mike's wedding.

Mike leaned closer. "So, is it me or are there a lot of women here checking you out?"

Brent glanced across the congregation. He couldn't help but notice that more than one lady sat up straighter, smiling wider. He grimaced. "It's pretty uncool if women are here checking *you* out on your wedding day."

"Everyone knows I've always been a one-woman man." Mike eyed him. "But you…"

How long would it take for him to live down the ladies' man reputation? Sure, he'd partied hard a few years ago, but since he'd started attending Reverend Josiah Abrahams' online Bible study group, he'd straightened out. He hadn't dated anyone for months, despite his teammates' offers of setups—and the loneliness that made some of those offers so tempting.

Brent stared down at his shiny black shoes. Maybe his mom and sister were right and he should make more of an effort to find someone with similar goals, who liked him for himself and wasn't obsessed with celebrity or the other superficial trappings of his sport. His mouth twisted. Like that'd be easy. How could you ever know?

The music in the background shifted, and the congregation turned to watch the first bridesmaid walk down the aisle. Brent's gaze lifted just in time to see Holly begin her approach. His eyes widened. With her pretty hair down for once and that pale green strapless gown accentuating her slender figure, she was…beautiful.

Mike snickered quietly. "Pick up your jaw, dude. You're embarrassing yourself."

Brent closed his mouth with a snap. He noticed some of Mike's teammates kept on staring as Holly moved gracefully down the aisle. His gut tightened. He'd made too many dumb comments this week. Holly's work ethic, loyalty, and sassy tease had intrigued him. She was nothing like the short, skinny, shy girl he vaguely remembered from seven years ago. Especially in that dress.

Her sunny gaze shifted to him. Brent smiled at her, catching the surprise in her green eyes before her lips thinned and she glanced away.

His lips hitched. Yeah, he definitely had bridges to mend.

"I KNOW IT'S HOT, but we need just one more of the groomsmen with their lovely ladies!"

Brent groaned at the photographer. Photos with Bree and Mike, photos with the bridal party, photos with various family members—on and on it went. His cheeks ached from smiling.

"Holly, move closer to Brent, please."

Holly sighed. Brent grinned, wrapping an arm around her waist. The photographer beamed. "That's it, Brent. Holly, let's see that lovely smile again!"

"I'm not six years old," she muttered through upturned lips.

That dress was definitely unsuitable for a six-year-old. "Relax, Holly, you look beautiful."

She arched her eyebrows, staring warily at him. Brent held her gaze. Her eyes were such a pretty green, like the sea, with violet rims and tiny golden flecks around the pupils—

"Brent! Holly! Pay attention!"

Brent ignored Mike's chuckle as he turned back to the photographer, trying not to squint as the afternoon sun beat down. The reception venue's rose gardens were super pretty, but his neck was getting sticky from Toronto's muggy heat. The photographer pronounced himself satisfied, and they were finally freed to go.

As they waited to be introduced to the cheering guests inside the function room, Holly looked up at him again. "Is my hair still okay? Hot weather makes it go frizzy."

He stepped closer and smoothed a few recalcitrant strands. "Relax. You look great." He leaned down, taking a delicate sniff. "What's your perfume?"

"It's Beautiful."

"Yeah, I know that. But what's it called?"

"My perfume?" Her voice was squeaky. "It's called Beautiful. It's by Estée Lauder."

"Oh, right." He glanced at her before focusing again on the door. "Suits you."

He caught the disbelieving side-eye as she raised her bouquet higher to match the angle of her chin.

"Ladies and gentlemen, let's hear it for our best man, Brent Karlsson, and the lovely maid of honor, Holly Travers." They stepped into the limelight and stopped for yet another photo before he escorted her to the bridal table and they turned to applaud the newlyweds' entrance.

The next two hours passed in a whirl of food and laughter as Brent chatted with numerous relatives and friends. He was listening to his grandmother when he glanced across the room to see Holly sitting at the main table, shaking her head at one of Mike's Calgary teammates. He frowned.

"Brent?" His grandma's faded-blue eyes peered anxiously at him. "Is something wrong?"

He quickly kissed her cheek. "Sorry, Gran, I need to go check something."

Ignoring the nearby group of smiling women, he strode over to Holly. Tyler Woletsky was too bold, on the ice and off. Brent sat down next to Holly and stretched his arm along the back of her chair. "Woletsky! Didn't see you there." Brent turned to smile down at Holly. "How's it going?"

Her eyebrows lifted. "Fine." She looked back to TJ, who still leaned against the table. "Thanks, Tyler, but I want to finish my cake." She smiled. "Besides, I'm not used to high heels."

Woletsky glanced between them, his blue eyes suspicious. "If you change your mind…"

"Thank you." The smile she offered was sweet as Woletsky lumbered off, then drained away as she faced Brent. "What was that about?"

Brent shrugged. "Woletsky doesn't always play nicely, especially with pretty girls."

Her eyes narrowed. She stabbed at her piece of cake. "And you think I can't take care of myself?"

He held up his hands. "Hey, I've seen you in the gym. I know you're tough." And super fit. The weights she could lift? "But, Holl, you need to be careful when you smile."

"What?" She twisted in her seat to study him. "What's wrong with my smile?"

"Nothing. Just that guys could get the wrong idea."

She blinked. "Are you serious? You sound like a caveman, blaming a woman for how a man acts, as if he can't be held responsible."

Huh? "I didn't mean it like that. I only meant to compliment you," he mumbled.

She stared at him for a long moment before shaking her head and looking away.

He followed her gaze back to the dance floor. "Want to dance again?"

"Once was enough. I hate dancing." Her smile held an abundance of sugar. "But don't let me stop you."

Dancing with random women sure wouldn't help him live down the reputation. Talking with Holly was far safer. "You're not that bad, for someone with two left feet."

"Two left feet? Hey, if you hadn't insisted on doing all that fancy twirly stuff, I might've been okay."

"Yeah, well, maybe I'm just a fancy kind of guy."

Her lips finally tilted up, and he felt like doing a fist pump to celebrate but settled for undoing his bow tie and slouching back in his seat. "So, are you having fun?"

"Yes. But I can't get over how big your family is." Her amusement faded as she picked off some icing with her fork. "Mine's so small now." She looked down at her plate, the white chocolate mud cake now thoroughly ruined. "I don't see them often enough."

"When do you go home?"

"I fly back to Brisbane tomorrow, but I won't get home to Wollongong until Christmas." Her face fell, and she started fiddling with the pretty paper rose place card she'd made, her slender fingers tracing the ruffled edges back and forth, back and forth.

Brent gazed across the chandelier-lit room, crowded with family members. It was amazing he'd been allowed to talk this long uninterrupted. "Big families aren't necessarily all they're cracked up to be."

Like his Uncle Ken, who sat in the corner, watching the girls dance. Bree had always found him slightly creepy. And there were those cousins who only ever called him when they wanted tickets to games, then got upset when Brent wouldn't work his connections to get them freebies. And as soon as he finished this conversation, he knew his grandmothers and aunts would buttonhole him to ask about that nice girl and wonder aloud when he'd get married.

He grimaced. "Hey, want to go outside?"

Holly cast another look at the crowded dance floor, raising her voice over the thumping disco music the DJ had begun to play. "But what about Bree and Mike?"

"I don't think they're going to miss us too much, do you? You know Bree. She never misses an opportunity to talk. And look, she's making Mike talk to every relative. They'll be here for hours."

"Poor Mike."

"And hey, if you disappear, Woletsky can't hassle you to dance again."

"Good point." Holly pushed back her chair. "Let's get out of here."

Brent found a side door that led to the reception venue's terrace, holding it open for Holly, then closing it firmly against the DJ's throbbing music. Her heels clicked on the tiles until they stopped at the far end near a marble fountain, lit up in the night by several spotlights. The stillness was broken only by the gentle song of insects and splash of water. The scent of roses filled the cooling air. Brent sucked in a deep breath, releasing it slowly. He looked over to see Holly standing still, her eyes closed.

"Are you tired? Want to go home?" Something about her today made him feel…protective. He swallowed. Like he would for his sister. That was all.

"No." She opened her eyes. "I'm just enjoying the peace and quiet. It's been a big week."

"And a big day." He leaned over the handrail, watching the water swirl around the base of the fountain. "But they seem happy, so all the hard work has been worth it." He glanced up to see Holly biting her bottom lip even as she nodded.

"I'm so glad. Bree's been like a sister to me." Holly blinked. "I'm going to miss that."

"You heard Dad before in his speech. Apparently, it's not about losing someone but gaining another." Brent shrugged. "But yeah, it won't be the same."

He frowned. It wouldn't be the same. Why hadn't he realized? Who would he call in the middle of the night to offload the stress for the day? Mike had been his closest friend for years. He totally understood the pressures that went with playing in the NHL. Brent knew his sister loved him, but he'd bet Bree wouldn't appreciate too many late night interruptions.

Was this why his mom had ramped up the *find a wife* mantra? He sighed.

"Don't get me wrong, I am really happy for them," Holly's quiet voice continued. "They're perfect for each other." She peered up at Brent again. "But it's nice to know someone else understands." She smiled.

Her smile... Whoa. He blinked. Dragged his gaze away. Weddings were notorious for making people act weird. "I think people should be best friends with the person they marry."

"I agree," she said.

So they agreed on a couple of things at least. He turned away to watch the water again. "So, do you want to get married?"

Man, he must be super tired. Had that seriously just come out of his mouth?

"Is that an offer?" She laughed. "You're lucky I never believe anything you say."

His stomach twisted. "Why not?"

Holly's gurgling chuckle came again. "Come on. You flatter and flirt all night and expect a girl to believe you?" She patted his arm. "It's okay. I know you can't help it."

Ouch. "When was I flirting?"

Her cheeks reddened as she looked away, pushing her hair behind her ear. "I've seen how you act with girls."

"Hey, I'm a friendly guy. Besides, I do think you're pretty."

She rolled her eyes and shifted away.

So much for building bridges. He gazed at a tree lit up in the garden, trying to ignore the knot in his stomach. Tonight's rich dessert had been a bad idea.

Awkwardness stretched between them. What to say, what to say...

"So, you want to compete at Vancouver, eh?"

She straightened, energy vibrating from her. "Have you ever had a dream you feel you're on the cusp of living?"

He nodded. "I could barely sleep the night before my first game in the NHL."

"Then you understand what it's like to devote your life to something, to wanting to be the best, feeling like it's in your DNA, like it's who you are, what you were born to do."

He nodded again, her passion oddly inspiring. He'd taken a lot for granted these past few years, but the recent Cup success had only cemented his drive to win. There'd be selections for Canada's hockey team next year. The thought drifted, stilled, anchored. Maybe he should focus a little more too.

"So, even if I met Mr. Right tonight, I can't think about a relationship right now. Not for another two years, anyway."

So, the romance of today definitely hadn't gone to her head. Still, her steely-eyed focus curled fascination within. She sure wasn't like any other girl he'd met.

"How about you, Brent? Is marriage on your to-do list?"

"One day. I want to focus more on my hockey right now. But down the line, it'd be good. It just needs to be the right time… and the right girl."

He glanced over at her again. She was rubbing her bare arms, the right sporting a silvery-pink scar.

"Are you cold? Here, have this." He removed his jacket and wrapped it round her.

"Thanks." She glanced up at him again before gazing across the moonlit gardens. He studied her profile: the classic nose, determined chin, her long-lashed, beautiful eyes that the evening shadows only seemed to enhance. He swallowed. Her skin looked so soft. He reached out a hand—

"Oh, there you two are!"

He swallowed a groan as Holly turned.

"Are you okay, Bree? Do you need anything?"

Bree shook her head. "Mom just wanted your help with something inside."

"No worries." Holly shrugged out of his jacket and handed it to him with distracted thanks, then quickly strode back to the reception room without a backward glance.

He watched Holly disappear before turning to his smirking twin. "Breanna?"

"Anything I need to know about, brother dear?" Bree raised her eyebrows. "Anything at all?"

"Nope." He shook his head, hoping to shake off the strange mix of emotions he felt.

"I can give you Holly's email if you like." Her expression held hope.

His stomach lurched. He ignored it. "Nope. I'm fine."

Holly might be nice and all, but she lived on the other side of the world and had made her opinion about him and relationships very clear. So what was the point? How on earth could that ever work?

CHAPTER 2

Nagano, Japan
November

"And in lane number five, representing Australia, Holly Travers."

Holly gave a brief smile and wave at the polite applause, adjusted her goggles, and snapped on the chinstrap of her yellow helmet as she skated toward the four other contenders for tonight's World Cup one thousand meter quarterfinal. "Good luck, ladies."

The American, Dutch, and German girls smiled at her. "You too, Holly."

Kate Jenkins, Australia's number one girl, ignored her. Oh well. Nothing new there.

Holly drew in a deep breath and exhaled slowly, working to ignore the Japanese pop music blaring in the background and the nausea that always threatened in these situations. *Thank You, God, that You're with me. Help me do my best.*

19

"Go to the start."

The arena hushed. Holly skated to the end of the pale blue line and found her starting dot next to Kate, wearing her high tech black-and-silver skates. Holly looked down at her basic grade boots and swallowed the bubble of envy. Focus. She had to focus. From this position, she'd need an amazing start to be in it at all. She balanced carefully on her right foot, the long silver blade of her left skate pivoting slowly on the ice. She edged the tip so it bit the ice more firmly.

"Ready."

She crouched lower, assuming position, waiting for the crack of the starter's pistol.

BANG!

With a series of short, powerful movements, she sprinted hard, then maneuvered her way into third position behind the American and German competitors, following their slipstream around the ice, slipping round behind them like a bead on a string.

They leaned into the first bend, then skate, skate, skate, repeating the moves: one lap down. Her legs felt good today. Hopefully that strength and jump would last all weekend. Heaven help her if it didn't.

Another lap down. Holly edged closer. Maybe this would be the race when she'd finally beat Kate. She sucked in another breath as they rounded the curve, her arm stretched out for balance as her blades slipped through the grooved ice. Time was running out to make her move.

The bell clanged for the last lap. Skate, skate, skate, skate. They headed around the penultimate corner. Holly drew closer, closer...

Movement flashed beside her: Kate. Where had she come from? A surge of adrenaline hit as Holly frantically looked for a way to pass. But Kate was too good, blocking every potential move. Holly pushed forward, her heart thumping loudly as they reached the last bend. Kate went a fraction wide. Holly slipped in close to the marker, scrambling upright, her leg thrust out in desperation as they crossed the line.

She glanced up at the scoreboard as the crowd's roar filled her ears. *Please, God...*

The scoreboard finally flashed the results, and Kate, breathing hard, turned and looked at Holly with narrowed eyes and a curled lip. "Loser."

Loser.

Forever the also-ran. The bridesmaid. Not good enough.

Holly skated past Kate, then put her hands down on her knees, struggling to breathe past the throbbing disappointment. She blinked hard. *Lord, help me not to cry.*

She sucked in a breath. She still had to prepare for tomorrow's five hundred and fifteen hundred quarterfinals. And even third was better than a poke in the eye with a blunt stick, as Granddad would say. She lifted her head, congratulated the other three girls as they finished a cool-down lap, and moved to exit when she heard her name called.

"Holly!" Jessica Wilton waved an Aussie flag from the barrier. "You almost had her."

Holly's smile slipped. She bit her lip to stop the sudden tremble. "Kate's just too good."

"Yeah, well, if you didn't have to work and could focus on training as much as she does, you'd be as good as her. Maybe even better."

But until someone wanted to sponsor second place, Holly would still have to work to find the means to pay for her dream. She glanced at Kate's dad, who had competed in Lillehammer back in 1994, and knew another tug of envy. If only Holly could win for once and Australia's Winter Sports Institute consider her chances good enough to earn a ticket to Vancouver. Not that wishing ever changed anything. Only hard work could.

Although, it seemed no matter how hard Holly worked, she never got ahead.

"Clear the ice."

She nodded to the official, then turned back to Jess. "I'd better go get changed. Catch up with you after? I want to hear how you did."

Jess nodded. "See you soon."

Thirty minutes later, her official duties done, Holly moved through the crowds. While she was friends with most of the girls, it was funny how often she felt a keen sting of loneliness. Unlike some girls on tour, her parents' jobs at the hospital and coal mine meant they rarely saw her compete. She finally spotted a familiar face. A quick hug later, she and Jess talked shop.

"So, how was your thousand time?"

"Almost two seconds faster." Jessica's face twisted. "I still think it's weird how someone who gets a slower time can advance just because they're in a different heat."

"That's short track."

"But you! You almost had Kate. I thought for sure you would beat her. I think all the Aussies thought there'd be an upset tonight."

Holly forced a smile. "Maybe next time."

The crowd parted before them, and Holly's confidence drained away at the sight of Kate standing with her World Cup medal-winning father and Coach Chan. They'd all seen Holly; she had no place to hide. *Put on a brave face.* Holly moved forward. "Congratulations, Kate."

Coach Chan gave a characteristic sharp nod as the two Jenkinses critically assessed Holly.

And found her wanting. Kate turned her back and started talking to her father.

Holly blinked, lifted her chin, and walked back to where Jess waited.

"Kate is such a b—" Jess glanced at Holly. "Witch."

Yep.

"I really hope you beat her tomorrow in the five hundred."

Jess wasn't the only one. But Holly had a funny feeling that pigs would sooner fly.

IT WAS LIKE A SCENE from the movie *Groundhog Day*. Same early start, same crowds and competitors, same results. Holly had tried. She'd come within 0.06 of Kate's time in the fifteen hundred—no point Kate thinking she could just mail in a first place. But Kate kept creaming the opposition.

Holly had tried to settle it with God last night. She'd prayed, read her Bible, and tried to give it over to Him. She hated carrying this disappointment and frustration in her soul. But wanting to improve wasn't bad, was it? It was what all athletes wanted—to be better, to just *win*.

"Ladies and gentlemen, it's now time for the women's five hundred meter quarterfinal."

Holly slowly moved around the ice, working to block out the noise and color around her. The five hundred was her favorite. She loved the energy and strategy it demanded, but so much came down to the start. She pulled her ponytail tighter under her helmet and skated toward the other four girls as they waited for the official. Yep, sure enough, her nemesis was beside her.

"Good luck, ladies," Holly offered. Not that the Canadian needed luck, world champ that she was.

Marianna grinned, shaking out her legs. "You too."

The Dutch girl echoed her with a "Stay upright, yes?"

Holly smiled at the Chinese competitor, who nodded, eyes focused on the ice track before them. No surprise there. Min never smiled unless she won.

Holly even managed a smile for Kate, but the blonde

scowled, lifted her nose, and looked away. Yeah, Holly could barely believe she'd made it this far either.

"Go to the start."

Five hundred meters. Four and a half laps. Every stride, every lean, every movement had to be carefully calculated. She had to place top two. She had to qualify.

"Ready." Holly crouched lower, balancing carefully on her left foot. *Lord, keep us safe.*

BANG!

After a chaotic scramble of thrashing arms and legs, they soon settled into position: Marianna in the lead, followed by Min, with Holly hot on her heels, the others just behind her.

One lap down. Holly blocked the roar of the crowded stadium, her eyes fixed on the girl in front, whose red skinsuit slipped around the corners elusively. Slowly, she inched closer. Three laps to go. Ignoring the burn in her thighs and the blood-like taste in her mouth, she searched for any hole in the Chinese girl's defense, a sign that her rival was going too wide or a stumble that would allow Holly to slide in and claim second position.

Holly rounded the bend almost horizontally, her left hand outstretched for balance, the razor-sharp blades of the skater in front a hairsbreadth away. Straightening up, she desperately lunged forward, passing the former gold medalist as she slipped into second place. Finally! If she could just hold position, all those sacrifices would be worth it.

Her senses heightened. The flash of Kate's skates, a fraction of movement as Min closed in, the burn in her thighs, the swoosh and scrape of their blades on grooved ice.

Another four strides, another lean. Her peripheral vision caught Min's blur as she frantically tried to close the gap around the bend. No! All those critics back home were wrong. Holly *could* do this.

Her heart thumped loudly. Holly gritted her teeth and

pushed forward. She was getting closer to the Canadian competitor in front. This was Holly's race, she could feel it. Her legs still felt good, with enough power despite the last two days' heavy schedule of heats. She could make it to the semis, maybe even make her first World Cup final!

They rounded the corner in a blur of movement, Min's golden blades flashing under the stadium's lights as they sped up to another bend. Kate slid past. No, no, no! Holly watched, disbelieving, as Kate's stride lengthened. How—?

Kate suddenly wobbled, toppled, crashing to the ice, taking the Chinese girl down with her. Holly struggled to move clear, but the flailing golden blade clipped her boot. *No, God! No!* She fell to the ice, and they spun round and round and round, those treacherous blades aimed directly at Holly's face. Kate shifted, sliding to crash heavily into the padded boards, the change in momentum pivoting Holly straight toward her. Holly angled her leg, hoping to avoid a gash from Min's skate, and braced for impact. Kate moved, straight into Holly's path. Oh, *dear God*, no!

SNAP!

Holly blinked. Pain. Cold. She lifted her head. Blood. Kate. Unearthly screams. Faces swam before her. Stay upright? No, no. Stay down. Loser. The world tilted.

Blissful blackness.

~

Detroit, Michigan

"Good game, man."

"You too." Brent Karlsson fist-bumped the goalie and permitted himself a small smile. With the first star of the night, yeah, maybe the coaches might consider him for Canadian team contention. The competition would be beyond fierce, so he'd take any chance to impress.

He moved from the lockers to the showers, had the world's quickest shower, changed, then it was media, more teammate ribbing, and out to where fans waited.

"Hi, Brent!"

"Brent, over here!"

"Excuse me, Mr. Karlsson, would you sign my jersey?"

"Sure." Brent nodded to the blond youngster wearing his jersey. "So, buddy, d'you play hockey?"

The boy nodded and began explaining about his youth team. Brent smiled. The boy's enthusiasm reminded him so much of his own passion and dreams as a kid. "Keep having fun, okay?"

He quickly signed his name and posed for a photo for the next group of fans.

The four boys started talking. "Hi, Brent. You were awesome tonight!"

"Yeah, that slap shot goal was wicked. The goalie never saw it coming."

The shortest one gave a gap-toothed smile. "And your hip check on Dmitry was so cool!"

Brent grinned. It was nice to be making a positive impression with the fans and the coaching staff—and maybe the Canadian selectors. He chatted briefly, signed their merchandise, and looked to the next fans in line. Uh oh.

The three young women wore skintight Detroit T-shirts and big red smiles. "Hi, Brent." The oldest girl couldn't be over twenty. She and her cohorts wore the shortest shorts he'd ever seen. She fluttered her eyelashes. "Would you sign our shirts?"

His heart sank. A few years ago he would've been very happy to do that and more. Now the idea made him cringe. "Sorry, ladies, I only sign stuff people aren't wearing."

They giggled, their catlike smiles growing wider. "Want us to take our shirts off?"

"No." His cheeks grew hot. How did girls get away with

acting like this? Hadn't their parents taught them better? "No, that's not necessary."

"Aw, he's so shy."

He turned to see rookie Doug Lehtonen, standing nearby, wink at the girls waiting for Brent. As they started tossing their hair, he grinned at Brent. "This is awesome."

Brent gave him a weak smile and looked toward the next set of fans, but the girls weren't finished yet. "Oh, but we wanted our photo taken with you too."

He forced a smile as they took photos with him, their bodies pushing into his. Gritting his teeth, he quickly stepped back. "Okay, girls." He motioned to the queue. "Gotta keep moving."

"Bye, Brent!" The boldest one gave him a kiss on the cheek while her friends snapped more photos on their phones. "If you ever need some company…"

So not calling you. He aimed for cool as he turned and surreptitiously wiped her lipstick off. Honestly, did they think the only way to get a man's attention was dressing like they were going to a night of roller disco derby? Not that he wanted a woman to dress like she was Amish, but still…

The next person in line was a woman who looked to be in her thirties, holding her son by the shoulders. She pointed to her left cheek. "You've still got some."

"Thanks." He shook his head, wiping at his cheek until she nodded. He sighed before looking at the towheaded boy. "Okay, buddy, what are we signing today?"

As he signed more autographs and posed for yet more photos, his mind kept flicking back to the girls from before. Puck bunnies didn't care about the sport, only about the players —or more precisely, what they could get out of them. He swallowed a big lump of regret. How had he ever thought girls like that were attractive? They were like the glossy veneer on that wooden table he'd ended up throwing out last year, the promise of oak peeling away as soon as he'd started digging out the dirt to refinish the piece. Some girls were just the same, full of empty promises with nothing of substance, exactly the sort of women who could derail his career—and his hard-won focus on God.

Thirty minutes after escaping the arena, he dropped his duffle bag in the darkened hall of the brick and plaster house he liked to call home. Some of his teammates had questioned why he wanted to buy such a modest place. He liked this part of Detroit. He liked the layout of the rooms and the trees in the yard. It kind of reminded him of his parents' place. He'd never understood the attraction of big open floor plan apartments. Sure, they might be equipped with the latest mod cons and not have a leaky bathroom, but they felt a little sterile to him, too much like all those expensively anonymous hotel rooms they always stayed in on road trips. This place, with its mock-Tudor features, scrolled woodwork and fancy fireplace, was home.

He moved to the renovated kitchen—last summer's project —grabbed a drink, and rubbed his shoulder. Tonight's game had felt way longer than three periods, the tied full-time score going to a shootout against Detroit's chief rivals—Jai's team, Chicago. Fortunately, Brent had scored, and the Wings had celebrated their first victory in three games. But tonight's checking had been tough, his body aching from where he'd hit the boards more than he liked.

He slumped onto the leather lounge, toed off his shoes, and flicked on the TV. News, an unfunny comedy, ads, some weird sci-fi drama, more news, a series rerun—lame the first time— more ads, a delayed broadcast of football. He tried following the game, but the lack of sleep from the past few nights was fast catching up. Flying home from Thursday night's game in Minnesota meant he'd arrived home at one a.m. Then last night he'd gone out with Doug and some others from the team, trying out a new restaurant that had opened near the river. Good food, but he'd struggled to sleep. Too much salt in the pizza.

He flicked off the TV, the standby light reflecting off the silver-framed photo Bree and Mike had given him after their wedding last June. He stood, picked it off the mantle, and moved back to his seat. That had been a good day. Bree and Mike's matching grins testified to the hard yards of a relationship that had endured through separation, as Mike had played in Boston, then Calgary, while Bree taught preschool in Toronto. Now living in Calgary, they seemed to love married life.

He peered closer. His parents stood with Bree, Mike, Holly, and himself. Despite her heels, Holly looked like a dainty green-clad princess next to the rest of them. He smiled, remembering her sass and determination. Yeah, definitely not a groupie. He fingered the simple silver surround. What was she up to these days?

He lay back, closed his eyes, and let out a huge yawn. He'd think about that later…

His phone buzzed.

Brent opened his eyes, his brain struggling, like trying to swim through thick syrup. Where was he? Oh, living room. Add a crick in his neck to the sore shoulder. His phone kept buzzing —he could feel the vibrations through the leather seat. He felt around for his phone and finally found it, slipped down the back of the sofa. He flicked it open.

"Hello?"

"Oh! Thank goodness someone's answering their phone!"

"Bree?" Brent rubbed the sleep from his eyes. "What's up? Everything okay?"

"No-o-o." His sister's voice quavered.

His stomach tensed. "What's happened? Is Mike okay? Mom? Dad?"

"I don't know! It's so late over there I didn't want to wake them. And Mike's phone is switched off because he's still at the game in L.A."

Brent blinked. This was getting hard to follow. Especially when he'd only gotten five hours of sleep last night. "What's wrong?"

"It's Holly." Bree's voice was shaky. She sounded close to tears.

"What's happened?"

"Oh, Brent, there was a terrible accident!"

His heart thumped, and he sat upright. "What happened?"

"She…she was competing in a race in Japan when the girl in front clipped her and—" Judging from the loud noise that ensued, she was blowing her nose.

"And what, Bree? Hello?"

"I hate that she does short track! It's so dangerous, Brent, and this is what can happen. I don't know why she insists on it."

Brent grimaced. He totally understood the intense desire to compete, to push your body to its limits, to win. How else could one expect to play in the NHL? But why wasn't Bree getting to the point? "What happened, Bree?"

"You don't need to yell at me." She sniffed again. "They…they hit the side really hard, and now she's paralyzed."

His heart dropped. *Dear God.* "She's paralyzed?"

"Yes!"

No. *God, please heal her.* Poor, poor Holly. He'd never dreamed just how extreme short track was. "Is it permanent?"

"Well, Holly's mother—she's a nurse—said that people can recover from fractured vertebrae, but it's a really long, tough road. But it's the severed artery that's the real concern."

His stomach turned. Severed artery? "That sounds terrible."

"Yeah, apparently when she slid to the side she cut into her left calf with her skate. Holly's mom said there was blood all over the ice."

The longer Bree talked, the deeper he could feel his frown become. He'd seen that once. A skate had cut the Kings' defenseman, and the intense play just prior meant the poor guy's heart had kept pumping blood out. The medics had rushed him to the hospital, but he no longer played hockey and now suffered recurring bouts of infections. How awful.

He drew a steadying breath. "Have you spoken to Holly yet? How's she coping with all this?"

He couldn't imagine what it would be like to suffer such catastrophic injuries. To not be able to walk? To have to give up on your dream after years of sacrifice?

"No, I haven't spoken to her." Bree sniffed. "Her mom seems to think she'll be fine."

Huh? That was a pretty big call to make, even for a nurse.

Bree continued. "It's a big shock, of course, and apparently she was pretty upset at first."

Well, yeah. Finding out you were paralyzed would be pretty upsetting.

His sister sighed. "Holly emailed earlier asking me to pray for Kate, but when I called her back, her mom answered, as she was asleep."

He was too tired. This was getting hard to follow. "Who's Kate?"

His sister groaned. "Haven't you listened to anything I said? Kate's the girl who got hurt. Apparently she's something of a—"

"Wait! I thought you said Holly got hurt."

His sister sniffled again. "Yeah."

He closed his eyes, trying to think clearly. "So is Holly paralyzed or not?"

Bree let out a sigh. "No, Brent, the other girl. Kate. She severed her artery, too."

God help the other girl, but he didn't know her. "And Holly?"

She sniffled again. "She got a mild concussion, cut her leg, and broke her little finger."

That tight feeling in his chest disappeared in an enormous sigh. "Thank God."

"What?"

After explaining how Bree really needed to work on her communication skills, then promising to pray, Brent finished the call and lay back on the couch in the darkness, heart jumbled with a million emotions. *God, please help Holly right now. Thank You she wasn't more seriously injured. Please help her sleep well. And be with this Kate girl. Heal her too.*

He picked up the silver frame from the coffee table, staring at the dainty figure in green with the beautiful smile, and studied the photo for a long, long time.

CHAPTER 3

Brisbane, Australia
One week later

"Then Peter said to the man, 'I don't have any money to give you, but here's something I *can* give you. In the name of Jesus Christ of Nazareth, rise up and walk!' Isn't that amazing?"

The children sat in a circle, watching as Holly read the big picture Bible. But seriously? This story? And today of all days? God sure had a funny sense of humor.

Holly leaned closer. "And then Peter took the beggar by the right hand and helped him up, and instantly the man's feet and ankles became strong. Can you imagine what happened next?"

"He woulda started running!"

Holly smiled at the brown-eyed boy. "That's right, Jackson." She turned to the others. "What else do you think happened?"

"He'd be so happy. He'd thank Peter, wouldn't he?"

"I can't imagine what it would be like to not walk." Lucy looked up with her huge blue eyes. "Can you, Holly?"

Holly swallowed. She had a pretty good idea. She'd visited Kate last week in the Nagano hospital. Well, tried to. Dale Jenkins would have none of it, cursing her, loudly telling the nursing staff that they should never admit Holly Travers to see his daughter. Holly had left the bouquet of flowers with a sympathetic nurse and fled.

"Holly?"

She wrapped an arm around the six-year-old girl's shoulders. "It would be very, very hard." She swallowed. "In fact, I have a friend who was hurt last week in a bad accident."

"Like you were?" Jackson pointed to her bandaged little finger.

Holly nodded slowly. "But this girl, her name is Kate, was hurt much more badly than me. She's in hospital and needs God to do a miracle so she can walk again."

The small heads all nodded and bowed. As their little voices started praying earnestly for "Holly's friend Kate," Holly tried not to squirm. Kate had never been her friend, not really.

She finished the lesson with a final prayer and said goodbye. "Don't forget your craft."

Jackson raced back in, his blond hair mussed. He grabbed his picture and gave her an enormous squeeze that almost toppled her. "See you next week?"

Holly shook her head. "Sorry, sweetheart. I'm going to see my family for Christmas."

"But you will be back?" The mischief was gone. The corners of his mouth turned down.

Holly nodded. These kids were so sweet.

"I like Miss Gina, but I like you best." Olivia snuggled close.

Holly gave her a hug and smiled. "See you next time, sweetie."

After clearing up most of the glitter, Holly made her way

outside to where the rest of the congregation still milled, talking. This small community church, only a few blocks from the skating share house, had proven to be such a blessing. A healthy mix of old and young, middle class and poor, these people were like an extended family, and after the tension and rivalry of competition, Holly always appreciated the simple love she experienced here. They accepted her for who she was and weren't concerned about what she did or how well she performed.

After fielding questions from several people concerned about her accident, Holly finally moved to where she'd parked her bike but then felt a light touch on her shoulder.

David Aldridge, the minister, stood with his wife, Gina. "You're off now?"

Holly nodded. "Thanks so much for those casseroles this week. And your prayers. I've really appreciated it."

Gina wrapped her in a hug. "How is Kate?"

Holly sighed. "She and her dad still blame me. There's a review panel tomorrow. If everything's fine, I should be okayed for travel to Europe for the next World Cup events."

"You know we'll be praying for you, Holly. Keep in touch."

"Thanks." She hugged them both, strapped on her helmet, then hopped on her bike for the short ride home.

This past week had been crazy. After spending hours in hospital getting her finger bound and her gash stitched up—twelve stitches, a new personal record—Coach Chan had eventually allowed her to join the team at the airport, where she'd emailed Bree. Of course, that email had unleashed a flood of concerned phone calls and emails from Bree, Bree's parents, even Brent. His email had been much like the others, expressing shock, concern, the usual. But it was his offer to pray for her that had touched her heart. He was...nice. Much nicer than what she remembered from June.

Holly pushed the pedals for the short climb up the hill to their share house. She had it to herself today. Jess was at work,

Kate still in hospital. Guilt spiked. *Lord, heal her.* The race officials had cleared Holly, and she shouldn't feel responsible. Stuff happened, especially in short track. But Kate's dad had never been less than pushy when it came to his daughter in this sport. And the way he'd spoken to Holly in Japan suggested tomorrow's meeting would not go well.

Lord, help me trust You. Please work this out. And help me get this assignment done.

She reheated a portion of Gina's chicken casserole and ate in front of her laptop, scrolling through the barrage of emails before tackling her health science assignment. Why didn't spam filters work properly? Delete, delete, delete…pause. There were messages from her parents, her brother, Bree, and—

Her heart gave a tiny kick. She peered closer at the name and opened the email.

> *Hey Holly,*
> *I thought you'd probably still be feeling a little down about*
> *your friend. I got sent this today and thought it might make*
> *you laugh. And check out 1 Peter 5:7, one of my favorite verses.*
> *Hope you find some peace. Take care. Stay up.*
> *Brent*

Brent? Why had Brent sent her another email? She chewed her lip and opened the attachment. It was a Gary Larson *Farside* cartoon of two deer, one with a target on its chest, the other saying *Bummer of a birthmark, Hal.* It made her smile. Shake her head.

And *Brent* was recommending she read Bible verses? He even had favorites? Who would've thought? She flicked open her Bible and read the reminder to cast her anxiety on God. Huh. So maybe he was more than just a jock. Maybe he was someone she could consider as a friend.

She hesitated, fingers hovering over the keys. Despite the

weariness of the past few days starting to bite, she summoned up enough energy to reply.

Hi Brent,
Thanks for your email. The bad thing is that Kate has never really been my friend. She blames me for her injury, so now there'll be a review. It's such a mess.

The accident flashed through her mind, the image of Kate lying with her leg positioned so awkwardly that everyone knew it was at least a break. She cringed. It still made her wake up in the middle of the night in a cold sweat. And now there was this stupid review.

Please pray for Kate. And that the review is fair and everyone knows the truth.
Thanks, Holly

Holly pressed send, took a deep breath, lifted her chin, and opened up the university course work.

Next day, Holly arrived with Jess at the rink and quickly changed. When they headed out to the ice, Coach Chan motioned for them to join the others from the squad who were standing in front of a group of serious men.

Jess leaned over. "Aren't they from the Winter Sports Institute?"

Holly nodded, her heart sinking. Yep. Judging from their frowns, she'd better kiss her dreams of golden glory goodbye.

Jess whispered again. "And isn't that Kate's dad standing there?" She motioned to the man standing with his arms crossed, his frown deep. His lean physique still bore traces of the World Cup-winning long track speed skater he'd been in his youth, and his hard expression—Holly had seen it on Kate's face a million times before.

Mr. Pearson was Australia's International Skating Union representative. "We've brought you all here today to clarify the situation concerning Kate Jenkins's accident in Japan." He shuffled some papers and looked up again, his eyes skipping over Holly.

Her hopes dropped further still.

"We wanted to have you all here so our position will be very clear and there can be no misrepresentation."

Holly's heart hammered hard. *Oh Lord, please help me.*

"There have been allegations that Kate may have been deliberately targeted."

"That's ridiculous," Jess muttered.

Holly glanced over to where Coach Chan stood, expressionless. Holly bit her lip. No help from that quarter. Mr. Jenkins was nodding away. Holly was ready to sink into the floor.

"I have been assured by Coach Chan that could not be the case."

What?

"The interviews we've conducted amongst the skaters involved and the spectators on the day attest to what Holly Travers claims"—he looked at her—"that it was the usual contact one would expect from short track, and if any contact occurred, it was accidental and definitely not deliberate."

Mr. Jenkins stepped closer, his face rapidly turning red. "But—"

Mr. Pearson held up a hand. "Furthermore, the video footage makes it very clear that it was Kate's fall that led to Holly and the Chinese competitor crashing out. Kate's injuries resulted from a series of extremely unfortunate circumstances. So, considering this material, we have decided to not pursue this matter any further, as it appears to clearly be an accident. Therefore, I do not want"—he glanced at Kate's father, who looked ready to erupt—"I repeat, I do *not* want to hear any further allegations or insinuations being made about any member of this team." He nodded. "I hope that's understood."

There were various murmurs of compliance, apart from Mr. Jenkins, who moved closer to Mr. Pearson, remonstrating.

Jess nudged her. "Wow, Holly, you're in the clear. Looks like it's your lucky day."

"I don't believe in luck." Prayers, however…

"You make your own luck, huh?" Jess laughed before chatting with someone else.

Mr. Jenkins stomped away, and Mr. Pearson beckoned Holly forward, his expression grave. "Holly, this is a very bad business, which is why we wanted to speak to everyone today, so there'd be no gossip." He shook his head. "You know how people can get."

She did. The competition for sponsorship and places was fierce.

Coach Chan's expression remained inscrutable. "You good skater, Holly. You our new number one girl."

"But—"

"You'll head to Europe for the next World Cup event, and as our top skater, you'll receive some extra funding," Mr. Pearson said. "It's designated for the top athlete attending the event, and if they can't attend…" He shrugged.

Ouch. This was a harsh business. But Holly nodded. *Thank You, God.* With this funding boost, maybe she could even quit her supermarket job one day.

Coach Chan's eyes narrowed. "You have ability. You must show it."

Holly nodded again. "I'll do my best."

"No distractions, understood? Distractions are enemy of success."

Those black eyes bored into her. What did Coach Chan

think? That Holly was going to suddenly find a man? She nearly laughed. Instead, she smiled. "No distractions. I get it."

~

Toronto, Canada
December

> *Hi everyone,*
> *Sorry this is a group email, but since everyone's been so inter-ested I figured it's best to share this ASAP. I'm cleared! Coach Chan not only found evidence that proved the crash wasn't my fault, but I've also been publicly endorsed as the new #1! Not exactly the way I wanted, but still... thank You, God! And thank you all for praying. I'll receive some extra funding, so I can cut back on my hours at work. I need to up my training though, which may affect uni, which is getting pretty stressful, so I'll need to make some decisions about that too.*
> *Anyway, thanks again for your support and prayers—it's SO appreciated!*
> *Love, Holly*

Brent reread Holly's email and shot up a prayer of thanks. It was cool to see how things worked out for good. But "love"?

He swallowed. It meant nothing—she'd sent this to others—but the word was enough to get him flustered. He allowed his brain to go there for a moment...

They had more in common than he'd first realized. Elite level sport meant the continuous pressure of travel, training, and competition, often demanding sacrifices on the relation-ships that made life worthwhile. Hockey was great, and he'd always loved it, ever since he first strapped on a pair of skates as a kid. But it could be very transitory regarding friendships. Guys got traded on team management's say-so, and suddenly a

40

buddy he'd been rooming with for the past few seasons was on the opposite team. It wasn't always easy.

And lately he'd noticed it more. This time of year the team always had functions where he could bring a date. He'd been careful over the past year to go stag—better that than getting some woman's hopes up—but he'd started noticing how the guys with wives or girlfriends just seemed so much happier, more settled. He didn't feel like that. Ever since Bree and Mike's wedding, he'd felt alone.

Pastor Josiah had talked about relationships with the hockey Bible study group recently, about being careful, not being unequally yoked. Jai, Beau, and Dan were also single and had shared—to varying degrees—about their hopes and frustrations with the whole dating scene. Most times people just thought that meant the whole Christian / non-Christian thing, but Jo had explained about shared values and interests, the things that kept people as friends long after the first flush of passion had worn off. While there'd been plenty of interest in the past, women who could really understand him and the demands of his sport were few and far between.

But Holly would…

His heart double-thumped.

But she lived in Australia, half a world away. How could that work?

It couldn't. It was way too hard. Not gonna happen. Impossible. No, even though he'd enjoyed these chats, he needed to find someone who at least lived on the same continent.

He shook his head and typed out a reply.

Hey Holly,
That's great news. I'm here in T.O. with the family for Granny
V's birthday, and we're all glad to hear your news. Thank God
people saw reason, eh? Regarding your stress, can you defer
your studies for a while or cut back on subjects? It may help

you find some peace amongst your busyness. Think, and pray,
about it.
God bless—and stay up.
Brent

"Hey, Brent, are you coming down to join us?"

He rolled his eyes at his sister's voice coming up the stairs. He pressed send, closed down his laptop, and headed downstairs to the lounge.

Bree was wrapped in Mike's arms. Man, this newlywed thing sure wasn't growing old for them. She smiled. "So, there's something we all want to know."

Uh oh. Judging by the way everyone was looking at him, this couldn't be good. He reached over to the snack tray on the coffee table and shoved a corn chip in his mouth. "What?"

Bree smiled wider. "How long has Holly been emailing you for?"

"Who?" his grandmother asked.

"Holly Travers," his mom said, picking up Bree's wedding photo. "Remember Bree's maid of honor?"

"Oh, yes. She's a sweet little thing. Is she someone special, dear?"

Brent nearly choked. "Just a friend, Gran," he mumbled.

"Just a *friend*, huh?" Bree said, eyebrows raised. "So, how long have you been emailing each other for?"

He scooped a stack of guacamole onto his next corn chip and began chewing really slowly as Bree squirmed. She so didn't do patience. He swallowed and looked his sister in the eye. "Why?"

"Oh!" She lightly punched him in the arm. "You're so frustrating. You know why."

"Nope." He picked up another handful of chips and stuffed them in his mouth. Should probably switch food substances soon. Too much junk food and his body would protest.

Bree turned to Mike. "You make him tell."

Mike held up his hands. "I'm not doing your dirty work. You're on your own with this one, hon."

Brent nodded to his friend. Yeah, Mike still had his back.

His father spoke up. "Why does it matter, Bree? Holly's email was addressed to many people. Are you going to accuse everyone of"—he raised his eyebrows—"'something'?"

"That's right. Surely it's Brent's business who he emails. And Holly's too." His mom sent him a smile. "But she *is* a very nice girl."

Yeah, he knew his mom had always been a fan.

Bree pouted. "She's my friend. You're my brother. I care."

Brent reached out and ruffled her hair, something she'd always hated. "It's just sometimes you care too much, sis."

Mike snorted back laughter. Bree turned to eye him. "Whose side are you on, anyway?"

His mom herded them toward the dining table. "I think it's time for dinner."

Brent slung an arm around Bree's shoulders. "Amen to that."

CHAPTER 4

Wollongong, Australia

"Holly! How's it going?"

Ben swung her up in a big warm hug. She'd missed this. After the stress and worries of competition, training, and too many late nights finishing assignments, the beach was exactly what she needed. She laughed. "Put me down! I'm fine."

"You sure?" His hazel eyes probed hers. "You've got dark circles under your eyes."

Holly glanced over to her where her mother was making a pavlova for Christmas lunch tomorrow. "Want to go to the beach? We can talk there."

He nodded, and she quickly slipped into her swimsuit, grabbed her boogie board and a towel, then walked the one block down to Austinmer beach with him. She smiled. With their bleached-blond hair tips and matching wraparound sunnies, they must look like the surfie twins, even though Ben's passion was for rugby and Holly would never have the great tan a true beach babe should have.

Ben slung an arm around her shoulders as they walked in step. She tried not to think about the last time a guy had wrapped his arm around her, back at Bree's wedding.

They found a patch of unclaimed golden sand and sat down amidst the families and teenagers who were making the most of this glorious summer day.

"Talk or surf first?"

Holly stood and grabbed her boogie board. "What do you think?"

She raced into the cold surf, squealed the obligatory "Oohh, it's so cold!" then headed deeper, past the little kids paddling, to knee high, thigh high, waiting for the perfect wave with enough power to take her to the shore.

She grinned over at Ben. "Ready?"

He laughed. "Watch and learn, baby."

She turned as the wave crashed into them and propelled her board toward the shore, zipping and zig-zagging her way through the other swimmers, laughing at the freedom. Boogie boarding was so much fun, like flying through water. She tossed wet hair from her eyes, looking over to see where Ben had landed. "Ha! I win!"

"Best of three." He grinned and turned, and she caught sight of the tattoo on his back. "Benjamin! What's that?"

He rolled his eyes. "It's called a tatt, Holly."

She made a face. "But how long have you had it?"

"Long enough."

She inspected it. "The coat of arms?" She smirked. "What, you're now officially endorsed by the Australian government?"

He laughed. "Come on. Race you again."

. . .

THEY LAY BACK against their towels, staring up at the big bowl of blue sky that seemed to stretch on forever as the hush of waves softly washed against the sand. Ben propped his head back on his folded hands. "This is the life."

Holly closed her eyes as she took a deep breath of the fresh, salt-tinged air, smiling as warmth permeated her pores. The pressure forever pulsing through her veins slowly eased. "I love Christmas."

"Yeah, me too." Ben poked her in the side. "Especially when I get to see all my favorite people."

Her smile faded. "I still can't get over how bad Granddad looked yesterday. He didn't seem himself at all." She drew in a breath. "I know Mum and Dad visit every few days, but I see him so rarely. I always feel so guilty whenever we leave."

"Holl, you can't blame yourself. I'm sure he understands."

Holly bit her lip. Granddad didn't seem to understand much of anything these days.

"So, what's got you so tense, Holl?"

"Didn't you get the memo? I'm always tense." Her laughter hitched.

"Might have something to do with your crazy busy life."

She sighed. "That's what they tell me."

"Who does?"

"Mum, Dad, Coach Chan, Bree." *Brent.* How weird she was even on his radar.

Ben propped his sunglasses on top of his head. "And are you listening to them?"

"What?"

"What are you going to change so you're not so stressed?"

She shrugged. "I've cut back on work a bit, and I'm dropping some of my uni subjects after first semester next year."

"Sounds wise."

He was starting to sound too much like a certain someone in Detroit. She blinked. *Stop thinking about him.*

"But, Holl, you know we're all proud of you." Ben looked at her seriously. "I don't think you realize just how impressed we all are by the way you've combined all this training and competition with your studies and work. It's been a really hard slog."

His face got a little blurry. "Thanks, Ben. That means a lot."

"No, I mean it. It's tough to maintain friendships, serve in church, and actually care about others. I don't know how you've stayed so close to Bree all these years."

"Yeah, well, God bless the Internet." She adjusted her sunnies as she looked away to the crashing waves of the Tasman Sea.

"I know I don't say this very often, but I love you, Holl."

She turned to smile back at him. Ben was the best. "I love you too."

HOLLY WIPED her hands on the kitchen towel. "Okay, that's the prawns done. What's next?" She looked over at her mum, who was finishing setting the table.

"Whose mobile phone is ringing?"

Her father entered the kitchen with the silver phone chirping away. Holly grabbed it with a smile. "Mine." She checked the caller identification and smiled wider. "Hi, Bree! Happy Christmas."

"Happy Christmas to you too. Well, almost Christmas. It's still Christmas Eve here."

"Been there, done that." Holly slipped onto the gray suede lounge. "So, did you get my present in time?"

"Yes! Oh, Holly, I love it! You know we always open presents on Christmas Eve, with the boys traveling on Christmas, but anyways, I got it. I love the fan!"

For years, Holly had been sending Bree charms for Christmas and her birthday from her travels around the world. "I bought it in Japan. It just looked like your kind of charm."

Bree excitedly filled her in for a few more minutes before saying, "Someone else wants to say hi."

Holly's heart picked up pace. *Please, don't let it be Brent.* It was one thing to email, quite another to know what to say to him on the phone. There was a brief murmur of voices in the background, then a deep male voice came on.

"Hey, Holly, merry Christmas."

"Uh, Brent?"

"Sorry to disappoint, it's Mike."

"Oh. Not disappointed!" She gave a high, fake laugh. "Happy first Christmas as a married man."

After chatting to him for a short time, the phone was passed to Bree's parents, who said hello. She answered their questions about her competitions before they asked to speak to Holly's parents. They'd gotten to know each other from phone calls during her student exchange days. She handed the phone over. Brent obviously didn't want to talk to her. Well, that was terrific, because she didn't know what to say to him anyway.

She stood and studied the dining table. Six place settings for her parents, grandfather, her uncle Richard, who was visiting from New Zealand, Ben, and herself. She placed the Christmas crackers on each of the plates and straightened the glasses.

"Thanks, Holl." Her mum handed her back the phone, and she held it to her ear in case anyone was still there. "Hello?"

"Uh, Holly?"

Her pulse skittered, but she'd already been caught out today. "Brent?"

"Hi. I just had to wait for everyone to leave."

Her heart beat strangely. She must be coming down with something. "Why's that?"

"I, uh, I just wanted to wish you a happy Christmas."

Was that all? "Wow. You're right. You can't have just anyone overhearing that."

A beat. "What?"

Maybe that had been a little too sharp. "Well, happy Christmas to you too, Brent."

She ignored the hooked eyebrow Ben gave her and moved through the living room to stand on the back deck overlooking the ocean. The silence deepened. Well, did he want to talk to her or not? She was about to hang up when she heard his voice again. "Holly?"

"Yeah?"

"Is everything okay? You sound a little tense."

How to explain that she didn't know what to say to him, that the sound of his voice made her palms sweaty? Maybe Mum should take her temperature. "Sorry. It's been a big few weeks, and I haven't figured out how to relax."

"It's summer there, right? Gotta admit I'm a little jealous. It's pretty cold here."

Her shoulders dropped a fraction. "Now mightn't be the time to tell you we're heading to the beach again after Christmas lunch."

He chuckled. "Nope. You definitely shouldn't tell me that. It's snowing here."

"Or that it's a perfect sunny day, and I can see the waves beckoning as I talk."

"Stop it, woman."

She smiled. "Hey, thanks for your emails these past weeks."

"I'm glad you're doing okay."

Okay might be overstating things. Surviving was a better fit.

She chewed her lip. He didn't seem in a hurry to hang up. She didn't understand why not. Ben glanced at her, palms up. She shrugged, dismissing his concern.

"So, when is your next game?"

"We play Nashville on the twenty-sixth. In Nashville, so that'll be fun. When is your next competition?"

"Not for a little while. I have this week off for Christmas, then it's back to training in Brisbane, then I fly to Bulgaria in early February."

"Another World Cup?"

He paid attention? "Yeah. Then it's Dresden, then the World Championships in Vienna in March."

"Sounds like you'll be busy."

"You know it." When was she not?

"Holly," her mother called through the open door. "It's time to eat."

She nodded. "I have to go."

"'Kay. Thanks for talking."

"You too. Merry Christmas, Brent."

"Happy Christmas, Holly."

She pressed end, studying the phone. "Well, that was weird."

"What was?" Ben moved closer, a slight frown on his face.

"Oh, nothing. Just an unexpected conversation." One that had left her heart feeling a little zingy. Not that she had time for that. "Now, are you ready to eat?"

～

Detroit, Michigan

JANUARY OPENED in a storm of plummeting temperatures and a streak of wins Brent hoped would see selectors taking note.

"Karlos, you're up."

Brent clambered over the boards and skated onto the ice. With only three minutes left in the last period, it'd be really nice to untie this game. Brent skated closer to the blue line as momentum shifted toward the Wings. Doug was getting hemmed in. He really needed to learn to pass. Brent dodged the Stars' center and skated to some open ice.

"Dougie!"

Doug passed the puck to him, then Brent deked the Dallas

defenseman, skating round him, moving closer to the goal. Their goalie might be an All-Star, but he wasn't gonna stop this baby. Brent took a swing. Slapshot. Five hole. Score!

"Great job." The captain, Erik, side-hugged him as his other line mates slapped him on the back. He skated over to the bench, did the high five thing, then resumed his seat. He studied the play overhead on the Jumbotron as he sucked down water. Yeah, that was sweet.

He watched the next minute of play. Ninety seconds on the clock. Now to protect their lead…

Another line change and Brent was out there again. The Stars were throwing everything at them. Brent kept his head up, trying to stay aware of the movement around him. Suddenly the puck came his way. He skated toward it when—boom!

His shoulder crunched the boards, and he twisted away from the hulking defenseman's weight. Payback. Thank God for shoulder pads. Ugh. Brent staggered to his feet and skated to the bench.

"Dude, you okay?"

"Yeah, fine." But he'd bet there'd be a pretty bruise there tomorrow.

The siren blared for the end of the game, and Brent joined the rest of the team on the ice. They lifted their sticks in appreciation of the crowd.

"Karls, they want you to hang around."

Brent nodded to the assistant coach, fighting back the smile. He fist-bumped Doug and waited near the bench as the announcer finished his spiel.

"And the third star of the night, with the game winner, is Brent Karlsson!"

Brent skated onto the ice, gave a quick wave and a smile at the applause, then headed back down through the tunnel to the dressing room, fist bumping the equipment guys on the way.

"Great game, Karls."

"Sweet goal, man."

He handed off his stick and headed inside. The guys were getting changed, sweaty jerseys thrown into the basket, equipment unstrapped, skates unlaced.

"Yo, Karlos!" Slaps on the back. "Nice one, man."

The music pumped. "Brent, they want you for media."

Great. He didn't mind the interviews, provided they stayed focused on hockey. He nodded and changed into his workout clothes. As the rest of the team disappeared to do some cooldown workouts, he shoved a hand through his hair, waiting as the assistant coach nodded and the media started streaming in. The camera lights were bright, and he tried not to wince as they crowded close, their microphones and recording devices in his face.

"So, Brent, tell us how you feel…"

BRENT COMPLETED a round of emails and text messages, replying to his MPFG sponsor kids, razzing Jai about Chicago's recent loss to Winnipeg—which scored him a line of face palm emojis. He set his phone aside, ready to finally enjoy the afternoon, when it buzzed again. He glanced at the caller ID. Doug. He always called him on their days off.

"Yo."

"Hey man, what's up?"

"Not much." Just the way he liked it. Man, he must be getting old or something.

"Hey, did you hear about the party down at the Mercury Bar?"

"I heard about it." The Wings regularly received invitations to all kinds of events. Like the movie premiere last weekend. His stomach tensed.

Taking Larissa had been a terrible idea. When Alex, his teammate, had practically begged Brent to take his sister, telling him she was desperate to go, he'd stupidly stayed listening when he should've walked out the door. Larissa was young, blonde, and super pretty, and feeling the desperate pinch of loneliness, he'd agreed. It had been way too long between dates. She was supposedly a huge fan of an actor who'd also be there. Not that she'd paid much attention to the actors or the movie, instead spending almost all her time cuddling up to Brent. And of course the media had been there. There'd been way too many photographs taken. He shook his head. What an idiot he'd been.

"So, are you going?"

The sun was setting, pooling gold on the tops of the houses. The perfect afternoon to just sit and relax. And avoid any of the complications caused by his random bouts of stupidity. "Nah."

"Come on, man. It'll be awesome."

"What's gonna make it that good?"

"They've got some sick bands playing."

As Doug started listing the bands that were performing, Brent felt a flicker of interest. "What time? We've got practice tomorrow morning."

"Man," Doug groaned, "we're not gonna get wasted, just have a good time."

Doug's powers of persuasion were good. An hour later, Brent was clutching a drink as he mingled in the dark recesses of the bar. The band was good, but this scene made him uncomfortable these days. He bit back a groan as Doug bounded over with another two bottles in hand. Doug was looking extra sharp tonight, working a fedora with flair.

"Nah, I'm good." Brent pointed to his almost full glass.

"You're too good, dude. You need to get a little bad." Doug's eyes widened, then he grinned. "Well, hello, ladies."

"Hey there." At the soft voice, Brent turned to see two girls almost falling out of their tops. "You're Brent Karlsson, right?"

He grimaced. Not again. "Sorry. Not interested." He glanced

over at Doug, who looked slightly crestfallen. "This is my friend, Doug."

They flicked Doug a brief look and even briefer smiles before moving closer. "But you're so *hot*."

Yeah, he was. It was way too warm in here. He stepped away and tapped Doug on the shoulder, yelling above the noise. "I'm outta here. See you tomorrow."

Doug nodded as he started chatting with the girls.

Brent shook his head as he disappeared outside into the light, punching in the numbers for a cab. What an idiot he'd been to come. He'd known what tonight would be like, but had felt sorry for Doug, had tried to connect with him on his terms. Brent closed his eyes, remembering the flash of phones as the girls were thrusting their wares in his face. His stomach turned. *God, please cleanse my mind.*

He opened his eyes at the sharp honk of a horn and heard a low voice next to him.

"Hi, Brent. Long time, no see."

And he turned and stared in disbelief.

CHAPTER 5

Sofia, Bulgaria
February

Holly blocked out the busy hum of Sofia airport, her fingers dancing across the computer's keyboard in the business lounge as she quickly read the messages of support she'd received via email over the past few days. She smiled. There really was a lot of love out there.

She started typing.

Hi all,
Sorry it's another group email, but I'm writing this in Sofia, knowing that when I land it'll be straight into mega busyness again. February in Bulgaria is so much colder than Brisbane right now! A quick update: competition went okay. I came 3rd in my quarters for 500m and 19th overall for 1000m, so okay, but not great. Hoping to do better in Dresden next week. Thanks again for your texts and emails. Can't wait to have more time one day to actually reply individually.
God bless, Holly

She hit send, then sat back in her seat and stretched, glancing at the clock. Due to a flight delay, she still had another thirty minutes until she had to head to her gate. That would provide another chance to get online and see if she could find what Bree had mentioned in her latest email. She clicked on the Internet and accessed Calgary's NHL website, where she found the photos from a recent charity event.

There was Bree looking beautiful as ever, dressed in a glamorous black dress and arm in arm with Mike, who looked very dapper in his suit. They looked so happy. She smiled, then clicked on the news articles Bree had mentioned, quickly scanning them. Yep, Bree was right. The report about the fundraising efforts of the Flames and their "better halves," as the team's wives and girlfriends were known, came across really well. Did other teams do this too?

She quickly clicked over to Detroit's website, looking through the news items until she found Brent's name. She glanced at the computer clock. Fifteen minutes to go. She clicked on his player profile and studied his photo. He was staring straight at the camera with a small smile on his face, like he was too cool to show how much he enjoyed this game. His dark hair was much shorter than she remembered from the wedding. She read his statistics: #25; 6′3″; 197 pounds; shoots left; birthplace: Toronto. There was information about when he was drafted and his game statistics.

Holly scrolled back up to the photo and tried to find the joker from Bree's wedding in the serious pose. Okay, so maybe she'd misjudged him. In all of his recent emails—and that phone call—he'd proven to be quite thoughtful and caring. He even seemed to share her slightly twisted sense of humor.

She glanced at the clock again. Ten minutes more. She clicked on the Wings' TV special, watching the video as some busty brunette got up close and personal, asking the players questions about their favorite movies, music, food. The guys all seemed to get on pretty well. There was a lot of joking about, and Brent often seemed to be at the center.

Scrolling through, she found a link to a site that talked about the players' girlfriends. Ignoring the sudden queasiness in her stomach, she pressed the link: *Brent Karlsson's girlfriend*. There was a picture of him smiling at the camera, his hunky pose showing off his biceps. She scrolled down the page. Dozens of anonymous writers were contributing to the discussion. She read through the comments: *He's so cute! Such a stud. He's, like, so totally adorable!* Holly grimaced. How old were the people who wrote these things?

She continued reading, her stomach tightening further. *I want to have his babies! I'm going to marry him.* Some girls sounded almost stalker-ish, telling people where they'd spotted him hanging out with other Detroit players. She frowned. Some girls seemed a little possessive, swearing at others, insisting they or someone they knew had dated him, had kissed him.

And worse.

She checked the date. This was only last week. He said he'd changed, but had he?

She slowly scrolled further down, and there, amidst the crazy talk from the stalker fans, she found it. Another photo. A recent photo. Proof.

Her stomach twisted. She clamped her lips together.

Brent had a girlfriend.

Detroit, Michigan

"Hey, Karlsson. You coming out tonight?"

Brent threw his towel into the hamper and shook his head. "Nah, I'm done. Gotta rest this old body of mine."

"And miss the media out there?" Doug nodded to the team's

locker room, where the media interviewed whoever they could after the players finished their showers and changed into street clothes.

Brent shrugged. "Maybe that too."

Fortunately, there was a door that led to the lounge where they could sit and relax—or escape to the parking lot. He nodded to a couple of teammates who were laughing in the lounge and was about to make his escape when he heard his name called.

"Yo! When you gonna call my sister? She's always on my case about you."

Alex Turner was a hulking defenseman with a nasty temper who tended to use his fists more than his brain. Best to not get on his wrong side. "Going to the movie was fun, but I don't think I'm the right guy for her."

Turner sneered. "No one's asking you to marry her. She just wants a good time."

Brent glanced over to where Doug and a couple of others were watching curiously. "Tell Larissa I said hi, but I'm not really in the market for that type of good time anymore."

"He's a monk. Never does anything." Doug shook his head. "Mr. Straight and Narrow."

"You never used to be."

Brent's cheeks heated as memories crowded in of the stupid way he'd previously acted and spoken about girls, like they were pieces of meat lined up for his selection. What an idiot. Believing his own hype had got him into this mess in the first place.

Alex took a step forward. "You got a problem with my sister?"

"No. Just don't want to be leading anyone on, okay?"

"Like Chloe?"

Brent repressed a shudder at the name. Thank God he'd woken up in time. "That was a long time ago. I thought we'd all moved on." Brent eyeballed the guys in the room, but nobody said any more, so he quickly escaped and drove home. He sped past the autograph seekers and soon turned onto Fort Street, but the choke of cars did nothing to shake the tension from before.

What would it take for people to believe he wasn't a player anymore? Of course, between going to the movie premiere with Larissa and seeing Chloe at the club, and his teammates' jokes and jeers, it wasn't gonna seem too convincing that he'd changed.

He entered his front hall just as his phone rang. He fished it from his pocket, held it to his ear.

"Anything you want to tell me?"

"Hi, Bree. Great to hear from you. Yeah, I'm fine, thanks for asking." He threw his bag down and headed up the stairs to his office.

She gave an exasperated sigh. "Anything about a particular girl?"

He rolled his eyes. Of course. "What girl? Holly? I haven't heard from her for a while." He moved to his laptop to check his emails.

"I'm not surprised." His sister's voice was tight. What was that about? "Fine, Brent, play it your way. Who is this Larissa woman?"

"Alex's sister?"

"Why did you go out to the movie premiere with her? How long has this been going on for?"

He groaned. "It was one time, Bree."

"What was she thinking, wearing an outfit like that? She looked like a…"

Yep. He'd thought that, too. But what was he supposed to do? She'd shown up dressed like that, and he couldn't very well tell her to go put on more clothes.

"Have you seen the stuff online about it?"

His stomach twisted. "No. You know I never look at that stuff. And you shouldn't either. It's full of lies."

"Brent, they're saying all kinds of crazy stuff." She sounded close to tears. "There were pictures of you and Chloe, too." She sniffed. "Tell me you're not back with her."

Brent closed his eyes. "Of course not."

"Then what were you doing?"

He shook his head. "I saw her outside the club. I was waiting for a cab and boom, there she was."

"How did she know you were there?"

"I don't know." He breathed out, past the spiking irritation. "She probably had friends inside who called her or something. I didn't ask. I just got outta there, ASAP."

"She seems a little obsessive."

"Yeah."

Bree didn't know the half of it. His soul shuddered at the memory of two years ago, when he'd woken up from a pre-game nap to find his girlfriend semi-dressed and trying to climb into his bed. He'd always suspected Chloe was a little needy, but he'd not expected the degree she'd go to show her affection. Nausea rippled through his stomach. Once upon a time he hadn't minded her advances and had actually really enjoyed her kisses. Thank God he'd always stopped things before they got out of hand. And thank God he'd woken up in time. If he hadn't...

"Brent? You still there?"

He sighed. "Yeah."

The longer Bree talked, the more his heart writhed. Taking Larissa to that movie event had created a storm in the social pages of the papers. It almost had him jumping at shadows, wondering if some photographer or teenager with a phone was going to take his picture. Everyone was wondering about the sudden interest Brent Karlsson had shown in his teammate's sister and whether the ensuing dynamics had affected their respective games. It hadn't helped that the Wings had lost a few times recently.

On so many levels, that date had been a really big mistake. He shook his head again. He was such an idiot.

"HEY, KARLSSON!"

Brent looked up at the Washington player, who smirked and pointed at the sign a nearby fan was holding. *#25 Stop scoring and start scoring!*

Brent chewed his mouth guard and skated past, working to hide his anger as he moved to the bench. So much for being a witness in the hockey world. Nausea rippled. Why hadn't he realized how impossible it would be to escape his reputation? Would anyone ever believe he was trying to live God's way?

Doug elbowed him in the ribs and nodded to the sign. "You're popular."

Brent shook his head.

He loved how everyone made judgments about his life with no real facts. He might be the face for the team, but it didn't mean he owed the fans full access to his heart. It wasn't like he could make some public service announcement either: *No, I am not interested in Larissa or any other girl who lives on this side of the planet.*

He watched from the bench as the Capitals scored another goal just on full time. Great. Yet another loss that would add weight to the speculation surrounding him. He'd missed a few chances again today.

"Karlos, that hot reporter from the sports channel's out there. I think she wants you."

"Which chick doesn't?" Alex snorted. "I don't get it."

"It must be his mystery man persona." Doug switched to falsetto. "Ladies, you can look but don't touch."

"You're real funny." Brent shuffled to the showers, avoiding the media that always barged into the dressing room way too soon. What a stupid predicament to be in. In the past, he hadn't minded the jibes from his teammates about the girls who wore his #25 jersey or held up signs with his name, but now their jokes stung harder.

Once showered and changed into street clothes, he made his escape and drove home. He flicked on the radio, listening idly as the sports summaries continued. Football scores, game summaries interspersed with banter. They started on the NHL. Calgary had won, Mike recording a Gordie Howe hat-trick: a goal, an assist, and a fight.

The commentators laughed. "And we bet his new wife is just thrilled with that."

"Come on, Lenny, she'd be used to it. Her brother is Karlsson from Detroit."

Brent's chest tightened as they continued.

"Speak of the devil, or the Red Wing in this case—"

"Haw, haw."

"He had a terrible game tonight, as did the Wings. Another loss, this time to the Capitals. Let's talk about that."

"Haw, haw. Then let's talk about some of those rumors about why Karlsson in particular is doing so poorly."

Brent switched it off. "Let's not."

He thought back to a team TV interview from a few weeks ago. The reporter had asked questions about who the most popular team member was with the fans, and apart from a few who chose the captain, the general consensus had him as the ladies' favorite. He groaned. He so wasn't that kind of guy, but people monitoring the Wings' website would come across this interview too, and it'd only confirm everything they apparently already thought. Not that he cared too much about what people thought, apart from his family, his pastor, and—

Brent swallowed. Bree had mentioned Holly wasn't emailing

him because she thought Larissa was his girlfriend. He hated that she had the wrong impression, that she thought him some kind of player. He'd tried to pray about it, had tried explaining some of it to Pastor Josiah from the online Bible study group, but all he got was this sense to keep the door open, to try and explain things somehow. *But how, God? She's ignoring my emails. What do I do?*

Ten minutes later he was back home, checking his email again. Still nothing. He flicked back to the one he'd sent three days ago. He'd tried to keep it simple and innocuous, but was it? He reread it.

> *Hey Holly,*
> *I haven't heard from you for a while and wondered how you*
> *are. I guess you're in Europe now. Your travel sounds more fun*
> *than mine. Good luck with your comps.*
> *All the best. Brent*

He checked the calendar, then the date of her last email. That much time had passed?

Frowning, he wandered down to the kitchen only to find an empty fridge. Bummer. He'd known there was something he'd meant to do. His phone vibrated. He hooked it out of his back pocket, staring at the screen. More mail. His heart tripped when he recognized the name in the subject line. Finally.

He flicked it open.

> *Hi there.*
> *The European leg of the ISU tour has just finished. Results*
> *improving slightly (made it to 500m semis but came 8th; 16th in*
> *1000m). Championships next, but can't wait to get home.*
> *Granddad is pretty sick with pneumonia. Please pray for him.*
> *Miss you, Holly*

He checked the message details and his heart sank. Bree had forwarded on a group email Holly had sent a couple of days ago. He shook his head again. He was such an idiot.

CHAPTER 6

Brisbane, Australia
March

"**Y**ou're here at last!"

Holly dropped her bags at the door, her weariness and frustration lifting as she enfolded Jess in a hug. "I'm so glad to see you."

"And me you." Jess squeezed, then stepped back. "How was your flight?"

"Long. Made even longer because the last connection got delayed by nearly two hours." Holly yawned, glancing around their small house. "How's everything here?"

"Pretty quiet with you and Kate away. You look like you need a cup of tea."

"I'd *love* one." As Jess moved to the kitchen, Holly grabbed a ripe-looking peach from the basket in the middle of the dining table. "Have you heard anything more about Kate?" she called.

"Apparently the doctors think she'll never have full use of her leg again."

Holly winced, the heaviness of past weeks weighting her soul even more. "What a waste." *Lord, heal her.* She bit into her peach. Urgh. There should be a law against selling sour peaches. She threw the rest into the bin.

Jess called from the kitchen. "Oh, your mum rang. She wants you to call her ASAP."

"Righty-o." Holly retrieved the box of macadamia nuts from her carry on and placed it on the table before picking up her bags and heading to her room. Macadamia nuts were Jessica's favorite form of comfort food, an always welcome present from the airport shop. She loved them as much as Holly loved Belgian choccies.

Holly retrieved her phone and dialed the familiar numbers.

Jessica's squeal of appreciation reverberated through the house. "Macadamias!"

Holly's lips lifted, her mum answered, and they chatted for a while about her results and travel. "I don't know how I'll ever qualify for Vancouver next year. My times just aren't cutting it." She sighed, swallowing the disappointment. Would she ever be good enough? "Anyway, enough doom and gloom from me. What's up?"

Several beats passed before her mother finally answered. "It's your grandfather."

Oh no. "What's wrong with him?"

Her mother sighed. "It's definitely Alzheimer's disease."

"Oh, Mum." Holly choked down the ball of emotion in her throat. "Are you okay?" If only she could be there to give her a hug. After losing Holly's maternal grandmother last year, this must be so tough.

"I'm okay. But we've decided to put him in a nursing home." Her voice was shaky. "It's not ideal, but your father and I can't keep taking time off work, and he really needs around the clock care."

Holly's eyes blurred. "He's that bad?"

"Yes." Her mother cleared her throat. "Holl, it'd be really good if you could make it back for Easter."

"Of course I will," she rushed to assure.

"I know your coach wants you to stay focused—"

"But not at my family's expense." Holly blinked away tears. "Will Ben be there?"

"Yes. He misses you, Holly."

Holly missed him too. She sucked in a deep breath. "Tell Granddad I love him very much, and give him a big hug from me. And if you need me to come sooner, I'll be there with bells on, all right?" No matter what Coach Chan might say.

"That's my girl." Her mum softly chuckled. "So, tell me more about Europe."

One paragraph to go. Familiar tension knotted Holly's shoulders, making finishing this essay so much harder. Worries pecked around her brain, stealing her focus. Worries about her grandfather's health, her results, her lack of money, whether she'd even qualify for the Australian team selection.

Her computer blinked with an incoming message. She glanced at it. Brent was online and wanted to talk with her. She rejected the invitation. No way. The last time she'd let herself become distracted, she'd let her emotions get the better of her, which was capital S for stupid. She should've known better. What was she doing letting him derail her focus, anyway?

But seeing that awful photo had spurred an investigation even Interpol would've been proud of. She'd trawled through years of photos posted online, her heart twisting a little more each time she saw Brent with some girl. As for that "Brent Karlsson's girlfriend" website—what an eye opener. Girls really talked like that about other people? She'd read online what the girls of Detroit said about him. Apparently, Brent was like the ultimate catch this Larissa woman had finally managed to reel in. And then there were all these other comments about his ex, Chloe. Her stomach tightened.

Seriously? How many girlfriends had he had? The comments were pretty mean-spirited, but even half a world away she got the message. And Holly sure wasn't interested in emailing or talking to someone who had a girlfriend, especially a girlfriend who dressed like she was a Playboy bunny. Yep, she'd sure picked his type correctly, and no, she wasn't about to let herself be made a fool of again.

Nausea threatened as a memory flickered of a naïve girl, the poor, sweet, stupid girl whose hopes for her first kiss had been so crudely disillusioned. She lifted her chin. Nope. With the exception of Mike and her brother, pro sports guys were all the same—only after one thing.

The pressure in her head ramped up another notch. She scratched at the skin on her hands, which had broken out again with eczema, as they did every time she got stressed. Coach Chan was right: distractions were the enemy of success. Holly needed to stay focused on what was important, what was real, what she could do something about, and not waste another thought on someone whose actions contradicted his words.

Holly squared her shoulders, lifted her chin, and resumed typing amid the brain fog. Finally finished, she wearily reread the essay, then emailed it off and closed down the computer. Thank God. Another item marked off the list. Another day done. Another day closer to the Easter long weekend and time with her family. She changed into her PJs and climbed into bed.

Wollongong, Australia
Easter

Nutmeg and yeast scented the air. Thank goodness her competition season was done. She could eat hot cross buns and chocolate without too much guilt this weekend.

Holly smiled at her grandfather, seated across from her, but his vague gaze held no hint of recognition. "Granddad?"

"Molly?"

"It's Holly, Granddad."

"Where's Molly?"

Her mother sighed, the animation since this morning's church service drained away. Molly was Granddad's sister, who'd been dead these past twenty years.

Poor Granddad. Poor Mum. Today had been tough—not nearly the fun holiday Holly had hoped for or imagined.

"I think we should take him back to the home," her mother said. "I suspect today was too much for him."

"I'm sorry, Mum. I'll clear up everything here."

"Thanks, sweetheart."

Halfway through stacking the dishwasher, her phone rang. Her heart lifted at the Canadian number. "Hi, Bree. Happy Easter! Well, I hope your Easter is happier than ours has been." Her voice wavered. "Sorry. Today has been a little tough."

A beat. "Holly?"

Oh. No. That deep voice definitely wasn't Bree. "Um, who is this? I thought this was Bree's phone."

"It's, er, Brent."

She closed her eyes. Great.

"I borrowed Bree's phone because I figured you might not answer if I called."

Clever man.

"Is everything okay? You haven't replied to my emails, and I was just wondering…"

She put the powder in the machine, shut the door, and pressed start. "I've been pretty busy."

"But you're not too busy if you've had time to delete me from your group emails."

His pause spurred defensiveness. "I...I'm not in the habit of sending emails to guys."

"So who are David and James? And who's Ben? You send emails to them."

Was he jealous? She bit back a laugh at the absurdity. "David is the minister of my church, and James is an equally ancient member of the congregation who heads up the prayer team. I email them because they and their wives are interested in how I'm going and they pray for me."

"Oh." The reply softened. "But I'm interested."

Air jammed in her lungs. Her heart altered its rhythm, quickening the beat. Did he mean interested generally or interested in her personally? Oh, why did she even care? She couldn't afford any distractions. Brent was a player, anyway. She shifted to the kitchen sink and turned on the hot water for the non-dishwasher-proof items.

"Would you include me again in your emails?" he continued. "I'd hate to think you didn't because of some misunderstanding."

She swallowed. "You mean that Larissa woman?"

"Holly, I went out with her as a favor for a teammate. She doesn't mean anything to me."

"That's not what the photo looked like." Images of a buxom blonde in a tight, short, low-cut red dress slithering over Brent flashed through Holly's mind. The sting caught her afresh.

"I hate that you think so badly of me. That's not who I am."

"Right." She squirted in the dish-cleaning liquid, then stuck the phone on speaker mode and commenced washing the silver-edged china. "So all those pictures on the Internet are just coincidences, are they?"

He sighed. "Holl, I don't know what pictures you've seen, but you need to believe me when I say I'm not like that. I've gone on one date in the past two years, and even that wasn't really a date." His laugh was edged with bitterness. "You'll probably say I'm just being egotistical, but some girls seem to hunt down where we go. It's crazy stuff. But it doesn't make it real."

Her lips twitched. If she didn't feel so fragile right now, she'd probably call him on the ego. And he *needed* her to believe him? Why?

"Honestly, Holly, I only went out with Larissa as a favor, not because I actually like the woman. I take my mom to stuff if I have to take anyone."

Her heart softened and her movements paused. That was actually kind of cute. Big tough hockey player taking out his mom. "I heard what your teammates said about you on that Valentine's TV special. Something about being the number one pick for the ladies."

"People say a lot of stuff. It doesn't mean it's true."

"Right…" She drew the word out.

"It's all marketing. It isn't real. It's about selling tickets to the fans."

"I wouldn't know. I don't really have fans." Let alone chat rooms filled with rabid stalker types.

"I'm a fan," he said softly.

She nearly dropped her grandmother's antique platter. Was it April Fools'?

"Please, Holly, I really want to stay in touch."

Had she misjudged him? Again? "Well…okay then."

"Thank you."

For some reason her throat grew tight.

"Hey, is everything okay? You sounded pretty down before."

She drained the water and wiped her hands. After taking her phone off speaker mode, she moved onto the deck to sink into the cushioned cane chair with its sea view. "It…it's my grandfather. He's not doing too well, and it's just been a little rough."

"You don't get the chance to see him often, do you?"

He understood? Moisture heated the backs of her eyes.

"I'm sorry, Holly. He's been in my prayers. I wish there was something I could do."

"It's okay." Not really. But Brent's call had—surprisingly—cleared some of the spiky clutter from her heart.

"Hey, it's been nice to chat with you."

"You too, Brent. I…I hope you have a happy Easter."

"It's happier now," he murmured.

What? She had no words, except, "Bye."

Holly ended the call, drawing in another deep breath of salt-tinged air as she studied the sea, trying to make sense of it all. What the—? Why had—? Oh, this was ridiculous. She smoothed her ponytail and headed back inside.

Ben appeared, eyeing her curiously. "Everything okay?"

She nodded and found her first genuine smile in weeks. "Yep. Things are better now."

~

Detroit, Michigan
April

Hi friends,
So I'm back in Brissy after a quick visit home, and I realised I never shared how the World Championships went. Let's just say Austria was pretty, and my results were pretty average. I got disqualified for impeding in the 1000m, crashed out in the 500m quarterfinals, and managed to cut my leg on another skater's skate, so I now have another beautiful scar to add to the collection. I also need to buy another skate suit now, as that one was too torn and the blood wouldn't come out. Sorry this sounds gory and depressing—it's a little tough to see any bright side right now.
Hope you're well and had a good Easter. Holly

Brent winced as her email revived memories of last November, when she'd been injured. Short track was high risk, and it didn't take much for his stomach to get queasy thinking of what could happen to Holly. *God, please keep her safe.*

He googled short track equipment costs, his eyebrows rising. It had been a long time since he'd needed to bother about purchasing much for hockey, but even so, a thousand dollars for a skate suit? He tracked down the page, and his eyes widened further. Over a grand for decent boots and blades? No wonder she sounded depressed.

He tapped the desk, struggling to think of anything that would be encouraging. He slowly tapped out a reply.

Hey Holly,
I was really sorry to hear about that. That's tough all round, huh? Jai led Bible study this week and talked about 2 Thessalonians 2:16-17. I hope it blesses you too. "May our Lord Jesus Christ himself and God our Father, who loved us and by his grace gave us eternal encouragement and good hope, encourage your hearts and strengthen you in every good deed and word." Hope you can find an upside soon. Brent

He reread it, pressed send, and prayed.

"Hi there."

"Hi yourself." Holly's lips lifted. "This is a surprise."

Brent shrugged, but he hadn't felt like going out, hadn't felt like watching TV. The thought had crossed his mind to see if Holly was online, and bingo, there she was. Who better to talk to? "How are you?"

"Good." She tilted her head to one side, her pretty hair swinging around her bare shoulders. "How are you?"

"Cold. It looks a lot warmer where you are."

"It's been in the high twenties this past week. That's Celsius, not Fahrenheit." She smiled. "Anyway, that's pretty warm for this time of year, even by Australian standards."

He loved how technology could lessen vast distances. "So your season is done now? You finished with the World Championships, right?"

"Yep. I have a bit of a break until training resumes in late June. My first comp is in August."

"Let's hope for a better result, huh? Disqualification must be tough."

"It's not fun, that's for sure." Her face shadowed. "Especially when half the time you don't even realize you've done something wrong. Officials can disqualify you for impeding when that wasn't your intention at all. We have a saying around here: That's short track." She shrugged. "It's the nature of the sport."

Respect mingled with sympathy for what she didn't say. "It's tough, isn't it, trying to stay positive when things don't go your way."

Holly propped her chin on her hand. "You mean like the Wings losing four in a row?"

He grimaced. "You noticed?"

She nodded slowly. "So, how are you feeling about that?"

He filled her in on the last disappointing games. "But you gotta have hope, right?"

"Right." Her lips lifted again, and his heart skittered.

Silence fell as she tilted her head and looked at him almost expectantly.

"You look great." Maybe a little thinner than their last video call.

"Oh. Thanks." Her cheeks flushed. "I'm going out soon."

His heart dropped. He hadn't realized she had a boyf—

"It's my birthday today."

Oh. Hadn't known. That would look lame to admit though. "Happy birthday, Holly."

"Thanks."

There was a vague murmur in the background. Holly turned at a voice off screen. "Spare towels are in the linen closet, Ben." She turned back with a sheepish smile. "Sorry."

What? Who was Ben? And what was this about towels? Strange hurt pinched his chest. "Where are you going?"

"To my favorite restaurant. I love seafood, and my family is up to help celebrate."

She grinned, but his heart refused to cooperate. "Who's Ben?" Subtle, he wasn't.

Her smile grew coy. "Why?"

He bit his lip as he caught sight of a muscled man in the background, wearing a towel around his waist. Wow. He never would've thought... "You look like you've got company. I'm gonna go—"

"Brent!" She laughed. "This is Ben."

The muscle man leaned forward and nodded unsmilingly. "G'day."

Brent nodded. "Hey." This was getting surreal. "Okay, I'll talk to you later." Real later. Like maybe never. This was kinda humiliating—

Holly turned back to the muscled surfer dude. "Ben, go away. I want to talk to Brent."

Ben's lips thinned, and he nodded again to Brent before disappearing. Brent's eyes narrowed. Did that guy have a tattoo on his back? What was Holly doing with him there?

"Brent—"

"Holly, you don't need to explain anything to me." He didn't want to hear about it. Talk about a sucker punch to the heart.

"It appears I do." She chuckled. "Ben is my brother. I thought you knew that."

"Oh." *Thank God.*

"I swear, for a second there—" She gave another gurgle of laughter. "You're so funny."

No, he was an idiot.

She leaned forward. "Ben and I had a bike race to Mount Gravatt and back. The loser had the second shower." Her lips lifted smugly. "I've already had my shower."

"Does he always go around in a towel?"

"No." Her smile broadened. "Not always."

His mouth finally echoed hers. "So, you're going out with your folks?"

"Yeah, I'm such a party animal. Some friends from training are coming too."

His heart tensed again. "Anyone I need to know about?"

"You sound exactly like my brother."

Not what he'd been aiming for.

"There's no handsome young man, if that's what you're asking."

Finally. His world tilted back into normalcy. "Ah, but what about short, plump guys? I seem to remember you prefer that type."

Her smile cooled, then slid off her face. What was that about? He was trying to joke…

"Oh yes, I'm surrounded by little men most weeks, but I'm sure there's not as many as the busty blondes who'd like to hover around a certain hockey someone."

Holly glanced down at the keyboard, her chest tight. She just needed one day of fun. Granddad's health was getting worse, her uni assignments continued to pile up, money was still super tight, and there were no more corners left to cut. Her family visiting today had been just the tonic, and she'd so looked forward to tonight as a rare escape from the grind. Brent's call had been an unexpected bonus. *Had* been.

She blinked and examined the charm bracelet on her arm which matched Bree's, fingering the little silver cowboy hat Bree had sent her earlier. She'd sent it with a card from Calgary that said *Wish you were here*. Ha. Living in Calgary would be a dream come true. It had one of the best short track skating programs in the world, and she'd get to see Bree more often. Holly swallowed. Impossible dream. Wishing sure never got her anywhere.

"You know, Holly, I never said that was my type."

She glanced up. "No? I seem to recall a certain conversation in a certain gym."

His blue eyes seemed to darken, grow more serious. "That was you, thinking you knew me."

"But—"

"Busty blonde is really overrated."

His smile warmed her insides. No point analyzing that right now. She nodded. "Clichéd."

"Right?" He grinned.

Was she such an open book? But despite these stupid emotions that resulted in silly banter like tonight, she couldn't let herself be distracted. Any relationship would need to be put on ice until after Vancouver next year—if she made the team. Besides, he lived so far away. An email relationship didn't count. Did it?

Brent leaned forward, an eyebrow aloft. "You might need to tell me about these short men of yours though."

"Oh." It was her turn to grin as the world suddenly leveled out. "You mean the little boys in my Sunday school class?"

CHAPTER 7

Detroit, Michigan
May

Brent gingerly moved off the exercise bike. Last night's game had left its mark in more ways than one. He rubbed at the bruise on his shoulder. The Chicago games were always hotly contested, and last night had been no different. He'd thumped Jai into the boards but come off second best, and the icepacks and cold whirlpool afterward hadn't helped much. Thank God today was a rest day.

He headed out of the spare room that he'd turned into a gym and walked up the stairs to the kitchen. Refueling time. He reheated the leftover pasta from two nights ago, watching the bowl spin slowly around as the microwave did its thing. Glanced at the clock. Most of his non-hockey friends would be at work.

At least he'd be able to make the Bible study this week. He'd missed too many recently, with away games and training eating into his time. It was good to hang out with Mike, Jai, Beau, Dan, and a few other Christians who played in pro hockey's major and minor leagues. God knew he needed support from others who tried to live for Jesus in such a money-hungry, celebrity-focused, results-oriented world.

The microwave pinged, and he opened the door, wincing as the heat seared through his fingers. Awesome. A burn to add to the collection of personal injuries over the past twenty-four hours.

His phone rang. He scrabbled it from his pocket and checked the screen. "Yo."

As Mike started filling him in on his past week, Brent shoveled the noodles in. Dropping sugar levels didn't wait for anyone. He swallowed with a loud gulp. "I hear you. This season seems way too long."

Mike groaned. "Don't tell Bree, but I'm starting to feel like an old man. I can't believe how much harder this season has been on my body."

Brent blinked. So didn't want to think about why that might be. He glanced out the kitchen window at the trees trying to pump out some green. "I'll just be glad to get out of the cold."

"Got any vacation plans for after the season?"

Brent slurped another mouthful. "Depends on how long you think our season is going to be."

"Yeah, I'm not sure our playoffs will last as long as yours. I've promised John Ramirez I'll visit the Philippines again and thought I'd take Bree."

"And visit your charity again?" Mission Possible for Future Generations was a charity that Mike fronted to raise awareness of the problems faced by children in Filipino slums.

"I figured Bree should meet the MPFG team, considering she's taken on so much of the administration of things. She's excited, but knows it will be a little confronting."

"Be great to see your sponsor kids again."

"Yeah, and to see how things are after the typhoon a while back. Anyway, I figured she might need some relaxation time after, and we wondered if you'd like to tag along."

"What? Married life too boring for you?"

"No. Just that we know you've wanted to get back to Hawaii."

Hawaii. Brent smiled. He'd only been there once, but it had been so good.

"Anyway, Bree thought it'd be a good chance to hang out. I think she misses you, bud."

Warmth filled his chest. "I don't want to be a third wheel."

"She's been dropping hints the size of boulders about all this shopping she has to do and massages she *needs*." Mike chuckled. "The thinking is that while she's doing that, you and I go play golf or windsurf or something."

"I'd be happy to just relax by the pool."

"Well, think about it. We can book it when we know how the playoffs go."

"Yeah, okay. Count me in. That sounds awesome."

Brent hung up, a smile in his heart. His body suddenly didn't ache so much anymore.

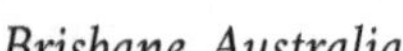

Brisbane, Australia

It was late. Everyone was tucked up in bed or at least watching TV, judging from the blue flickers behind curtains as Holly pedaled home from the supermarket. How nice would that be, to just sit and relax like a normal person instead of having to get her head in the right space for tonight's assignment. Holly finally pulled into her driveway and fished free her keys.

She unlocked the front door and wheeled the bike inside. "Hey, Jess, I'm home."

No answer. She sniffed the air and sighed. No magical dinner, either. Oh well, it looked like another apple for her meal tonight. She plucked one from the fruit bowl and went to her room, powering up the laptop while she jammed her feet into Uggs. This past week's cooler weather had left its mark in more ways than one. She coughed, then frowned at the burn in her chest. Good thing Mum wasn't around, otherwise she'd be forced to lie in bed for a week.

Holly scrolled through the emails, quickly replying to one from Bree before noticing that Brent was online too. She smiled, unsurprised when he sent an invitation to chat minutes later. She accepted, ignoring the little voice that whispered *assignment*. So what if she hadn't started it yet? She needed a break. She *deserved* a break. Brent often made her laugh, and she hadn't laughed much at all lately.

"Hey, Holly. It's nice to see you." His smile was so nice, like an advertisement for joy.

"Nice to see you too. Congrats on doing well in the playoffs. I saw your interview the other day after your goal." She snickered. "You looked like you had a classic case of helmet head, red marks and all."

"Oh, that." He rubbed his forehead as if it were still marked. "Well, it's nice to feel like I'm contributing. I hope the selectors notice."

She nodded, coughed, then pasted on a smile as he raised his eyebrows. "I've got a bit of a cold." How crazy to be coughing and spluttering before winter had even begun. At least she wasn't trying to compete with such reduced lung capacity.

"I thought you sounded a little different." He shifted in his seat, his smile fading a notch. "So, has life slowed up for you any now your competitions are all done?"

She tried to laugh, but it sounded wheezy. "Not really. I'm working double shifts at the moment, trying to boost my savings for next season."

"You don't have sponsorship?"

"I get my flights and accommodation covered and little else. This isn't the NHL, Brent. This is Australian short track. The only time Australians maybe even think about us is once every four years when it's the Games. Nobody's keen to sponsor no-names like us."

"Wow. I didn't realize."

She shrugged. "So I have to keep working. Nights, I keep up with my health science course."

He frowned. "I thought you were deferring some of that."

"Yeah, next semester, when training and competition pick up again. But if I want to graduate before I'm one hundred, I need to keep studying."

He gave a slow nod. "You look tired."

"Thanks." Why did people always feel you needed to hear that? Of course she looked tired. She *was* tired. These days she always felt tired.

"Uh, I meant to say—"

"Brent, it's past ten o'clock here, I've been on my feet serving cranky customers all day, and I've had the flu for a week. So yes, I'm feeling tired."

He bit his lip. "Are you taking care of yourself?"

Tears blurred her vision, and she looked down. She didn't need his pity. She needed sleep. And more money.

"Holly?" She chanced a quick glance at the computer screen. His brow had furrowed. "You're looking a little thin."

She swallowed. He wasn't the first to say that. Mum had made a comment a couple of weeks ago. Jess had noticed she wasn't eating very much. Even Gina at church had said something. She shrugged. "You know I need to watch my weight."

"But I don't want to watch you fade away." He frowned. "Is everything okay?"

A sudden desire to laugh hysterically came over her. No. Everything was not okay. Granddad just seemed to get sicker.

She had to work like a slave and watch every cent to afford the equipment to be competitive. A new skate suit had pushed her savings down another grand, pushing back the planned purchase of better boots and blades.

But where could she cut corners? It wasn't like she ever had any spare cash to splash. No way was she going to deny her MPFG sponsor child just so she could eat meat. Brent sure wouldn't understand. She couldn't ask her parents for help—they'd sacrificed enough to help pay for her dream over the years. So if it meant skipping a meal here and there and not buying the usual stuff she ate while she was in training and competition mode, that was the price she had to pay. She'd been a little lightheaded every so often, but that was really only because she was still recovering from the flu. She knew about eating disorders. She sure wasn't skipping meals because she was worried about her appearance. It'd just be nice to have some more money for groceries.

"Holly?" Brent's searching glance was disconcerting as he shifted closer to the screen. "You are taking care of yourself, aren't you?"

She swallowed again. There was no place to hide from his scrutiny. "You know, you sound just like my mum."

"She's worried too? Holly, what's going on?"

If he kept pushing, she was going to lose it. She crossed her arms and prayed her voice would hold steady. "Brent, I know what I'm doing, so stop hassling me, okay?"

His eyes widened. "Okay, okay. I know I've got a big mouth, but you don't need to jump down my throat." His laughter sounded forced but helped break the tension. He leaned forward. "People care about you, Holly."

The concern in his eyes made hers mist again. Gee, she wasn't supposed to be such a wimp. This flu was playing havoc with her emotions. "Thanks." She couldn't look at him. It was time to go anyway. "I really have to get my assignment done. Good luck with the playoffs."

"Thanks. And thanks for talking. Bye, Holly."

"Bye." She clicked off the computer and rubbed her eyes. She should've just done that stupid assignment after all. What a mistake talking to Brent had been.

"Holly? Is this your phone?"

Holly looked up from the lunch table at Cheryl, the plump, brown-haired supermarket manager, who was holding a chirping silver phone. She wearily reached for it. "Thanks."

She glanced at the caller ID and, spirits lifting, sank down in her seat. "Hey, Bree."

"Hi, Holly! How are you?"

"Fine." She coughed.

Bree laughed. "Sure you are. I was on the phone with Brent yesterday, and he mentioned you'd been sick."

Great. Holly stifled the sigh.

"I emailed you, but no answer."

"Sorry. I've been that busy. But you're going to the Philippines? How cool!"

"Well, I don't know about that. I hear it's pretty tropical. But I'm excited to be going somewhere with Mike and meeting the Mission Possible team. And our sponsor children."

"You'll have to say hi to Desiree for me."

"Will do. Hey, where are you anyway?"

Holly closed her eyes and propped her head in her hands. "I'm at work. I've got twenty minutes until my next shift starts."

"Wow, Holl. You're so busy all the time. You really need a break, don't you?"

Thank God Cheryl had left and there was no-one else in the room to see how dangerously close to tears she was. She pressed her fingers against the headache forming in the middle of her forehead as Bree continued.

"Holly, I've been worried about you. This past year's been really tough, and you've been so stressed. You really need a good break—somewhere warm where you can relax and just enjoy yourself."

Yeah, she totally needed something like that. The stress was there all right: knotted in her shoulders and neck, pounding away in her head, boiling away in her stomach, breaking out on her fingers and interrupting her sleep. Worry about her grandfather, worry about her finances, worry about the wisdom of committing her life to this sport. Uni had left its mark on her soul, as permanent as the scar on her leg from the last competition. She'd love to get away from it all.

"Holl?"

She cleared her throat. "Yeah?"

"Would you let me arrange a break for you?" Bree's voice was gentle. "I miss you. It'd be so nice to hang out again."

"Sure, why not whisk me off to paradise?" Holly's laughter ended in another cough. "Now, back to those of us living in the real world."

Bree sighed. "Can you take some time off soon? You need to be careful not to overdo things. I know your study is demanding and so is work, but can't you manage a little break?"

Holly bit her lip. She had a tiny window of opportunity partway through June, after uni exams finished and before training ramped up again at the end of the month. "Maybe."

"Great! Email me the dates when you're free and I'll organize everything. And don't worry, you won't have to pay a cent."

"Bree, I hate feeling like the poor cousin. I always feel like a charity case."

"Holly!" Bree sounded shocked. "That's just your pride talking. I can't help it if Mike gets paid so much. And I'm worried about you. You're my best friend, and I don't want you collapsing or going crazy just because you're so stubborn you can't accept a gift given with your best interests at heart. Please say yes."

Holly sighed, even as hope flickered in her heart. "Fine, be like that then. Organize it all, but remember, Bree, I want five star all the way." A gust of laughter escaped with a wheeze. "Jokes, Bree."

"Ha. It'll be great to see you."

"You too, Bree." Holly smiled. "And thanks. I can't wait."

June

TEN HOURS in a plane to a tropical island seemed a fairly steep price to pay when there were plenty of similar destinations so much closer to home. But that had been the only price. Holly glanced out the aircraft's window, marveling at the blue, blue water. God bless Bree and Mike. Flying from Sydney had meant she'd had some time with her family. They'd been pleased she had the chance to get away. Mum had expressed further concern at how thin Holly was getting. "Sweetheart, you really need to take better care of yourself."

"I'm fine, Mum." Sandwiches and fruit were food, cheap and easy to prepare, not horrifically calorie-laden, and it wasn't like she was very hungry anyway. When she got in from work, the last thing she felt like doing was cooking a proper meal, and she much preferred to see a healthy bank balance than care whether there was meat on her dinner plate.

She was surviving okay. Unlike Granddad, whose health seemed to steadily worsen. Mum and Dad were obviously worried. Holly had even contemplated staying behind, but they'd insisted she go. "There's not a lot you can do, sweetheart. He doesn't recognize anyone these days." So even though her heart had been torn, she'd boarded the plane, having given them all—and especially her grandfather—a big kiss and hug.

She shifted in her first-class seat with its first-class view. Bree was so naughty going to such expense. The food was pretty nice, the size of the seats meaning Holly had actually managed to get some rest, unlike in the cramped space she was used to in economy class. She leaned closer to the window for a better view of the white breakers rolling across the blue Pacific, her heart dancing in anticipation. She couldn't wait to go boogie boarding again. It'd been way too long between surfs.

"Aloha, ladies and gentlemen. Please fasten your safety belts as we approach Honolulu airport."

Half an hour later she'd landed, collected her luggage, and made her way through the gates, the warm air hitting her like a just-opened oven. The scent of frangipani wafted nearer. This truly was paradise.

"Holly!" Bree's big smile and bigger hug were so much better than any phone call. "It's so good to see you."

"And you." Holly squeezed tightly and stepped backward. "Wow. Check out your tan. Your emails made it sound like you enjoyed your time in the Philippines."

"Oh, it was so amazing meeting John and Rose and the other leaders. It's such a beautiful country. Mike took all these photos that we'll use for another fundraising calendar this year."

"Sign me up for a few."

"Will do." Bree held her hands. "How are you? You're looking kinda skinny." She frowned. "Is everything okay?"

"It will be." Holly managed a chuckle. "So, where are we staying? I've gotta admit, I don't mind turning left when I board a plane. First class was pretty special."

Bree hooked her arm through Holly's and walked to the parking lot. "You said you wanted five stars. I aim to please." She pointed to a red convertible hire car.

"Really?" Holly laughed. "I bet Mike loves driving that." She loaded her suitcase in the back. "Where is he, anyway?"

"Back at the hotel beach having a surfing lesson."

"Surfing?" Holly settled into her seat. "Mike?"

"I know! That's what I thought, too, but Brent talked him into it."

She blinked. "Brent? Is he here?"

"Didn't I tell you? Oh." Bree giggled. "My bad."

Holly's pulse picked up pace. "Bree, this isn't some wacky matchmaking scheme, is it?"

Bree started the engine and looked over with wide eyes. "Me? Matchmake? Come on, Holly, you know me."

Holly groaned. "Yes. Yes, I do."

THAT HAD BEEN FUN. Yeah, ice was nice, but after such a deep run of games only to lose by a whisker in the Conference final, sand and surf weren't bad either. Trudging back to the room, Brent stopped abruptly as Mike paused in front of him. "Hey, darling."

Brent shook his head. It still kind of weirded him out to hear his best friend talk to his sister like that. "Good to see you too, Holly."

Holly? What was she doing here? Brent rubbed a hand through his hair, brushing sand from his shoulders and wishing he'd worn a T-shirt or something. Mike gave Holly a quick hug and then there she was, standing before him, her gaze shifting from his chest to his face.

"Hey, Holly."

She still looked too thin, her cheekbones sharply defined. She was paler than he remembered, too. Of course, it was winter in Australia, but she sure looked different from a year ago. Shadows underscored her eyes, as if she hadn't slept well for weeks.

"Hi, Brent." She seemed as wary as him, her smile tentative.

"What? No hug for Brent?"

Bree's smirked comment seemed to elicit enough motivation for Holly to step forward, so he moved and gave her a hug. Whoa. She felt far too good but far too fragile in his arms. He released her and stepped back quickly. There was only one way to play this.

"So...they didn't tell you I would be here either."

"No." Her mouth hitched up on one side. "They didn't."

He reached down and picked up her bag, hoping she'd play along. "D'you think their marriage has gotten so boring they have to mess with other people's lives to get excitement?"

She glanced back at Bree and Mike. "It appears so."

He looked at her room key. Yep, right near his. Figured. "So, did you tell them?"

He'd started walking to her room, but Bree and Mike were still within earshot. "Huh?"

"About us?" He winked at her.

She stopped, staring at him. "Us?"

He took her hand. "I know you didn't want to say anything." He gently squeezed, willing her to play along.

Eyes widening, she finally nodded. "You're right. I didn't. But what's a girl to do?" She glanced back at Bree and Mike, who were watching them, open-mouthed. "Thanks for arranging all this, Bree. You'll never know how much it means to us."

Holly glanced back up at Brent, smile in place, before wrapping her arm around his waist. His breath hitched. She fit way too well.

"Will you show me my room?"

He nodded, suddenly unable to speak.

～

"HA! That was so funny. Did you see their faces? Serves them right." Holly laughed. She'd never seen such a flabbergasted look on Bree's face. Chuckles kept spurting out. Oh, she must be tired.

Brent lounged against the mirrored doors of the hotel room wardrobe, his muscled arms crossed over his equally muscled but now-covered-with-a-T-shirt chest. "You know we're gonna have to keep this up for a little longer."

"But how? Bree will figure it out soon enough."

Brent sighed. "I'm afraid you'll just have to pretend you like me. I know that's a challenge, especially as I'm not your type or anything, but if you smile at me, let me hold your hand, and act like you think I'm funny, that might work. I'll do the same for you."

Holly's mouth dropped open. "You're as sneaky as your sister."

"I prefer to think of it as using my gift for spontaneity for good. Come on. It'll be fun to mess with them. It's not like we have to kiss or anything."

Holly's cheeks heated. "Good."

Bree knocked on the open door. "Hey, what are you two talking about?"

Brent quickly glanced at Holly before replying slowly, "We're just talking about what we'll do over the next few days."

Holly nodded. That was true enough. She didn't mind the pretense, but outright lying wasn't right.

Bree glanced at Holly with upraised eyebrows. "How long has this been going on?"

"Not long at all." Holly caught Brent's gaze as he grinned. Her heart squeezed, releasing an extra beat or two.

"Holly." Bree's arms crossed. Any minute now she'd start tapping her foot.

Holly offered a smile she hoped appeared coy. "Well, you know we've been emailing."

"Yeah, but I didn't know you *liked* him."

Brent snickered. "I am standing right here, you know."

Bree ignored him, giving Holly a dark look. "I'm going to need all the details."

"Seriously, there's not much to tell." Holly caught Brent's gaze, and the amusement there echoed hers and escaped in a chuckle. Yep, this could be pretty fun.

❧

MIKE TEED OFF, his ball arcing through the air before dropping onto the green two hundred yards away.

"Nice." Brent placed his ball on the tee, practiced his swing a couple of times, then glanced at his friend. "What?"

"Nothing."

He shrugged. Mike's mock innocence sure didn't look like nothing. He swung, the club connecting with the ball, which arced out to the rough, sending a bunch of unsuspecting ducks scattering. He groaned. "Man."

"You might do better if you concentrated on the game."

Brent plucked the tee from the ground, ignoring his friend's chuckle and the truth of his words. He hadn't been focused, not since that unnerving encounter two days ago. Holly's blush about the kiss comment had kept him awake way too late the past two nights. What was that about? He trudged to the spindly grass. He'd promised God two years ago that the next woman he kissed he'd make his wife, so it was a good thing they weren't trying to be that convincing.

He found his ball and knocked it gently toward the green. The pitiful way he was playing meant he might as well hand Mike victory now. Not that it mattered how this game worked out. Not when something else was working out so well.

His lips twitched. Holly could've majored in drama the way she had Bree fooled. Each time Bree looked at them askance,

Holly would do something—touch his arm, grab his hand, lean forward and give him a special smile—that would make his heart miss a beat. Man. If he didn't know better, he'd really believe she meant it. But this was about fooling Bree, not about letting his emotions get carried away and fooling himself.

"Dude?" Mike was peering at him funny. The girls had gone off for a massage while he and Mike spent the morning playing golf. "You can't fool me."

"Whaddya mean?"

"Look, I know you're just trying to get even with Bree." Mike smiled. "She does kind of deserve it. But you shouldn't mess with Holly, man."

"I'm not messing with her. She knows what's going on."

"I wondered." Mike chuckled before looking at him thoughtfully. "But do you?"

"Huh?" Mike had always been able to read him like a book. What had he seen?

Mike shot Brent another disconcerting look before grinning. "Nothing."

$\mathcal{H}$olly took a long sip of her fresh pink lemonade studded with pieces of tropical fruit. "This is *so* good."

"Glad you're enjoying yourself," Mike said.

She grinned at him, appreciating the quiet man's generosity and mellow ways. "I think I've been enjoying myself a little too much."

"At least we can't see your ribs anymore, Holly," Bree said.

Holly sighed. "Bree, I thought we'd settled the fact that I'm never going to look like you." She noticed the two men watching them and felt itchy with embarrassment. She so didn't want to get into a conversation about her body shape. "It's not like I don't eat."

"We've noticed." Mike leaned forward to clasp Bree's hand. "You seem to hold your own in the food stakes, Holly."

She exhaled, thankful for Mike's willingness to ease the strained atmosphere. Yeah, the food here had been a little too good. Seeing as Bree and Mike were footing the bill, she hadn't skimped like she normally did. Good thing there was a well-equipped gym and so many great activities to work off all those extra calories.

"Yeah, Bree. Holly's an athlete. She knows what she's doing." Brent turned serious eyes on her. "Don't you, Holl?"

His scrutiny was so piercing it felt like he could see right through her. She nodded stiffly before looking away at a nearby clump of palm trees. Yes, she knew she had to eat better, and she would try harder when she got back home. She'd have to, anyway. Training demanded so much more of her body.

Brent's hand found hers on the table. Her breath hitched. Her smile quivered. This pretending business was a little tough to remember sometimes.

"I still don't get it," Bree said, looking between the two of them. "I didn't think you even liked Brent."

"Wow. Harsh, Bree," Brent said, gently squeezing Holly's fingers.

Holly opened her eyes wide, glad for the distraction from the previous topic—and the juddery sensation in her veins at his touch. "Oh, but I *do* like Brent." She liked him, sure. As a friend.

He leaned in closer. His eyes were such an interesting color today—almost green, like the lagoon they'd paddled around yesterday. He touched a wisp of her hair that had escaped her ponytail. "The feeling's mutual, babe."

Was he for real? Sometimes it was hard to tell if he was messing with her as well as Bree. She'd catch a look in his eyes that would set her tummy fluttering. That same intensity was there now. She drew closer, lowered her voice. "You know this is pretend, don't you?"

Brent murmured, "I think it's important to stay in character."

Holly laughed. "I think you're crazy."

~

Brent stared out at the waves, trying to enjoy the warmth but unable to stop thinking about the woman on the sun lounge next to his. She was eating properly here—anyone could see that—and she seemed brighter than when she'd first arrived, but still…

"Hey, Holly." He waited until she looked up from her book. "You are doing okay, aren't you?" He shifted closer, so Mike couldn't overhear. Bree was asleep on the sun lounge. "You are eating properly now?"

"I'm doing better."

"Can I ask…?" This was tricky. Would she admit to the truth? Holly turned to look at him more fully, waiting warily. "What was going on?"

She pushed her sunglasses on top of her head. "I told you I'd been unwell."

"Yeah, but it wasn't really that, was it?" He leaned nearer. "You weren't worried about what you look like, were you?"

Her eyes widened. "You're kidding, aren't you?"

Okay. So it definitely wasn't that.

"Brent, if I cared what I looked like, I'd be trying to put weight on." She shook her head. "I'd love to look more like Bree." She stared out to the beach, and he followed her gaze to where a couple of bikini-clad Barbie wannabes were strolling along. He quickly glanced back to Holly.

"I think you look fine." Her eye roll suggested she didn't believe him. "So, if it's not that, then what?"

She huffed out a breath. "Money's been tight, okay? And I don't want to talk about it anymore." She dropped her book and picked up a bottle of sunscreen.

"Yes, ma'am." But she was sacrificing her health because of a lack of money? That so wasn't right. He sat back on the sun lounge and chewed his bottom lip. She obviously had a lot of pride, otherwise she would've asked for help. Maybe he needed to talk to her parents. But would that just be meddling? Maybe he should talk to Bree. *Hey, God, what should I do?*

He didn't get any impression apart from the usual *be a friend.* But simple friendship wasn't so simple anymore. Holly was fast becoming entwined in his thoughts and emotions, and in these past few days, he'd become aware of all sorts of things about her. He sighed and settled back, trying to watch the waves, but his eyes kept straying to her.

Holly had great legs. Long, nicely shaped. For an elite athlete, she sure wore her muscles well. He didn't want to notice, but the scar on her leg hadn't fully healed yet, and the pink gash glowed against her pale skin, drawing his attention. "That must've hurt."

She glanced over from where she'd begun rubbing sunscreen on her arms. "A little."

The understatement ratcheted up his admiration another notch. "I gotta admit, Holly, you just don't seem the type to do such an extreme sport."

Her eyebrows rose. "And why is that?"

Uh oh. Sounded like he'd offended her. "I just mean…you're soft."

"Soft?" Her eyes narrowed again, her voice pitched higher.

"I mean, you're nice and"—he swallowed—"sweet…and a lot tougher than you look."

Holly stared at him for a beat before shaking her head and standing. "I need a swim."

She walked down the beach, entering the water without a qualm, striding through the breaking waves until she dived through one.

Brent turned to encounter Mike's bemused face. "What?"

"You've certainly got a way with the ladies."

Brent heaved out a breath. "I don't know what her problem is."

"I'm guessing she's thinking exactly the same thing about you." Mike laughed. "So, you *do* like her then."

"Well, yeah." Mike's shrewd look cut through the haze of his heart.

Oh.

Yeah.

Whoa.

He'd had so much fun pretending with Holly these past few days that it had taken until now to realize he didn't really want to play pretend anymore. Brent grabbed his water bottle to wet his suddenly dry mouth as Mike continued to stare, mouth curved on one side.

Brent shrugged, aiming for a cool he didn't feel. "If this helps get her to like me, that's a bonus."

"You're as bad as your sister." Mike nodded to where Holly was bobbing in the water, chatting to some tanned he-man. "You might need to try a little harder then."

"Yeah." Brent frowned at the bright water for a few minutes before the glare started eating into his retinas. He stood. "I need my sunglasses."

He cast another look at Holly before striding off to his room.

When he returned, Holly was sitting with Mike and Bree, who had woken from her nap. Holly shot Brent a quick glance as he resumed his seat before her attention returned to Bree, who now animatedly shared. "The worst one was when he was rammed into the boards a couple of years ago. That was so scary! I was in Toronto and Mike was playing in Florida, and I saw it on TV."

"What happened?" Holly turned to Mike.

"Concussion, cracked a rib or two. I was out for a few games."

She grimaced. "Concussions happen with us too, but mostly it's ankle and knee injuries."

Mike nodded. "So, what's your worst?"

"Oh." Holly wrinkled her forehead. "I had a stress fracture in my foot, which took a while to heal. And there's been a few cuts, of course." She pointed to her leg. "These gashes are less common with the better suits we wear these days."

Bree's nose wrinkled. "There must've been so much blood."

Holly shrugged. "A little."

Brent guessed from the way her face stiffened that *little* was another understatement.

"I could never do it, Holl." Bree shivered. "You travel so fast. It's scary dangerous."

Holly smiled at Bree. "I used to have bad dreams about crashing and getting injured, but now I just think it's fun." She caught Brent's eye, her smile fading as she looked away.

Brent couldn't stop staring at her. It was still so hard to reconcile the calm, quiet girl lying on the sun lounge with the adrenaline-fueled sport she did. Bree and Mike moved to the water, and Holly picked up the book she'd been reading earlier. Now was his chance to make amends.

"Hey, Holl." He waited until she looked up at him. "Look, I'm sorry about before. I didn't mean to upset you."

She shrugged and focused on her book again.

"I really do think you're amazing." Her sunglasses had slipped down slightly, and he caught her eye roll. "You're so pretty it's hard to remember just how tough you are. I like that about you. You're different to most girls, that's for sure."

She turned a page, then her lashes lifted and her gaze fused with his. "Well, if you can keep talking like that"—her lips curved, and his heart took flight—"you're forgiven."

HOLLY HADN'T LAUGHED like this in years. Grasping the board in her hands, she waited until the exact moment the wave surged, hoisting herself up as the crest of the wave pulled her in to shore. What did it matter that most of the other boogie board riders were young kids or teenage boys? This was so much fun.

God bless Bree. Twisting her arm to take a break had been such a good idea. She flicked wet hair from her eyes and headed back out for the next wave, laughing to herself about the teenage boy who'd tried chatting her up. Only about ten years too young, but the attention was flattering—nothing fake there, at least.

Holly turned and caught another wave in to shore, holding on until her knees scraped the sand in the shallows. She laughed, clambered upright, and glanced over to see Brent watching from the sun lounges. She tucked her hair behind her ears and gave him a small wave before heading back out again. The water sparkled in the sun, crashing enthusiastically against the shore. She'd thoroughly enjoyed trying windsurfing and the jet skis yesterday, but the best had been the stand-up paddle surfing. It had been tricky at first, but the years of core strengthening had soon proven itself of obvious benefit, and her sense of balance had impressed her instructor. She seemed to have impressed Brent, too. Every time she glanced up she'd caught him watching. It was a little disconcerting, but maybe it helped keep up appearances.

After the initial shock of seeing Brent, she'd grown accustomed to his company, but she still wasn't sure about the lengths he went to to "prove" things to Bree. It kind of went against the grain to have a guy open doors and hold out her chair for her—things she was perfectly capable of doing—but it added to the pretense, so she let him. He *was* fun to be around, full of jokes and laughter, and his flattery was nice to hear, even if it was only to maintain this ridiculous charade. Mike wasn't fooled and seemed to enjoy the joke, but Bree still wasn't sure what was going on. It was fun to mess with her, especially as she'd proven to be so conniving herself.

Holly clutched the board to her chest and floated on her back in the water, her eyes studying the plum-colored nail polish on her toenails. Catching up with Bree had naturally entailed pedicures and massages and shopping at designer outlet stores. Bree had bought her some dresses and some super high heels that made walking difficult but did show off her legs and helped her feel slightly more feminine. It'd be nice if she had the nice tan so many others had and more figure to fill out her modest black bikini, but hey, wishing couldn't change that.

Anyway, what did it matter? She rolled over and smiled. This vacation had been exactly what she needed. Over the past five days, she'd felt something of the old spark return, the worries of the last few months effectively chased away. *Thanks, Lord, this is fantastic.*

A big wave dunked her, and she stood up, gasping.

"Hey, babe, you okay?"

Holly glanced over to the blond muppet from before. "Thanks, I'm fine."

She giggled as he swam off, his words sparking memories of what Brent had started calling her. Feminist Holly cringed at being called *babe*, but another part loved seeing the expression on Bree's face each time he said it. He'd even taken to giving her a hug good night—all for show, of course—but the hugs sometimes seemed to go on slightly longer than necessary. It made her wonder…

Nope. Stupid to think that. Guys like him didn't go for girls like her. Anyway, she had her career to focus on. She closed her eyes, floating in the water as the sun blessed her with its warmth. Ah, this was the life. *God bless Bree.*

~

HE COULDN'T BELIEVE she was still out there. All Brent wanted to do was relax, but Holly was still going strong. He smiled as she gave another full-throated gurgle of laughter as the waves propelled her back into shore once again on her boogie board. She loved that thing.

He lay back, hat propped slightly forward to shield his face, as the whine of two competing jet skis filled the air. Yesterday had been pretty fun, racing her on the jet skis. She was so competitive. He'd teased her about losing, then fought laughter as she tossed her head. "That doesn't count. I've never done it before, so I should have a head start."

"Holly, you're lighter than me, so you'll go faster. So I win."

She'd huffed. "Well, let's make it best of three then, now I've had some practice."

And a short time later it'd been "Best of five. I think my motor thingy just doesn't go as fast as yours. Maybe we need to swap machines."

He'd grinned. "Come on, admit defeat. You tried but got beaten by a true champion."

"Your humility constantly amazes me."

"Yeah, well, that's the kind of guy I am."

Her snort of laughter had made him smile. For all her bluster, she was having the time of her life. He loved the independence she displayed too, happy to do something by herself even if no one else wanted to. She was different to Bree, for sure.

He frowned, watching as that young kid from before swam back over to Holly and started talking again. She laughed, then picked up her board and slowly walked through the shallows, oblivious to the fact that the guy was still watching her. But it wasn't surprising. She seriously had to be the fittest girl on the beach, even if she showed a lot less skin than the stereotypical beach babe. How many other women here had a six-pack the envy of most men? He'd noticed guys checking her out, turning to give her second glances whenever she got out of the pool or walked up the beach. A few times he'd even had to shoot some men a warning look, not wanting to see her the subject of any crude advances.

It was only what a brother would do, he told himself. He'd been by the pool the other day when some random guy tried to hit on her. He'd seen Holly smile at the man, and the chest twinge he'd felt still surprised him. What was that about? Surely he wasn't jealous. He swallowed. No. It was that Holly had no idea how attractive she was—and that made her even more attractive.

She wandered up to where he lay on a sun lounge near where Mike and Bree were lying. Holly's cheeks sparkled with water droplets. "That is just so much fun!"

"It looked like it."

"You should try it." She picked up a towel and wrapped it around her.

"Nope. I like being warm."

"You like being boring. Where's your spirit of adventure?" She leaned to one side and started squeezing out her long hair.

His mouth drained of moisture. For some reason, that looked just so…

"Brent?" She raised her eyebrows.

He swallowed and finally found his voice. "Uh, must've left it behind in Detroit."

"Weren't you surfing the other day?"

Mike laughed. "Trying to, anyway."

"You weren't much better."

"I think I'd like to try parasailing next." Holly glanced back at the water, where they could see a boat pulling a parachuted person behind. "That looks like so much fun."

Bree stretched out on the lounge. "You're such an adventure girl. Why not relax?"

"You wanted me to have fun, and I am!" Holly grinned at Bree. "God bless Bree and Mike."

She glanced at Brent, her smile spilling over, bathing him in fresh sunshine. He soaked up the warmth and the feelings flooding his chest. God bless Bree and Mike, for sure.

"WE'LL BE BACK LATER"—BREE glanced at her husband—"or not."

Holly rolled her eyes at Brent as the couple departed, hand in hand. "I'm thinking not."

"I'm with you. They're having way too much fun."

He shifted on the sun lounge next to hers and glanced over to catch her staring at his chest. She looked up and quickly glanced away. "What's wrong?"

"Nothing." She finally met his gaze again. "I didn't realize you had a maple leaf tatt."

"We all got them after we won the World Juniors a few years back."

"You're so hard core."

"Tough is my middle name," he agreed meekly.

"I can't believe I've never noticed it."

"You've obviously never checked out my body before."

She hid behind her book. "Obviously not."

"Look, if it makes you feel any better, I didn't know you had a six-pack."

"A six—oh." Her gaze met his. "Lots of core exercises."

"I bet you have great skinfold test results, too."

Her lips twitched. "They're not bad."

"I'm not surprised. I've seen you here in the gym. Impressive stuff."

She shrugged. "Training starts again in a week or so. Then my first comp is early August."

"No rest for the wicked."

"Or for those of us who want to go to the Games next year. Of course, I don't know what my chances are, especially after the World Championships, but you've got to keep trying, right?"

"Right." Her commitment to her sport was inspiring.

"I've told God that a World Cup final would help." Her smile was edged with wryness. "A win would be even better."

"You'll make it," he assured her. "Hey, maybe I'll see you in Vancouver."

Her eyebrows shot up. "Are you in the team?"

"I've been invited to attend the training camp in August."

"How awesome!" She sat up, her lips widening into genuine happiness. "Wow, congratulations. I didn't realize you were keen to go."

"No hockey player worth his salt would ever turn down a chance to represent his country. World Championships, the Games, it's a great stage to play on."

She nodded. "Most people think the Games are the pinnacle of sports, but World Champs are just as important to us skaters. I guess the Games are considered more special because they're only every four years, so there's less chance to win gold. Not that I could ever hope to do that."

"Why not?"

"Please."

Her withering glance told him now wasn't the time to push her on the lack of self-belief. "So, when did you first want to skate competitively?"

Her gaze turned shy. "Probably when I first learned to skate back in Toronto."

He barely remembered those months when Holly had stayed with them on high-school exchange, his life jam-packed with hockey training, plans, and dreams. "How d'you mean?"

"I remember when you and your dad first showed me how to skate, how it felt to fly on the ice. Then, when I saw footage of Steven Bradbury winning gold at Salt Lake City, I realized I wanted to do that too."

"You will, Holly. You're the most determined person I know."

"But determination without opportunity can be a recipe for frustration. Sometimes I don't even know why I do this sport."

Her sigh seemed to draw up from the soles of her elegant feet, stuffing his crack about the Yoda-like comment back down his throat. "You inspire me," he encouraged softly, willing her to believe him. "You motivate me to do better."

"Really?" Her raised eyebrows showed her skepticism.

He nodded, wishing he could show her his real appreciation.

But she turned back to her book, and the moment was lost, relegating him to contemplation.

"Phone call for Miss Holly Travers."

Holly lay asleep. At least, Brent guessed she was. She'd barely stirred these last twenty minutes. He caught the attention of the waiter and leaned across to gently shake her arm. "Hey, Holly, wake up. You've got a phone call."

She yawned, rubbing her eyes as she sat up. "What?"

"Miss Holly Travers?" the waiter asked.

She nodded, and the waiter handed her a phone. Brent chewed his lip. Why would she be getting a phone call?

"Ben!" Her face lit.

Brent's chest tightened. Then he remembered Ben was her brother. He exhaled, shaking his head. Man, what was wrong with him?

"No. I'm on the beach. My phone's back in the room. Why? What's up?" The relaxed expression drained as she sat upright. "No!"

Heart twisting, Brent stayed silent as she listened, her hand covering her mouth.

She leaned forward, shaking her head. "Tell them I'm on my way." She ended the call, then sat ominously still, hair curtaining her face.

"Holly?" Brent leaned forward, touched her knee. "Holl, what is it?"

She finally glanced up, her eyes filled with tears. "My

granddad just died. A heart attack." She gulped. "I need to get home."

She rose unsteadily, and he stood too. Where was Bree when he needed her?

"I'm so sorry, Holly." He wrapped his arms around her, her sorrow dampening his chest. She dragged in a shaky breath, and he rubbed her back. Conscious of curious eyes, he murmured, "Come on, let's go back." He picked up her towel, hat, and book and walked her to her room.

He unlocked the door and inserted the keycard to turn on the lights. Her room was a mess, with clothes strewn across the floor. Huh. He wouldn't have picked her for a slob. "Looks like housekeeping hasn't got here yet."

"What?" She followed his gaze. "Oh. I don't ask them to clean my room. It's my mess, my responsibility. It's not fair to ask them to clean up stuff just because I'm lazy."

Holly was considerate, even to cleaners. Man, he liked this woman. "What can I do?"

"Nothing." She looked around distractedly. "I have to pack. I..." She placed a hand to her head. "I just need my ticket home. Do you think it'll cost much to change it?"

She was worried about money at this time? "Don't worry about it. I'll take care of it."

Her face held a stricken, dazed look. "Granddad was sick for so long. I knew he was bad, but everyone said to come." She glanced up at him, her green eyes shimmering. "I should've stayed home. I could've been there."

He gently rubbed her shoulder. "It sounds like there was nothing you could do."

She stared at him with big, sad eyes before moving to shift clothes to her suitcase. "Would you tell Bree? This is such bad timing. I'm so sorry she wasted her money."

"Holly, stop worrying." He wished his sister were nearby. She could've helped so much more. *Lord, what can I do?*

An idea sparked. "I'll be back in a moment."

He raced next door, called reception, who promised to send someone around to help, then called the airline. Didn't have a sense of adventure, eh?

CHAPTER 9

Holly settled back in her seat, gazing out across the wide, blue Pacific Ocean, tears never far from her eyes. Unbelievable. Only hours after receiving the phone call, she'd managed to get on a direct flight back to Sydney, first class again. She'd be seeing her family in just over ten hours. It had been so quick they hadn't even had a chance to tell Bree. She sighed, grabbed her water bottle, swallowed a mouthful.

Her seat companion nudged her. "You know, Bree and Mike will think we've eloped or something."

She gasped, almost choking on the water.

"I'd love to see their faces when they find out." Brent grinned. "It certainly adds credence to our story."

She studied him as he flicked through his in-flight magazine. "Why are you doing this?"

"Some people think I'm boring, apparently."

"Hopping on a plane spur of the moment might change that."

"I've always wondered what it would be like. Have passport, will travel."

"The beauty of money, huh? And for a minute there I thought you cared."

His laughing eyes turned serious. "But I do care. Besides, I couldn't let you go like that." His lips lifted on one side. "Especially when you were, you know, crying all over the place, sobbing hysterically and stuff."

"I wasn't—"

"You don't need to be embarrassed about it." He patted her hand. "People understand, babe."

"Babe?" Any further desire to cry fled. "What is it with the *babe* business? I'm not your babe. It makes me sound like a child. Do you know how sexist it sounds?"

She glanced behind him at the other first-class passengers, who were staring at them like they'd never heard a raised voice before. Warning, warning: crude passenger alert.

Brent held up his hands. "Hey, I'm quite happy to be your babe, babe. Just say the word."

She snorted and shifted away.

"Sorry, what was that? Do you want me to leave? Do I jump out now?" He nudged her arm.

She turned to study him—his small smile, those blue-green eyes alight with mischief.

He leaned closer, the mischief draining away, leaving only warmth. "Holly, I'd never abandon you at a time like this."

Oh. All his joking around was about helping her keep it together so she could get through these next few hours until she could finally be home. All this was born from his consideration for her. His kindness curled around her heart and drew fresh tears to her eyes. She blinked and bit her trembling lip.

"Holl, what is it?"

She swallowed. "Thanks for all you've done."

His smile flooded warmth to her aching heart. "You're welcome. Babe."

~

Brent walked slowly into the bustling arrivals area of Sydney airport, his eyes on the wilting woman beside him. He touched her arm. "How are you holding up?"

"I'm okay." She offered a small smile that didn't exactly convince him.

He shook his head as another yawn threatened to erupt. "That flight seemed so long."

"Ten hours isn't that long, Brent. Not for a real tough guy, anyway."

He smiled, glad to see the return of her sass. These past hours had been an emotional rollercoaster as he'd fought to help her maintain her equilibrium, shielding her from the prying eyes of other passengers as tears dripped onto her cheeks at regular intervals, yet trying not to make it obvious he'd noticed, let alone done something to help. Ms. Feminist would never approve.

"Oh! There's Ben!"

Holly left his side and raced away to be swept up in a long hug with her brother. Brent struggled with a wave of envy. If only he could be the recipient of such warm affection from Holly and not those awkward hugs where he could feel her stiff shoulders and don't-mess-with-me manner.

Ben looked over Holly's shoulders, his features melding into a frown. As Holly stepped away, the disapproval became more pronounced, Ben slinging a possessive arm around his sister's shoulders as his watchful dark eyes narrowed. "So, you're Brent."

Holly had mentioned that Ben had played professional rugby and now coached at a fancy Sydney private school. Judging from the extra firm handshake, it seemed Ben had the muscles and no-nonsense attitude to prove it.

"And you're Ben." Brent squared his shoulders, conscious he was being sized up. He still couldn't fully account for why he'd come. He knew if he'd left Holly in the lurch then his mom and sister would have had something to say about it. Not that he was that worried about what they'd say. He'd just been thinking about Holly. She'd looked so sad…

Ben turned to Holly, eyebrows raised.

She shrugged. "I couldn't stop him. He insisted."

"Hmm." Ben looked at him askance. "Where are your bags?"

Ah, bags. Didn't have time to go back to the hotel for his things. After finding out what time the first available flight left, he'd barely had enough time to hustle Holly and her luggage to the airport, only grabbing his wallet, passport, and phone, figuring they'd all be helpful in getting her ticket changed. Then, when the airline representative looked at him asking *Is that all?*, he'd looked over to where Holly was standing looking dazed and teary and a sudden surge of compassion made him discreetly ask about any spare seats. She'd smiled, nodded, and quickly fixed him up. Holly's look of shock when he followed her through security to the lounge was one he'd remember forever. He smiled to himself again before Ben's piercing gaze cut through his memories.

"I travel light."

Ben still didn't look convinced, but Brent no longer cared. Holly was drooping, each blink getting longer, the shock and emotion and the lengthy flight finally taking their toll. "Hey, Holl, you okay?"

"I'm fine. I just want to go home. I need a cup of tea. I'm so tired."

"Okay. Well, thanks for stopping me from being too boring."

"What?" Her eyes widened. "You're not going back now?"

"You didn't think I'd crash your family at a time like this, did you? I'll just hang around here and stay at an airport hotel until I catch a flight back."

Those green eyes opened wider. "Don't be ridiculous. You've come all this way—you can't go back now. You're staying with us. I insist."

He gave Ben a resigned shrug as Holly grabbed his arm and led him out to the wintry Sydney sunshine.

∼

How completely bizarre.

Holly sat on a recliner in her parents' living room, half watching the Australian Football League game on TV, the rest of the time puzzling out her guest who sat opposite, watching a sport he'd never heard of but getting into it all the same. It was the pinnacle of the past four days' weird alternative reality: Brent, here, the evening after her grandfather's funeral today, looking comfortable in shorts and a T-shirt while the rest of them wore comfy tracksuits. Strange, but it felt oddly right, too.

"Wow. That's insane." Brent leaned forward on his seat, watching the replay as a Sydney Swans player took a mark, leaping on the back of the Collingwood player to catch the ball. He shook his head. "Man, that's amazing stuff."

"Come on, Swannies!" Her dad was a little passionate about his Aussie Rules.

Holly swallowed a smile as Brent asked Ben a question about some rule. She tuned out, using the cover of darkness to study him more closely. Throughout the flight, then the trip home to Wollongong and her parents' startled looks as she walked up the drive with Brent, the questions had swirled around her brain and heart. Why had he accompanied her here? And why, for that matter, had she insisted he stay with them? She could've died when those words escaped, but he'd been so generous and kind that to send him home had seemed the height of rudeness.

But questions had been raised. The first moment they were alone, her brother had started investigating. "You know guys don't usually jump on planes like that, Holl."

"I'm not an idiot, Ben. Like I said, he's my friend. He was

there when I found out about Granddad, and he felt sorry for me."

He hadn't seemed convinced. "I'm a guy. I've seen the way he looks at you."

Heart flutter. Really? "How's that?"

Ben just shook his head. "He likes you."

"Yeah, well, he's just pretending." She'd filled him in on their scheme in Hawaii.

Ben raised a skeptical brow. "But, Holly, why would he continue doing that here?"

"I don't know."

Surely not. No. She suddenly felt dizzy.

"Think about it, Holly." Her brother's sandy eyebrows had pushed up. "And fill us in if there's something we need to know about, all right?"

She'd nodded, unable to say a word.

"Holly?"

She blinked and looked up. Brent's face was mere inches from hers. Her heart beat double time. "Yes?" She winced at how breathless she sounded.

"I asked if you wanted another drink. Coffee, tea? What can I get you?"

Her father muted the advertisements that signaled the half time break in the game. "I'm making Beth a cuppa before she starts her shift tonight." He headed out to the kitchen, and she heard the glass kettle begin its dull roar.

"Holl?"

"Oh." She swallowed. Hopefully her normal voice would reappear soon. "Um, nothing, thanks. I'm still going." She pointed to her cup of tea, delicately poised on the fat armrest of her chair. And knocked it off with a clatter. "Oh no!"

Brent leaned forward just as she reached across to grab the box of tissues, banging into her head. "Ow!" Amidst the stars, the lights clicked on.

"Oh, Holly! I'm sorry. Are you okay?"

She rubbed her forehead. "I'm fine. Are you?"

She glanced down at the shattered cup and pressed her lips together to stop the quiver. Her grandmother's prized Royal Albert teacup would never hold tea again. She dragged in a breath. Funerals were crazy for messing up her emotional equilibrium.

"I'm okay if you're okay." He picked the pieces up off the carpet before glancing up again. "But you're not, are you?" He bit his lip. "Was that cup special?"

She flicked at an errant tear. "It was my grandmother's."

"I'm really sorry."

"It wasn't your fault. Anyway, it's just a cup, Brent. I'll live." She forced a wobbly smile.

"But sometimes it's nice to remember special people with certain things, isn't it?"

She nodded, unable to speak, his empathy overwhelming. How unexpectedly sweet and thoughtful was this man?

He felt around on the carpet. "If it's any consolation, I don't think it had much tea in it."

Ben's deep chuckle made them both look over at him. "Are you two finished? Any more tricks up your sleeve, Karlsson?" He shook his head. "You've sure got some smooth moves."

The chagrined look on Brent's face made Holly swallow a hysteria-laden snicker. He turned back to her. "I guess I owe you another cup of tea, don't I?"

"I guess so."

"Come on." Ben shook his head. "I'll show you how it's done."

Brent glanced at her as if to check she was okay. At her nod, he disappeared into the kitchen with Ben, and she could finally exhale.

Uncle Richard looked over from his chair nearby. "Your boyfriend seems a nice chap."

"Oh!" Holly chuckled nervously and dropped her voice. "He's not my boyfriend. Just a friend."

Her uncle's muddy green eyes, so like her mum's and Ben's, twinkled. "Well, your *friend* is very solicitous, shall we say. He's asked some very interesting questions about my research in Antarctica."

She pulled up her legs, hugging her knees.

Her uncle's silver head nodded. "He's much nicer than that other silly fellow. What was his name again?" His brow furrowed. "Darryl? Darren?"

"Uncle Richard, that was years ago." She cast a quick look behind. Uh oh. Ben and Brent, now thoroughly bonded over their mutual love of sport, were balancing cups as they re-entered the room.

"What was years ago?" Ben placed a coffee mug on the table in front of Uncle Richard as Brent carefully gave her a fresh cup of tea and a warm smile.

"Nothing." Holly took a hasty sip of tea, trying to chase away the icy shiver in her soul.

"Darren. Darryl." Her uncle shook his head. "Whatever happened to that Darren fellow, Ben?"

Trust her uncle to keep asking the questions. While that trait might be excellent for his environmental research in Antarctica, she didn't appreciate it regarding her personal life.

Ben frowned. "Not Darren Mortdale?"

Her heart sank as Brent shifted her direction. "Who's he?"

"No one," Holly muttered and sank deeper in her chair, gazing at the muted commentary on the television screen. As her uncle started explaining, she shook her head. "Yes. I am invisible. I'm not really here. I like being ignored, and I really *love* my personal life being talked about."

Ben chuckled. "Darren Mortdale was a guy I used to share a house with in Sydney, when we both played for the Waratahs. He was something of a ladies' man, shall we say."

Holly stole a quick glance at Brent, who'd gone very still.

"This story has entered family folklore." Her uncle cleared his throat. "It started when Holly went to visit him, is that right?"

She caught Brent's eyes on her and quickly dropped her gaze. "I'd just got my driver's license and drove to Sydney to visit Ben. Ben, not anyone else." *Liar, liar, pants on fire.*

"Sure you did." Ben's skeptical look would never get the truth out of her.

Of course she'd had the world's biggest crush on Darren—he'd been every girl's dream. And her big brother *knew* him. Her friends in year twelve had been so jealous. Little did they know there'd been nothing, absolutely nothing, for them to be jealous of. And if they'd ever had an inkling as to his sleazy behavior...

Ben loudly slurped his coffee. "Anyway, I'd just finished a morning run and got home to see Holly kneeing him in the 'nads." He shook his head. "And after she told me what he said, I waited till he was upright and decked him again." He gave Holly a small smile. "Moral of the story: Don't mess with Holly, or she'll take you down." He raised an eyebrow at Brent. "And so will I."

She shivered as the memory of that day rose in all its terribleness. Her stupid, stupid crush on someone so utterly worthless. That giddy joy when she'd thought it was just Darren and her alone in the house. That leer on his face she'd mistaken for a smile. Those words... *"Well, look who's all grown up."* He'd looked her up and down before settling his eyes on her woefully undeveloped chest. *"Babe, you're a little scrawny, but I'm prepared to make an exception, knowing that you're so...young."* He'd moved closer, grabbing her arm.

It was only when he started touching her that she finally mobilized out of her state of shock, and with a swift knee to the crotch, she'd felled him to a whimpering mess on the floor, just as her brother walked through the door. She shivered again. *Thank You, Lord, for keeping me safe.*

She propped her head on one hand and peeked through her hair at Brent, whose face looked carved in stone. Obviously he was disgusted now he realized she wasn't as sweet and innocent as he must've thought. She breathed past the tight feeling in her chest as she pretended interest in the muted game on TV. No way was she going to run and hide. *Put on a brave face…*

"What happened to him?" Brent asked.

She couldn't answer. If only people did really reap what they sowed.

Ben sighed. "He busted a knee and got into TV. He's now on *The Footy Show.*"

"Did you report him?"

Holly glanced at Brent and nodded. "He got off. Insufficient evidence."

Brent's gaze grew sorrowful. "That's rough. I'm sorry, Holly."

"You've got nothing to apologize for." She shrugged, aiming for nonchalance. "Some guys are sleazy."

He nodded, his eyes intent on her. "Some guys. Not all."

Warmth stole into her heart, heating her cheeks. No, some guys were definitely not. Some guys were thoughtful and kind and caring and sweet and—

"What's the score?"

Holly blinked as her father re-entered the room, grabbed the remote control, and pressed the button so the room filled with sound. She gazed unseeingly at the blurry screen. *Lord, please help me leave the past in the past. And help me keep it together. I'm so tired of being an emotional yo-yo.* She hugged her knees tighter and wiped her wet cheeks on her sleeve. *And, Lord, I hate to admit this, but I really don't want Brent thinking less of me.*

The game continued, the Swans outplaying Collingwood, but the score didn't matter. She peeked across at Brent, who still watched the game intently. Her uncle was right. She'd noticed several times over the past few days when Brent had displayed a kindness and thoughtfulness she never would've expected to see a year ago. He'd been great this morning at the funeral, just quietly there, offering a quick hug when she'd needed it. She'd been sad, but Granddad had been old, sick for such a long time, and really ready to go to heaven to see the wife he'd adored so much. But Holly had struggled at the gravesite. The problem with small families was that any member's loss left that much more of a hole. The six people making up her entire family in all the world had become five, the older generation now all gone. She didn't want to be morbid, but who would be next?

She'd felt panic rise until Brent's soft touch on her shoulder brought calm, his sympathetic smile helping her blink back tears. Afterward, at the RSL club, she'd witnessed more of Brent's kindness as he listened to an old gentleman from Granddad's war days go on and on about his crook leg. She'd looked over from where she was chatting with some people from Mum and Dad's church and studied Brent as he nodded and asked more questions, kindly interested. He'd looked up and caught her gaze and winked, which had been enough for her to turn back to Mum's nursing friend and pretend she wasn't flustered.

"C'mon, Swannies." Ben stood and muted the ads that now signaled three-quarter time. He turned, screwing up his nose. "Those flowers really stink." He gestured to one of the artful arrangements that had come flooding in over the past week. Everyone from the Aldridges in Brisbane to Bree's parents had sent something. Ben sneezed. "Whew. I'm getting a headache."

Holly rolled her eyes. "You're such a sensitive little petal."

Her uncle stood too. "Those lilies are a trifle overpowering."

"Not everything can smell as good as Gran's roses." She gently touched the beautiful blooms her mother had picked from the Double Delight rose bush she'd transplanted from Gran's old place. Soft as velvet, with a rich, creamy center and deep, ruby edging, the sweet, spicy scent always reminded Holly of time with her grandmother. She carefully picked out a rose, shook off the water droplets, and inhaled, closing her eyes as various footsteps tromped out toward the kitchen. She let out a sigh, then opened her eyes to see Brent's gaze fixed on her. He smiled, then propelled his long body out of the chair to join the man crew in the kitchen, leaving her feeling flustered. Again.

She wanted to burrow under the sofa's cushions. Why did he keep doing that? It was uncanny how often he'd peered into her soul this past week, seeing those raw, ragged parts of her heart she rarely admitted to possessing, let alone showed anybody. And his unexpected sensitivity kept throwing her off balance, leaving her with this feeling of…fluster.

The ads ceased their flicker as the Australian Football League's familiar logo flashed up.

"It's back on!" Holly grabbed the remote control and flicked the volume back on as the men moved back into the room and resumed their seats. She drew up her knees as the light from the TV flickered over the room, then glanced across to where Brent lounged on the seat opposite as Ben tried to explain another rule.

Brent really was very good-looking. She'd noticed his body back in Hawaii—what red-blooded woman wouldn't have?—and recognized the results of hours of working out. Great abs, muscular arms and shoulders, a physique that could have been on a calendar somewhere. He was handsome, too. Nice eyes, nice nose, nice eyebrows that weren't too thick or thin. His dark hair was a little long, but everything else was just right. Her lips quirked. He'd certainly looked very right today, all dressed up in a newly bought suit for the funeral. She studied him now, as the television light flitted over his features—the strong jaw, his hair curling at the base of his neck. Those lips…

Brent turned and looked at her. "Hey, Holl." Those lips turned up into a smile. "Are you enjoying it?"

Her stomach clenched. Thank goodness it was dark and he couldn't tell how hot her cheeks were. "Yes."

"So, how long have you been a fan for?"

She swallowed to prevent another squeaky answer. "A while."

Ben chuckled. "Dad's been a diehard supporter for years and made sure we all knew the right team to barrack for."

Her father smiled. "It's called training your children in the way they should go."

Brent nodded, his lips still flicked up. She wrapped her arms around her knees as he studied her a moment longer then turned back to the game. Her breath released.

"They must be really fit with all that running and jumping." Brent shook his head.

Ben told Brent about his friend who was a trainer for the Swans and what some of their training involved. Holly glanced back at the TV, but it held no interest.

No. Ben had to be wrong. Brent really was only here as her friend. The way he'd been acting toward her in fooling Bree wasn't to be taken seriously. Although, now she thought about it, he'd never once looked at any girl, either in Hawaii or on the plane…

Apart from her.

Her tummy fluttered.

No. She *had* to be imagining things. That couldn't be real. She was just tired and still suffering the effects of an emotion-packed day. Besides, she couldn't afford distractions. She pressed her lips together as Brent high-fived her brother for another Swans goal. No. Ben was wrong. Brent might be thoughtful and kind and considerate, but that was only because he was a good friend. She blinked. He was *only* a good friend.

～

"Brent, thanks for looking after our girl."

"My pleasure, Mrs. Travers. Thanks for putting me up—and putting up with me."

Brent smiled at Holly's mother, dressed in her blue nurse's uniform from this morning. The startled look of five days ago had transformed into the warm smile she was giving him now, the awkwardness of that first day now well and truly over.

She gave him a hug, then he turned to the man next to her. "Thanks, Mr. Travers."

"It's Beth and John, son." Holly's father gripped his hand. "Better luck next season."

"Thanks." He held out his hand to Holly's brother. "See ya, Ben."

This time Ben's firm grip held camaraderie, not suspicion. "Brent."

"All the best back in Antarctica." He shook Richard's hand.

"Well, it's New Zealand for the next four months, but I'll get back to my penguins soon." Richard nodded. "Happy travels."

"Thanks."

He kind of understood the Travers family now. Down to earth, get-on-with-it people who weren't especially demonstrative except for their fierce loyalty to each other. Maybe it was a small family vibe, the way they closed in on themselves, looked after each other. He couldn't imagine having so few family members. And after last night's story, it was no wonder Ben was protective of his little sister. He'd barely slept last night, trying not to imagine what had been said to Holly that had made her act so ferociously and look so fragile. No wonder she had issues with some guys. He'd like to slapshot that Darren guy from here to—

"You ready?" Holly held the keys in her hand.

He nodded, tossed his bag in the back, and got in the small red hatchback.

The drive was fairly quiet. Holly drove much like she seemed to handle most things, with confidence and a calm grace that still showed her need for speed, right on the limit. She didn't seem inclined to talk, but he didn't mind. He was too busy trying to get his fill of the scenery.

He stole another glance at her. The afternoon sun highlighted the freckles on her nose and the blonde streaks in her hair that he guessed were a legacy from Hawaii. No make-up, but then she didn't need it. She glanced across, and he averted his gaze outside. The beautiful blue water with its large ships near small islands and the escarpment filled with eucalyptus trees sure was different to home.

Home. He didn't really want to go back, but when Holly had murmured something about needing to get back to Brisbane after the funeral, he'd made sure to book the first available seat home. He'd been half-tempted to follow her to Brisbane, but figured after this week, Holly really needed some space.

He cast a last look at the blue sea as they sped up the mountain and veered right, following the signs to Sydney. Despite the sadness that had underscored everything, these past few days had been good. He'd taken Holly's family out for a few meals, attended a service at her parents' church, and checked out the beach, which was as awesome as Holly had described, even in winter. They'd gone bike riding this morning, which had proved a nice way to clear out some of the sadness from yesterday. Holly really was super fit, beating him as they pedaled up the hills. When he'd assured her it was because the ocean views distracted him, she'd just thrown him a skeptical look. He chuckled. No, she wasn't competitive at all.

Holly glanced over for a second. "What?"

"It's been nice getting to know your family this week." He studied her profile as she concentrated on driving. "And you."

Her cheeks pinked.

Cute. He liked that about her. This innocent modesty and vulnerability coupled with the independence and tough competitive spirit sure made her a fascinating contrast to most girls he'd met. He liked her calm demeanor. What was it Granny Violet had always said? *Still waters run deep.* There was plenty of depth to Holly, for sure. He liked her family, their relaxed warmth and hospitality. He liked her hometown of Wollongong. He liked Sydney. Two days after he arrived, Holly and Ben had taken him for a day's sightseeing, insisting that no visit to Australia was complete without a couple of token tourist things. So they'd visited Bondi Beach, done a Harbour Bridge climb, and taken a ferry to a place called Manly. He snickered again.

"You keep laughing. What is it now?"

"Manly."

She smiled, her eyes on the road. "I still think that's where all you wannabe tough guys should live."

"Wannabe? Babe, that's uncalled for."

She smiled wider and pressed harder on the accelerator to overtake a semi-trailer. He settled back to watch the last of the bush disappear as the suburban sprawl of Sydney suddenly yawned in front of them. He chewed his lip at the sight of planes taking off over the big bay. He really wished this car wasn't getting there quite so quickly now.

They finally pulled into the airport parking lot. "You can just drop me off, Holl."

She gave a little smile. "I know." She zoomed into a large parking area and smoothly parked. They got out, and he picked up the small backpack he'd ended up purchasing. Staying for a few days had necessitated a quick trip to Wollongong mall that first day for a few clothes, including a suit. It would've been dumb to buy more, especially when he was heading back to summer in Detroit. He smiled. He loved winter in Australia. It felt like spring. How funny seeing all these Aussies dressed in warm clothing, complaining about the cold. Hello? These people really needed some perspective.

He got his ticket processed, then found a nearby coffee shop where he could wait with Holly until his flight. Despite the reason for it, he'd really enjoyed his time with her. It was yet another fascinating insight into what made Holly Travers tick.

"So, will you miss me?"

Holly spurted out her coffee as her face pinked. "Um, sure, a little bit, I guess."

"Good." He sat waiting for her to make a similar comment, but no, she would not bite. He had to admire the self-control. Bree sure didn't have much. "Yeah, okay, okay, I'll miss you too."

She took another sip, her quick glance revealing her amusement. "That's nice to know."

"So, Holly…" He waited until her eyes were on his. "Does this mean your tastes are changing?"

"What?"

"Maybe you're not such a fan of short, plump guys after all."

She leaned back in her chair before shrugging. "Maybe." Her smile peeked out, grew. Man, he liked her smile. "And maybe you're not such a fan of the busty blonde."

"You're right. I'm not." He leaned forward, suddenly nervous. "You know, I was thinking…" He put his coffee cup down on the table, his fingers grazing hers. He couldn't help but notice her little jump, like she felt the electricity here too. "Holly, I really want to keep on, you know…" Oh man. Why wouldn't the words come? It wasn't like this was high school.

She was looking at him, puzzled. "You mean keep emailing you? Well, yeah, of course."

No, he hadn't meant emailing. These past ten days had opened his eyes to further possibilities. He opened his mouth to speak—

"Hey, isn't that your flight that's boarding soon?" She gestured to a flashing screen nearby.

Awesome. He downed his coffee, pushed back his chair. "I'd better go."

She stood, and they walked to the departure gates.

"Thanks again for all you've done." Holly looked up at him. "You've been a good friend."

"Friend, eh?" After studying her for a moment, he stepped forward, wrapping his arms around her. She stiffened, then slowly relaxed. He rested his cheek on top of her head and inhaled the floral scent of her shampoo. Man, she felt way too good in his arms. "Take care of yourself."

He felt her nod, heard the quiet "You too" before she stepped back and he reluctantly let her go. She gave him a final, beautiful smile. "See you, Brent."

"Bye, Holly."

He picked up his bag, and with a sore heart and a last wave, walked away.

CHAPTER 10

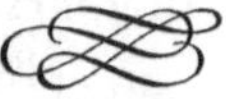

Brisbane, Australia
Late June

Unbelievable. Holly sat in her bedroom, her laptop opened to a new email message while she studied the small plastic card that had arrived this morning. It bore the mark of the supermarket where she worked and a number that had made her eyes almost fall out of her head. She tapped the card again, shook her head, and started typing.

Hi Brent,
Thanks for the gift card, but I don't need your charity.
Holly.

She sat back in her chair and frowned. Nope, that just sounded too rude. She pressed delete, watching the letters disappear one by one, and tried again.

Hi Brent,

Thanks for your help before. Your gift card was very generous —but unnecessary.

But thank you anyway! Holly

She chewed her lip for a minute, then pressed the delete button. That just sounded dumb. Take three.

Hi Brent,

Back in Brisbane now. Hawaii seems so long ago. Thank you once again for all you did before. Your gift card certainly was unexpected but way too generous, so I hope you can get your money back. I appreciate the thought though.

Holly

Her fingers skipped across the keys, and before she knew it, she'd pressed send. Whoops. She winced, wrinkling her nose as she reread it, shrugged, then turned off the computer. She padded out to the bathroom, brushed her teeth, then went back to her room and changed into her flannelette pajamas. Winter in Brisbane was tropical compared to much of the world's wintry standards, but there was enough chill in the air to keep her feeling cool. She got into bed, read her Bible for a while, then turned off the light and shut her eyes. If only she could shut off the questions.

Why had he sent it?

Brent was a nice guy. He'd proven to be a lot of fun in Hawaii, then incredibly sweet and thoughtful afterward. But a thousand-dollar gift card? She sighed and rolled onto her side.

Jess was wrong. Just because Brent cared didn't mean he had any ulterior motives. She chewed her lip, recalling this morning's shock. When she opened her mail, her gasp had been enough for Jess to pick up the letter from where it had fallen on the dining table. She'd read it, sworn, then looked at Holly with upraised eyebrows.

"Who on earth did this?" Jess had narrowed her eyes. "I bet it was Brent, huh?"

"It's anonymous." Holly had held up the letter and frowned. But it could only have been Brent. He was the only one who knew about her money problems and could afford to do something so extravagant to help. She pulled out her phone and made a quick call. Sure enough, Cheryl, the supermarket manager whose kindness had always helped Holly with her shifts, had received a call a few days ago from an anonymous someone asking for a gift card to be arranged and sent to Holly. When questioned further, Cheryl had admitted that the "someone" had transferred money—no credit card details—and "had a very nice deep, sexy voice. And he was American."

Holly had smiled to herself. Mr. Maple-Leaf-on-his-Chest would love that. Not.

She'd thanked Cheryl, ended the call, and nodded at Jess. "Brent."

"Why'd he do that?" Jess had looked at her cynically, eyebrows raised. "What did you have to do for him?"

Holly had sat back in her seat as if slapped. How sad Jess thought like that. "He's just a nice guy. He cares about people."

"Just a nice guy? Wake up, Holl. All guys want something."

Now, Holly rolled over again and punched the pillow. No, Brent wanted nothing beyond friendship. Definitely nothing like the insinuations Jess was making. For some reason, Brent just seemed to care about her, and his actions demonstrated his concern. Anyway, thinking anything else was ridiculous. Wouldn't work for her skating dreams. So she'd best guard her heart. Last Sunday at church, David had preached about vigilance in quickly dealing with heart matters like envy or offence before they could gain a foothold, to be careful not to stir up feelings of love...

Nope, it was best to put thoughts of love on ice and keep treating Brent as a friend.

Nothing more.

Even if she still couldn't stop remembering how good his arms felt around her.

Or the flutter-inducing scent of his aftershave.

Or the joy she felt when she discovered an email from him.

No, no, no. She had to treat him as a friend. He could never be anything more.

She rolled over again.

Could he?

Hey Detective Girl,
Too bad.
Brent

Hi Brent,
What do you mean 'too bad'?
Holly

Hey Holly,
Non-refundable. Stop being stubborn. Eat. Use your savings
for new boots or something in Hong Kong.
Brent

Hi Brent,

*Fine then. Have it your way. I'll just have to force myself to eat
steak now. There. Happy? I do appreciate it—and you.
Thank you.
I started training again this week, and it's like my legs have
forgotten what squats feel like! I enjoyed my time off though. I
just got another weird email from Bree about Hawaii. I can't
believe she still hasn't figured things out! I still think it's pretty
funny.
I hope you're well and enjoying your break.
Take care, Holly*

~

Detroit, Michigan

BRENT EXHALED as he read Holly's most recent email. Finally. He
hadn't wanted to embarrass her, but a couple of veiled questions
to her folks had led to the idea. He hoped it made life easier for
her. He'd suspected Little Miss Independent would be too
proud to accept help, but with Cheryl's assistance, he'd managed
to make it impossible for anyone but Holly to use.

The sound of bathroom tiles clattering to the floor, accompanied by a muttered curse, drew Brent's attention, pushing
him to yell out the study door, "Swear jar!"

Doug groaned. "You're sending me broke, dude."

"You're kidding, right? You're sending yourself broke. It's
your mouth, man. Remember: you volunteered to help. Nobody
forced you."

He caught Doug's faint mutter of "Somebody had to get you
out of the seventies, dude."

Brent laughed and went back into his office to reread the
rest of Holly's email.

Oh yeah, he'd received plenty of emails and phone calls. On
his crazy long flight home, he'd had to swing by Calgary to

collect his stuff from Mike and Bree, and sure enough, the questions that couldn't be asked on the phone had started as soon as he walked through the door. His mother had been almost as bad. As much as she liked Holly, the turn of events had surprised her. He thought his muddled explanation had gone some way to mollifying them all, but everyone had an opinion. Even Dean had got in on the act, FaceTiming him from Vancouver the night Brent finally made it home to Detroit.

He winced as another crash came from the room next door, followed by another oath.

"Swear jar!"

"Dude, are you coming to help me?" Doug sounded a little desperate.

Brent grinned. Ripping off the ugly mustard-and-brown swirly tiles in the bathroom in the height of end-of-June heat was fair payback for all the times Doug had pried into his personal life.

Another oath. "I didn't mean that!"

"Swear jar!"

Brent clasped his hands behind his head and stared out the office window. It was funny how the Hawaii charade then his impromptu visit to Australia had really helped clarify his feelings. He wouldn't settle for just anyone. He really liked Holly. And he was going to trust that God could make this work.

Brisbane, Australia
July

"So, do you miss me?"

Holly smiled, leaning closer to the computer screen. "No, not at all. Have you missed me?"

"Nah. I haven't thought about you at all for months, Holl."

Holly laughed, recalling the almost daily emails he'd been sending these past weeks. "You like to mess with people, don't you?"

The teasing glint in his eyes disappeared. "I'll never mess with you, Holly."

She sat there, wishing it were a phone call so she had some place to hide her confusion as her heart shifted all over the place. "Um, thanks for the flowers."

He smiled again. "Getting invited to the Aussie team event is worth acknowledging."

Joy spurted again. She'd recently attended a special Winter Games team function in Sydney, rubbing shoulders with several famous former athletes, listening to their encouragement and stories. She'd been measured for uniforms, had information collected for accreditation. She'd even done some video interviews for a few media outlets. Her heart danced. She was one of the prospective athletes for next year's Vancouver Games! As the number one-ranked female short track skater in Australia, it seemed quite likely she would go. She swallowed. There still was so much to do—like qualify—before she could really get her hopes up, but competing at the Games! It would make everything worthwhile. *Please, God.* "I totally wasn't expecting that. To be honest, I don't feel like I should talk about it much in case I jinx things. What if I don't go?"

"I didn't know you believed in jinxes."

"Okay, I know I should have more faith and not worry about the future."

Brent looked at her seriously. "You can trust God with everything in your future, Holl."

She nodded, knowing he was right. Again. *Lord, I'm sorry I worry instead of trusting You. Help me remember that You have good plans for me.*

He tilted his head. "Anyway, you should expect to do well. You're great!"

"Yeah, expecting to do well doesn't always equate with actually doing well, does it?" She shrugged. "I can feel great, be performing well in training, but all it takes is for one person to fall and bang, I'm kaput." Like Kate. The last she'd heard was that her father was trying to get her to the U.S. for some radical therapy to help her walk again. *Lord, please heal Kate.*

"Holl?" Brent's eyes were fixed on her. "Do you always expect the worst?"

Whoa. This conversation wasn't supposed to be getting so serious. "Why? Do you always expect the best?"

His lips pushed up on one side. "I expect God to work things out for my best. So yeah, I have faith that whatever happens will ultimately be for my best."

She ducked her head. Why couldn't Mr. Charming be content with shallow flirtation?

"Hey, Holl." He waited until she looked up. "I think you're a superstar."

Oh. Her heart grew tight. She couldn't cope with much more of his kindness. "Well, that's nice to know." She smiled. "Thanks for being a good friend, Brent."

He leaned back. "Friend, huh?" He appeared to consider something before he shifted closer to the screen. "You should know something, Holly." His voice was husky. "I don't send my friends flowers."

What?

He grinned again. "Gotta go, Holl. I'll catch you soon. Take care—babe."

Making a face at that last comment, she managed a final smile before switching off the computer, sitting in the early morning darkness of her room. He didn't send his friends flowers? What did he mean?

. . .

"HOLLY, stop daydreaming. You need more focus. We want World Cup. Pay attention!"

Holly lifted her chin and skated back to where the guys waited. This season she'd started training with the men in order to stay competitive, as none of the other girls could touch her times. Aaron and Craig were nice enough, but she didn't have the same camaraderie as she did with Jess. They were both a couple of years younger than her but highly focused on making World Cup qualifying times at the Desert Classic in Utah next month.

"Okay. Remember, focus on yourself, not worry about others. You control your actions."

Holly nodded. It was weird, but she still had a tendency to be tentative when in close proximity to others, even though the accident with Kate had been months ago now. She was working to let go of the fear, but Coach Chan's frequent reminders couldn't come often enough. Short track was all about the individual. Holly against the world.

She skated back to the start line. The whistle shrieked, and another sprint start began.

Push, push, push, push. The guys were tough to beat at the start, their height and explosive power giving them an edge, but Holly's extra year of training with Coach Chan showed at the finish. Her stamina had improved. Those long bike rides and jogs over the past months had helped too.

They completed another lap, got closer to the red line, then—

"Now!"

Holly pushed lower, her muscles screaming as she sprinted harder. These training drills were great practice for the intensity of competition, when she felt exhausted but had to kick things up a gear to strive to win. Closer, closer. She skirted around the outside of Aaron, her right arm pumping as she closed in on Craig. She could do this.

One more bend. She slipped in between him and the marker. Yes! She crossed the line, breathing heavily.

"Woo hoo! Go, Holl."

Jess gave a thumbs up from the center of the ice as Holly skated a cool-down lap. Coach Chan looked up from her stopwatch and gave a sharp nod. Holly smiled. That nod was the equivalent of a jubilant fist pump for anybody else.

"Okay, everybody. Stairs."

Holly sat next to Jess, tugged off her skates, and laced up her sneakers. Stair workouts involved running and jumping up the steps. It worked the muscles in her quads, hips, calves, and ankles, making for a great contrast to the long gliding motion on the ice. Two feet jumps were followed by single leg hops, all helping to improve her agility, precision, and power. Her heart was racing after completing the thirty minutes.

"Thank the sweet Lord that's done." Jess wiped her face with a towel. "I need a shower."

"Holly." Coach Chan beckoned. "You doing okay, but could do better. You still work?"

Holly nodded. "But I'm cutting back my hours come—"

"You need sponsor." Coach Chan frowned. "Need more training, not distractions like work or studies. Or men." The black eyes peered over the red frames. "Understand?"

Holly nodded. Could Coach Chan read minds?

"You have ability. You must show it."

"Happy birthday, Brent."

"Thanks, Holly." Brent settled back on his seat with a smile that made her heart dance. He looked like he was really glad to see her.

"So, what have you been up to?"

He filled her in on his prep for the Canadian hockey team

evaluation camp in late August. "I know I need to pick up speed. Some of the other forwards are just so fast."

"I wonder if you'd get more speed if you drop your body a little and get your center of gravity closer to the ice," she offered. "That's the problem with being so tall. You've got a better stride, but you're not always as fast as those of us who are shorter."

"Huh." He sat back, nodding slowly. "Okay, I'll give that a go tomorrow at training."

"Hope it helps." She wondered how to bring up that last conversation that had her puzzling over the "friends" comment. If she wasn't his friend, what was she? She wasn't even really sure that she wanted to know the answer. If he was really interested, then how on earth could a long distance relationship work? That would be crazy. And after last week's warning, Coach Chan would definitely not be impressed.

He grinned again, and her tummy tipped. Why did he have to be so good looking? "Bree was telling me about the special handmade card and charm you sent her for her birthday."

"Oh, the palm tree? Yeah, I thought she might like it."

"So." He leaned closer, his face alight with interest. "Is my present still in the mail?"

"Sorry, I didn't know you were expecting something. What were you hoping for?"

His lips turned up on one side. "You."

She stared at him. Why did this man make her feel so off kilter? "What do you mean?"

"I'm just going to make a wish when I blow out my candles later, that this time next year you'll be around."

"Why's that?"

"Because I miss you, Holly."

"You've said that before."

"So sue me. It's true." He smiled.

Her insides quivered. "I thought we were done pretending."

"Holly, I was done pretending weeks ago."

Oh. Her heart beat erratically. "What exactly are you saying, Brent?"

"I'm saying...I can't wait until you're over here."

The disappointment at his answer surprised her. Why couldn't he be serious and actually say something real? She hoped she'd kept her face impassive enough. "Well, lucky you, I'll be in Utah next month, then Calgary in October." August's Desert Classic was ice racing's first event, followed by the Asian leg, which included Taiwan then the first two World Cups in Korea and Beijing. Calgary's Oktoberfest short track event was the week after Nationals. After that would be the next two World Cup events that were Games qualifiers in Montreal, then Michigan. Surely she'd get the chance to see him—if he was fair dinkum about wanting to see her, of course.

She told him the dates, but he sighed. "Maybe I can see you in Utah, but the others probably won't work, as the season will have begun."

She'd known it was stupid to get her hopes up, but this level of disappointment was shocking. She shrugged, finding a smile. "Oh well. It's not like I'll get a chance to see you play. Guess that makes us even then."

His eyes grew serious. "I am really sorry, Holly. You know I'd love to come see you."

Why was her chest feeling so tight? Why did she feel like she wanted to cry? This was ridiculous. She shrugged and looked down at the crumbs in her computer keyboard. "I need to go. I've got training." In another hour, but she couldn't sit here any longer. This was excruciating. She chanced a last glance at the screen, hoping her smile hid her true feelings. "Hope you enjoy your day. Bye, Brent." And with a simple click, the screen went dark.

~

SHE WAS UPSET.

It hurt that she was upset, that she might think he didn't want to see her. Brent pushed back in his chair, threw his hands through his hair. What could he do?

He glanced at his phone and calculated the time zones. He'd been doing that a lot lately. A few taps later and Bree's voice came on the loudspeaker.

"Brent." She sounded surprised. "You okay? I'm heading out for dinner soon."

"I hope Mike is taking you somewhere nice."

"Very nice, thank you. Most birthday appropriate. How about you?"

"Oh, Mom's cooked something good."

"You're not going out?"

Put like that, his life sounded sadly pathetic. "Staying in this year."

"Wow. How the party king has fallen."

"You know it."

"Seriously, you should go out. Do something. Stop being miserable just because Holly isn't there."

His heart sparked. "Yeah, about that."

"Oohh, this sounds promising."

"Has Holly mentioned competing at the Desert Classic in Salt Lake City?"

"Yes. I was planning to go." A beat. "Why? Do you want to come too?"

He chewed his lip. If he said yes, then that really was taking things to another level. But surely pursuing her meant making the occasional big call?

"Brent?"

"Um, yeah. That'd be cool."

"Cool? I think it'll be awesome. Brent and Holly sitting in a tree, k-i-s-s-i-n-g!" She laughed.

He rolled his eyes. "How old are you? Seriously, Bree, go put Mike on the phone or something."

"Maybe you should come stay with us for a while. Your evaluation camp is here in Calgary, isn't it? Holly could come visit too."

"I think she has a comp in Asia not long after that."

"You have been keeping tabs on our girl, haven't you?"

He shrugged—was about to deny it when he realized that was untrue. The more time he spent talking with Holly, the more he wanted to know. She fascinated him. Her passion, her dedication, her commitment to God and family—he wanted more of Holly in his life. More importantly, he wanted to see if she—Olympic-focused, elite skater girl—wanted him as more than a part-time distraction.

"I really like her, Bree," he finally confessed.

"Yes!"

"Did you just fist pump?"

"Maybe." She laughed. "Mike is looking at me funny."

"Yeah, you'd better go."

"Oh, I'm so excited!"

"Yeah, sorry to have kept you. Enjoy your dinner."

"No! I mean, yes, I'll enjoy my dinner, and I'm always excited about going out with you, aren't I, honey?" she said, the last part obviously to Mike, as her voice grew a little fainter and a sound suspiciously like a kiss was followed by a muted giggle. "But what I'm really excited about is seeing you and Holly together."

"Yeah, you might need to back that one up a bit, Bree. We're hardly together."

"What?"

Too late he remembered the facade he'd been keeping up. "I mean, we're taking things slow." Was that a lie when he didn't even really know if Holly liked him like that? Still, she had to like him a bit to be upset that he might not see her, right? "I mean, it's tricky trying to figure this out when we live in different parts of the world."

"Yeah. You didn't go for easy this time, did you?"

His gut tensed, defensiveness rising in his chest. Was that a loaded question?

"Oh! I didn't mean it like that. Although, Chloe wasn't exactly playing hard to get, was she?"

No.

"Anyway, I'm extremely glad you're finally seeing reason and you and Holly have a chance to make this work. She's pretty special, Brent. I hope you know that."

"Yeah." He was coming to realize that more each day.

Another giggle. "Look, I need to go. We'll set up details soon, okay?"

"Thanks, Bree. Enjoy dinner."

"You too. Say hi to Mom and Dad again for me."

The call ended, and he slouched in his seat. He loved his parents, but what he wouldn't give to have a girlfriend he could celebrate with. Maybe the Desert Classic might help reveal whether Holly might consider giving him that chance.

CHAPTER 11

Salt Lake City, Utah
August

The first event of the season was always a great chance to catch up—to find out who had done what, been where, or was with whom after months away. Holly's stomach fluttered. Would she one day be able to say she'd met someone, be able to share photos or even introduce a special someone to others like Marianna was doing now?

She glanced across the Salt Lake City arena to where Marianna's compatriot and fellow skater held her in a movie-worthy embrace. Holly's stomach tugged, remembering the feel of Brent's arms around her in Hawaii, fake as that had been. It had to help, to live and train together in the same country, to share the same sport. Maybe that was the only way to have a relationship and remain competitive. Or be like Bree, willing to live full time in one location while her man got to live out his dream. She bit her lip.

"Holly?" Coach Chan. "You look worried."

"Oh! No, I'm fine." She straightened her spine, glanced around the building. How amazing to think this was the venue where Australia had won its first gold medal in short track all those years ago. *Lord, please.* Desperation, like a panicked flame, rose within. She exhaled. Stretched out her gloved fingers. *Trust God.* "I'm imagining what it would've been like skating here when it was an Olympic venue."

"You want Vancouver, then you must focus now."

"Yes, Coach Chan." Enough wondering about what might be. She needed to concentrate on what she could do right now, not the *ifs*, the fairytales, and what-would-never-bes. She exhaled. Bree had said she'd come watch her skate, a gesture Holly appreciated so much. It had to help, knowing there'd be at least one person in the crowd willing her to succeed. But it was enough to make her wonder why Brent—

No. She wouldn't think about him. Since that last awkward conversation, he'd not said anything more about seeing her, and she sure wasn't going to push him to come. She had no desire to act like the pushy wannabe girlfriend. It wasn't even like she was his real girlfriend or anything. Besides, Coach Chan was right. If Holly wanted to compete at an elite level, then she couldn't afford distractions. And the amount of space Brent took up in her thoughts made him a fairly big distraction.

"Competitors, to the ice."

Holly smiled at Jess, here with the Aussie men, and they joined the rest of the women being marshalled for the five hundred meters.

As per other competitions of this stature, there was a mix of novice, juniors, and the opens in which registered skaters would compete. It allowed for a more relaxed atmosphere, even though Coach Chan seemed as driven as ever.

Holly nodded to Alana Matthews and Tori Popovic, two girls she'd come to know over the past year who trained at the

Calgary Olympic Oval program. Envy spiked. Coach Chan was a good coach and had helped Holly succeed beyond her teenage dreams, but to have world class training partners and rinks devoted to short track that weren't used by recreational skaters… *Lord, is it selfish to want more?*

She pressed at the headache forming between her eyes. "Lord, direct my paths."

"Did you say something?" Jess said.

"Just praying aloud."

Jess looked at her askance. "O-kay?"

Holly shrugged. Her efforts to show Jess God's ways seemed to fail dismally at times. Maybe she was too stressed. Or too busy. Or too focused. *Lord, help me be a friend to Jess. Help her come to know You. And help me trust You too. With everything.*

"Look, there she is! Number 101 helmet." Bree pointed to a group of skaters at Utah's Olympic Oval. "I don't think she's seen us yet."

Brent nodded. "Good. I don't want her distracted."

"You sure about that?" Bree's eyebrows rose.

"This is her world, her life. She needs to concentrate."

"So why exactly are you here then?"

He chewed his lip. Was it unfair to turn up unannounced? Was it right to want to seek more when Holly wanted to win gold? Or was this a window of opportunity provided by God to see if this could work out?

"Bree, honey." Mike wrapped an arm around her. "Let the man make his own moves."

"Oh, fine then." She huffed. Groaned. "Oh, she's so skinny."

Brent swallowed. He wouldn't have said that exactly. He couldn't help but notice that Holly had a few more curves than last time he'd seen her. Dressed in a dark-green skate suit, she

looked super fit, the suit leaving little to the imagination—
though he could just imagine what Doug would say if he could
see her. She looked amazing. Her focused expression made her
look fierce, and her telltale ponytail hung down her back under
the yellow helmet that showed how dangerous this sport
could be.

The announcer introduced the competitors. Holly gave a
quick wave and skated to the line. The stadium's noise level
dropped. Brent could feel the blood pulsing through his body.

"Go to the start." Holly bent down into a peculiar stance, like
a lazy sprinter's squat.

"Ready."

BANG.

With a blistering start, Holly quickly maneuvered her way
into the lead before leaning into the first bend. Brent held his
breath. The girls seemed so close to each other that the slightest
miscalculation would mean they'd all fall. They powered
through the straight, Holly pulling farther in front. She seemed
to possess a kind of graceful strength that made her skating
seem almost effortless. She leaned around the next bend, and he
held his breath. What sort of training would that require? She
seemed to defy gravity as she stretched almost horizontally
around the bends. He shook his head, unable to drag his eyes
away. The roar of the crowd grew as Holly continued, her lead
never really in question as she completed the race in 45.81
seconds. His heart could finally slow its rapid pace.

"Wow. That is intense." He'd learned to deal with the pressure of NHL playoffs, but it sure was different when it was his
girl-who-was-a-friend out there. No wonder her coach always
demanded focus. Distractions could be deadly. He couldn't get
over how wild the sport was. And people thought hockey was
dangerous. "Full on adrenaline."

"You should see how intense it gets during a World Cup,"
Bree said. "I saw her compete in B.C. last year. Did you know

they have to do the five hundred meters maybe five times in the space of a couple of hours, then turn around and do the thousand the next day?"

"That's amazing." No wonder training and competition took it out of her.

They kept watching in case she noticed them, but her attention was on what her coach was saying. Anticipation throbbed. Brent didn't want to distract her, but he couldn't wait for her to be surprised. Uncertainty streaked through his chest. He hoped she thought his visit a nice surprise.

Next was the thousand. He watched, heart in his mouth, as Holly raced around on the ice. Times weren't as essential as placings, so the fact she was in the first two finishers was what really mattered. She'd qualified for the next day's quarterfinals in each distance.

"Ready?" Bree glanced up at him with a sly smile.

He pushed back his shoulders, willed his expression to appear cool. "Sure."

"You can't fool me. You're excited, aren't you?"

He exchanged glances with Mike. "Does she do this to you too?"

"All the time, man. All the time."

"I can't help it—ooh! Look, there she is!" Bree hurried to the sidelines. "Holly. Holly!"

Holly turned, her face lighting as she skated to the rink board and leaned across and hugged Bree. "You came!"

"Of course I did. Actually, *we* did." Bree turned, her arm sweeping out like a game show host.

Holly's gaze met Brent's. Her mouth sagged.

"Hey, Holly." Warmth filled his chest as she stared at him as if she thought him a mirage. Like a parched man in the desert, he drank in the sight of her. It was one thing to see her via a computer screen but quite another to see her in real life. He drew closer.

"Hi." Her smile widened, sweetened.

"I'm here too," said Mike with a small wave.

She blinked. "Oh! Hi, Mike." She took her helmet off, tugged her ponytail smooth. "This is such a wonderful surprise."

"Holly." A stern-faced Asian woman beckoned her.

"Oh. That's my coach. I'd better go."

"You still free for dinner?" Bree asked.

"I think so." Holly's gaze drifted back to Brent. "I still can't believe you came."

"You were amazing," he said. "I knew you could skate well, but wow, you just flew."

"Thanks. That was the easy bit though. The finals tomorrow are where it's really at."

"Holly?" Another competitor, an Aussie judging from the same style suit as Holly's, glanced at them curiously. "Coach Chan is getting cranky."

"I'd better go. See you soon?" Holly's gaze found his, her question aimed at him.

"We'll be waiting."

Her smile stretched and she turned, skating off to the competitors' area, turning around once as if to check he was still really there.

Mike's chuckle broke into the bubble of satisfaction.

"What?"

"That was worth it."

"Oh, she was so happy to see you!" Bree exclaimed, leaning her head on Mike's shoulder. She sighed. "How adorable."

Please. Brent exchanged glances with Mike, who simply laughed. "I think they call this payback, dude."

But he didn't mind. Not really. It was that good to see Holly again.

∼

Holly's heart beat strangely. He was really here? She removed her neck guard and protective gloves, stripping off to change into her street clothes.

"Who were they?" Jess asked curiously.

"My friend Bree. Remember when I went to Hawaii? She's here with her hubby and brother."

"Is the brother the tall, hot one?"

Holly nodded. Yes. Yes, he was.

"He's the guy who sent the gift card?"

Yes. Yes, he had.

From farther in the room she heard whispers of *Karlsson* and *Red Wings* and *Flames*. Her pulse ratcheted up. So others had recognized Brent and Mike. Had they linked them to Holly yet? The short track community was pretty small, so it wouldn't take much for whispers to make their way back to Coach Chan. "Come on. Let's go find Coach Chan."

"But aren't you going to see your friends? I'll go see them for you if you like," Jess offered. "Especially the tall guy. He's a bit of all right."

Protectiveness surged. Jess might only tease, but judging from the surrounding conversations, she didn't think Brent's presence here would go under the radar for much longer. And this friendship with him—for really, how could it be anything more?—still felt too fragile and precious to allow others to offer their opinions yet. Could it work? Why else was he here? She dug her fingers into her brow.

They headed back into the main stadium, Holly's senses alert for Brent and co. whilst also eager to avoid further scrutiny from Coach Chan.

"There she is," Jess said, pointing.

"Who? Oh, Coach Chan."

"Who's she talking to?"

Holly's mouth dried. "I think that's Dan Mathieson."

"Who's he?"

"The coach from the Calgary program I told you about."

"Ooh." Jess glanced at her. "Are you thinking what I'm thinking?"

Holly's gut tensed. *Please, God.* "I don't want to say it out loud in case I get my hopes dashed."

"You deserve it though."

"It's likely too late in the season for me to join this year."

"Never say never." Jess coughed. "Don't look now, but he's looking at you."

"Dan Mathieson?"

"No. Hot guy. Your *friend*." Jess chuckled. "Tell you what, you can hook me up with a friend of his any time you like."

"Jess. There's no hooking up."

"What? You mean you're not a thing?"

Holly sighed. What exactly had she told Jess about Brent? This must be why God despised lying. Messing with others seemed to have a way of messing with one's own head too.

"Don't tell me you haven't even kissed the man!"

She shivered, suddenly wondering what his lips would feel like on hers.

"Holly?"

Stop it! She was here to develop her skating, not develop feelings for someone she couldn't be with. She glanced up. He still watched her, smiling. He lifted a hand.

Her face heated. She gave him a small wave.

"Oh, Holl. You've got it bad."

She shook her head. "Stop it, Jess. We'd better go see what Coach Chan wants before she gets mad."

They hurried to join the Aussie boys, who were listening to Coach Chan as she advised on how they could each improve. Holly pushed to her toes, searching the building. Dan had left, was nowhere to be seen. Her heart sank. Did that mean he wouldn't offer her a place after all?

"Holly." Coach Chan's terse voice snapped her attention back to her coach. "Pay attention."

Holly leaned in, listening, focusing as best she could to her coach's instructions about turns and depth and reach. But her heart wanted to chase down these other fascinating lines of thought. What had Dan Mathieson been talking about so avidly with Coach Chan? And why exactly was Brent here?

"Holly." Coach Chan finally turned to her. "I need to speak with you a moment longer, please." She excused the others to go have dinner, with a reminder to not have a late night.

Jess squeezed Holly's hand. "Good luck."

"Thanks," she murmured, not entirely certain whether she meant with the skating program or with Brent. Not that that should matter right now. Especially not with Coach Chan looking at her so seriously.

"You skate well today. You were noticed."

Holly swallowed. "I saw you talking to Coach Mathieson."

Sharp nod. "He quite impressed. Is good trainer."

"And...?" *Please, God.*

"And would like you to talk with him now."

"Now?" Brent was waiting. But he'd understand, wouldn't he? "Um, sure. I just need to tell a friend I might be a little longer."

"You want Vancouver medal, or you want this friend?"

Holly's breath suspended. Did it really have to be one or the other? Marianna was a World Cup champ who'd succeeded and still sustained a relationship. Couldn't Holly do so too?

"He is waiting for you."

Holly half turned, then realized Coach Chan wasn't talking about Brent. She exhaled, moved to follow, then, "I'll just be a moment."

She ran back to where Bree stood with Brent and Mike. Best to make it look like her friend was Bree. "Hi again. I'm really sorry, but I have a super important meeting with someone, so I can't come just yet." She glanced up at Brent, saw his look of disappointment. "I'll be as quick as I can, I promise."

"Holly, we don't mind. Text me when you're ready." Bree cleared her throat, dropped her voice. "Your coach is coming this way. She looks a little scary."

"She is scary," Holly murmured, flashing Brent an apologetic smile before hurrying to forestall her coach from interrogation.

"Who are they?" Coach Chan frowned over Holly's shoulder.

"You remember the wedding I went to last year? That's Bree and her hubby." Avoiding mention of Brent might be best. She gently steered her coach away. "So, did Coach Mathieson say anything about when I could start?"

"Nothing definite. Just meeting you. That is all."

"Oh." Her heart dipped. Still, the fact he wanted to meet her at all was encouraging. Even if the ensuing introduction and conversation revealed—as she suspected—that there was no place in this year's program, there might be one down the track.

Which further showed that she might need to choose between golden glory and pursuit of other appealing goals.

By the time Holly left the air-conditioned rink, Brent was ready to melt. The Desert Classic certainly lived up to its name —Utah in August was hot enough to cook an egg on the car's hood. He'd borrowed Mike's hire car as soon as Holly texted Bree.

Brent hurried to help Holly with her bags. She looked a little dazed. "Can I get these?"

"Uh, sure. Thanks."

He gestured to the car. "Good meeting?"

"I think so."

"You okay?"

"Yeah. I'm just tired now."

He understood. Games took it out of him, too. Still, he knew a throb of concern. "Holl? What is it?"

She shook her head. "Sorry, I'm still processing."

Processing what exactly? "Hey." She glanced up. "You can relax now."

She nodded, but the wrinkled brow didn't smooth. Was she concerned about her results? What had her coach said to her?

"Bree and Mike are back at the hotel."

She nodded, still quiet. He sagged, pretending her bags were heavy. "Did you pack rocks in here or something?"

As he'd hoped, his tease tugged forth her energy and smile. "I didn't figure you for such a weakling. Let me know if you can't manage."

He laughed, and the knot of concern dwindled. He placed the bags in the trunk and opened her door. "Your chariot, Miss Travers."

"Thanks." She sank into the leather seat and sighed, looking suddenly, unutterably weary.

He moved around to the driver's side and started the engine, fiddled to make it cool. "Air-con good?"

She nodded, still too quiet.

Concern threaded him again. "You okay, Holl? We don't have to do anything. I can just drop you back at the hotel if you prefer."

She shifted to face him. "But you came all this way."

"Yeah. But I completely understand if you'd rather sleep than talk to me."

"You're really sweet."

"You know it."

This time his humor fell flat as she bit her lip, and for a moment, he thought she might cry.

"Holl, I'm joking. Sort of." He pulled the car to the curb, reached for her hand, clasped her palm in his. "What's happened? You don't seem yourself."

She studied their hands, her brow still furrowed.

"Holly? You're starting to scare me."

Her gaze met his again. "I'm sorry. It's just I have some decisions to make."

"Want to go back to the hotel then? You can go rest in your room, do some thinking. I'll make your excuses."

She shook her head.

"Okay, then shall we drop your bags first or just go find the others?"

She squeezed his hand and released, then straightened, as if determined to shake off her trouble. "Let's go find the others. I'm starving."

"That makes two of us."

"Why does that not surprise me?" Her smile flickered, then she exhaled. "Okay, that reminds me. What are we going to say to them?"

"About?"

"About you…and me."

"You know Mike knows the truth, but Bree still doesn't."

"Okay. So just more like what we did in Hawaii?"

His skin tingled, remembering just how good it had felt to hug her. Yeah, he'd be up for more of that, except… "Not quite like that, no."

"What do you mean?"

"I was serious before, Holly. I want to know where this can go."

"Sorry, I'm so tired. Where what can go?"

Perhaps this wasn't the best time to talk about trying to figure out how to turn their fake relationship into something real. She seemed so tired that anything he said would likely be forgotten or misconstrued. "Never mind. We'll talk later. What do you want to eat?"

Half an hour later, they were eating at the hotel restaurant with Bree and Mike.

He watched, fascinated, as Holly steamrolled her way through her steak and scallops, only coming up for air when she'd mopped up the last of the sauce with her dinner roll.

"Wow. That's seriously impressive, babe. I don't think I've ever seen a girl eat so fast."

She frowned.

"No, no! I'm glad you enjoy your food. It's just something else we have in common." He shook his head. "I hate when people pick at their plate, like the animal died for nothing."

"Sometimes it's a bummer, liking food as much as I do, knowing I have to be careful how much I eat." She smiled sweetly. "But then, that's the good thing about eating with you. I never feel like I'm being too much of a pig, because you eat so much more."

Mike and Bree laughed as Brent glanced down at his empty plate. When it had become clear Holly had simply needed refueling and not conversation, he'd tackled his fifteen ounce steak with gusto.

They soon moved to a slightly more quiet lounge area, Holly sinking into the plush sofa as if she was ready to nest there forever. He sat next to her, swallowing a smile at Bree's look of approval as he reached for Holly's hand.

"So, what did your coach want?"

Holly glanced at him before shifting her attention to Bree. "Well, it's exciting, but nothing is definite yet."

"What is? Stop keeping us in suspense."

"Coach Chan spoke to the head coach at the Calgary Olympic Oval training facility."

"And?" Bree's face lit, like she might explode from excitement.

"And he's offered me a place there—"

"Wow! That's fantastic! I can't *wait* to have you near."

"—next year."

Disappointment shaded Holly's eyes, and Brent swallowed

his own. For a moment he'd seen a way forward. Perhaps the questions over the status of this relationship could be resolved if distance weren't such an issue. It'd help to live on the same continent at least.

"That's great, Holl." His thumb stroked the back of her hand. "So, you said yes?"

She nodded. "It's a great facility. It'll be awesome to train with people who are world class skaters. I need more experienced people to push me." Her shrug held a measure of resignation. "It'd be nicer to have it happen before next February, but I guess God knows what He's doing."

Swift inhale. That's right. This wasn't happening by chance. And Brent's future wasn't a matter of randomness, either. He really needed to trust God with his future. With *all* aspects of his future. He squeezed Holly's hand again.

CHAPTER 12

Taiwan
End of August

Hi everyone!
So I've just left Utah, and next stop is Taipei. These warm-up
competitions are great to iron out the kinks before the first
World Cup event in Korea next month. My Desert Classic
results were good, not great. I managed to make the final in the
500m, even if I did get disqualified. Oh well. That's short track.
Hope you're doing well. Appreciate your prayers.
Love, Holly

Holly pressed send, then dragged in a breath. She didn't want to share last week's discussion with Coach Chan and Dan Mathieson with her supporters yet. It still felt too tenuous and a little unreal. She'd discussed it with her parents, who'd shared the excitement of Bree and Mike. And Brent.

Except she still wasn't sure what Brent *really* thought. She'd wondered for a moment if he'd hoped to have her nearer, if maybe his words about making this relationship real were actually true. His showing up at her event, the way he'd looked at her, the way he'd later hugged her goodbye—her insides curled as they had each time she remembered *that*—were enough to almost make her believe that this wasn't a show, that he really wanted a future with her. But she couldn't reconcile that with what Dan Mathieson had said, with what Coach Chan had always said—that to be the elite skater who might make Australia proud would mean even greater sacrifices. Such as time with family. Time for a relationship.

Others might manage such a balancing act, but it still seemed impossible for her. And it wasn't like she could ask Brent to clarify exactly what his intentions were.

Could she?

~

Calgary, Canada

THE END OF AUGUST saw the Canadian hockey team evaluation camp, which meant long hours at Pengrowth Saddledome. But time in Calgary meant time snatched with Bree and Mike, too. Brent's video call with Holly—she was in Taiwan—had to be kept short.

She wore a sleeveless top, her hair was mussed, and she had no makeup on, like she'd just tumbled out of bed. Brent swallowed, chaining his thoughts from going there.

She propped her head in one hand. "So, you're on the red team?"

He nodded. "Against the whites. These games help the coaches see who works well with others." He rubbed his shoulder where he'd been pushed into the boards. "Everything gets considered. Particular skill sets, techniques, strengths and weaknesses, who can do what. Which is why your tips with speed have helped."

"I'm glad." Her smile finally appeared. "So, what happens after this?"

"Team training camps start in a few weeks, then some of us fly overseas to start the season, so this is really our only chance to get together before the Games in February. Over the next few months, each player gets assessed to see who has form, which guys are healthy, and who's playing well against the players from other teams. It'll be interesting, because the coach is from Detroit, so here's hoping that means more chances to impress."

"Not that you want him being accused of favoritism."

"Except maybe it wouldn't hurt."

Her lips tilted higher. "How many go to Vancouver?"

"Around twenty or so."

"So it's pretty tight competition."

"Yeah. But at least I've got a better chance as a forward."

"They need more forwards than defensemen?"

"Yeah. Mike got cut, but he's not too sore. Says he's got enough excitement at the moment." He glanced at the time. "Hey, babe, I've gotta go. Talk soon."

"Let me know how you go."

"Pray I make it through this next round."

"Will do."

"Oh, and I hope things go well in Taiwan."

"Me too. Bye."

Detroit, Michigan

Hi y'all.
I need a new passport! Can't believe this one's filled already.
Taipei was interesting. Loved the food, skating was okay. The

Chinese and Korean girls are SO good it's a real achievement when you can beat them. (I haven't yet.) Still, looking forward to the first World Cups in Seoul and Beijing next month. Jess, my flat mate, sprained her ankle and had to fly back to Brisbane. Please keep her in your prayers.
Hope all is well with you.
Love, Holly

BRENT REREAD THE GROUP EMAIL, sensing Holly's frustration, and wondered how she was doing. Did she get lonely? He knew she had friends in the skating community, but not having Jess there might add to a sense of loneliness. During their last video call, he'd sensed a slight withdrawal, the distance between them greater than mere miles. He wished he could peer inside that pretty little head and know what she really thought about him.

He took a moment to pray for Jess. Holly had mentioned Jessica didn't believe in God and that Holly struggled to show her God's grace at times. He thought of Doug and could so relate. Trying to be salt and light in a world that didn't seem to care was a challenge.

As was trying to show that he cared about a certain girl who always seemed to be too far away. He reread the last line. *Love, Holly.* His heart flickered. Maybe these feelings went deeper than he'd realized. Despite the challenges, she certainly was distracting, intriguing, and—dare he admit it—lovable. He picked up the wooden photograph frame on his office desk, studying the picture of Holly and himself in Hawaii, grinning at the camera over a seafood feast. If only the love she signed off with were something she actually meant. Maybe it was time to find out how she really felt.

"HEY, HOLLY."

"Hi, Brent." She looked and sounded weary, her face and voice lacking animation.

"You seem tired."

Her lips flattened. "So, the Canadian team tryouts are done?"

"Yeah. We won't know who's in the team until after Christmas, so we're back in Motor City for training camp, staying in a hotel. Coach wants us to bond more. It means I'm sharing with Dougie, which he's enjoying."

"I bet."

"How about you? China, huh?"

"Beijing in September is hot and loud and smelly. I kinda want to be home." Her lips tipped up, but there was no joy in her expression. "Don't let Coach Chan hear me say that."

"What can I do?"

She laughed, a sound edged with bitterness. "What can you do? There's nothing you can do, Brent."

"Holl, are you okay?"

"Yes. No. I don't know. My results just aren't good enough, and there are all these expectations to perform, and then I always fall short." She rubbed her forehead. "I used to love this sport and thought I was born to skate, but it's just so hard sometimes—"

"Holly, you're strong. You can do this."

"Can I?" Her gaze connected with his. "I don't know anymore. Maybe I might be able to do the skating thing, but I really don't know about whether I can do *this* anymore." She gestured to the screen.

"What do you mean?"

"I mean, I don't even know what this thing between you and me is. You hold my hand, tell me you aren't messing with me, but I really can't see any future, can you?"

What? No. This conversation wasn't supposed to go this way.

"We're rarely in the same country, let alone the same time

zone. Call me crazy, but I think most people would think this is too hard. And right now everything else feels too hard, and I—" She gulped. "I don't want to keep pretending this is real when it's not."

No. No, no. "Holl, I really like you."

"And I like you. But I feel like you've spent months teasing me, saying all sorts of stuff, and for what? This?" She motioned to the computer screen again. "I don't even know what you want this to be."

A relationship. A life together. Something real. He swallowed. "I wish this could be easier, but it's not, and I'm sorry that's so frustrating."

"No, it's crazy, that's what it is."

"Good thing I don't mind a little crazy—"

"Yeah, but I do. I've got competitions I have to focus on, and I can't afford to have emotional drama get in the way of what I need to do."

"So don't let it."

She snorted. "Brent, I'm not in the mood. I need to go. See you later."

The screen went dark.

Dear God. No. How had that escalated so quickly? Concern grew for her emotional wellbeing. No. She must have been speaking from tiredness and tension. She couldn't really mean things were over. Could she?

He was still frowning at the computer screen when Doug walked back into the room. "Karlsermeister!" Doug dumped his stuff on his bed, then looked around. "I swear I heard voices. Is someone else here?"

Brent pointed at the laptop. "FaceTime."

"Right." Doug jumped on his bed and lay back, arms folded under his head. "Was that the chick you keep emailing?"

Brent nodded. "Holly."

"The Aussie skater?"

"Yeah."

"How's that work?" His fellow forward eyed him curiously.

"We email, text, FaceTime. That's how it works." Except when it didn't. His stomach swirled with uncertainty. At times like this, the crazy clash of their schedules seemed so unfair.

"So you're friends?"

Were they? Of course they were. Although, he might need to settle for maybe-friends in the short-term. "Why?"

"Just wondering. You're different these days, and I'm wondering what's got you that way. Makes sense if you're in lurve."

Brent threw a cushion at him. "You gotta stop watching those chick flicks, man. They're screwing with your head, dude."

"You're the one screwy in the head, having a relationship with someone you barely see." Doug threw the cushion back and disappeared into the bathroom as off-key singing began. "Karlos is in lurve…"

Brent banged on the door. "Don't give up your day job, man. Better yet, give it up—then I won't have to listen to you anymore."

He heard the shower start and escaped down to the hotel's gym. He got on the treadmill and started a slow jog, ignoring the muted TV as he mulled over Doug's comments. Holly. He liked so many things about her—her sense of humor, her drive and determination, that gorgeous smile. Spending time with her in the middle of the year had grounded the friendship, and their emails in these past few months had gradually become more personal, covering faith, values, and their perspectives on some of life's bigger issues. He'd never experienced such a depth and honesty with a girl before.

He flicked the speed switch up several notches and started running faster.

Sure, there'd been times when he'd wondered if pursuing a friendship with someone on the other side of the world was the best use of his emotional energy. And it was obvious Holly felt the same. But she was different. For as long as he could remember, hockey had been his only focus, but over this past year, Holly had definitely slipped onto his radar. But did she like him? He thought back to the video call. The fact that she was upset sparked hope. She must like him to some degree, otherwise she wouldn't care. He cared. He prayed for her, wanted her best, wanted to help her as much as possible.

But love? He swallowed the dryness in his mouth. Did it really go that far?

"Karlsson! What have you been doing this summer?"

Brent looked up at Coach Reynolds. It was the second last day of summer training camp. The week had been super intense, the fans crazy wild. But it was nice to get back with the guys, to play with people whose moves he could anticipate, whose plays he understood and didn't have to second-guess like he'd had to with the other Canadian team hopefuls in Calgary.

"Karlsson?"

Brent shrugged, balancing his stick on the ice. "Training."

"No, what have you been doing different?"

"He's been getting tips from his girlfriend," Doug said.

Brent ignored his teammates' sniggers as his coach stared at him. "Your girlfriend?"

"She's a short track skater."

Man, Doug had a big mouth. "She gave me some hints on my sprinting." Brent still wasn't sure if Coach Reynolds was pleased or not. He kept looking at him oddly.

"Short track?"

"Yeah. She's going to Vancouver next year." It wasn't settled for sure, but who else would represent Australia as well as Holly?

His coach was still looking at him funny. "Huh. Well, it's working."

Brent released a quiet breath. At least something was working right.

What could he do to make things right with Holly?

CHAPTER 13

Beijing, China
September

"You still tense, Holly?"

Coach Chan continued kneading Holly's shoulders, trying to loosen the muscles as Holly sat on a hard gray seat in yet another monotonous airport terminal. Oh yeah, she felt tense all right.

She ducked her head and pulled at a loose thread on her track pants. Her results in Taiwan and Seoul had been okay—better than the disaster of Beijing, at least, even if she hadn't lived up to her practice times. Her disappointment had nothing to do with Brent. Nothing. At all.

So what if he kept emailing her? Words were cheap. Disappointment and frustration swirled around her brain, peaking and subsiding. She'd reverted to sending him group emails, unable to answer the more personal questions he asked. No way. It had been easier to maintain the illusion of friendship, keeping him on the group address list. No way was she going to admit her dissatisfaction with his non-answers and the hurt that her foolish hopes had buoyed. She couldn't really blame him. For how could a relationship between them ever work?

"Thanks, Coach Chan." Holly rolled her shoulders and pasted on a smile. "I'm better now."

Liar, liar, pants on fire. These past weeks had been an exercise in tension. Ever since that last online call, her shoulders were always tight, and she'd started snapping at some of her team-mates' teasing as she tried to focus, focus, focus on short track. But all the focus in the world didn't stop her feeling like the color had been turned down on life. And it didn't stop the occasional tear from leaking out onto her pillow at night.

"Ladies and gentlemen, the passengers in rows twenty-eight to forty will now begin boarding."

Holly sighed and stood, savoring the last chance to stretch her legs before the ten-hour flight began. She followed the shuffling queue, had her ticket scanned, and a smiling red-lipped cabin crew ushered her to the right, into economy. Right—where she belonged. No more first class for her. She stowed her hand luggage, retrieving her iPod and a book before sinking into her window seat. *Thanks, God, for a view.* Even if it was over part of the wing.

Disappointments. China had been full of them. With Jess out of the picture, Holly had gone there with Coach Chan and the guys, who were hoping to improve upon their eighth position in the relay back in Taipei. But it was like the Aussies were cursed or something. She'd finished last in her fifteen hundred quarter-final. She, Craig, and Aaron had all crashed out of the thousand meters—thank God they'd only suffered some bruises. The men's relay team had been ousted in their heat.

Disappointments were nothing new—that was short track.

But her disqualification in the five hundred semi was bitter. Blocked by the competitor in front, she'd gone around the final bend and only realized she'd touched the competitor next to her after the race concluded. She hadn't tried to touch them, having zero desire for a repeat of Kate's accident, but in this sport, if it was perceived by the officials she'd hindered another competitor, then it was considered intentional, regardless.

Coach Chan had argued with the officials—to no avail. "Officials must be blind!"

Holly had just lifted her chin and shrugged. Nope, that was short track.

"Ladies and gentlemen, please fasten your seatbelts. We are about to commence takeoff."

Holly fastened her belt but turned away at yet another safety demonstration. She'd seen so many over the years she could probably help her entire row escape in an emergency with her eyes shut. She peered out the window at the fog-covered runway, hunching her shoulders so nobody could see her face. She was tired. Stressed. Her skin had broken out, her hands were covered with eczema. This sport was so brutal, exhausting, emotionally and financially draining. Once upon a time she'd found this sport exhilarating. Now it was tainted with expectations, fueled by a panicky need to prove herself and win. She blinked back tears. *God, honestly, what is the point? I feel so stupid. I've wasted my life on short track, and for what? Do You even want me to do this? Should I just give up and study full time? Can You please show me if this is what You want?*

She closed her eyes and leaned against the hard plastic headrest, pulling the thin blanket closer, trying to rest, trying to stop the whirl of worries: money, health, career, her future…Brent. *Is there any point in pursuing a relationship? Is it just more distraction?* She feigned sleep as the questions ebbed and flowed. *Lord, what on earth do I do?*

When she finally arrived back at her share house, Jess met her at the door on crutches. Holly dropped her bags and gave her a hug. "Poor thing. How's your ankle?"

"The doctor is giving it four weeks. We'll see."

Holly winced. Jess had already missed the first two World Cups. What a waste. This sport was really cruel. "I'm so sorry." She gingerly bent down to retrieve a box from her bag. "I got you something."

She handed the box over, noting that Jess's eyes lost their disillusioned look from before. "Thanks, Holl."

Holly smiled, glad her gift of macadamias had lifted her friend's spirits for a moment.

Jess grasped the box as she slowly made her way inside. "China sounded tough."

Holly's mood dived. "It seemed pretty unfair." There was so much more she could say about the officials involved, but it was never helpful to dwell on the past, so she bit her lip, conscious Jess was watching her.

"You don't badmouth anybody, do you?"

Holly mustered a smile. She wanted sleep, not a deep and meaningful conversation. "Sometimes a little venting is good for the soul, but usually it just makes me more upset." And she had enough worries in her life. She didn't need to add further stress.

Jess shrugged. "Well, here's your mail. And there's something on your bed that might make you feel better."

Holly slumped heavily into the dining chair, the bruises on her hip from her crash still causing some discomfort, and sorted through the various letters until she came to a familiar logo. Opening the envelope, she read the words in disbelief. A major manufacturer of custom-made speed skate boots had agreed to sponsor Holly for the next three years. She vaguely remembered approaching a representative at a meet earlier in the year and sending off the required paperwork, but due to some less-than-stellar performances this season, she'd assumed their silence meant they weren't interested. But this—this was wonderful, an absolute answer to prayer! *Thank You, God!*

After sharing her news with Jess, she limped into her room to discover a lovely bunch of roses—Double Delight roses at that—lying in the middle of the bed, their delicate perfume filling the room. She read the card: *You're always a winner in my eyes. Brent.*

Oh. The roses blurred. How sweet. He must've remembered… Regret kneaded her heart at how she'd treated him. This distance over the past weeks had hurt so much. Maybe she needed to treat him a little more considerately.

After a shower and some food, she powered up her computer and started typing.

Hi Brent.
Thanks so much for the flowers. They're beautiful. You made
my day. I was feeling so low about my results I wanted to quit.
Thanks for still being my friend. Holly

She pressed send, then went straight to bed.

Detroit, Michigan

WHEN BRENT GOT HOME from training that day, he opened his email from Holly. She'd sounded so discouraged when she emailed everyone her results from China. He was glad he'd cheered her up a little. He went online, surprised to see Holly was awake and at her computer. After calculating the time difference, he sent her an invitation to talk online.

"Hey, stranger."

"Hi, Brent." It wasn't too early in the morning, was it? She looked and sounded so weary.

"How are you?"

"Tired. I've only got a few minutes. I was just checking emails. Training starts in an hour, and I still need a shower."

"Do your showers always take that long?"

She didn't smile. "Coach Chan is pretty strict. No rest for the wicked."

"I don't think you're that bad."

Holly yawned. "So, what's up?"

"I just wanted to clarify something about your last email."

She raised her eyebrows. "I said thanks, didn't I? Honestly, I was pretty impressed. I didn't think you could get that type of rose delivered."

"Yeah, well, I've got skills. But it wasn't that I wanted to clarify."

Her eyebrows pushed up. "Then…?"

He swallowed. "I really don't want to be your friend."

"What?" She blinked at him. So cute. "You don't?"

"I'd really like to be more than that."

"I'm really tired, Brent." She sighed, rubbing her forehead. "And haven't we gone through this enough already? Just how on earth could that work?"

"We write, we talk, we stay in touch. We pray and share, and one day we meet up again."

The laughter sounded brittle. "One day?"

"How about this: I promise to see you next year."

"Oh, wow." Her voice was flat. "Can't wait."

So, she wasn't impressed. He chewed the inside of his lip, wondering what to say.

She gave a small smile. "Sorry for being such a grouch. I hardly slept last night. I hurt my hip in China, and it's still giving me grief."

He winced. "Beijing wasn't all you hoped, was it?"

"That's short track." She shrugged. "That's why your flowers were such a nice surprise." Her green gaze caught his for a long, long moment.

Man, he hated this distance between them.

"I'm glad you liked them."

"Did you remember from my mum and dad's place?"

He nodded, and she bit her lip and blinked, looking down. Oh. He didn't want her to cry. "Holl—"

"Did I tell you my good news?" she interrupted, looking up again, blinking furiously as if determined to put aside the emotion. "I'm getting some sponsorship! I'll get custom-made boots from one of the top skate manufacturers. It's such a miracle."

"That's awesome!"

"Yeah. I know my head has been a bit of a mess lately, so it was nice to feel like this was confirmation to continue. Which is just as well, I suppose, because if short track is what I feel like I'm meant to do and who I am and I'm always failing, then what does that say about me?"

"You are not your results, Holly."

"Try telling that to my coach." Her lips twisted wryly. "Hey, I really need to go now."

"Okay." His heart sank. He hated ending these calls. He wished he could be with her, to uncover what she really thought about herself. And he wished these calls weren't always limited by their schedules. "Holly, I've missed you."

"Oh." Her gaze dug deep into his heart. "I've missed you too."

Thanks, God. "Take care of yourself, okay?"

"Okay." Her smile held a note of wistfulness—or was that just his hope? "You too. Pray for me."

"Always. Bye."

Stockholm, Sweden

"HEY, babe! Or should I say hallå? It's good to see you."

Brent drank in the sight of her. Holly's hair was down, flowing around her shoulders, and she wore a green T-shirt and that smile he loved so much. She seemed different today—more energized, like the pensiveness of past calls had been put aside. She shifted closer, and he could see her better through the computer. "How does it feel to be settling back into life Down Under?"

"I've gotta say, it's great being back here where it's *warm*."

"I bet it is."

Her smile was genuine. He could tell by the light in her eyes. It'd been ages since he'd seen her smile like that. Heart threads eased. "So it's been nice catching up with people?"

She nodded. "My church family had a nice little lunch for me last Sunday. Lots of hugs from the little blond guys."

"Now who's a celebrity?"

Her lips twitched. "So, you're enjoying Sweden?"

"We haven't had too much time to be tourists, but yeah, it's super pretty. There's so much water. It sure is a long way to go for preseason games though." He yawned. "But definitely a nice part of the world. I think I'd like to come back when I've got more time to look around." He caught her gaze. "It'd be nice to see it with you."

She bit her lip and looked down.

"Holl?"

Her eyes found his again. "Have you tried any interesting food yet? You know, pickled herrings, that kind of thing?"

"I didn't, but some of the others did. They just *loved* it."

Her lips lifted in amusement. "I bet."

"You doing okay? You've got your Aussie championships this weekend, right? You ready for it?"

She nodded. "Then it's Oktoberfest the following weekend. Speaking of…"

"You mentioned you had something big to share?"

Another nod, a bigger grin. "I got an email from Dan Mathieson."

"Who?"

"The head coach at the Olympic Oval training program in Calgary. A spot opened up, and I can go straightaway, so when I go for Oktoberfest, I'm actually going for good."

"Really?"

"Yes! Isn't that great? I have to defer my studies for the next few months, but the extra training means I'll be far more competitive come February, and I'll be able to see Bree more. Maybe even other people who might care to venture west sometime."

"I think I'll definitely be venturing west sometime."

Her smile sparked warmth in his chest. "Do you know your schedule yet? Bree mentioned about inviting the Aussie team to have Canadian Thanksgiving with her and Mike."

He glanced at his desk calendar. "I wish I could, but with a game Sunday night and a road trip starting Tuesday, it's just not gonna work out."

Her joy faded, the slump in her posture plain. "Are you sure you can't come?"

"Holl, I'm really sorry."

A beat. "It's okay."

He wished he was close enough to read her eyes. "You sure?"

"I'm fine." She gave a small smile. "I miss you."

"Oh, babe, I miss you so much." It was ridiculous how much he missed her. "Hey, have you heard from Bree yet?"

"Not recently."

"I'm sure you will soon."

Later, as he finally said goodbye, he couldn't stop the sweeping feeling of discontent. It didn't seem to matter that he'd found his form so early in the season and was already scoring goals and racking up the points. While it boded well for a good season, and he hoped it impressed Canada's team selectors, this separation was getting really hard. He sucked in a deep breath and exhaled loudly. *God, I do trust You, but when will it be the right time?*

CHAPTER 14

Hi all,

Woo hoo! Finally, I am the fastest woman in Australia on ice in all short track categories! (I got a new Aussie record in 500, so that was an extra cool surprise.) It's so nice to be declared the Women's Senior Champion, especially here in Sydney.

Mum, Dad, and Ben were there to help celebrate, which was wonderful. Now I'm off to Calgary for the Oktoberfest short track event, and then I'm joining the Olympic Oval training squad there! I've had a fantastic time training in Brisbane, but the calibre of the Calgary coaching and expertise is second to none. Skaters from many countries train there, and it has produced many medal winners - so please pray for a miracle!

Love, Holly

Calgary, Canada
October

*H*olly threaded her way through the crowds attending the Oktoberfest competition, enjoying the energy that still pulsed through the room. She waved at a few competitors she knew, exchanging compliments on races hard fought and well won. These past few days had proven encouraging, her results boding well for upcoming contests. But now she had to find someone she'd longed to see…

"Holly!"

She turned, smiling as Bree wrapped her in a hug.

"That was awesome! You looked so cool out there."

"Come on, you just love the suit. You want one of your own, right?"

"That lime green color does nothing for your complexion, I've gotta admit," Bree said, shaking her head.

"How are you? Brent mentioned there was something you wanted to say."

"Oh, I'm so glad you're here in the flesh so I can finally tell you. I'm pregnant! I'm going to be a mother. How crazy is that?"

"Wow!" Holly clutched her in another hug. "Is this good news?"

"It's *wonderful* news," Bree continued. "I'm only twelve weeks, so the baby will be born in April. And you must be my baby's godmother."

"Of course I will." Bree's baby would be born after Holly's World Cup season. She squeezed her again and let go. "Congratulations. I'm so happy for you!" And maybe the teensiest bit envious, too. How good it would be to have some form of certainty in life rather than living this weird rollercoaster of travel, suitcases, and unmet expectations.

Bree led Holly to her car, and they were soon driving to Bree's house. "Now, did you ask them? Can your squad come to Thanksgiving?"

Holly nodded. "They'd all love to come. But including my

coach, that's an extra seven people, Bree. How's that going to work?"

"There'll be room. We cater large in case any of Mike's teammates need a place to come. But there's only two of them plus both sets of parents this year. Mike's parents have already arrived, and my folks get in later tonight." Bree tilted her head. "You know Brent can't make Thanksgiving, right?"

Holly's heart tensed, and she nodded and glanced away. "Yeah, he mentioned that last week." She swallowed the spike of disappointment. Was this even a relationship when they never saw each other?

"So, tell me, how are things going with Brent? I noticed you've demoted him to group email status again."

"It isn't a demotion. It's just easier to send the same info to everyone once rather than a million times."

Bree lifted a skeptical eyebrow.

"Well, okay, maybe it was a bit of a demotion."

She chuckled. "So, what's really going on?"

"Well, he sent me some flowers."

"And?"

"And yeah, but this is ridiculous. I like him a lot, but I still can't see how this can work. I'm here, he's there. It's just so hard, especially when I barely see him to know how he really feels. Maybe I'm reading too much into everything." She swallowed. "Anyway, what's the point if I never see him?"

"Come on, Holl, you know he likes you. Every time we talk he's always asking after you in case he's missed out on the latest news from Holly world."

"Does he?" Her heart started slow dancing again.

"Yeah. He's smitten, Holl. He's never been like this with anyone else. You know he even called me to find out what your favorite chocolates were?" She slapped a hand over her mouth. "Oops. I don't think I was supposed to mention that."

Yet living in different locations with all the clashing schedules and other logistical hurdles meant that unless God did something amazing, it would remain unworkable. "But it can't—"

"Holl, how many other guys are out there trying to pay you attention?"

"Bree—"

"Short track won't keep you warm when you're old and gray, Holly. Just sayin'."

"The way we're going, I won't be seeing him until I'm old and gray."

Bree smiled. "It's not that bad, Holly. Anyway, does God love you? What does Jeremiah twenty-nine verse eleven say? Does God have good plans for your life?"

"Yes." Why was it so easy to forget that? She really needed to memorize that verse.

"Trust Him. And when it all seems too hard, trust Him again. I'm praying for you."

"Okay, okay. I'll try to play nice."

"Don't play too nice though. Keep making him chase you."

"Yes, oh wise, married mother-to-be. I will heed your great wisdom."

Bree laughed. "Finally. Now, are you ready for dinner?"

"Yep." Beyond ready. She loved her teammates, but sometimes it was necessary to spend time away from the squad, away from her coach, so she could really relax and be herself. Today had been cool, tomorrow promised to be fun—and a great way to round off time with her Aussie team before the challenge of knitting into a new training squad began. Maybe time with Bree tonight would help get her head back in the right space after the roiling tension of Brent's absence.

Ten minutes later, she followed Bree back inside her large house, the neutral tones soothing and calm. A quick meal with Bree and Mike, then she'd need to leave to ensure a good sleep before tomorrow's early training. She said hello to Mike's parents, who were reading in the spacious living room and told them Mike was in the kitchen. But when they went there, it was to find Mike on his laptop, talking to someone with a familiar deep voice, a voice that drew an insistent tug low in Holly's gut. No. She wasn't ready. She hadn't figured out how to pretend his absence didn't feel like rejection.

"Hey, look who just walked in." Mike smiled at her. "Brent's online. You want to talk to him now, Holl?"

"Or would you rather talk *later*?" Bree's eyes carried mischief.

"Uh, now's fine," Holly said with a shrug, striving for indifference.

Bree chuckled and rushed Mike from the kitchen, leaving Holly to sink into the seat and summon up a smile. "Hi, Brent."

"Hey, Holly. How's my superstar?"

His superstar? "I'm fine. How are you?"

He sighed. "Bummed I'm here and not with you."

She lifted a shoulder. She refused to go back there. Why did it matter if he didn't see her? She didn't have time for a relationship. She couldn't afford the distraction. She needed to focus—

"Holly, I really am sorry."

Her chest, her smile grew tight. "You don't have to keep apologizing. I know you've got a game tonight and a road trip starting Tuesday." She shrugged again. "You've got your work, I've got mine. That's how it is."

"I wish…"

She leaned closer to the screen. "Wishing changes nothing, Brent. Never has, never will. Now, do you want to talk some more with Mike? Or should I get Bree?"

"Holly—"

"What?" Frustration suddenly surged. She dropped her voice. "I'm having Thanksgiving with your parents and Bree tomorrow, who all seem to think we're some sort of couple. But we're not."

Are we? If only she had the guts to ask that.

He sat there, chewing his lip. "Holl, I wish I knew what to say."

"That makes two of us."

"Holly, plenty of people balance long distances with successful relationships."

"I know that. But—" She didn't want to be one of them. She propped her head in her hands. "This is seriously doing my head in."

"Holly, please—"

"I'm sorry, Brent." If she stayed any longer, she was going to scream—or cry. "I have training early tomorrow and need to go. I'll see you later." And pushing back her chair, she walked away.

BRENT STARED at the empty screen. What had just happened? One minute they were doing the banter thing, the next she'd huffed off.

Mike slowly ambled into view. "Hey, bud."

"Hey."

The chair squeaked as Mike sat down. "So, there's trouble in paradise?"

Brent sighed. "What did she say?"

"Nothing. But I'm guessing any minute your sister's going to be out here wanting an explanation. So, anything you want to tell me so I can broker a peace deal?" The smile slid off Mike's face. "Have you been messing with Holly? She looked kind of upset."

"She's still disappointed that I can't see her."

Mike leaned back. "I suppose from her point of view she feels like she's come all this distance and it looks like you can't be bothered coming a few hours out of your way to see her. I get that she's upset, especially if you've been talking up how much you miss her and stuff."

"Have you seen my schedule for the next few weeks?" After tonight's game they had a day off, then a week and half road trip to the west, followed by back-to-back games in Detroit, after which Holly would be heading to her next comp.

Mike folded his arms. "Been there, done that with your sister. It doesn't fly. They need to know you care. Words and presents don't cut it as much as showing up."

"But—"

"Dude, there were plenty of times I got back from a road trip just to jump on another plane so I could see Bree for a few hours before I headed home again." Mike shook his head. "It was really tough, but really necessary."

Mike studied him with that look in his eyes that said he saw far more than Brent wanted him to. He leaned forward. "If you want this to work, you've gotta put in the hard yards. Otherwise someone else will."

Brent frowned. "What do you mean?"

"TJ will be here tomorrow."

"Woletsky?" Brent's gut tightened. "What's he doing there?"

Mike's eyes narrowed. "He's from Nova Scotia, man. He needed a place to go for Thanksgiving, and we were offering."

No. His stomach roiled at the memory of Tyler's interest in Holly last year. "But is she—"

"No, of course not." Mike shook his head. "But I get the feeling she's a little confused about where things stand."

She wasn't the only one. Brent chewed his bottom lip as Mike continued.

"It's called a long distance relationship, man. It won't be easy, but it will be worth it." He smiled. "You want to talk to anyone else?"

"Nah. Catch you later."

Mike nodded. "Later."

And the screen went dark.

~

Thank God Bree's house had so many bathrooms. It had taken almost ten minutes of deep breathing before Holly felt calm enough to face Bree. She finally unlocked the upstairs bathroom door and came face to face with Mike, lounging against the opposite wall.

"Hi, Mike." She tried out her smile. Yep, still worked. Just. "Sorry for hogging the bathroom."

"No problem." His shrewd eyes studied her. "You okay?"

More fake smile. "Never better!"

He nodded slowly. "You know, Bree still doesn't know about that time in Hawaii."

What? So how much did he know? She dropped her gaze to examine the blue-gray hall carpet. "It was kind of funny." Had been. Now it just hurt.

"And you know, when Brent went to Australia with you, that really seemed to seal the deal."

She shrugged and looked up. "I still don't know why he did that."

"You don't?" Mike had a knowing smile on his face.

Exasperation rose again. "He's not exactly been very clear about what he intends."

"No?"

Why was he looking at her like that? "Look, Mike, if he really cared, don't you think he'd find some way to see me?"

He nodded slowly. "I said that to him."

He had? Well…good.

"To be fair, he did come and see you in Utah."

"Yes, well…" That was true. But, "It's not like I'm in the country all the time."

"I know. But he does have games he's committed to."

"I understand that. But it's so ridiculous with him there, me here." She lifted her chin and pushed back her hair. "Anyway, I can't afford distractions. You should hear my coach. You probably will tomorrow. She's always going on about focus, focus, focus, and Coach Mathieson is just the same, and I—"

"Short track isn't everything, Holl."

Except it often felt like it was.

"You still have a life to live," Mike said gently.

But who would she be without short track? She blinked and studied the floor again. "I can't get my hopes up. It's impossible anyway."

"Hopes, huh?" His voice was gentle. "Holly, is anything impossible for God?"

She sighed, but his question continued to linger in the back of her mind, even as she ate dinner, even as Bree drove her home, even as she showered and tried to sleep.

The next morning, she trained through a haze of sleep-fuzzed concentration.

"Holly! You must focus!"

She nodded, exchanged a look with Jess, and went through the motions. But her legs had no jump today, as though the hard work of the past days had drained all energy away.

At least today's training session was shorter, as they had the chance to enjoy some real Canadian hospitality. Staying with the squad at a cheap motel near the University of Calgary's Olympic Oval meant meals had been pretty basic. She'd bet a million gold medals that today's meal at Bree's would not be.

"Welcome! Nice to meet you, nice to meet you." Bree was at her sparkly best as Coach Chan, Jess, Craig, Aaron, Chris, and Sean traipsed inside, everyone dressed in their nicest clothes. "It's so great to finally put faces to some names I've heard for so long."

Jess stared around Bree and Mike's home, her brown eyes

wide. She leaned closer to Holly. "I didn't realize they were so rich." The rest of the team perched on the leather lounges in the open-concept living room. "No wonder she can afford to send you on vacation."

"They're just normal people, Jess."

"Yeah, well, I could do with some of this becoming my normal."

The doorbell rang, and Mike excused himself to answer it. There was a soft murmur, then two men followed Mike into the room. "Everyone, this is Carl and Tyler, two of my teammates." He motioned around. "And this is...everyone."

"Hi, guys!" Bree stood and started introductions.

Holly looked up, her chest tightening as Tyler's eyes lit. "Holly, isn't it?"

She nodded, her heart sinking as he sat next to her and started chatting. Memories sparked of Bree's wedding, of Brent getting all macho protective when Tyler had wanted to dance. She nodded and tried to act polite but couldn't help feeling the sting at the fact that the one guy she wanted wasn't here while Mr. Unwanted was.

"It's incredible!" Bree's warmth and animated face had obviously captivated the male members of the Aussie squad as they sat around the huge dining table, eating the first course. The conversation so far had centered on sports and the Oktoberfest competition. Bree had kept her parents and in-laws enthralled as she described the relays she'd witnessed the previous day. She shook her head. "You guys are so amazing."

The youngest two members of the men's relay team flushed. Holly caught Jess's eye and bit back a smile as Coach Chan gave a little cough. "They work very hard. Start training young."

Mr. Karlsson glanced at Holly with a smile. "I can't get over how good Holly has become in such a short time. Did you know she first learned to skate when she stayed with us?"

"That's right." Bree grinned slyly. "My brother taught her to skate."

Holly's cheeks heated at the looks she was receiving from Coach Chan and Tyler.

Tyler leaned forward. "You're a skater?"

Jess batted her eyelashes. "We all are."

Mr. Karlsson nodded. "I still remember how amazed everyone was when this girl who had never been on ice before showed how fast she could be."

"Until you crashed." Mike smiled at her. "Remember that? Brent felt so bad." He gazed at her thoughtfully.

Holly touched the small scar at her hairline, the tiny reminder of that huge crash into the end boards. She'd been so intent on proving she could skate fast, that she wasn't just this shy kid who talked funny. Learning to skate hadn't been that hard. If only she'd learned how to stop.

Mrs. Karlsson sighed. "It's such a shame Brent couldn't be here today, isn't it, Holly?"

Coach Chan frowned. "Who is this Brent?"

Holly's cheeks burned as the rest of her squad looked at her. Uh oh. Here goes. "Um, he's a friend."

"Yeah, right. He's way more than that, isn't he, Holl?" Bree grinned and started sharing, swapping notes with Jess about just how good a friend Brent had been over the past year. Holly sank deeper and deeper into her chair, studying the intricate lace edging of the linen tablecloth. The charade was coming full circle and now starting to bite. If only she hadn't said quite so much to the others. This was beyond embarrassing.

She lifted her eyes to glance around the table. Mike's parents and her teammates looked interested, Mrs. Karlsson wore a big smile, and Mr. Karlsson looked mildly surprised, as if he'd discovered a secret side to his younger son. Tyler had his thick lips pursed, and Coach Chan's frown had deepened. Holly swallowed.

Aaron and Craig were whispering. They looked up. "Is Brent your boyfriend?"

"No!" She could feel her cheeks getting redder. "He's just a friend."

Coach Chan's frown looked like it would have to be chiseled off. "Just friend?"

Holly nodded even as her stomach lurched. "No distractions, right?" Brent *was* only a friend. It didn't matter what he said. Talk was cheap. His absence today proved his real feelings.

She glanced down at the end of the table where Mike was studying her with his mouth teased to one side. He glanced at his phone, smiled, then looked up and interrupted Bree, who was halfway through the Hawaii story. "Well, that smells like the next course is ready. Bree, Holly, can you help me in the kitchen?"

Holly recognized the cue for distraction. *God bless Mike.* She stood. "Sure."

The doorbell rang. "Mike? Are you expecting more company?" his mother asked.

He was halfway to the kitchen. "Holly, seeing as you're up, would you mind getting the door?"

"Uh, sure." She tugged down her knee-length dress. Bree had insisted Holly dress up, although she seemed a little overdressed in comparison with some others here. Oh well.

She moved to the entryway and swung open the heavy wooden door. And gasped. Then slammed it closed.

"Holly? What's wrong?"

The doorbell rang again, followed by a firm knock on the door.

"Holly?" Bree called. "Is everything okay?"

Emotion heated the back of her eyes. Everything was okay now.

She opened the door, conscious everyone was looking, and stepped outside onto the tiled porch, drawing the door closed behind her. "You."

"Hey, babe."

Brent opened his arms and she rushed into his embrace. He held her close. She could feel his lips in her hair, his heart beating against her ear.

"It's so good to hold you," he murmured.

It was so good to be held. To feel wanted. Safe. Secure. She relished the peace she found in his arms.

She squeezed him tighter, then drew back, tilting her head to see him properly. "I thought you weren't able to come."

"Turns out I needed to be here."

He needed to be? Warmth filled her chest. "But don't you have a road trip starting?"

"Tomorrow morning."

"Then you're here for the day?"

His lips pulled to one side. "Yeah, a little less than that. I've got to get back to the airport in two hours."

"Seriously?"

He nodded. "But seeing you is worth it. Hey, are you cold?"

No. With his arms around her she felt deliciously warm, thank you. She snuggled closer. "I'm sorry I was pushy," she murmured. And sorry for letting insecurity win.

"You've got no idea how glad I am to be here," he said, squeezing a little tighter. "But, um, I think we have an audience."

She peeked over her shoulder, saw faces at the window. Oh dear.

"Are you two ready now?" Bree said from the reopened door.

"You knew!" Holly said.

"I hoped," she admitted. "We only arranged it late last night." She hugged her twin. "Hey, bro. Glad you could make it."

"Me too," he said, eyes fixed on Holly.

A delicious shiver trembled up her spine. She drew him inside. "My coach is here," she whispered.

He nodded and stepped away as Bree introduced Brent to the gathering—to his parents' delight, Tyler's consternation, and Jess's and Coach Chan's wide eyes and raised eyebrows.

Holly resumed her seat, and Brent grabbed a chair and placed it next to hers at the end of the table. "Hi again," he said.

Heat rushed to her cheeks, and she desperately strove to appear calm. "Have you met my coach and the rest of the team?"

She introduced him, and he stood and shook their hands before slipping back next to her, his fingers threading through hers under the table. "Hey, TJ. How's it going?"

"Fine," Tyler said, looking anything but.

Bree reentered the room. "Dinner is served."

What followed was a feast of turkey and trimmings, laughter and thanksgiving—delicious to eat and fun to share. But really, how could she concentrate on food when Brent was beside her?

The fact that he'd come—he was here, holding her hand under the table whenever a pause in eating allowed—said he was intentional, he prioritized her, even as his father questioned the wisdom of flying a total of ten hours for only two hours here.

"Oh, don't scold him," Mrs. Karlsson said, smiling at Holly. "It's obvious he's in—"

"I couldn't miss Thanksgiving with those I care about," Brent said, squeezing Holly's hand.

Tingles skittered over her skin as her heart thrilled and danced and sped like a comet around a galaxy of stars.

"Not your boyfriend, huh?" Jess said later, after dessert.

"No distractions," Holly said, with a gritted-teeth smile at Coach Chan.

"Hmm. Might take a bit more to convince her. Not that I have any problem with it. He's really hot, Holl."

"Is he?" she said, glancing back to where Brent laughed with his parents and Mike. She shrugged. "I hadn't really noticed."

Jess chuckled, drawing the others' attention. "So, what are you doing talking to me when he's the one you want to spend time with?"

"Diverting Coach Chan's suspicions?"

"Good luck with that."

And it seemed that Holly would need a bit more luck when Bree asked if she could borrow Holly for a little while, promising to return her back to the team's accommodation, while Mike murmured about Brent needing to return to the airport.

"We can take you, son," Mr. Karlsson began.

"Oh, it's fine, Dad," Bree rushed to say. "Mike and I have it under control."

"Good to see you all," Brent said. "Nice to meet you." He nodded to Coach Chan and Holly's teammates.

Coach Chan gave her narrow-eyed nod, eyeing Holly in a way that suggested tomorrow's warm-ups would be even more intense than usual. But she didn't have time to care now. Bree was tugging her to the garage, where they met Brent, waiting in the backseat, patting the space beside him invitingly.

Bree hopped into the driver's seat and clicked the garage door opener. "I've always been thankful for the short distance to the airport," she confided, "but today it seems too quick."

Holly shifted to face Brent. "I'm still so stunned you came all this way for such a short amount of time."

"I couldn't have my best girl wondering how I feel about her, could I?" he said, his voice holding husky tones.

His best girl? "How many girls do you have?"

"Only one." He pressed his lips to the back of Holly's hand. "Well, I *hope* I have her."

Bree glanced at them in the rearview mirror. "Oh, judging by that expression, I think it's safe to say you have Holly."

How embarrassing. But Bree was right. His actions today proved this relationship did hold something real. Now if only she knew if he wanted to kiss her.

She shivered, and Brent looked at her questioningly. She shook her head, content to hold his hand, listening as brother and sister continued bantering.

Bree pulled up outside the airport's glass entrance doors. "Text me when you're ready, Holl."

"What? I'm not going anywhere."

"You don't want to come inside and say goodbye?" Brent asked.

And finally grab a moment of—relative—privacy with him? Well, okay.

She slid outside, suddenly conscious of the cooler temperature, which Brent seemed to notice as he wrapped his arm around her shoulders and drew her to a quieter corner. "I should've made sure you brought a better jacket."

"It's okay," she assured him. "I'm warmer now."

"I'm so glad I came, Holl."

"I'm so glad you came too. It means so much. I bet it'll be exhausting with all these flights."

"I can always sleep on a plane. But seeing you makes it all worthwhile."

Her heart swelled. His words, his smile, his actions all made her feel valued.

"I'm sorry it was such a short time, but tomorrow is Buffalo, then we're heading to Arizona and the west coast. But we're back in Calgary on the thirty-first."

"I can't wait."

"And your next competition?"

"The Olympic Oval Invitational is in ten days. The next World Cup is in Montreal, November seven, then Marquette the weekend after that. They're the Games qualifiers, so they're the big ones."

"And they're both a little closer than Calgary. I'll check my schedule. Maybe I can see you there."

She nodded. Maybe they could have a future, if they snatched moments such as this.

He cradled her face in his large hands. "You know, my mom was right before."

"Right about what?"

He smiled, shook his head slightly, his eyes darkening as he studied her like he wanted to etch her features in his mind for eternity. He pressed his lips to her forehead, then wrapped her in his arms. "I have to go in a moment."

"Do you need to check in?"

"Did it online back at Bree's. It's security that takes the time." He sighed. "Can't wait to see you again."

"You too." Her voice wobbled.

"Hey, don't cry."

"I'm not crying." She drew in a ragged breath, even as he smiled tenderly and thumbed a renegade tear away.

His gaze dropped to her lips, stayed there a long time, then he sighed, leaned his forehead on hers, and closed his eyes.

She shut her eyes and breathed in his skin-tingling nearness, breathed in his scent, breathed in the assurance that she'd see him again in just a few short weeks.

Around them, the buzz of the airport continued, but this warm space of shared breath held tenderness, trust, and calm. Her heart quietened, the worries of her world fading in the peace found in his arms. God was good. She could trust Him. And she could trust Brent, too.

A crash shattered their serene cocoon. Her eyes flew open to see fallen luggage from a nearby trolley.

He drew back, lips pulling ruefully to the side. "Guess that's my cue."

She propelled to her toes and hugged him fiercely, willing

God to keep him safe, wishing she could shrink into his pocket and live next to his heart. "Stay safe."

"You too." Another peck to the forehead. "Bye, Holl. Miss you already," he said hoarsely, releasing her.

The loss of his embrace cooled her even as his words renewed a fire within.

He smiled, saluted, and moved through the gates into security, her eyes following until his tall frame slipped past a corner. She took a step back, then another, trying to reconcile what had just happened.

The rush of people and noise seemed to float past like she was in a bubble, and it wasn't until she settled into the passenger seat of the car and Bree was talking that she finally snapped to.

"So, did he kiss you?"

She guessed Bree didn't mean those gentle brushes on her forehead. "No."

"Really? Wow." Her brow furrowed, cleared. "He really *has* changed. Well, good for him. Anyway, it's better to take it slow and be sure and get it right."

Holly nodded.

"Don't worry. I'm sure he wants to. Anyone with half a brain can see he's totally into you."

Her heart spasmed. So Coach Chan could see that too? She felt like she should protest. "He said he came to spend Thanksgiving with his family."

"Yeah, he hasn't minded missing a few before. Besides, I think his words were 'those I care about.' And that's you." Bree laughed delightedly. "Oh, this is so exciting!"

Holly drew in a deep breath. As thrilling as this was, as much as it seemed an answer to her prayers, she couldn't help asking one question. What would all this mean for her skating career?

CHAPTER 15

The next few days passed in a blur of travel, games, training, and...Holly.

Thoughts of her couldn't be contained. All the way home and on the next day's flight, Brent had questioned the wisdom of what he'd done. He'd wanted to kiss her, desperately longed to know the softness of her lips, but hadn't wanted to rush things nor push her somewhere she wasn't ready to go. So he'd held back, leashing the old desires, fighting the instinct to press his mouth to hers. He yearned for her to trust him, to know that he'd changed, and he sensed kissing her too quickly would only confuse matters. Besides, he'd made a promise to God, so any deeper display of his affections would need to wait, at least until Holly could see an enduring future with him.

But it was hard. Hard to rein in his thoughts as his team-mates talked about their girlfriends. Hard to not dream about what kissing her—and more—could be like. His past experience made the yearning a greater challenge. Had he really been the type of guy to not consider how such actions messed with emotions? *God, help me* was a constant prayer as he wrestled with his memories, desires, and dreams.

His phone buzzed. Hi! Are you free to talk online?

He tapped out a reply, then sat at the computer. With travel taking them in opposite directions, they'd been emailing and texting daily. The phone calls were so hard to end. Even hanging on the phone, not saying anything, helped him feel closer to her.

"Hey, Holl." She looked tired but happy. Playful, even.

"It's good to see you."

Gee he liked her smile. "You too."

"Sorry about your last game. That was a bit rough."

"Shootouts are always tough to lose."

She laughed, pushing the hair behind her ears. Man, even her ears were pretty. "You looked like you were enjoying being in the penalty box."

"Let's not talk about it, okay?" He was still getting grief from the media about the water bottle incident. He sure hadn't meant for it to escalate like this.

"Oh, but it's fun! Some of those fans seem to take hockey a little too seriously."

"Yeah, that's why I thought they needed cooling down."

She grinned. "I don't think I've seen you lose your cool before, so that was pretty funny."

"Sympathy, Holly, the man needs sympathy."

She laughed softly, that gurgly laughter he hadn't heard for a while.

It was so nice to be back to this easy banter. "You going to pick on me all night, babe?"

Her head tilted. "You know, you really should come up with something that doesn't sound quite so sexist and demeaning."

"I'm happy to call you whatever you like, Holly. Darling, sweetheart, sugar plum, honey…"

Her cheeks pinked. "Holly will do nicely for now."

"For now?" He raised an eyebrow. "Just let me know when

that changes. I'll be more than happy to oblige. So, how was your day?"

"I'm just gonna put this out there: Coach Mathieson is a sadist. Or is it a masochist? Whatever, he and Coach Chan both push so hard. But in a good way."

"Does that make you the masochist? Thriving on pain?"

She chuckled. "I'm not exactly thriving, Brent. But I will admit that I'm enjoying seeing how my body responds to being pushed even more by training with girls like Tori and Alana. They've been fantastic—really welcoming, like I've been part of the squad for ages."

"So going to Calgary has been a good move, eh?"

"It's been fantastic. There are still some things that need to get sorted because of moving from one country to another, but it really helps to be staying at Bree's. She and Mike have been so kind."

"I'm glad it's working out well."

She sighed happily. "So well. Did I tell you my new boots arrived? They're gorgeous, and so light I just know they'll help me do better. Every night I go to bed with this happy song in my heart. I'm so thankful God is working things out. Even to talk with you, knowing there's only two hours' difference between us instead of fourteen—oh, things feel so much easier."

"God is good."

"All the time." She grinned.

His heart caught. He loved this ease about her, seeing her more settled and confident.

"And you. I still can't get over you spending so many hours in a plane to see us."

"To see you," he corrected softly.

She shook her head. "Brent, I...I..." Her confusion was so sweet. "I still can't even find the words to say how much I appreciate it."

"We can make this work, Holl."

"You know, for the first time, I agree. It actually feels like we can."

Gladness bloomed within. The exhaustion the next day had been worth it if his visit had really helped undergird hope for their future.

"And it won't be long until you're here again."

His smile grew wry. "I don't know if we'll have much of a chance to talk after the game. History tells me it's usually a case of a quick hello, then getting back on the bus, getting back on the plane."

"I don't mind. Just seeing you in these brief moments is like oxygen in my lungs. I'll take whatever you can give, Mr. Karlsson."

His heart double-thumped. Was this the answer he'd been praying for? "Careful, Holly. I might hold you to that."

"Please do." Her voice dropped. Her gaze lowered to his lips, lingered.

He exhaled heavily. "Now you're making me think things."

"What kind of things?"

"Maybe that your tastes really have changed."

"Maybe they have." Her gaze crept back to his and held.

"So, you're definitely not into short and plump anymore?"

"No. I think I prefer my men to be tall."

"Your men?" He raised an eyebrow.

"Generally speaking. I'm just describing a type."

"Oh. No one specific?"

"You asked me what I prefer. I'm telling you."

"So, is that tall, dark, and handsome?"

Her lips twitched. "I didn't say he had to be handsome." Her voice lowered. "I'm not really into clichés."

"I see."

"But I am prepared to make an exception."

"You are, are you?" His grin grew. "And what else does this mystery man need to be?"

"Well, he needs to be a Christian, that goes without saying."

"Of course."

"And we would need to share some common interests."

"Like?"

"I happen to enjoy skating, so it'd be good if he knew how to stand up on ice at least."

"Noted. What else?"

"He needs to make me laugh."

"Wow." He sat back in his chair. "That guy would have to be pretty amazing."

Her lips curled further to one side. "He would."

"I guess such amazing men aren't too easy to find."

"They're not."

"You didn't find one in Australia?"

"Surprisingly enough, no."

"That's too bad." He grinned. "I may know of one guy like that."

"Really?"

"Yeah. But I think he's already taken. Seems he's gotten really attached to this wonder girl from Down Under."

"Oh, he has, has he?" Her eyes sparkled.

"Yeah. He really likes her, but sometimes has a bad way of expressing it, so he wonders if she knows just how special he thinks she is."

"I'm sure she'd just like to be told."

He stared into her eyes. "Holly, this guy thinks that girl is really beautiful and truly realized it when he saw her at his sister's wedding. He's super impressed by her love for others, and can't get over what she does for a living. He thinks she's really smart and has juggled all kinds of responsibilities really well. There's a lot this guy loves about her."

Her eyes were so wide. Surely she got the message. "Loves about her?"

He'd said that, hadn't he? He nodded slowly.

"Oh."

They said nothing for the longest time, just gazing at each other through the computer screen.

"I wish I was there with you, Holly."

"Me too." Her voice sounded squeaky.

"I miss you so much."

"I miss you too."

Lord? He sensed peace. Swallowed. Wiped sweaty palms on his jeans. "Holly, I just wanted to know...if maybe, one day, you'd consider letting me kiss you?"

Her eyes widened further. "What?"

"I don't want you confused about how I feel, Holly. I want you to know I'm very, very serious about you."

She gulped. "Oh. Wow." The silence stretched between them as a smile played on her mouth. "Well..."

"Yes?"

"Maybe."

"Maybe what?" He leaned forward, heart beating in anticipation.

She smiled fully. "Maybe I'll consider it."

Calgary, Canada

HOLLY GLANCED at the huge banner advertising the *Olympic Oval Invitational* that hung against a wall. It was funny how the reality of living one's dream didn't always measure up. For so long she'd envisaged what living and training in Calgary would look like. But this...this was so much better.

A new weight training regime, slightly different balance and core exercises, and classes on strategy, nutrition, and mental preparedness combined with the twice daily sessions on ice were refining her technique, her skills. This was why the

Olympic Oval training was so highly regarded. She breathed a prayer of thanks, as she'd done every day for the past ten days. Thanks for this opportunity, thanks that the uncertainties surrounding her future—in many areas—seemed to have clicked into God-ordained place.

The five hundred finals were on the last day of the Invitational. This morning's fifteen hundred meters had been disappointing, coming third in her quarterfinal, but that distance wasn't her strength. She shook out her legs out as she waited. Her body was feeling the strain of the previous two days. *Lord, help me stay strong and focused.* But so far, so good. She was proving her time with the Calgary training squad was valuable. She'd come first in her quarter final and led her semi, her time a new Australian record. High expectations preceded the final.

She moved to join the others to warm up before today's five hundred final—yet another opportunity for vital experience with high caliber competitors prior to the Vancouver qualifiers at the World Cup in Montreal in two weeks. She knew she could make the qualifying times, but in this sport, skill wasn't always enough. A good measure of luck—or God appointed blessing—was necessary to avoid the catastrophic falls that sometimes saw medal contenders miss out on selection.

"Hi, Holly." Tori and Alana, fellow training partners, skated closer.

"I tried that recipe for chicken and sweet potato last night," Holly said to Tori. "So good. My friends loved it."

"It's a great dish. And so good for you."

"Come on, ladies," Coach Mathieson called over the barrier. "Enough chat. Focus. Get in the zone."

She glanced at the other girls, shifting mentally from friend to competitor. Up against Alana and Tori, plus Germany's Ilse Schuster and a Korean and Chinese skater, Holly knew a little of what to expect. Coach Chan had always emphasized the need to know your opponents. Alana was dominant in starts, Tori had a powerful finish, and Ilse was strong on the turns.

Stomach roiling, she briefly waved as her name was announced, then adjusted her ponytail under her helmet, watching as Alana waved at the crowd like a B-grade celebrity on the red carpet. Holly bit her lip. How could she be so relaxed? *Please, Lord, help me not throw up.*

"Go to the start."

Holly assumed position. The past two days of encouraging results had boiled down to this. She took a deep breath, let it out slowly.

"Ready." She assumed her stance.

BANG!

Skate, skate, skate. Holly pumped her arms, her skates eating up the ice. Yes! She was in the lead. She scooted around the corner, her left hand hovering over the ice. She had to maintain the pace and not to get outwitted on the turns. Alana and Tori were too good. On the second lap, Ilse started to make a move. Holly adjusted her position accordingly. No more impeding disqualifications allowed on her watch.

Skate, skate, skate, lean, then straighten until the next bend. The crowd's roar was encouraging. They'd probably like to see one of the skaters from the Calgary group beat the Korean and Chinese girls, who'd been so dominant in every other race. Third lap and again Ilse was trying to pass. Holly dug deep, her thighs burning. The bell rang. One lap to go. She skated around the penultimate bend. Where were the others? Coach Chan's refrain sang softly: *Don't worry about others; think about yourself.* Strong strides to finish...and she'd won?

Holly glanced up at the scoreboard. She'd won!

Her heart hammered with adrenaline and excitement. Laughter bubbled free. After congratulating the others, she skated the cool-down lap and looked up to see Bree waving madly from the stands. Holly waved back. Hello, world! Here's a contender for the Vancouver Games.

"Holly! Awesome job, girl." Coach Mathieson gave her a quick hug.

Holly collected her guards before heading to the athlete's area, where she changed and hopped on a stationary bike, pumping out the lactic acid as she cooled down. She grabbed her phone and texted Brent the good news. She pressed send, and within the minute, it was ringing.

"Hey! Congratulations, superstar! How d'you feel?"

If he could only see this smile that threatened to split her face in half. "Pretty good right now. It's still a little hard to believe."

"I'm proud of you! You've worked so hard—you deserve to reap the rewards."

Wow. Yeah. Maybe she did. And this was what success felt like. Laughter spilled again.

Holly grinned as Tori gave her a big thumbs up as she walked to her relay heat.

"So, how are you?"

She and Brent chatted for a while but were soon forced to say goodbye, as the officials conducting the drug testing demanded her attention. Later, at the awards ceremony, she looked out at the sea of faces. Rare contentment filled her soul. God had given her the gift to skate really fast, really well. This moment was worth savouring, as was the knowledge she'd see Brent again in just a week. *Thank You, God.*

"COME ON, MIKE!" The matchup between Calgary and Detroit was in full swing at the Calgary Saddledome. "Come on, Brent!"

Bree's divided loyalties were almost as entertaining to watch as the amazing spectacle that was an NHL game. After years of hearing about it or seeing recaps online, to actually be here at a game was fantastic. First, Calgary would make a good play and Bree would cheer, but then her brother would provide a great assist and Bree would call out "Go Brent!" The nearby spectators had to be confused.

The stadium was loud, the vocal crowd a sea of red with a sprinkling of Halloween-inspired outfits. The special family room where they sat amongst the players' wives, girlfriends, and other family members was equally partisan, making Holly, dressed in jeans and a Detroit #25 Karlsson jersey loaned by Bree, feel even more conspicuous.

Holly watched carefully whenever Brent was on the ice, marveling at the skill it took to weave and pivot, her heartrate soaring whenever defenders came at him as he moved toward the goal. He seemed to be on the ice a lot—unsurprising when his line had the most shots on goal. He skated behind Calgary's net and tipped the puck in, something she only realized from the flashing light and groans and the replay on the giant screen above. She cheered a little less loudly than she would have had they been in Detroit. At least Brent's coaches would be happy with him. He was on the ice for his fourth shift in the third period when a rough hit to the shoulder sent him back to the bench. Holly winced. *God, keep him safe.*

The match finished, Detroit winning three goals to one.

"Holl, I'll be right back," Bree said.

Holly nodded, and settled back and watched people catch up with different team members. Her heart caught as a little girl gave her daddy a big cuddle followed by a harried looking woman carrying a newborn. Holly bit her lip. Was that what life would be like if she and Brent sought a future together? She, the little woman looking after the kids, watching from the sidelines while he did his thing? Feminist Holly resisted. But how could she remain competitive and be a mother? Trotting off for competitions around the globe wouldn't be fair to a child.

"Holly." Brent, still in uniform, sweat glistening on his face that still showed the red marks of his helmet, grinned at her.

"Hi." She smiled, suddenly shy, conscious of the curious eyes on them.

Brent stepped forward to give her a careful, sweaty hug. He seemed so much bigger than normal. Must be all the padding underneath. "How's my superstar?"

"Pretty good. Congrats on your goal."

"Thanks. Hey, I like what you're wearing."

"Why am I not surprised?" She smiled, his eyes holding hers captive.

"Did you enjoy the game?"

"It was so exciting. It amazes me how you have to be so quick to even see the puck, let alone do something about it."

"Yeah, sometimes it's almost instinct. It was a good game."

"I guess a win always makes for a good game."

"Karlsson, coach wants you." A teammate dressed in the Wings' white away jersey was gesturing to the locker room. "Hey, you must be Holly, right?"

Brent introduced Doug, who came over and took hold of her hand, grinning broadly. "Hi, Holly. It's good to put a face to the name."

"Nice to meet you." She tried to slide her hand away, but Doug retained his firm grasp.

"Just release her, man." Brent none too gently shoved Doug in the shoulder, who smirked and disappeared. "Holly, I've gotta go get changed, then get on the bus to go catch our plane." He stepped closer. "But I'm real glad I got to see you again."

"Me too." This was it? He was leaving, and they'd barely talked?

"Hey." He drew near again. "I hope I can catch you after your World Cup next week. Do you get a day off?"

One day. Still, that was better than none. "I think there's one scheduled after Montreal. I'll need to check."

He nodded. "Maybe we can have a proper date then."

Where he might follow up his comment about wanting to kiss her? Her heartbeat quickened. "That'd be great."

"Yeah." He tugged her closer to a corner, eyes darkening.

Her pulse kicked up a gear. Was he finally going to kiss her? She inched forward, nestled closer, wrapped her arms around his waist.

"You know I want to kiss you," he whispered.

"I want you to kiss me," she murmured back.

"But I don't want our first kiss to be in a crowded space. I want it to be the right time, the right place."

Disappointment was chased by the faintest relief, then reluctant admiration. This wasn't a man free with his affections. He was purposeful. Intentional. Honorable. And he wanted to kiss her. She shivered.

"Karlos!"

Brent sighed. "I'd better go. I can't afford to tick off the coach."

"Especially when he might be making final selections for the Canadian team, huh?"

"I didn't want to say that, but yeah."

She laughed, and he swept her up in a hug, kissed her forehead, and with a final "bye," disappeared through to the players' area. She sank into a nearby chair, working to restrain her emotions. This would be her life now, snatching a few hours here, a couple of days there, time together a precious commodity until hockey finished and they'd have maybe two, three months before the short track season began. Her stomach lurched. That is, if she continued short track…

"Look who I found." Bree returned, holding Mike's hand. He was freshly showered and changed into street clothes.

"Good game, Mike."

He gave a tired-looking smile. "Not as good as it could've been, but the Wings are hot right now."

"Hey, Mike, Bree." A bunch of Calgary players nodded as they made their way outside.

"Hey! Holly, right?"

Holly turned. Oh. Tyler Woletsky. She forced a smile. "Hello."

He grinned and her heart sank further. "I didn't realize you were still around."

She nodded. "I'm staying with Bree and Mike."

"Right. Hey, maybe we could—"

"Sorry, you'll have to excuse me." She pulled out the sleeve with its embroidered 25. "I came to watch my boyfriend." Those last words sounded so strange. But despite no kiss, Brent still counted as her boyfriend, didn't he?

"Karlsson?" She nodded, and he sighed. "I knew it. Man." He offered a weak smile. "Well, lucky him I guess."

"Thanks." Holly turned to find Bree and Mike watching with amusement. "You ready now?"

They nodded and left by the players' door. Several fans waited nearby, and Mike patiently signed pucks and other items while Bree and Holly waited.

Holly leaned close to Bree. "Has Mike ever had a problem with strange fans? I've heard some girls can be pretty mean to the players' wives and girlfriends."

Some of the online photos she'd seen were unbelievable: girls at games standing near a player, holding signs that said *Divorce your wife and marry me.* Seriously? Who did that?

"Mike hasn't"—Bree gave her a sideways glance—"and I don't think Brent has either. But some people out there will try anything and wreck relationships. I think it's important to stay close and be interested in what Mike's doing so he finds validation at home and doesn't have to look elsewhere." She sighed. "Oh, Holl, some advice? Never read Internet fan forums. They can be brutal."

Holly bit her lip, remembering those comments made about

Larissa and Chloe months ago. "But what about when I'm away so much?"

Bree looked at her, compassion creasing her lips. "You've got to trust him, Holl."

But later that night, as Holly tried to sleep, the swirl of uncertainty lingered. Could this really work? And how would a future with Brent affect her future with short track?

CHAPTER 16

"Sorry I'm late." Holly gave her coach a brief explanation, then quickly changed and headed onto the ice. Warm-ups, then practicing sprint starts tried to claim her attention, but the questions still bubbled away. Would Brent prefer her to be the little woman? Would she have to give up her career? She stabbed at the ice with the tip of her blade, waiting.

The whistle shrieked. Skate, skate, skate. Her legs pumped and arms fought to sprint with maximum speed. Whistle. Heart racing, she straightened up and skated slowly back to the start.

Holly lined up with Alana and Tori, who kept glancing her way. "You okay, Holl?"

She nodded. Bent over, waiting. She knew Brent was moving slowly on purpose with her, but this yearning to know his kiss was intensifying each day. How much longer would she have to wait?

Whistle. Skate, skate, skate. Whistle. Go back to the start.

She skated back, hands on her hips, studying the grooved ice at the start line. How many girls had he kissed? How many wanted his attention?

Whistle. Skate, skate, skate. Whistle. She skated back to the start.

Whistle. Missed it.

"Holly? You're not focused. Come on!" Coach Mathieson yelled.

Was this why Coach Chan had warned her not to get involved in a relationship? Maybe she'd been right after all. Maybe it was impossible for two people to succeed in sport and love. Love? This was—

"Holly." Coach Mathieson skated closer, frown etched, motioning her to the side as his assistant continued the sprints. "What's going on? You're distracted. We leave for Montreal in two days. Do you want a World Cup or not?"

Yes! She sucked up the emotion to give the remainder of the practice session her full attention. Afterward, emotionally and physically exhausted, she begged off a coffee with Tori and drove home. She opened the front door, called out a "Hi there" to Bree, and hurried up the stairs.

"Holl? You okay?"

She paused and turned. "Sorry. It's been a tough day."

"What's up?"

Holly slumped to sit on the top step. "I'm just trying to figure out some things."

Bree arched an eyebrow. "Brent kind of things?"

"How did you know?" Holly freed her hair from her ponytail, and it fell forward over her face.

"He likes you, Holl. Stop worrying and trust God."

The words pricked inside. "That's so easy to say but so hard to do."

"I know," Bree said softly. "But you don't need to have all the answers. God's got this sorted."

The words slammed into her brain. That's right. God did, didn't He? Holly exhaled, then hurried down the stairs to give Bree a hug. "Thank you."

"For what?"

"A necessary reminder. For all of this. You're such a good friend to me."

"I know."

Her Brent-style reply drew Holly's laughter.

"Hey, have you started packing for Montreal yet?"

Another thing to do. "Is that your subtle way of offering to help?"

"Maybe."

"Give me a moment to have a shower and get changed."

Twenty minutes later, Bree perched on the chair in Holly's bedroom, fashion editor of the wardrobe that was taking Holly east. "No, not that one. That color does nothing for you, Holl."

"It's not supposed to be about looks, Bree. I have to stay warm too. It's going to be cold. And I don't think there are too many glamorous tracksuits in the world. Not for real athletes, anyway."

"But lime green?" Bree arched a brow. "Will you see Brent when you're there?"

"He mentioned he wanted to visit after the competitions." Holly closed the suitcase, mentally ticking off her clothing essentials. Skinsuits, warm-up outfits, casual clothes for her day off—she had to see as much of Montreal as possible—a dress for the closing banquet, jumpers, underwear, shoes…

Bree nodded. "Hmm. In that case, I think you need to take something that will be a sensation. You want to give him something to remember you by. Not that he seems like he'd ever forget." She grinned. "He's a goner, Holl."

"I'm glad you think so."

Bree sat forward in the chair. "You don't think that? Come on. Everyone can tell he loves you. The question is more do you love him."

Holly stared at her, the words spinning in her heart. Did she love Brent? Truly? She admired so much about him—his kindness, his thoughtfulness, his godly focus—but she hadn't even said those words to Brent, so to admit it to Bree felt a little bold. "Yes, I do."

"Ooh, I knew it!" Bree clapped her hands. "You're pretty good at holding your cards close to your chest, Holl. So, does this mean one day we might hear wedding bells?"

"Bree!" She couldn't afford to think like that.

"Holl, surely God can work things out. Just look at what's happened in the last year."

Maybe she needed to stop worrying and start believing that God actually wanted to bless her. Maybe things *could* work out well. Like being the Australian champion or training here in Calgary or winning the Invitational. And maybe part of that blessing was Brent in her future. Permanently. Hope suddenly suffused a golden vision of her walking down an aisle, dressed in white, as Brent stood waiting, watching her draw closer with tender delight…

Bree laughed. "Wow. I don't know where you just went, but that must be a happy place."

Holly blinked. "You're right. I do need to trust God more." She smiled. "I do love Brent, you know." So much that the ache these separations caused was eating a hole in her heart.

"Yeah? So go make a sensation then." Bree frowned. "But from what I've seen…"

"I don't really have anything too fancy." Why did that sound so shameful?

"Sounds like we need to go shopping then." Bree disappeared out the door. "Mike, Holly and I have to go out, okay?"

There was a faint "okay" from down the hall, then Bree grabbed her hand. "Come on, we've got some work to do."

Two hours later they were in Bree's favorite boutique, the salesperson waiting patiently as Holly tried to decide which of the three outfits was best. Bree and the saleslady had gushed over how good she looked in each of them, but that was the saleslady's job, and Bree was never less than enthusiastic. But truth be told, even Holly had found her appearance gobsmacking, unable to recognize plain, simple Holly in the mirror. A decision was impossible.

Bree muscled in, retrieving her purse from her leather bag. "That's it. We'll take all three."

"But, Bree—"

"Holly, you've done so much for me." Bree handed over her credit card to the saleslady, who beamed and started carefully removing tags. Probably counting her commission, too. Bree started ticking off her fingers. "You've helped around the house, you've cooked meals. You're my best friend, and he's my brother. I have a vested interest in making sure you look sensational so Brent knows what he's missing. So, too bad, Holly. You'll just have to keep the clothes and like it." She gasped. "Oh no!"

The saleslady looked up, startled. "What's wrong?"

Bree clapped her hands. "She's going to need shoes, too!"

The saleslady sagged with relief. "Right this way then."

Holly shook her head, smiling. Now she'd definitely need to repack her suitcase for Montreal.

Detroit, Michigan

BRENT SKATED around the San Jose player, protecting the puck as he raced to the goal.

"Karls!"

Brent flicked it toward the center, watching as Doug shot to the net—

SLAM.

Fire ripped through his shoulder as he staggered from the boards while the Shark skated away. An oath slipped from his mouth as he clutched his arm and motioned to the bench. A minute later he was shuffling down the tunnel to the medic station. Five minutes more and he was gritting his teeth as the doctor carefully examined him.

"It doesn't appear to be broken, rather a contusion. I'm afraid it will be quite painful for a time." Dr. Feeney eyed him. "So that means not travelling for the Toronto game."

Breath hissed out. What would this mean for Montreal—and seeing Holly? "Can I travel at all?"

"I wouldn't recommend it. The best thing you can do is to ice and rest. I'll give you a sling to use, but I'll want to see you in a couple of days anyway."

Brent calculated quickly. "You want to see me on Saturday?"

Feeney slid his chair back and glanced at his diary. "I should be able to squeeze you in first thing. Eight too early for you?"

"It's fine."

"You can have ibuprofen for the pain, and we'll see on Saturday whether another pain medication might prove necessary."

"Sure thing, doc."

An hour later he was at home, on the phone with his parents. Knowing them, Dad would be on the phone in the study while Mom had the kitchen extension pressed to her ear.

"So it looks like I won't be in T.O. for the game after all." He explained the situation to them.

"Oh. That's a shame," his mother said. "Will this mean you're out for a few games?"

"Dr. Feeney will make that call on Saturday."

"Do you think this will hurt your chances of team selection?"

His guts twisted. "Hopefully not. Especially if it's only a game or two and I recover fast."

"We'll pray you heal quickly."

"Thanks, Dad."

After he hung up, he found a missed call from Holly. He called her back straightaway.

"Hi, I left a message," she said.

"I like your messages, but I like talking to you more."

"How funny! Me too."

He shifted, sinking into a seat, trying not to grimace at the pain spreading from his right shoulder.

"Are you okay?" she asked quickly. "I got in late, so I missed your game tonight."

"Yeah, that."

"Brent? What happened?"

"Just got banged up a little. I have to miss the Toronto game and probably Montreal. They'll call it an upper body injury. It might just be my shoulder, but I'll call it a sore heart at the thought of not seeing you."

A beat. "I'm so sorry. Of course you need to rest and recuperate. Maybe we can catch up after Marquette instead."

"You know there's nothing I'd like more than to see you."

"I get that impression, yes."

He chuckled, the action spreading more fire through his injured joint. He ripped open his pain meds, popped two pills, swigged some water. "So, your flight is tomorrow."

"Yep. Then it's preliminaries, then the thousand heats, then the fifteen and five hundred finals on Saturday afternoon."

"You'll do great. How do you feel?"

"You know, I'm actually feeling a little confident."

"That's my girl."

He heard voices in the background. "That's Bree. She's dishing up dinner. I'll try to call you again tomorrow, but it may be a little hectic, so I can't guarantee what time."

"No problem. I'm not going anywhere."

The words fell into the void between them. Fresh regret filled his chest.

"Can't wait to see you," he assured.

"Me too." Her voice was sad. "I really should go."

The call soon ended, and he slumped, conscious of her disappointment—disappointment that was only exacerbated when he listened to her voice message.

"...oh, and I can't wait to see you on Monday! It'll be so good to spend the day together. Can you believe it'll be our first proper date, just you and me? Talk soon. Miss you, Holly."

He pressed to hear her message again, the excited lilt in her voice, the anticipation lining her words—knowing their conversation just now had snuffed it out.

Disappointment kneaded within. "Lord, this is crazy. What can I do?"

An idea sparked. Maybe he needn't spend the next few days stuck at home feeling miserable, waiting around for others to give him permission to leave and live again. Hope ignited in his heart. He had more phone calls to make.

CHAPTER 17

Montreal, Canada

Holly leaned closer to the plane window, peering down at the tree-covered hills and wide river. Montreal was so beautiful; she couldn't wait to explore. Anticipation flooded her veins. Four days of competition, a day off to see the sights, then she'd travel to Marquette for the second Vancouver qualifier—and to see Brent. She couldn't wait. Of course, the World Cup was important, but seeing Brent again soon? Priceless.

The plane landed, and soon began the chaos of settling into hotel rooms and orientation meetings before she joined the rest of the Calgary team for a couple of practice sessions on the ice. She caught up with Coach Chan, Jess, and the Aussie men's relay team at dinner, and afterward rang her parents in Australia, then spoke to Bree and Brent. The heady rush of love and encouragement about her recent success soothed the nerves and helped her sleep.

The first day began with the fifteen hundred preliminaries and heats, giving Holly a chance to get a feel for the arena and spectators. Considering it wasn't her favorite event, she wasn't too disappointed to miss the cut. The preliminaries for her pet event, the five hundred, were next, and she safely made it through to the next round. Day two was similar, except this time it was the thousand, followed in the afternoon by relays. Again, safely through, Holly enjoyed watching the drama of the relays as team members pushed each other around the laps.

Day three dawned. First up was the fifteen hundred, and Holly tried to relax until her afternoon competition. Stretches, Pilates, music, Bible reading, prayer—whatever it took to keep the nerves at bay.

"Okay, ladies, five hundred quarters." The official glanced around at the girls in the heat box, checked his clipboard, and began reading out names. Holly breathed out and took a last sip of water. She was up next. She stood and moved to the side, dropping her blade guards in the plastic container balancing atop the boards, then slowly skated to the girls in her group. Brief introductions, repeated in French, a briefer wave, then it was time.

"Go to the start."

Eyes fixed on the ice, she tucked in her bottom lip and assumed her start position.

"Ready." *Thank You, God...*

BANG!

Skate, skate, skate, skate. She propelled her body forward, angling for the front and closest to the inside. Whoever controlled that position usually controlled the race. Skate, skate, skate, lean. Hira Ito from Japan slipped in front of her. Holly controlled the fear. She didn't have to finish first. Second would get her through too. Skate, skate, skate, lean. The pace was good, but not spectacular. There was still a lot of racing left; she needed to keep something left in the tank. Skate, skate, skate, lean. The Japanese girl wasn't budging, so she'd have to settle for…second. Holly straightened up. That was okay. Her legs felt good. And she was through to the semis.

After a cool-down lap, it was off to the stationary bikes to pump out the excess adrenaline and listen to music as she prepared for the next race. The other quarterfinals concluded, and it was her turn again.

This time she was facing off against Ilse, the pushy German competitor from the Summer Classic, Su Kim from Korea, and the USA's Kelsey Hendry. Nerves rushed up her throat, and she took a deep breath against them as she tried to enter the quiet space, visualizing the turns ahead.

She pulled her ponytail tighter, adjusted her helmet, and waited for the crack of the pistol.

BANG!

She wanted this. Hunger drove her into the lead. One lap down. She angled her arms, careful not to impede as she took the next corner. Two laps down. *Concentrate. Stay in the zone. Don't worry about anyone else. Focus on yourself.* Three laps down. Her legs were tiring. *Ignore the pain. Keep going.* The bell signaled the last lap. Her peripheral vision caught Ilse's sudden advance. No! Holly swung in hard through the last turn and sprinted for the finish. Yes! She'd won the semi.

She congratulated the others, then skated to the side, breathing deeply to ease the nerves scampering in her veins. *Don't get ahead of yourself, even if this is the furthest you've ever got in a World Cup. Keep calm and carry on.*

This time there was a slightly longer wait as the men completed their semis, followed by the women's five hundred final B, the placings of which would help with World Cup point scoring. Her final, final A—final A!—was next.

Lord, fill me with peace. Thank You I've made it this far. Help me glorify You, no matter what happens. Lining up for the last time that day, Holly glanced at her fellow finalists. Ilse from her semi,

Min Weng, last year's World Cup Champion from China, and Stacey Green, Canadian national champion. She took a deep breath. Put on a brave face.

"And representing Australia, Holly Travers." She smiled, waved, and adjusted her goggles. *Thank You, God, that You are with me.*

"Go to the start."

Help me not be sick. Her mouth was dry, her heart beating loudly as she skated to the start line, her left skate's blade poised for flight.

"Ready." She crouched deeper.

BANG!

Skate, skate, skate, skate. She slid into the first turn, close behind the Chinese girl. Skate, skate, skate, lean. One lap. Her legs had revitalized and felt good. She sucked in another breath as she leaned into the corner. It was all about strategy in this race. She completed the second lap, hand out for balance as they rounded the turn. She needed to find a loophole in the Chinese girl's defense but was running out of laps to do so.

Skate, skate, skate, lean. She blocked the crowd's roar. *Focus on yourself.* Skate, skate, skate, lean. Controlling the bend, she surged forward as the bell sounded for the final lap. Carefully maneuvering her body, her lungs threatening to burst, she leaned deep into the curve. Heart pumping, eyes focused, she spied her chance as the Chinese girl went slightly wide. Holly slipped through. She was in the lead! Now to maintain it.

Skate, skate, skate, lean. Final turn. The Chinese red skinsuit flashed on her right. No! Holly dredged up her last ounce of energy to sprint. Skate, skate, skate, finish!

Gasping, hands on her knees, she looked around the frenzied stadium. *Decision pending* flashed on the scoreboard. She skated around to where Coach Chan stood with Coach Mathieson. They were screaming at her, pointing to the scoreboard.

She turned around.

First: H. Travers. Australia. 44.125 seconds

Second: M. Weng. China. 44.155 seconds

She'd won! She'd just won her first World Cup competition!

She clapped a hand to her mouth. No wonder the crowd was still going wild. She'd beaten a World Champion? By three hundredths of a second?

This was surreal. The other girls patted her on the back, congratulating her, but all she could do was nod and smile, her ears barely retaining their words. She was the winner? Seriously? She checked the scoreboard again. Apparently everyone else thought so.

"Holly! You did it!" Coach Chan was jumping up and down? Smiling? Threatening to squeeze the life out of her with an enormous hug? "I knew you could!" Who was this woman?

"Girl, that was outstanding!" Coach Mathieson gave her a hug as the other coaches nodded, offering polite congratulations as she skated past to cool down. Rounding the last bend of her cool-down lap, she noticed an Australian flag waving at her from the sidelines. How cool—and tonight of all nights! She skated over, beaming, only to see the faces of Brent and his parents as they peered around the edge of the flag.

She nearly fell over and had to hold on to the boards to stay upright. "Hi!"

"Congratulations, sweetie." Mrs. Karlsson kept waving her corner of the flag.

"I knew you had talent." Mr. Karlsson looked as proud as if she were his own daughter.

And Brent… The world faded compared to his warm smile. "Hey, wonder woman."

"Hey." She smiled, sinking into the way his eyes held her, caressed her, assured her, loved—

"Clear the ice!" a track official yelled.

Holly glanced back at the Karlsson family. "I'm so glad you're here."

"We'll be here again tomorrow." Brent leaned over the railing and squeezed her hand. "So proud of you."

This smile was never coming off. She turned and skated back to the competitor's area, accepting the congratulations that poured in from all corners while team officials filled her in on her World Cup points. Unbelievable. She completed her cool-down exercises, underwent the mandatory drug test, then rang her parents, who sounded as excited as Coach Chan.

Media interviews—who didn't love an underdog story?—then instructions for the next day before, finally, they were herded onto the bus back to the hotel. Holly leaned against the cold glass of the bus window, her heart full. *Thank You, God! Thank You, God! Thank You, God.*

"HOW ARE YOU GOING, SON?"

Brent looked up to see his dad eyeing him in the rear vision mirror as they traveled back to their hotel. "I'm really glad we could come see her. Thanks for making it happen."

The doctor had been very clear that the only way Brent had any chance of a quick recovery was if he took extra care on this trip and refrained from undue physical exertion. Even that stretch to hold Holly's hand had put some strain on him. Not that he'd ever admit that to her or anyone else. Seeing her, touching her, had been like water to a thirsty man.

That night he lay in bed, staring up at unfamiliar shadows filling the ceiling, unable to sleep as a cavalcade of highlights raced by. Watching Holly race. Her stunned expression when she won. Coach Chan's funny hugging-jumping dance. Holly's shock when she saw him. Her delighted smile. Her joy. His Holly. His love.

His heart thudded loudly in the stillness. Maybe God had allowed his injury to occur so Brent could use this enforced rest to more deeply connect with Holly. Maybe this could work out for good. *Hey, thanks, God, that You know what You're doing.* He smiled, and peace filled his soul.

~

DAY FOUR MEANT an early start for warm-ups prior to Holly's thousand quarterfinal. The months of training in Calgary had improved her stamina, and despite the workload of the previous days, she made it through to the semis, where she came third.

Disappointment flowed as her heart thumped and muscles protested. As she skated to cool down, she lifted her eyes and saw Brent gazing intently at her. She gave him a small wave, her heart lifting. There was final B to think about now, then she'd have the rest of the day to spend with Brent. Holly raced hard, and her sixth placement was still enough to see Coach Chan crack another rare smile. Her results meant she'd qualified for Vancouver in the five hundred and the thousand, and that was a super amazing accomplishment. The Games! Her goal was within reach.

Released from her official duties and rugged up in her track-suit and puffer jacket, Holly made her way out to the stands while the first of the relays began. Thank goodness that wasn't her. Her muscles were crying out for a bath—or at least a long sit down next to the man of her dreams.

"Hi there."

Brent's parents hugged her and briefly chatted before scooting farther along the seats.

"Hey, beautiful." Brent stood and smiled, drawing her close in a long, tender hug.

She let herself relax, the tension draining away as she smelled that delicious aftershave and heard the solid thump of his heartbeat. Oh, she could stay here forever.

He drew back slightly, sliding a hand down her hair, tracing heat down her cheek, stopping next to her lips. He studied her lips for a long, long time. Wow. He wanted to kiss her now? Here? In front of his parents and all these other people? Amidst the crash and chaos of relays? Not that she minded. She'd waited this long for him to keep his promise. She held her breath as he sighed and ducked his head—and gave her a quick kiss on the cheek. Oh.

"Holly, remember what I said back in Calgary?" He cradled her face in his hands, his eyes now dark with emotion.

She nodded. How could she forget?

"You know I want to kiss you properly, more than anything in the world."

Did he?

He tilted his head down, his eyes searching hers. "It just has to be the right time"—a memory tingled—"because I've found the right girl."

Ohhh…

She nodded, and he drew her close again. One day. Soon. Hopefully.

"Excuse me? Didn't you win the five hundred yesterday?"

Holly turned and looked at a young girl who was sitting two rows above them. "Uh, yes."

The girl smiled hopefully. "Would you sign my program, please?"

"Sure." Holly grinned, signed away, and posed for a photo before resuming her seat next to Brent.

"I always said you're a superstar." He took her hand again, and she snuggled closer as they watched the rest of the competition, the excitement and spills of the relays for once unmarred by any great controversy.

During the time, she caught up with Brent's parents. "I'm so pleased you could come. It's great to have support."

Rob Karlsson smiled. "Montreal really isn't too far from home. Not when something as important as this is taking place.

Besides"—he glanced at his son—"someone here was coming to see you, come hell or high water. So we thought a brief vacation was in order."

A tap on her shoulder and Holly turned to see a team official beckoning her. "I've got to go. See you later!" She flashed a smile before hurrying away.

~

SHE WAS AMAZING. And so talented. And so beautiful. And so deserving of the admiration that surrounded her. And to think, if Brent hadn't been hurt, he'd have been off playing somewhere and would have missed it. *Hey, God, thanks for this. I'm really glad You know what You're doing.*

He stood off to one side as the interviews and photographs continued. Fortunately, only a couple of sportswriters had recognized him and hadn't yet put two and two together. Or worked out that one plus one made two. His lips pulled up. He definitely wanted to fly under the radar today. When Holly was finally free of the interviewers, he moved closer.

"Hey, Holly."

"Hey, you."

He drew her close, carefully wrapping his arms around her, ignoring his shoulder twinge. "I'm so proud of you."

Her smile... Every night he drifted off to sleep remembering her gorgeous smile, that one she was showing him now. He liked to dream what it would be like when they were married and—

A bright flash suddenly punctuated the stillness as a photographer tried to get a picture. "So, uh, Brent, have you got anything to say?"

Nothing that he should say right now, so "No comment."

He shot the photographer a dark look, and the man blustered away.

Holly didn't need any extra pressure right now. No way was he going to advertise their relationship until things were absolutely settled. Which would be soon. Really soon. He hoped.

Holly was gazing at him, her expression cooling. He tugged her closer. "Holls, I don't want to hide you, but you can't let people know too much, otherwise they keep coming back for more and it becomes all-consuming. What we have is worth protecting." He looped his finger around a tiny tendril of hair that had escaped her beloved ponytail. "Can you leave, or do you have other duties?"

"I have to collect my things. Tonight there's a party at the hotel, if you'd like to come."

"Of course I want to come. And tomorrow?"

"We've got a day off."

He smiled. "Great."

THE HOTEL FUNCTION room was loud with the buzz of conversation and international pop music. Scores of people mingled over finger food and drinks, the mix of nationalities doing the UN proud. Brent soon found Holly in the middle of conversation, dressed in a purple top and a black knee-length skirt and heels that showed off her fantastic legs.

He captured a glass and stole to her side, stealing his fingers through hers as she continued to hold court. "Hey there, beautiful."

Her eyes lit. "Hi!"

The next hour was a blur of faces and noise as Holly introduced him to countless people. Remembering names was pointless, so he concentrated on absorbing the beauty of the woman beside him. Her hair shone, her skin glowed—Holly was joy personified. They moved around the room, chatting easily with the officials, athletes, and support staff. A few people stood out: Coach Chan, Coach Mathieson, Jessica, Tori, people he'd met or names he'd heard before. A few people looked at him speculatively, nodding. Then it was speeches and toasts before the crowd began to slowly disperse.

"So, Miss Superstar, what do you want to do now?"

"I want to spend time with you, but I'm exhausted." She yawned as if to prove her point.

He laughed. "Okay, I believe you. Don't fall asleep on me now."

"Ha." He walked her upstairs to her door. She smiled up at him, wrapping her arm around his waist. "I hope you had fun tonight."

Her smile made his heart dance crazily. "I did." He pulled her closer. "I wonder…"

"Wonder what?" she whispered.

"About that kissing thing." His gaze lingered on her mouth. "Whether you'd mind—"

"I don't mind at all."

He drew her nearer, bent down, and she closed her eyes. He felt the magic of her lips at the ever-so-light touch of his own. "That's a promise," he whispered, "for the next time we meet."

Her breath came haphazardly. "Can't wait."

"Goodnight, beautiful." He leaned in and kissed her cheek. "See you tomorrow."

"Goodnight."

CHAPTER 18

*M*orning sunshine streamed through the hotel restaurant's windows as Holly ate her muesli and fresh berries topped with plain yoghurt. She sighed happily.

"I do like to see a woman who enjoys her food."

She looked up at the owner of that delicious voice. "You must really like seeing this woman then."

Brent's lips curved. "I do."

She laughed. "Good morning."

"It is now." He sat down at her table. "Sleep well?"

"Like a log."

He pinched her second last strawberry. "Mom and Dad are revisiting their old haunts from when they honeymooned here, so today it's just you and me."

"Much as I love your parents…"

He chuckled. "I'm up for whatever you want to do."

"Some of the girls talked about visiting Old Montreal, seeing the historic section, and while I want to do that, I don't really want to share this day with them. Tori and Alana still can't believe you're *the* Brent Karlsson."

"Call me selfish, but I don't want to share you either." He

picked up her hand, pressed it to his lips. "I'm happy to follow your lead and do anything."

"Anything?"

"Anything." His gaze dropped to her mouth, his smile sending a shiver up her spine.

This, their first proper date, made every moment significant. The laughter and conversation, just holding his hand and being able to give him a hug whenever—her heart was full. After breakfast, they took a taxi to the top of Mont Royal. The beautifully landscaped park with views across the city was a mid-city haven of natural tranquility and friendly squirrels. Once they'd taken the requisite photos, the icy November breeze saw them explore Old Montreal, whose shops, historic architecture, and general French vibe proved so interesting. She wasn't in Wollongong, that was for sure. She made some purchases at a vintage-styled paper crafts store, then they stopped for coffee and people-watched at an antique-filled café.

"Good thing we had our walk before. This chocolate croissant is so good."

"You don't have to hurry," Brent said. "We've got all day."

He looked so good today. Indigo jeans, walking boots, topped by a cream sweater, brown leather jacket, scarf, and a woolen beanie that looked like it could keep out a blizzard. Henry Cavill had nothing on him.

She kept wondering about that kiss, but even that was okay. Just being with Brent, catching his eyes on her, his special smile just for her—it was enough. She smiled.

He echoed it. "What's up?"

"I'm just enjoying you."

His grin widened. "Ditto." He picked up her hands, caressing each finger, before pressing his lips to the back of her hand.

More shivers, leading to a desperate desire to not let him see how much his touch affected her, rushed her to say, "So, um, how are you feeling?" He'd done pretty well, considering all the walking they'd done.

He squeezed her hand. "I'll probably be a little sore tomorrow, but we've kept it pretty easy with enough breaks, so I'm feeling good."

After visiting the very beautiful Notre Dame Cathedral, they wandered down an art gallery-lined street as a horse-drawn carriage clip-clopped near on the cobblestones. Brent motioned to the driver, who took them on a tour of fairytale-like Old Montreal, dropping them near the old port, where they continued to enjoy the European-like atmosphere as they caught the mighty St. Lawrence River at its shimmery afternoon best.

"This has been heaps of fun," Holly sighed happily. "Thanks for such a great day."

"Have you seen everywhere you wanted to?"

"All except the botanic gardens. But we don't have to—"

"The botanic gardens it is then."

A taxi took them to Montreal's Jardin Botanique, next to the former Olympic site and its angled cauldron.

"I saw this garden on a calendar once," she confided, "and since then I've had something of an obsession with visiting Japanese gardens."

They passed a tall Chinese-style pagoda, then a stand of white-trunked pines. Her breath held as they rounded the corner to see the scene she remembered from her calendar.

"Oh, how beautiful!"

They moved to a small pavilion, its stone seat perfectly positioned to capture the scene. The pond gleamed with golden sparkles, reflecting the late afternoon sun and stillness around them. Carefully coiffed conifers draped a small island as, beyond, the artful placement of stones and waterfall balanced the scene of soothing loveliness.

Brent tugged her close, and she leaned against his chest,

drinking in the stillness, the beauty, his scent. Oh, the pleasure of being held in his strong arms, tucked close to his heart, feeling the slight rasp of the stubble of his cheek bent next to hers. It was a moment that both soothed and heightened every nerve to tingling awareness.

"Is it like what you imagined?" His voice was husky.

"Well, it's not autumn, so the trees haven't got their color, but it's still so tranquil. Just what I needed after the past few days." She sighed, snuggled deeper into his arms. "I could do this forever."

"Look at this view?"

"And just be. Just breathe. To be here with you—it feels so right."

"You and me are so right, Holly."

He shifted, his head tilting, his eyes searching hers. Butterflies filled her stomach at the intention in his eyes. Then he lowered his head, paused for a delicious second, his mouth a breath away, and finally lowered his lips to hers.

She'd known from last night's caress there would be wonder in his lips—just hadn't quite anticipated the utter sweetness of the sensations rolling through her as his mouth possessed every millimeter of hers. As his lips clung to hers, so firm, sweet, and warm. As he made her feel cherished, chosen, and special. As longing flickered and flamed into more.

"I love you," he murmured before drawing in for another soul-tingling kiss.

She pressed closer, melting further, hands up behind his neck. She loved this man. Loved him with every fiber of her being. This godly, patient, oh-so-right-for-her man. She smiled up at him. "I love you."

His smile lit the depths of his eyes, and he dropped another kiss to her lips. "I could do *this* forever."

"Me too." She pressed her face into his chest and closed her eyes, breathing in his spicy-sweet scent, lingering in the precious moment. He seemed as entranced as she, barely moving, as if he wanted to preserve this minute in time for eternity.

"*Pardon.*"

A voice intruded into their cocoon of contentment. Holly opened her eyes and saw a dark-haired woman dressed in the attire of the park workers smiling at them.

A flood of French, which Brent fortunately seemed to understand, had Holly shifting from his warmth. "The park is closing."

"What a shame. It's been so lovely being here, just with you."

He rose, gently tugged her upright. "But the day is not yet done. Well, the day might be," he said, pointing to the sunset, "but I've made a reservation for dinner."

"Oooh. What sort of restaurant?"

"French."

"Ooh la la! Do I need to wear a nice dress? You want me to try and impress?"

"You don't need to try. I'm already impressed."

He dropped her off at her hotel with a quick kiss, promising to knock on her door within the hour. She raced upstairs. A hot shower, then she found the dress bought last week with Bree—the one that made her feel like a supermodel. Skin tight aerody-namic suits, goggles, and helmets sure didn't make her feel like this. The silky knee-length black dress gently accentuated her curves, strappy heels highlighted her legs, and she brushed her hair until it shone and left it to tumble around her shoulders. Makeup, perfume, jewelry, handbag, and warm-yet-stylish jacket. Finally. Even Bree would be impressed. She was ready.

She was sitting on the bed, trying to ignore the butterflies dancing in her stomach when the knock came. She opened the door.

"Wow." Debonair in a dark suit and carrying a long coat, Brent looked especially handsome.

His smile grew soft as he stared at her. "Oh, Holly. You look amazing. I didn't know I could be this impressed." He gazed at her like she was a prized jewel, then cleared his throat. "Are you ready?"

She nodded. They walked quietly through the lobby to a waiting taxi. Holly waved at Alana, staring at them open-mouthed, but she didn't stop to talk. She wanted to preserve this illusion of being the heroine in a romantic film for as long as possible.

They gazed out the taxi windows as the old buildings they'd seen earlier came alive through the artistry of streetlamp and moonlight. Soon, the taxi pulled up in front of a tiny French bistro in Old Montreal. Brent squeezed her hand. "This place has a great reputation for delicious food. It's been here for over thirty years." He smiled. "Let's see if it's as good as everyone says."

They walked through the front door of the tiny restaurant to be greeted by delicious aromas, flickering candles, and tables for two. Brent's reservation had secured them a private table overlooking a little courtyard out the back, overhung with vines and festooned with fairy lights. It was magical, the most romantic place Holly had ever seen.

Dinner passed in a series of golden moments: the food, the ambience, but most of all the company. All the delays and hiccups and frustration seemed to fade as she savored this time, drinking up every moment.

Holly sighed. "Oh, Brent. This is just so amazing."

Amazing was an understatement.

Brent leaned forward. "Holly, I'm so glad you moved to Canada. I love spending time with you. Today has been the perfect day."

She looked down at their intertwined fingers. "It has been wonderful. I mean, living here, being with you, today. Everything." She glanced up again. He could get lost in her beautiful eyes.

He reached across and touched her face. "Holly, you're so beautiful. I love being able to see you without distance or some computer screen in the way."

"Me too."

Their meals arrived with flair and a murmured *"Bon appétit."*

Dinner was delicious: veal blanquette, duck confit, grilled bison, a range of flavors synonymous with Quebec cuisine. Brent loved how this modest girl had a huge appetite for trying fresh adventures—that she'd visited so many parts of the world, had experiences he'd yet to learn, yet somehow still seemed to feel at home with him. She was fun, she was feisty, she was courageous, she was sweet. She was perfect. And so perfect for him.

She wiped up the remnants of sauce on her plate with her finger. "That was the best meal I've had, probably ever."

"You're so fun to be with." He scooted his chair closer to hers, gently grasping her hands in his. "You know, Holly, I love being with you, talking, laughing—it doesn't really matter what we do, I just love to be with you."

"I love to be with you too." Her eyes were luminous in the candlelight. "I'm so glad you could make it here after all."

"I couldn't have missed seeing you prove to everyone else you're the wonder woman I've always known."

She chuckled. "Always? I didn't think I rated so highly with you before Bree's wedding."

"Before Bree's wedding I was blind. But now I see."

"And what precisely do you see?"

"I see a future. A future with you." He swallowed. "I just hope you feel the same."

"Oh, Brent." She spoke his name in a whisper, then leaned

closer, placed a hand on his cheek. "How can you not know that?"

Her green eyes, lit like stars, invited him to another kiss, another question his lips asked met with a yes, then their plates were cleared, dessert was served, and the meal continued.

Conversation turned to future plans, to upcoming travel. Holly's bus left for the airport at eight, so this night of promise and magic would soon need to end.

But Brent now felt renewed assurance that his future would be one which Holly shared.

CHAPTER 19

The dining room was filled with bustle, the clank of plates and cutlery, and the chatter of her teammates. Holly finished her cereal as she read the congratulatory replies to her recent email about her World Cup success. Yep. She smiled. God answered prayers, all right. She touched her lips, glanced at the time. Where was Brent? He knew she had to leave soon...

"Hey, babe." An arm snaked around her shoulder. Lips kissed her cheek. "I'm sorry we were late. Traffic."

She twisted in her seat and faced him. "You're here now."

"Hi." Brent smiled, leaned in and kissed her. Beautifully, reverently, possessively.

Oh. Lightheaded! "Hi."

He wrapped her closer. "I could hardly sleep last night. Yesterday was the best day of my life."

"Me too." Knowing she was loved, knowing his kiss, had poured assurance over any lingering doubts about what this might mean for her career. They'd *have* to make this work. She wasn't going to miss out on his kisses now she knew just what they meant.

They shared smiles, holding each other's gaze until he heaved out a breath.

"Are your parents here?"

"They thought they'd give us a moment alone."

The noise level around them pitched to new heights. "And they're taking you to the airport?"

"Yeah. I'll grab some time with them this morning before the flight at noon."

She was about to reply when Pam Karlsson appeared, followed by her husband. "Oh, Holly, I'm so glad we caught you before you left."

"Thank you so much for coming. You don't know how much it means to know there's someone out there cheering for you. And with my parents unable to see me, you're the next best thing."

"Oh, sweetie. You know we already consider you like a daughter."

Pam's close hug certainly testified to her words, while Rob's glance at his son made Holly wonder whether they carried an even deeper significance .

"Now, we were wondering if you had plans for Christmas. If you're not heading back to Australia, then maybe you'll consider spending Christmas with us this year."

And experience a white Christmas? "If I'm not in Australia, there's no place I'd rather be."

"Excellent." Pam clapped her hands, her enthusiasm such it was easy to see where Bree's vivacity came from. "And of course, your family would be welcome too."

"That's so very kind. I know they're planning to come in February for the Games, so I'm not sure if they could get that much time off work, but I'll definitely mention it to them."

"Good. Well, we'll leave you to it. Brent, we'll be in the car when you're ready."

"Yes, Mom," he said, like a little kid.

Holly laughed as Pam pinched his cheek. Pam and Rob gave her last hugs, wished her well in Marquette, and they were left to themselves again.

"Airport bus leaving in ten minutes." Coach Mathieson looked stern. "Ten, people."

Brent held her hand, gently stroking the back of it with his thumb. "Are you all set?"

She nodded. Her luggage sat in the designated zone, ready to be loaded on the bus that would take her away. She drew in a breath. Nope. Not going to think about how this was yet another separation. "How is your shoulder this morning?"

"I've been too distracted to notice it much." He seemed surprised. "That's good, because when I get back, the doctor might be happier about letting me play."

"Who are you up against next?"

"I play Jai in Chicago, so we'll see what happens."

"Five minutes, people!"

Holly wrinkled her nose. "Just don't damage anything. I want you strong and healthy."

He tucked a loose strand of hair behind her ears. "Same goes for you. Don't go making any crazy moves or feel the need to prove anything in Michigan. You've qualified for Vancouver—"

A thrill raced through her.

"—and I want you to stay healthy."

"Yes, sir."

He smiled.

"Time to go!"

They stood and moved slowly to the lobby. Brent wrapped his arm around her waist. Breath caught at his nearness. "Holl, if I can get to Marquette, I will. Things really depend on what the doctor says. Is that okay?"

She nodded. "Totally okay."

"Holly!" Coach Mathieson mustn't have slept well.

"Coming!"

They walked out to the bus, which idled noisily as it waited. Her luggage had already been stowed in the hold below. This was it. Brent turned, wrapping her in a bear hug that said a bruised shoulder didn't matter. "I love you, Holly."

He eased back, his heart in his eyes. She so didn't want to go.

"I love you too." She pressed up on her toes and kissed him one last time. Oh…to do this forever!

The cheers and applause of her waiting teammates made for a noisy backdrop.

"Bye, sweetheart," he whispered.

"Bye."

Her travel time to Marquette, Michigan, was peppered with questions and commentary from teammates, most of whom wanted to know how Holly had managed to snavel one of the NHL's most eligible bachelors. She didn't mind sharing—some —details, such conversations both reiterating her joy and providing further distraction from the nerves about the upcoming meet.

Brent might be Mr. Right in so many ways, but he was wrong about this upcoming event. The tightness in her stomach underscored her mind's agitation: that she *did* need to prove that her victory in Montreal wasn't just a fluke. Not that anyone had said—or even hinted—that. But backing up her Montreal results with good results here would lock in her standing as a contender for Vancouver, proving she could do this.

She swallowed. Glanced out the window at the banners of North Michigan University, green and gold—Australia's colors —lining the streets. Was it foolish to dream of a medal in Vancouver? Any color would be good. Gold was an impossibility, of course, but silver or bronze would be lovely. Her chest tightened. Released. What was it that made people always chase more? Some might say she should be content with having won a World Cup, but God hadn't given her this talent to see it squandered, and she longed to see what potential still lay in her skating future.

That last word ticked her memory back to yesterday, when Brent's serious talk had made her heart dance with the possibility of a proposal. A tiny part of her had been relieved when he hadn't—although she knew as soon as she returned to Calgary that Bree would prod and tease and wonder aloud why he had not. She was enjoying this wondrous space of feeling wanted and cherished and prized. Another part wanted to hear him say the words, to secure this future they talked around, to define what this might mean for her skating career. A truly serious future relationship—one which involved marriage and one day, possibly, motherhood—would impact her world in ways she wasn't sure she was ready to deal with. What would her life look like without skating?

"Holly? We're here."

She shook herself. She needed to get her head into gear, to pull herself out of fairyland and start doing what Coach Chan had always said: focus, focus, focus.

Detroit, Michigan

If ONE HAD to prove oneself fit to play, it sure didn't hurt to score two goals in one's comeback game. Nor another goal against Vancouver the next night. Brent pulled off his helmet and wiped sweat away, watching as Detroit pulled ahead of the Ducks in what looked to be another win. Three wins straight. And the way they were going here tonight, three games where he'd scored the game winner.

"Great goal, man." Dougie fist-bumped him as he shuffled along the bench.

"Cool pass from you."

"Yeah, it was, wasn't it?"

Brent grinned, attention on the game. He had another minute or so, then their line would be back on the ice. He grabbed a drink, wondered how Holly was doing—her five hundred final was tonight—shot up a quick prayer for her, then pulled his thoughts back to the play.

"Karlos, you're up!"

Brent nodded, grabbed his stick, and sped onto the ice. He scooped up the puck and wove his way through the Ducks' defensemen before belting it to Dougie. A quick deflection, then the puck slid back. He outpaced Anaheim's captain and shot to goal. *Ping*. Rebound off the posts. He shot again. Goal!

He skated behind the net, teammates pounding him on the back, then back to the bench, swigged his drink. Thank God his shoulder had healed in time. Thank God his pace had improved, thanks to Holly, and his body could do what he'd been born to do.

Born to do. His thoughts swung back to Holly. He'd checked his phone during the interval, but no message. Maybe he'd find one after the game.

~

Marquette, Michigan

"Good luck, Holly."

"You too!" Holly smiled at Tori as they hurried to the warm-ups.

She stretched, listened to Coach Mathieson's instructions, and prepared as she had a thousand times before, working to block out the nerves and noise.

"Okay. Breathe, focus, get there in your head. We all know the fourth quarterfinal allows more time for nerves."

That was for sure. Holly swallowed. *Thank You, God, that You're with me.*

"At least we know who's gone through. Now, the girls in your race..." They discussed her rivals' strengths and weaknesses, then it was time to head onto the ice.

Holly glanced at the others in her group. Irina Svechnikov, a Russian champion, Stacey Green, the Canadian favorite, and Mai Lee, another Korean previous World Cup winner. Stiff competition. Holly had recorded the slowest time of the four and was in the outermost starting position, but she'd won from position four before. The announcer began the introductions, and Holly waved at the crowd and gave a brief smile, then skated slowly to the pale blue start line.

"Quiet please." The crowd was noisy tonight.

"Ready."

Holly's blade pivoted slowly. *Thank You, God—*

BANG!

Skate, skate, skate, skate. Irina pounded into the lead, followed by Stacey. Holly skated around the outside to lock in the third position. The plan was to avoid going too hard too fast; she'd tire too quickly that way. Just stay in the slipstream, maintain pace, and not fall or be knocked over by others.

One lap down. Mai Lee was angling. Holly gritted her teeth and picked up her pace. Irina was stretching out her lead. If Holly was going to progress, she'd need to make a strategic move really soon. As the second lap neared completion, she inched forward, and on the curve, smoothly slipped between Stacey and the marker. She was now in second place.

On she pushed, her legs letting her know she'd worked hard over these past few days. *Stay smooth, stay focused, stay up.* Holly concentrated on her breathing: deep breaths in and slow release. Round the next bend. The bell rang. That was three laps down.

She could hear the swish and hiss of their blades, the quiet grunts of the girl behind her, vague shouts from the side where the coaches yelled encouragement. She rounded the next bend, glimpsed a Korean blue skinsuit. Her heartbeat hammered louder. Mai Lee was too close. Holly tried to straighten. She felt a slight push on her side. Oh no. Her legs wobbled. She thrust out her right leg to regain balance, but it was too late. Holly crashed to the ice, was sliding, spinning off to the blue padded boards, her right leg outstretched, the crowd, the officials, the lights a desperate blur. *Lord, help me!*

Ooofff!

A scream.

Darkness.

CHAPTER 20

Detroit, Michigan

"So, Brent, tell us, how does it feel winning the second star of the night?"

Brent squinted into the camera's intense spotlight. "Great. But really, it's a team effort. Nobody can play good hockey by themselves. I'm so thankful for these guys, the fact I get to spend my days playing this game I love."

"You've had a remarkable few games, bouncing back from injury the way you have. Any secret to your success?"

Brent glanced at the interviewer, considered who might be willing to hear. "Actually, yeah. But I don't think it's a secret. I'm a Christian. I prayed, and I believe God healed me."

"Oh." The smile wilted, the interviewer glancing at her notes, then hurrying on. "And I'm sure your recent performance is something selectors are taking note of for the Canadian team for Vancouver. Anything you want to say about that?"

"I'd love to represent my country, but with so many

outstanding players, I know it's going to be a tough task. I'm sure we can trust those with such an important responsibility to pick the best possible team to win gold for Canada."

He grinned at the expression on the proud American's face and took the moment to step back, salute the camera. "Meanwhile, go Wings! And thank you fans for your incredible support."

He was still chuckling when he returned to his stall in the dressing room and finally had a chance to strip off his gear. After a shower, he dressed in street clothes and chatted with the remaining guys for a few more minutes, then remembered. He tugged out his phone.

Huh. Still no word. Maybe Holly was just held up by something.

"Karlos! There you are. Hey, caught your interview."

Brent ran a hand through his hair. Doug had never been particularly forthcoming about what he believed. "What did you think?"

Doug shrugged, glanced about, but didn't leave.

Huh. Brent had a choice: revert to teasing, as he usually did, or push a little deeper. Maybe it was time for deeper. "You knew I'm a Christian, right?"

"Well, uh, yeah. I thought so."

Hmm. Can't have shone much Jesus if that was the response.

"I mean"—Doug shuffled his feet—"yeah, of course I knew."

Phew.

"But I just don't get it. How can you know it's real?"

"Know what's real? Jesus was a real person. Historians from the early centuries who had no reason to lie wrote about a Jewish man who died and came back to life."

Doug shook his head. "I can't believe that."

"Just because something seems impossible doesn't make it untrue. What if I told you all the times I've prayed and seen God answer?"

"How do you know it's not just coincidences?"

"Come on, man. You know statistics, right? You know the probability of that is pretty low. How can you account for God pulling out these miracles time and time again? But more than that, perhaps the biggest thing is that I've changed."

Doug eyed him, hands folded, expression wary. "What d'you mean?"

"I mean"—Brent took a breath—"I used to play hard, party harder, treat women as if they existed for my pleasure. I used to do all sorts of things, look for fulfilment in winning, in pushing my body to extremes, but it never satisfied. Even the rush of winning a Cup or winning World Champs doesn't satisfy forever. Nothing satisfied. Except God."

"Yeah, right." Doug raised a skeptical brow. "Not even Holly?"

"This was way before Holly. But yeah, if I'm honest, I won't find ultimate fulfilment from being with her either."

"Wow. Diss your girl, why don't you?"

"I'm not dissing her. She'd say exactly the same thing about me. If I'm looking for someone else to meet my deepest need, eventually they'll fall short. But God won't."

A trainer moved into the room. "Hey, Karls—"

"Give me a minute, Joe." This conversation with Doug was important.

"I really think—"

"A minute longer, please."

Joe finally nodded, walked away.

"Where were we? That's right. God loves you, man."

Doug looked away, shifting his feet, clearly uncomfortable.

"You can deny it all you like, pretend He isn't there. But I dare you to pray and ask Him to show Himself as real."

Doug met his gaze with a cynical raised eyebrow. "And when he doesn't?"

"What makes you think He won't?" Brent smiled. "Hey,

anytime you want to talk, or if you want to come to Bible study with me, you're always wel—"

"Brent." Joe returned. "I really think you ought to hear this."

"What?" What could be more important than finally having this conversation with Doug?

The trainer sighed. "You've got a message from your sister—"

"Bree?"

"—asking for you to check your phone."

He tugged it out, checked the screen. One message. He clicked it open.

Holly seriously injured. Please call asap.

Heart drumming, he stabbed the numbers to return Bree's call. "Bree?"

"Oh! Finally!"

He shifted, angling away from the men's attention, and slumped in his stall. "What's happened?"

"She's unconscious."

"Unconscious?" The word stabbed inside. "What? How?"

Bree's sobs reached through the phone, each one piercing his heart.

His throat clamped. No. Holly would be okay. She *had* to be. *God, let her be okay.* "Where is she now?"

"They took her to a hospital," Bree said.

"Which hospital?"

"Holly's in hospital?" Doug whispered.

He met Doug's wide eyes. Nodded. Leaned forward and pushed his head into his hand. "Which hospital, Bree? I'll go there straightaway."

Joe shifted closer. "I'll tell front office. Where is she?"

"Marquette. She was competing tonight and is unconscious, and—" He couldn't continue, fear clutching his chest, clamping his throat. *God, help her!*

Joe patted Brent's shoulder and moved to the door. "I'll make some calls."

Brent nodded, swallowing. "Bree? Are you still there? Where is she?"

"She…she's at Marquette General, I think."

"Okay. I'm catching the next flight I can."

He pressed end, stared at the phone for a minute. Seriously? How had his world turned upside down so quickly? His thoughts trickled slower than frozen maple syrup. What should he do? What *could* he do? He could only pray. *God, be with her. Heal Holly, please.*

"Dude, it's late. It might be tough to get a flight right now. I could drive you."

Heat stung the back of his eyes at Doug's unexpected kindness. "Thanks," he rasped. The overwhelming magnitude of it all pressed in, squeezing out his admission. "I…I don't know what to do."

Doug studied him a moment. "Give me your phone."

Brent handed it over. Watched Doug press some buttons. Hold it to his ear.

"Bree? This is Doug Lehtonen. I'm here with Brent. He's a little shell-shocked. We need to know how you got your information."

He held the phone out, Bree's voice now on speaker. "…called me as next of kin as they couldn't get Brent."

"The hospital called?"

"Coach Mathieson. He's with her."

"Is she conscious now?"

"Yes."

"Thank God," Brent murmured, scrubbing his eyes.

"…thinks she hurt her knee badly too. But they're most concerned about brain injury."

Brain injury? The weight that had just eased sank heavier than before. "I need to be there."

"Thanks, Bree. That helps." Doug lifted the phone to his ear again, listened to Bree some more. "I'll pass that on. Hey, don't worry." He eyed Brent. "Apparently God listens to Brent's prayers."

Oh man.

Before Brent could say anything, Joe returned, followed by Coach Reynolds. "Brent? This is your skater girl who's injured?"

"Holly. She...she was competing in the World Cup in Marquette. She won her event just last week in Montreal, and now..." He lifted his hands, shook his head, bit his lip as emotion cramped his chest. *Keep it together.*

"I just got off the phone with the team manager. He's arranged a flight for you." He glanced at Doug. "You too, if Karls needs a friend."

What? "I...I..." No words.

"You leave in an hour. Get your stuff, Joe here will drive you to the airport. Take as long as you need. Tomorrow's a day off anyway, and we're not on again until Dallas on Wednesday. Just let us know how she is, okay?"

He drew in a breath. He needed to pull himself together. "Thanks, Coach. Please pass on my thanks to—"

"I'll tell him. Get going now, son."

Brent nodded, Coach Reynolds patted his back, and he turned to his locker. What to take? Couldn't think. *God, I need Your help.*

"I'll get your stuff, man," Doug said. "Go with Joe. I'll bring it with me."

"You're coming?"

"You better believe it." Doug smirked. "Someone needs to hold your hand."

IT WAS past midnight when they touched down in Michigan's Upper Peninsula. By that time Brent had spoken with Coach

Mathieson, texted Bree, then Holly's parents and his own, emailed an urgent prayer request to the Bible study guys, and viewed the video her coach had sent him of her accident a few too many times.

"Wow." Doug's voice held awe. Or was it fear? "She's so tough. She'll be okay, you'll see."

Brent hoped. He prayed.

But the image of Holly falling heavily, then sliding too fast to the padded boards and lying crumpled and all too still wouldn't go away. Her sport wasn't an adrenaline rush. It was a death wish.

And concussion? He'd suffered a mild dose before, knew it knocked a person around for some time. But Holly had lain motionless, unconscious for a minute or so. He wasn't a doctor, but that simple fact meant this case was way more serious than anything he'd faced. How would she pull through? Would she recover for the Games? What did all this mean for her, for her skating, for them?

The plane taxied to a stop, a car met them, and thirty minutes later they were rushing through the hospital doors.

"Brent?" A man Brent vaguely recognized from a week ago pushed up from a row of plastic chairs. "Dan Mathieson."

"Hi." Brent shook his hand. Anxiety was making him antsy. "How is she? Where is she?"

"Stable. She's this way." He eyed Doug, but Brent was too weary to do introductions. They were big boys. Let them figure it out.

They trailed down white corridors interspersed with waiting areas designed to soothe or distract, past desks of nurses who glanced up as they passed. It was quiet, and lights were dimmed, the austere surroundings adding to his trepidation. *God, be with her, please.*

They rounded another corner, drew up at a desk. The older nurse looked up, glasses perched atop her head. "Yes?"

"We're here to see Holly Travers."

"Are you family?"

"No. I'm her coach, Dan Mathieson. I was in before. And this is her boyfriend, Brent Karlsson."

"Family only, I'm afraid."

"Her family is in Australia," Brent said. "Please. I think they listed me as an emergency contact."

She peered at him, then glanced at her notes. Sighed. "Very well. But no disturbing her."

"Yes, ma'am."

Her frown deepened as she glanced at Doug. "And who are you?"

"Doug Lehtonen, moral support for my man Brent here. And fellow player for the Red Wings."

Her eyes widened. "Well, that's something that might impress my son, but if you're not family, you can wait there." She gestured to a seat.

Brent knew a ridiculous urge to laugh at the chagrined look on Doug's face, but he stifled it as the nurse led the way to Holly's room.

A soft, dim light shone, illuminating the golden strands in her hair as Holly slept, the bed's white blankets covering her form. She was so still, the only sign of life the way her chest rose slightly as she breathed.

"She was conscious when brought in but will need to be monitored for the next few days," the nurse said. "Her knee also took a beating and will need to be assessed before we can release her."

Brent stole closer and stroked Holly's hair, then touched her face, careful not to disturb her. Her eyelashes fanned in a dark fringe upon skin too pale, her mouth parted softly as she slept. Had it really been less than a week since they'd kissed, since her vivacity had drawn the declaration he'd withheld for months?

Emotion made him sway, and he stole to a nearby plastic chair and sat, watching her breathe.

"She'll be okay," her coach murmured, but he frowned as he studied the bed. "Concussions happen, but it's her knee that could be problematic. Holly took a hard fall, and the swelling means it's hard to know the extent of injury. Not helped, of course, by the fact she's concussed and probably won't be up for standing or using her leg for any length of time in the next little while." He sighed. "And she was just finding her form, too."

"But she's qualified for Vancouver, right?"

"Yes, but as I explained to her parents when I called them earlier, it'll take a miracle for her to bounce back in three months. These sorts of injuries take time, and concussions affect people differently." He glanced at Brent. "If you're a praying man, you best start praying."

"I have been."

"Good, good." Her coach yawned. "I probably should go. We've got another big day tomorrow."

"Thanks for all you've done."

Coach Mathieson nodded. "You're staying?"

"For as long as I can."

"Good. She'll appreciate a friendly face when she wakes. Oh, and just a heads up: her former coach was most insistent on coming and was not happy when I insisted she not. So if you're here tomorrow, you'll probably see her."

"Noted. Thanks." Awesome. Coach Chan had never liked him much.

They shook hands and Coach Mathieson left, leaving Brent to sigh and slump deeper into the seat. He scrubbed at his face, uncertainty roiling within. Was this visit just an overreaction? Her coach was right. Concussions happened. It didn't mean the end of a career. Neither did a knee injury. Maybe Holly didn't need him here...

The door wheezed open again and Doug stole in. "How is she?" he whispered.

"Stable and asleep. Which is probably where you should be." He exhaled heavily. "I feel like I dragged you up here for no reason."

"I don't recall any dragging involved. Besides, there's nothing I like more than midnight flights and hospital runs and hanging with my main man."

His comment spurted stupid amusement again, tempered by fresh appreciation. "Doug, thanks for your help."

"Don't go getting all mushy on me, man. So, you're staying?"

"Yeah. Go check in at the hotel, and I'll see how long I can stay until Nurse Ratched kicks me out."

"Good luck with that." Doug dumped a backpack on the spare chair. "Here's your stuff. I'll go now. Hey, but if she wakes —when she wakes—give her a kiss from me, okay?"

Brent rolled his eyes and made a shooing motion, but didn't mind his teammate's tease. He'd proven himself a true friend tonight.

Now if Holly could wake, Brent could prove his love for her, too.

CHAPTER 21

$\mathscr{A}$ scent of disinfectant drifted to her nose, twining inside to rouse her nerves. Holly stirred, shifted, the heaviness in her head, her limbs, pinning her down. She heard a distant clatter. Flinched. Somewhere nearer was another sound. Breathing. Was that a snore?

She lifted weighted eyelids and peeked through a fringe of lashes. Blurry. Too bright. She closed her eyes again. Sucked in a breath. Exhaled. Forced her eyelids open. After a moment, the fuzziness cleared. She was in a room. White walls. Dark shadows. A metal bed. And there, at the foot of her bed, drooped a man, seated in a chair, his face on folded arms on the mattress.

She recognized that dark hair. Too long. Soft to touch. The wisp of curl. What was his name? Too hard. Head hurt. She closed her eyes and drifted back to sleep.

"Holly?"

Faint voice. Low voice. Sweet voice. Who?

Eyelids lifted. Same man. Awake now. Shadowed jaw, shadowed eyes, studying her. Her skin prickled.

"Holly? Sweetheart? You're awake."

Was she? Or was this a dream? Bad dream last night. Racing. Wobbling. Crashing. White heat. Skidding, spinning, everything a whirl of dizzying lights.

Head hurt. She shut her eyes.

"Holly?"

Someone touched her hand. She jerked away. How dare someone touch her?

Footsteps. Anxious voices. More footsteps. A different voice. "Holly? Can you wake up, please?"

No. Would rather sleep. *Stay down, loser.*

"Holly, the doctor is here."

Why couldn't they go away? Would waking make them go away? She pried her eyes open. Three faces. The dark-haired man. Another man. A woman…dressed as a nurse?

"Hospital?" Her voice sounded weird, slurred, like a drunk's.

"I'm Dr. Yannick. You're in the hospital, Holly." The second man, graying hair, mustache, picked up a folder from the end of her bed. Flipped papers.

"Why?"

"You crashed in your race last night, sweetheart." The man from earlier picked up her hand, like he thought he had a right to.

Who *was* he? She pulled her hand away. Groaned. The pain in her head sharpened. Nausea churned. She pressed her lips together.

"Holly, we need to do some tests," Dr. Yannick said.

"Sleep."

"You can do that soon. Right now we need to check your knee and look at your head and eyes. Okay?"

No. Not okay. But, "All right."

"You want me to stay?" the first man asked.

"Who are you?"

The man's eyes widened, his face falling, even as both doctor and nurse swung to him, their faces holding suspicion.

"I'm Brent. Your boyfriend."

"No. Not." She didn't have a boyfriend, did she? No time for men, no time for distractions. *Focus, focus, focus.* But hadn't he been here a while now? "Head hurts."

"I'll give you something for the pain." The doctor nodded, and the nurse disappeared. "Now, I'm going to take a quick look at your knee."

Bedsheets lifted. Coolness. Leg exposed. The Brent guy winced. She shifted to see what had him concerned. Nausea rumbled. She slumped back on the pillow, hand on her mouth. Couldn't contain—

"Are you feeling unwell? Oh dear…"

She retched her stomach's contents down the side of the bed. Gross. Managed a "Sorry," then lay back, head swimming, and closed her eyes. Wretched, wretched her. Moisture gathered against her eyelids. Emotion rippled up her throat, spilling out in a sob.

"Sweetheart."

A touch on her arm brought comfort. A damp wash cloth wiped her mouth. She peeked through wet lashes. Tenderness. Undeserved. Oh, her head hurt. Darkness.

BRENT NEEDED SLEEP. The tiredness weighting his brain was surely responsible for the insecurity wracking him. Had she truly not recognized him? It might be the result of her concussion, but it still hurt.

His phone buzzed. It was low on battery. He needed to recharge. He needed—

Coach Chan entered the room.

Not her.

Brent braced, waiting for the dislike he'd always felt emanating from her, but after shooting him one quick glance, she moved to the bed where Holly still slept. "How is she?"

Brent reported all he knew, finishing with "I messaged her parents last night."

"I called them."

Score one for her. "How are they?"

"Beth wants to come, but tricky timing. Costly."

He should call them too. And update Bree. His parents. His coach and team. The Bible study guys. Responsibilities massed, weighting his shoulders.

She shifted to study him. "You look tired. Been here long?"

"Since one a.m."

Sharp nod. "You care for her?"

"That's why I'm here."

"Hmm." A double beat. "She do well in Montreal."

Montreal and all its magic seemed a lifetime ago. "She was amazing."

"She do very well." Her dark eyes scrutinized him. "Hmm. You may be good for her."

A twisted smile escaped his lips. "She's good for me too."

His phone buzzed again. Doug. Bless him. "Excuse me. I need to take this."

He moved from the room to a quieter alcove. "Hey, Doug."

"How is she?"

"Much the same. Doc thinks she'll be out of action for weeks, if not months." There went Vancouver. His heart hurt for her.

"Man. That's rough. Hey, you planning on staying?"

"If you want to get back, that's cool. I'm really not sure what I'm doing yet."

He wasn't sure about so many things.

∼

"ANYTHING I CAN GET YOU?" a middle-aged nurse asked Holly.

"No. Thanks."

This second sleep seemed to have helped. Or maybe that was these new meds. She had the vaguest sense of her actions before, of something not being right. Of course, so much about this wasn't right. Holly closed her eyes, trying to focus. *God, You see this. Please don't let this be a serious injury.*

She'd had an MRI on her knee earlier, but diagnosis remained unclear. "We suspect there may be a small tear in the tendon, but until the swelling goes down we won't really know how bad it is," Dr. Yannick had explained. "You'll need to limit movement, so I'm recommending you stay at least another night."

And continue to face the storm of concern? Mind you, she was pretty tired. Her ears still seemed to ring all the time. And when she tried to sit up, she still felt dizzy. Maybe a little more resting would be okay.

Thoughts seemed to slip and slide, her mind unable to hold on to them as they drifted like fast-moving clouds, lacking substance or form.

She opened her eyes as the nurse reappeared, holding a cup. "Take this for the pain."

"Thanks." Holly swallowed the pills and some water.

A figure at the door. A knot unraveled in her heart. "Brent."

His lips tweaked up. "You remember me."

"Of course. Wait—did I not before?"

A wry chuckle escaped, and he drew near, pulled up a chair. "Doesn't matter now. You seem much better."

"My knee is still really sore." And it hurt to look at light. Her stomach rumbled. "I'm so hungry."

"Yeah, you might want to take that slow."

"Why?"

He shook his head. Threaded her fingers with his. "I spoke to your mom. She's going to fly out here as soon as her visa can be arranged."

"What? Why?"

"You were seriously injured, Holly. She was worried."

"But how did she know?"

"Coach Chan. Coach Mathieson. Bree. Me."

"Was I that bad?"

"The doctor said you sustained a grade three concussion. You lost consciousness for nearly a minute. That's pretty serious."

"But I feel better now. Once this knee is sorted, I can get back to skating, back to training. Vancouver is only a few months away."

His brow lowered. "Holly, the doctor says it's gonna take weeks, if not months. You can't rush things. You'll need to see what the doctor and your coaches say."

"They'll say I'm fine," she insisted, panic squeezing her chest. She had to be. "I hate that I've let everyone down."

"What? It was an accident, Holly."

"Coach Chan was here before, telling me what I could've done better. And I haven't trained for all these years to not succeed. I'm going to the Games, Brent. Nobody can stop me."

He squeezed her hand but said nothing. And in his silence, she knew. He didn't want her to go. He was worried for her. Was being overprotective. Like he thought she didn't know her own body well enough to make wise decisions. She drew her hand away.

"Holl? What is it?"

"You don't want me to skate, do you?"

"I want you to be careful."

"Careful and short track aren't exactly compatible, Brent."

"Concussion isn't something to gloss over either."

"I'm not glossing." She tried to hide the agitation in her voice and heart with a tight smile. "But I'm a short track skater. That's what I do, it's who I am. I have to skate!"

His lips pressed together, then he sighed. "Holly, I love you. I want you to be safe so we can have a long life together."

What? Was this some kind of oblique proposal? She pressed at her forehead's pain. "Sounds like you want someone like Bree, happy to be Suzy homemaker while her man goes off and does his thing. Well, that's not me, Brent. Never has been, never will be. If that's what you want, for me to give up my career and stay home and have kids, well, you don't know me very well at all."

"That's not what I'm saying."

"So you don't?" Did that mean he didn't want a happily-ever-after with her? Oh, this conversation was making her head swim. Or was that the meds? "I think you should go now."

"Holly—"

"I'm really tired."

And she was. Tired of people who didn't think she could do it or wanted to stuff her into their box of narrow expectations. She didn't need that sort of negativity in her life.

He nodded, murmured a farewell, and left, leaving her feeling wretched, frustrated, headachy, and sad.

EVENING SHADOWS CRAWLED across the room as worries stole across Brent's heart. Holly's words earlier had forced him to face his fears. Did he really want her to give up short track? Well, no. But he did want her to be safe. Did he want her to settle for being a housewife? Again, no. One of the things he most admired about her was her grit and fierce determination. But getting her to believe it was another thing. He'd managed to snatch a few hours' sleep back in the hotel, then he'd tackled the phone calls now that the hours were better for those farther west—and in Australia.

Doug had returned home, and Brent had called Coach Reynolds about missing tomorrow's practice. He planned to stay another day at least, even if Holly still seemed reluctant to see him. He knew that was simply her stress talking. Wasn't it?

He studied her now, held her hand, and prayed yet again for God's healing.

She stirred, opened her eyes, blinked, smiled. "Hello."

"Hey, sweetheart. How are you feeling?"

"A little better." Her lips flattened on the sides. "If you ask me often enough, maybe one day I won't have a headache."

What?

"Sorry, I sound like a grouch, don't I?" She pushed up, winced. "My head is improving, but I still feel a little woozy."

"A bit more rest needed, eh?"

"That's what they tell me." She sighed.

"Hey." He leaned closer, kissed her hand. "If this had to happen, then it's good it's now and not a week ago."

"True."

"It's good it's now and not a week from the Games."

"Are you trying to cheer me up?"

"Is it working?"

"Maybe." She swiped hair from her eyes. "Perspective can be a good thing, right?"

"For sure."

Her smile faded, her gaze lowered, and he wondered again at what was going on in that pretty head of hers.

She glanced back at him, seemed to draw herself up. "So, how did you get here? When did you arrive?"

"Early yesterday morning. Real early. The organization was kind enough to arrange for a private plane."

"Wow." Her gaze shifted to the ceiling. "That was really kind. Please tell them thanks, even though it wasn't necessary."

Wasn't necessary? Hurt crawled through his chest.

"I mean, I'm glad you're here, but I'll be okay really soon. I *am* okay, apart from this dumb knee."

"Take it slow—"

"Thank you, Dr. Brent. I know what to do." She heaved in a breath. "Sorry. I'm being snappy again, aren't I? I'll be fine. Please don't worry."

This time her smile held more of the Holly life he loved. His heart eased.

"The team must really like you to go to such lengths."

"Yeah, I think they do."

A small chuckle. "Don't make me laugh. It makes everything blur a little more."

"Didn't you just say you're fine?"

"And I *am*." Her smile appeared forced. "So, when's your next game?"

"Tomorrow, against Dallas."

"So you head back tonight?"

"You keen to be rid of me?"

A beat. "No."

His chest pinched tight.

"I'm sorry." Her expression was penitent. "I keep saying the wrong things. Maybe because I'm so tired."

"I'll let you sleep then."

"Thank you. And thanks so much for coming all this way."

"Holly, I can come back tomorrow—"

"I don't need you to. You have work to do, and I'll be flying back soon anyway."

"But your parents—"

"Right. I need to talk to them. Make sure they don't waste their money by coming here. Hey, would you please pass me my phone?"

He found it and handed it to her. She squinted at the screen, blinked a few times.

"You okay there, Holl?"

Her brow lowered. "It's nothing a good sleep won't fix. I'll contact them later."

"Want me to help?"

She nodded, winced, and he collected the phone. Followed her prompts, scrolled through and found *Mum*.

He quickly calculated time zones. Dialed. It shouldn't be too early there…

"Hello? Holly? Oh, we've been so worried. How are you, darling?"

"Hi, Beth. It's Brent. Here she is." He handed the phone to Holly.

"Mum?" The strain lining her face finally eased.

At the exchange of conversation, Brent settled back in his seat, glad he'd done something right at last. He looked at his own phone. Tapped out a reply to soothe his own mother's worry. Pressed to open his email. Scrolled down until he found Holly's last email—one she'd sent a few days ago, before her competition had started. He reread the last lines:

…looking forward to all that Marquette holds. Then it's a break, Christmas, then the Games in Vancouver! Can't wait! Thanks for all your support. Love, Holly.

"But, Mum…"

He glanced up. Holly's brow had wrinkled.

"I really don't need you to come. I'm heading back to Calgary tomorrow anyway. I'll be fine." The friction in her voice suggested she wasn't. "Mum, I need to go." A beat. "Yes, I'm tired. Love you too. Bye." She shoved the phone onto the side table.

"Everything okay?"

Her face wore a mulish look. "I really wish you hadn't worried her."

Huh? "She's your mother, Holly. She's supposed to worry. It's called caring about someone."

She glanced away, lips pressed together, then faced him again, the smile on her lips not reaching her eyes. "I really am tired, Brent."

"You want me to leave?"

A small nod. Another tight smile. "Thanks for coming. Have a good flight tonight."

Really? That was it? He bent down, hoping for a kiss, but she turned her head, wincing as she did so, so he kissed her cheek instead. "I'll talk to you later, Holly."

"Okay."

She offered him a sleepy smile, one that grabbed him around the heart and made him wonder what it would be like to—No. He pulled his thoughts back. "Good night, Holly. Love you."

But there was no return proclamation of affection, which again made him wonder just how much this crash had knocked her around.

He left the room, walked down the corridor slowly, nearly bumping into her Calgary coach as he rounded a corner.

"Still here?" Coach Mathieson said, eyebrows pushing to his hairline. "How is she?"

"Yeah, she's not quite herself. Keeps saying she's fine, talks about getting straight back into things, and thinks she's returning to Calgary tomorrow."

"When she returns depends on what the doctor says."

"I tried to tell her that, but I don't think she heard me. She might pay more attention to you though." Brent managed a wry smile. "I get the feeling that I'm not her favorite person."

"But last week, I thought—"

"I thought that too." But today?

"Maybe a good rest will do you some good too. Give you clearer perspective."

"Maybe," Brent agreed wearily.

But he had a funny feeling things would get worse before they got better.

~

Holly had just finished breakfast when the doctor appeared. He agreed with her that the swelling had decreased substantially. "Let's see how it goes when you move it."

The nurse assisted as Holly gingerly placed the injured leg on the floor. She stood, winced, then quickly sat down on the edge of the mattress.

Someone knocked, and at the call of "Enter" Coach Mathieson moved inside and stood at the end of the bed. "How's she doing?"

"We're just finding out. Now, Holly, I want you to try and walk. Hold my hand."

Holly held onto the doctor and nurse as she took one step, then a second, then another.

"It's not too bad. It hurts, but nothing like yesterday."

The doctor nodded. "Okay. Let's have you walk back."

Holly slowly made her way back to the bed. "It's *so* much better."

As the nurse helped her back onto the bed, the doctor scribbled more notes. "It looks like it may just be a contusion. The impact was so great that the muscle damage probably felt a lot worse than it actually was, because of the swelling."

"So what now?" Coach Mathieson asked.

"We continue icing it. She rests. No unnecessary movement. We take it a day at a time."

Holly took a deep breath. "So, how long do I stay here?"

"Eager to go?" The nurse smiled.

"Yes. Much as I love your company…"

"Well, if you can promise to place no undue strain on it and to keep the ice up and your leg elevated, then we could consider letting you go. But the concussion complicates things."

"How?" Holly asked.

"Ah. That's what we're going to have to monitor very carefully. Most concussions of this magnitude require a minimum of several days' rest in hospital. The CT scan looked okay, but I'd feel more comfortable if we can keep you here another day and complete the neuropsychological and cog-tests. We need to assess that your learning and memory skills are where they ought to be before we can consider releasing you. Even then, you'll need to report to your medical team back home."

Home. Where was that? Wollongong? Calgary? Did she really want to inflict her sorry self on Bree? But how else was she going to get back into training? She sucked in a breath, summoned all her energy. "So I just need to pass some tests and you'll say I'm okay and can go home?"

"Holly, you need to be really cautious with head injuries."

"I promise to be careful."

"Promise not to push it?" Coach Mathieson eyed her with a raised brow.

"Of course."

She'd do anything to get out of here and away from the pain and frustration this part of the world had brought.

Detroit, Michigan

"Hey." Brent pasted pleasantness on his face at the Zoom meeting with the other Bible study members.

"Dude, you made it," Beau said, a retro Arizona poster prominently displayed in the background. "We weren't sure after your last email."

"How's Holly?" Jai asked.

"She's out of hospital, back in Calgary."

"That's good," Dan said.

Brent nodded but couldn't really agree. Was it good she didn't seem to want to talk to him? Bree had told him to be patient, that Holly's headaches meant she barely left her room, but he wondered if that was all. Despite his prayers, he still couldn't shake the feeling that she was pushing him away.

Fortunately, Pastor Josiah Abrahams joined at that moment, and after Brent deflected his queries regarding Holly, the Bible study began.

An hour later his heart still felt a mess, despite the offers of best wishes and prayers. Maybe he should call Bree—Mike was playing away in Edmonton—and see if Holly wanted to talk tonight.

But when he did, Bree sighed and said Holly was asleep—again—and he was left with torturous thoughts of rejection and the feeling that a future with her was not certain at all.

~

Calgary, Canada

"She's not doing too well."

Holly's ears—despite the constant ringing—sharpened at Bree's voice. Did the *she* refer to Holly? Irritation rose. Who was she speaking to? Probably Brent.

The door opened. Holly closed her eyes, pretending to be asleep.

"Holly?" Bree whispered. "It's Brent. Are you awake?"

No. She wasn't awake for him. She was barely awake when her parents talked. Everything hurt so much. She slowed her breathing, feigning sleep.

A week after landing back in Calgary, the intense pressure inside her head sometimes made her wonder if her face might explode. Maybe the doctors had been right and she shouldn't have flown so soon. They'd been right, she'd been wrong. Again. But this pounding in her brain, the facial tightness, the dizziness —it was all she could do to lie on her bed in the darkened guest room. Bree and Mike both insisted she see a doctor, but she had no energy, and she was scared her migraines would worsen, as they did each time light triggered them. How could she get in a car, risk motion sickness and matters getting worse?

"She's asleep again." Bree sighed, her footfalls fading from the room.

The door closed, and Holly breathed freely once more.

She hated this wretchedness. Hated this soul-deep agitation. Hated feeling she was so inferior to the strong athlete she'd always striven to be, and that she'd let everyone down. How could someone win gold at a World Cup, then fall so far so quickly? At times it seemed a bad dream, then reality by way of nausea or neck pain would swamp her and she'd know it was only too true.

Coupled with this was her knee pain. Icing and elevation had helped, but she still couldn't walk properly and needed Bree's help with such humbling things as taking a shower and using the toilet. She barely ate and could feel herself growing weaker, but somehow, she found she didn't care.

What was the point of it all? Why had she spent so long training—for nothing? How could she get so close to her dream only to see it slip through her fingers? Her life was a joke. A cruel joke. She'd be better off giving up, letting someone else make the most of the opportunities she'd squandered.

A light tap came at the door. "Holls? Brent insists on talking to you."

Holly bit back a sigh. The man was so persistent. Too persistent. She cracked open an eye, mumbled a thanks, reached for the phone, and propped it nearby so she could lie and listen and talk without holding it to her ear.

"Holly?"

Despite everything, his voice still held the power to soothe.

"Holly, are you there? You okay?"

Oh. Right. Should talk to him. "Yes," she rasped.

"Thank goodness. I was wondering what was going on, seeing as you haven't answered any of my calls."

Or his FaceTime requests. Or his texts. Or emails. Moisture lined her eyelids. She was a horrible girlfriend. A horrible person. She should never have allowed herself to get swept up in emotion and be distracted by this man. He'd be better off without her.

He gave a hoarse chuckle. "Although, I don't know if you *not* talking to me on these calls makes it any better." A beat. "Holly? What's going on?"

What could she say? "Nothing." Quite literally. She was banned from training, banned from books and TV, banned from socializing. Banned from life, it seemed. Not that she cared. She was too tired to care. "How are you?"

He exhaled. "We had a game last night against the Leafs. Played against Dan—remember my friend from the hockey Bible study? Went to shootout, so that was fun."

"Did you"—what was the word again? That's right—"score?"

"Game winner."

She heard the pride in his voice. "Well done, you."

"Thanks. So, Holly—"

"Who next?" She scratched her fingers, which had broken out in eczema again.

"Who do we play next?"

She nodded.

"Holls? Are you still there? Are you okay?"

"Yes." Why did he keep asking that? If he asked again, she'd end the call.

"We're in Nashville."

"And who will you play?"

A beat. "Nashville, Holly. We'll play Nashville."

"That'll be nice."

"Yeah." His voice sounded puzzled.

Too tired. Talking was exhausting. Thinking drained her brain. She shifted to her side, careful to make allowances for her bruised knee, and listened. His voice sounded so far away.

"Holly? Sweetheart, are you listening?"

No.

"Are you still there? You okay?"

She'd warned him. She yawned and pushed the phone off the bed. Couldn't do this anymore.

~

B*rent* *ended* *the* *call*, staring at the phone in frustration. Something was seriously wrong. It was like talking to a zombie. Was it the meds or simply her injury? He didn't want to take it personally, but it almost felt like she didn't want to speak to him.

But what could he do? Ever since the accident, he'd felt her slowly drifting away, like she was caught in concussion's riptide, being pulled away from his world. Were his expectations unrealistic? How could he be supportive when she refused to admit she needed help?

He texted Mike, who called him back straightaway. "Man, am I glad to talk to you."

"What's up?" Mike asked.

"What else?"

Mike's sigh spoke volumes. "I wish it was better news, but she's still a mess."

"We were talking, and…Mike, she wasn't making sense. Has Bree spoken to her coach yet?"

"Wait while I go find her. We'll put you on speaker. Give me a sec."

A minute later, Bree's voice chimed in. "Yo, bro."

"Breanna." He swallowed. "She's not herself."

"That's normal with concussions, remember? Just like the irritability is too."

"Have you spoken with—"

"Coach Mathieson? Yes. He wants to send out a concussion specialist to assess her again, but every time I go into her room she's asleep. And the worse thing is, I can't even be sure she *is* asleep. Sometimes I think she's just faking."

"I've wondered that too," he admitted.

"I know we have to take things slow, but this is really hard."

"Are you coping, Bree?"

"Well, yes. Mostly. She's not doing anything. Doesn't go anywhere. She's not allowed to, anyway. She barely joins us for meals—"

"She's not eating?" Concern throbbed within.

"Oh, Brent. I don't know what to do. Should we call her parents again?"

"Maybe." *Definitely*, a little voice whispered. "Leave that to me."

"I'm just so scared. She's so irritable some days, then seems nearly normal the next. I never know what to expect when I go to her room."

"Get Coach Mathieson to call in ASAP and anyone else he thinks can help. Holly obviously isn't thinking clearly, so we need to think clearly for her."

A short time later he ended the call, plunged his head in his hands, and prayed.

Weariness clutched him. This was so hard, caring from afar. But what else could he do?

Footsteps drew near. "Karlos, we've got practice." Doug tapped on the doorframe.

"Sure. Be there in a moment."

He checked the clock, calculated time zones, jabbed in another number, listened to the dial tones. "Hello, Beth? It's Brent. I think we have a problem."

"Look what Brent sent!"

Holly glanced up as a gigantic blue bear entered the room. Her lips lifted. Her heart didn't.

"I told him the bear is ridiculous, but he thinks it's gonna help Mike Junior grow up strong and brave."

"You're having a boy?" Hurt cramped her chest. Why hadn't Bree told her?

"Holly." Bree placed the bear on the floor and drew closer to the bed. "We told you last week after the ultrasound."

Oh. Didn't remember. The hurt on Bree's face shamed her. Why couldn't she remember? "I'm sorry." Tears welled. "I'm such a terrible friend."

"Holly, no. You're injured. These things take time."

"But I don't have time." Panic reared again, shooting shards of fear into her bloodstream. "I have to get better, get back to training. The Games are so close, and I'm never going to get better in time at the rate I'm going."

"Holly, listen to me. Short track won't last forever, but your brain needs to. You have to take this time and really rest."

"But I can't. I feel so sick, so tired, so awful all the time." Her breath sped. Heat filled her chest. Heart palpitations. Was this a panic attack? She covered her face with her hands and obeyed as Bree encouraged her to calm, to breathe slowly.

"Holly, Coach Mathieson is coming soon."

"Coming where? Here? Why?"

"He's your coach. He has some advice. You need to listen to him."

"No. No, I won't. He'll just tell me to rest too. He doesn't want me to win. He'll want a Canadian girl to—"

"You're being ridiculous," Bree said gently. "Here. Let me help you dress and brush your hair, and we can go downstairs and talk to him."

"I don't want to."

"Shall I ask Mike to carry you downstairs?"

Well, no. "I'll come."

Holly didn't look at the mirror as Bree fussed with clothes

and hair. Hopelessness weighted her, dragging her limping steps to the door.

After a careful descent—to keep dizziness at bay—she made it to the large living room, where a cheery fire crackled in the large stone fireplace. She sank into a seat and awaited her fate.

Ten minutes later, Coach Mathieson arrived, accepting Bree's offer of a cup of coffee. As he and Bree exchanged small talk, he looked at Holly a few times, but he said little to her except a quick greeting and an enquiry about how she was feeling.

So what was the point of this? She scratched her hand. She might as well return upstairs. She would—if she didn't need Bree's assistance.

Finally, the small talk ended, and Coach Mathieson's attention turned fully to her. He asked Bree to stay, and she shifted to the couch beside Holly, her presence comforting.

"So, Holly, I know you said you were fine before, but I really need you to be honest. How are you doing, really?"

She pressed her lips together, willed the tears away. They insisted on appearing anyway. Great. With Bree sitting beside her, she couldn't lie—or at least not own the truth.

"My head still hurts," she admitted.

"All the time?" he questioned.

"Yes. Things seem foggy still. But I do feel I'm improving."

"How?" He shifted on the lounge. "What measures do you assess your improvement on?"

Why was he using such big words? She glanced at Bree, who studied her with a frown.

"Holls." Bree captured her hand. "Honey, I'm sorry, but you're not getting better." Her smile held sympathy, then she turned to Coach Mathieson. "She's still vague, forgets things, gets cranky, is a little slow at understanding."

Holly cringed. She sounded like a—

"That's normal," he said. "And it's normal to find that frustrating, Holly. You have to be kind to yourself."

"But Vancouver is so soon! I have to train. I have to do short track. It's who I am."

"You're not what you do, Holly," Bree protested.

Yes, she was, she thought stubbornly.

Her coach leaned forward. "Holly, I know you always want to be the first one at training and the last to leave. I know you're committed to this sport, and you've seen that dedication pay off. But now is not the time to push."

"But—"

"Holly, muscle memory never degrades. You can afford to take time off and be assured that when you return to training, your body will know what to do. But more important than that is getting your motivation, your zest back. And that won't happen by pushing too hard too soon. Look, I think it's fair to say that these next few weeks will be hard, but trust me. In the long run, you'll be okay."

Emotion cinched her throat, leaked from her eyes. Bree handed her a tissue box, and Holly blew her nose. "So you're saying I have to stay here and rest?"

He nodded.

How could she rest with all these questions hovering over her? "When will I know I'm better?"

"You'll know. But the key is rest. Resting your body, resting your brain from too much stimuli, and also resting your heart and mind."

"But I can't! I'm worried about what this means. What if I don't recover for the Games? I'll be too old in four years' time. What if this continues and I can't skate again? It makes all these years of training"—and her life—"seem like a giant waste of time."

"You have a World Cup, Holly. That's not exactly wasted."

"Yes, but I want more. I want to *win*."

"Why?"

To prove herself. To be enough. She reared back at thoughts she couldn't admit aloud. "I don't know. Ask anyone. Why do Mike or Brent want to win each game? Why do they push to win the Stanley Cup? It's human nature, isn't it?"

"I know Mike and Brent have fun along the way," Bree said slowly. "Do you have fun, Holls?"

Sometimes. But if she was really honest, she hadn't for a long while. This sport seemed to have overtaken her life, consuming her, obsessing her thoughts, her time, her body, her decisions. Worry about her times, worry about her weight, worry about money and travel and constant comparison to others. When had she lost the joy of flying on the ice? When had she allowed short track to define her? Emotion swelled, forcing her to wipe at her eyes.

"Holly," Coach Mathieson continued, "if all you have is your sport, then you're always thinking about what you're doing next, not about what you're doing now. That just leads to anxiety and stress about the future."

Like her questions about a future with Brent and what choices she'd need to make about kids and career. Ugh. She scratched her broken skin. This conversation was making her head hurt even more.

"Holly, let this be a time to rediscover what you love and focus on that. What you love, who you love."

She felt the weight of Bree's gaze.

"Short track will still be there in a few weeks, in a few months, however long it takes," he continued. "But *you* need to be back. One hundred percent healthy physically, mentally, and emotionally. You know your best performances come when those things are in balance, so do what it takes to get it sorted, okay?"

She nodded. Winced. Managed a small smile.

He soon left. Bree returned from seeing him off and held her hands. "Holls, I'm sorry if that was hard to hear. But it makes sense."

"It just feels so wasteful and self-indulgent to lie about on a couch all day."

"You need this time, your brain and body need this time to rest. Be refreshed. Find the Holly that we all know and love again."

"I've been such a pain, haven't I?"

"You've been *in* pain. And we love you and want your best."

Holly's vision blurred again, but this time from emotion. She hugged Bree in a gentle clasp. "You've been so patient with me. You and Mike. And Brent."

"He loves you, Holly."

And he'd proven it time and time again. Tears filled her eyes and spilled.

CHAPTER 23

Detroit, Michigan

Hi everyone,
Sorry this is so short, but I can't use screens for too long other-
wise my headaches get worse. Just wanted to say sorry for
letting you all down and a big thank you for your prayers. I'm
slowly getting better, knee is improving, but they've advised me
not to resume proper training until after Christmas and to rest
and spend time on things I love. The doctors aren't sure that I'll
be ready for Vancouver, so I really need a miracle. It's really
hard to go from feeling like a hero to feeling like a zero, but I'm
trying to trust God, that He still has good plans for me.
Love, Holly

Brent reread Holly's email, his heart tipping and turning with what she'd left unsaid. *Spend time on things I love.* Did the fact she barely spent any time with him mean she didn't love him? He wished he knew where he stood with her. He certainly wasn't feeling much in the way of love. Try dismissed. Unheeded. Every phone call or FaceTime invitation either too short or ignored. He was trying to be understanding, but it was so hard sometimes, walking this tightrope between hope and dread.

He put away his phone. He needed to focus on training. But even on the ice, his turbulent emotions spilled over. They were practicing shooting, and some of Brent's slapshots had garnered attention.

Erik chuckled. "Karlsson, it's not Vancouver yet."

Sure wasn't. Brent gritted his teeth and struck again. Straight to the back of the net. He barreled a bucket load of pucks. Goal, goal, goal, rebound, goal, rebound, goal, goal.

"No selectors here today, dude."

Brent skated around Alex, ignoring him as he upended a fresh bucket and repeated the exercise. Goal, goal, rebound, goal, goal, rebound, miss, goal.

He finally skated over to where Doug stood by the bench. His line mate looked at him with a frown.

"Karlos, you okay?" Doug's eyes held concern. Brent turned away to watch the next forward practice shots. "You look like your dog's died."

"Don't have a dog, man."

"Oh." Doug skated in front of him, in his face as usual. "So, is it Holly? How is she?"

"Improving." That's what her email said. Whether or not it was true, well, who knew? Why did she have energy to write a group email but couldn't be bothered talking to him?

Doug turned to the others. "Did you guys ever see Wonder-girl fall?"

Brent closed his eyes. *God, give me patience.* "Dude, don't."

Doug skated off, soon returning, iPad in hand. "Watch this."

He settled the iPad on top of the bench, pressed play, and

footage from the Marquette meet came up. Why Doug insisted on watching this was a mystery. He had to be a sadist, for sure.

Despite having seen this footage several times, Brent's stomach still twisted in knots, knowing it was his Holly out there. It was like watching a horror movie, where you knew something awful was going to happen but couldn't drag your eyes away.

"That girl is so fine!"

Brent raised an eyebrow.

Doug held his hands up. "The Russian, not Holly. Not that Holly isn't smokin' hot—"

"Don't make me come and hurt you." It was a promise. His fist had "accidentally" connected with Doug's jaw the one time Brent had heard him make a comment about Holly and the other girls wearing that Lycra. Doug had apologized and not done it again. Not that Brent had heard, anyway.

Brent skated to the net, collecting pucks, wishing he could slapshot Doug's iPad away. But when he heard the scream, his eyes swung back, his heart clenching as he watched Holly topple to the ground and spin on the ice only to slam into the blue padding and lie ominously still. "Dude, why are you showing this?"

"She's still not moving." Erik frowned and glanced over at Brent.

Brent nodded. "She was unconscious for nearly a minute."

"Wow."

The video continued as the camera zoomed in on Holly, lying on her side, still immobile on the ice but now surrounded by a bunch of guys in different team uniforms. Each time Brent saw the way they touched her, he felt this bizarre mix of jealousy and relief that they'd been there to help. His stomach churned. He'd read some of the comments from others who'd watched this footage. There were some really sick individuals out there, and some others he'd like to hunt down in a dark alley and throttle until they—

He let out a deep breath. *Sorry, God.*

Alex swore and peered closer at the screen. "That looks bad."

"Yeah." Doug glanced at Brent and picked up his iPad. "She's getting better now, right?"

Was she? Or was she pretending? Like she'd apparently pretended to be asleep instead of talking to him…

"Sorry, man," Erik said. "Wasn't she going to compete in Vancouver?"

"Was. It's unlikely now." Brent glanced away, studying the advertising lining the far end of the rink. Poor Holly. His emotions were all over the place; he couldn't imagine how she was feeling. To have trained so hard for so many years to simply crash and suddenly have your dreams savaged? God forgive him for taking things so personally. "It'd take a miracle to recover in time, and she'd need time to get back into competition form. But you never know."

"Miracles happen, though, don't they?" Doug said, skating backwards.

"Yep."

Erik nodded. "It's a miracle Brent has put up with you this long, Dougie."

Brent summoned a laugh, but caught the flash of hurt on Doug's face. He skated to his side, then punched his shoulder. "Actually, he might be a pain, but he's also there when you need him, like when I first found out about Holly's accident." He turned to face him. "Thanks again, man."

"Dude, I'm choking up here."

"As long as you don't choke in our next game," he razzed.

Erik nodded. "Yeah. Some people here might have their shooting under control, but others"—he glanced at Alex —"could probably work a little more. Come on. Get back to it."

An hour later, Brent could finally draw out his phone again. Saw he had a missed call.

His shoulders tensed. He nodded goodbye and walked to his car, glad to have privacy in which to listen.

"Hi. It's me. I...I'm really sorry for how I've treated you. Can we talk soon? Please?"

Holly's voice sounded subdued, even a little shaky. He went to press redial, then stopped. He was tired and still needed more time to get his churning thoughts and attitude adjusted, to ensure whatever he said wouldn't come from a place of rejection and hurt. For the next twenty minutes as he drove home, he prayed, pleading for wisdom. He was still bombarding the gates of heaven while he walked up the tiled steps and inside his front door.

He ceased pleading and just stood, letting the quiet of the house surround him. Without the rush of emotions or words, at last he could hear wisdom: *Don't let the sun go down while you are still angry.* He hadn't exactly been angry. More disappointed, frustrated, and feeling unwanted.

But now, in the stillness, he felt God's peace fill him, and he knew a deep rush of tenderness for the woman who had burrowed inside his heart like nobody else had. Like nobody else ever could.

He glanced at the clock. Calgary was two hours behind Detroit. She should still be up. It was definitely worth heeding that verse from Ephesians and speaking with Holly now, before his stupid emotions doubled back to offense and rejection. He dialed her number.

"Holly?"

"Brent. Hi."

Just the sound of her voice spiked longing to be with her. "Hey, can you FaceTime? I'd really like to see you."

A beat. "Uh, sure."

She sounded distant, but maybe that was the connection. It

didn't take long before he was seeing her in her room that looked as messy as the last time they'd spoken like this. She wore a green sweater and, judging from the damp hair, had recently showered. She offered a small smile. "Hi again."

"Hi, sweetheart. How are you feeling?"

"Not great. My head still hurts, especially when I look at screens. It's why I could only send a group email earlier. I felt nauseous, so I didn't reply to you. I'm really sorry."

"Hey, it's okay." It was now, anyway. "Were you avoiding me?"

"You. Everyone. But Coach Mathieson came and saw me. Told me I needed to rest, that short track will always be there. It helped. A bit."

"I'm glad."

She propped her head in one hand. She still looked so weary.

"In your email you mentioned feeling like you let us down. You haven't let anyone down," he assured her. "It was an accident. Stuff happens."

"Maybe. But I still feel that way. It's hard dealing with other people's expectations and not taking it personally."

"You mean like Coach Chan?"

She nodded. Winced.

"You're not your performance, Holly." At her shrug he persisted. "People care for you, not for how well you do."

She pressed her lips together, her expression unconvinced. He swallowed a sigh. Looked like God was going to have to convince her of that truth.

"So, you mentioned spending time on things you love. What kind of things?"

"Well, it's hard to concentrate on anything for long. Movies move too quick and make me feel sick. I try to do puzzles, but they make my brain hurt. I saw a doctor who said it's best I don't fly yet, so I can't travel to see you." She looked down, a chunk of hair falling to hide her face, but not before he saw her blinking rapidly, as moisture slid down her cheek.

"Holly?"

She put her face in her hands.

"Holls, don't cry. It's okay."

"It's not okay," she whispered. "I feel awful, and I...I know I've treated you badly, and it's so hard to not feel like myself anymore, to not even like myself anymore." She wiped underneath her eyes. "I feel so weak, and I hate this. I *hate* not knowing if I can ever skate again. I hate thinking I've missed my chance to compete at the Games. I hate thinking I've wasted my life on something that might be over. For years I've thought skating was my life, and now that it's gone, it's really scary."

His heart throbbed with compassion. "Holly, honey—"

"And I *hate* how I've treated you. I'm such a horrible person. I'm so sorry. Please forgive me."

"Of course I forgive you."

"I don't deserve it," she said with a sob. "But I want you to know I *do* love you. Even though I mightn't always show it, I love you, Brent."

His heart eased. *Thank You, God.* "And I love you." His lips pushed to one side. "I can't help wishing you were closer so I could help should something happen, even if it's just to hold your hand. I guess I need to trust God more and worry less."

"You and me both."

"We can trust Him. And regardless of the Games, God has good plans for you, Holly."

"For both of us," she whispered.

Her words arrowed into his heart. He needed to remember that.

Seconds ticked away. Her lips lifted. She wiped her cheeks and pushed her chin into her hands. "I need to go soon. But, Brent, thank you. Thanks for being so patient with me. I know I haven't dealt with things as well as I could've." She sighed.

"Short track is such an individual thing—me against the world, my choices that affect the outcome of my race. For the last few years, I've really only had to consider my career and not think too much about anyone else. So I'm sorry you bore the brunt of that."

"It's okay," he assured her.

"These past few weeks have been"—her voice wobbled—"some of the toughest of my life. I've felt so sick, and anxious and stressed too."

"But you can take some time to relax now."

"I'm going to try, anyway."

"Try *really* hard at relaxing, okay?"

She chuckled. Winced. "I need to go."

"Love you, Holly."

"Love you, too. G'night."

The screen went dark, but his heart was the lightest it had been since Montreal.

~

Calgary, Canada
December

"Darling."

Holly held tight, the fragrance and strength ones she'd known all her life. "I'm so glad you're here."

"Brent refused to take no for an answer," her mother murmured. "He's a good man, Holl."

"I know." Paying for her mum's flight to Calgary so she could stay with Holly until Christmas was yet more evidence of his kindness and generosity.

Her mother released her, looked at her seriously. "How are you doing? Really?"

Holly sank into the couch, glanced at the framed black-and-white photograph of Bree and Mike above the fireplace. "I'm getting better. Really, I am. The headaches are clearing, my brain isn't as foggy anymore, and the ringing in my ears has stopped."

"And your knee?"

Holly tugged up the bottom hem of her velvet track pants—or "deluxe lounge wear," as Bree called it. "It's lost most of the awful green-and-yellow blackness from before but is still sensitive to touch. But at least I'm cleared for walking and some light exercise now."

Last week's appointment had gone better than expected. According to the physiotherapist, Holly might have full range of movement by Christmas.

"That's encouraging."

"Oh, Mum, you've no idea."

"I have some idea." Her mother smiled. "And is there any word yet on what this means for Vancouver?"

A sigh escaped. "I'm not sure I even want to know if the answer is no. I've qualified, but I'll need medical clearance regarding the concussion, and that means passing a bunch more tests in a few weeks' time."

Her mother grasped her hand. "I've been thinking about this, Holly, as I've been praying for you."

She'd sensed those prayers in recent weeks, seen the times when the fog would lift and she could suddenly think clearly again. In those moments, she was sure someone had just prayed.

"Holly, I have to ask, is competing at Vancouver for short track your ultimate goal?"

"Well, not my ultimate. But it's why I've been training for so long."

"So what *is* your ultimate goal? If short track was not in your life, what would you be doing?"

Studying again. Spending time with Brent. Marriage, one

day. Kids? She gulped. "Are you saying I shouldn't go to Vancouver? I feel like short track is what I was born to do."

"Holly." Her mum held her hands. "You are not what you do. You are so much more than just your skating."

Holly bit her lip. Hadn't Bree said this? Brent too?

"As good as you are, no one can remain competitive forever. Eventually, you'll age out and transition to something new. I just want to make sure you keep the bigger picture in mind. Holly, I know you're good at this, but do you really think God is more interested in your success or in the state of your heart?" Her mother lifted Holly's hand, touched the broken skin. "I don't think God wants us stressed and anxious all the time. And you've been that for many years now, haven't you?"

Holly ducked her head.

"*You* are enough, Holly. Regardless of short track, you *are* enough. Your life, your opportunities are in God's hands. You can work hard to be the best, but for how long? The nature of competition is that, sooner or later, there will always be someone who gets a better time." Her mother smoothed a hand down Holly's cheek. "Darling, you've always been a winner in our eyes. Your family loves you. Brent loves you. Bree, Jess, so many others. Take the pressure off, and let God be your true measure of success."

Let God be her true measure of success? Holly exhaled. *Help me.*

HOLLY SLOWLY CUT the special paper she'd bought in Montreal. This was to be a special card, so it needed to be perfect. Another cut, then two folds. There. One side down. Three to go.

"Holly?"

She glanced up at her mother. "It's getting there."

"I think she'll love it."

"I hope so. She's a special part of his life, and it'll be nice to be there."

Her mother nodded. Her arrival a week ago might have added to Bree's houseguests, but her presence, her conversations, had gone a long way to helping Holly feel greater peace. How Mum had scored this much time off work was still a mystery, but each day Mum was here, each day Holly spent resting, listening to music, getting back to the paper crafts she used to do, seemed to settle her spirit and add ease to her heart.

Bible reading had helped too. She'd found encouragement in Psalms, the enforced time of quiet allowing for meditation on the promises found there. To not just skim but soak in God's word, to listen as truth was imparted into her life.

Mum's words had sunk deep. How long had Holly put her pride in being seen to be successful? How long had she put her own interests above God? Yet time and again, this had come at the cost of her peace of mind, her relationships, her health. Striving in her own strength had only shown how weak she truly was, and she'd spent her rest time the afternoon after the conversation with her mother in her room, not resting but repenting and releasing, asking God to restore her relationship with Him. Confessing her selfishness. Realizing that she needed to seek first God's kingdom above her own desires. The peace from that encounter had soaked in as the weight lifted, false expectations crumbled, and she came to a fresh understanding that her identity, for so long entwined with her performance, was based not on what she did but who she was. *Whose* she was.

She didn't live for skating. She lived for God. She was God's child, loved by Him no matter what. And whatever happened in her future—Vancouver, skating, Brent—she had deep assurance that God would be with her, continue to help her. That she would learn more of her value within the promise of His love.

Prayers of *help me do my best* had become *help me live for You,* a reminder to stay upward focused, to remember God's purposes were bigger than her feelings or success. She was enough because she was God's child. Because of what Jesus had done, Holly had nothing to prove. She was loved. She had assurance. She now knew peace.

"Oh, I love this song. It's by one of the singers from that group Heartsong Collective." Bree turned up the sound system, the room filling with a song that spoke of love waiting. The music, a delicate strum of guitars and an ethereal husky voice, led Holly to sink back against the cushions and close her eyes.

The words so closely followed her relationship with Brent. He'd been waiting, so patiently waiting for her, his actions going far to hold back the dark of pain and regret. She could see now where she'd taken him for granted, allowed her hopes and plans to override his. All this striving, this focus, had eroded who she was. The fact he was so patient, remained patient still in spite of his many games and road trips and training sessions, yet still found time to connect with her...

She found her phone, texted him. Christmas couldn't come soon enough.

Toronto, Canada
Christmas Eve

"That's lovely, dear," Granny V said, holding the birthday card Holly had labored over. "You are very talented, aren't you?"

Holly shrugged modestly, smiling as the elderly lady unwrapped the jigsaw puzzle. "Oh, this looks fun. Shall we?"

The jigsaw puzzle, an ornate decoupage-style picture, proved an enjoyable way to spend time with this lady who was fast becoming like her own grandmother. Granny V was sweet, sincere, yet holding that spark of fun Holly was slowly rediscovering in herself.

The offer from Pam and Rob to host Holly's entire family for Christmas had proven their generous natures yet again. "It's no trouble at all, Beth," Pam had assured Holly's mum. "Holly shouldn't fly for long, so going home to Australia was out of the question. And seeing you were already here, well, it makes sense if you can all come and enjoy a white Christmas."

So, after a doctor's consult and careful preparations, Holly and her mum had taken the four-hour flight and arrived a few days ago, leaving Bree and Mike to themselves—something she was sure they were thankful for—until after Mike's game on the twenty-third, when they would join them in Toronto. Dad and Ben had arrived yesterday—Uncle Richard choosing to remain in New Zealand—and Holly had reveled in their hugs, assuring them she truly did feel symptom free.

"You look so much happier too, darl," her father had said.

"I am."

She no longer had the angsty worry of wondering if she'd ever be good enough. If she passed her tests next week and could compete in Vancouver, well and good. If she couldn't, well, that was something to think about another day. She was trying to live each day more fully present, choosing thankfulness instead of worry, that desperate drive to succeed no longer steering her world. She was trying—as much as possible—to release her worries to God. Minute by minute, hour by hour.

"Holly?"

"Oh, sorry, Granny Violet. I lost my train of thought."

Her mother looked up with a faint frown. Holly shook her head and smiled. Returned her attention to the puzzle. "I think that piece goes...here."

She snapped it in, pleased with herself for finding the patience to master this type of activity. Once upon a time she'd had so little, too busy focused on the short track to her goals. She'd learned a lot in recent weeks.

The door rattled. "Oh, I wonder who it is," Pam said.

Holly's heartbeat escalated. Was it him?

The door opened. "We're here!" Bree walked in, Mike at her side holding small bags.

Her shoulders dropping, Holly smiled from her spot on the

floor. Bree looked so happy. These past days with no houseguests had been a welcome reprieve, if the glow on her cheeks
was any sign.

"Hey, Holl." Bree squeezed Holly's hands after Bree's belly
bump was exclaimed over by Pam and Granny V. "Is Brent here
yet?"

"Not yet."

"He'll be here soon."

"I know." Holly looked past Bree to Mike. "Sorry about the
Canucks."

"At least shootouts mean we get one point."

Holly introduced her father and brother, and soon they were
chatting about—what else?—sports.

She returned to the puzzle, glad her concentration now
allowed for this. Only a few more pieces remained, then the
picture would be complete. She couldn't wait to see Brent—to
hold him, to kiss him. Five weeks since Marquette, and so much
to make up for.

She exhaled. He'd be here soon. *Release the worry. Trust God.*
Her heart eased. He'd be here soon enough.

The scent of roasting dinner drifted from the kitchen with a
further trace of spice and sugar. The Karlssons celebrated
Christmas on Christmas Eve, and she was looking forward to
the differing traditions. She'd helped Pam make gingerbread
yesterday, helped Mum make a pavlova this morning, and set
the table—basic assignments that suggested her domestic skills
needed more work. Oh well.

Another piece snapped in. *Lord, thank You for the chance to be
here. Thank You for all Your goodness. Thank You for—*

The door rattled. Opened. She looked up. Heart thrilling, she
propelled to her feet, then raced over, leaping over a small
ottoman to jump into his arms.

～

Holly slammed into Brent's chest, and he staggered back a pace. Dropped his bag. Clutched Holly more tightly. Smiled at the wide eyes and dropped jaws. "Excuse us."

He carried Holly, her arms around his neck and her legs koala-hugging him, and moved to the den. She'd pressed her face into his neck, and the feel of her, the scent of her, she was home to him.

"Hey, sweetheart." He gently disentangled her. "It's so good to see you."

"It's so wonderful to see *you*," she said, the light in her face, the peace in her eyes something he'd never seen before. Then she kissed him.

All the questions, all the doubts, were answered in that kiss. Her mouth was soft yet gently insistent, igniting his passion as he hungrily kissed her back. Her lips melding with his, her body melting against his—this was perfection. This was bliss.

"I missed you," she whispered against his jaw a short time later.

"Oh, sweetheart." He drew her to the small couch and sat with her legs across his knees, his arm cradling her shoulders, his other hand touching her cheek. She looked so good—vibrant, luminous even. After weeks apart, he couldn't stop touching her face or tangling his fingers in the silk of her hair.

"I'm so happy to see you."

"Ditto, Holls." He pressed another kiss to her mouth, then pulled back, smiling as she slowly opened her eyes and sighed. "You look happier."

"I feel so much more content."

"I'm glad." He kissed her hand. "So, what's changed?"

Her lips pulled to one side. "I realized you were right. Coach Mathieson, Mike and Bree, Mum—you've all been right. I need to have the big picture in mind, because short track won't last forever. And I can't let my short track goals take the place of seeking God. All this time, I've been wanting to prove myself

when God has been saying 'just trust Me.' So I've released it all
to Him. I'm trying to do my best to live more in each moment
instead of with my worries about the future. And knowing this,
really knowing this here"—she touched her chest—"and not just
here"—she touched her brow—"I feel so much happier, so much
more at peace."

"You've been working so hard for so long it's natural to get
caught up in things."

"And I allowed myself to get a little too caught up. I'm sorry."
She snuggled closer. "I never meant to do or say anything to
hurt you."

She pressed a kiss to his jaw. His heart stuttered. "So we're
all good?" he murmured, the faintest question in his voice.

"Absolutely." Another kiss. Man, he'd never tire of her
displays of affection. "God is all good. And we're along for the
ride."

~

HOLLY GLANCED around the Karlsson's fully extended dining
table, the faces included her favorites in all the world: her
parents on one side, Brent on the other, and Ben sitting opposite near Bree and Mike. The rest of the table was filled with a
klatch of Karlsson relatives, with Brent's parents sitting at
opposite ends. The turkey was delicious and so were the sides,
but as the conversation flowed, Holly took a moment to just
breathe. The past thirty-six hours held a collection of golden
moments that shone as brightly as the precious German heir-
loom ornaments on the Karlssons' Christmas tree.

At the exchange of gifts last night, the highlight for Holly
had been a mysteriously large, oddly shaped parcel from Brent.
He'd merely grinned, so she'd torn off the gold paper to find a
bubble-wrapped cardboard box, inside which she'd discovered
a Royal Albert teacup—an exact replica of the one broken six

months ago. Tears had rushed to her eyes at his thoughtfulness.

Unwrapping the rest had revealed her favorite Belgian chocolates and an exquisite painting of the Japanese garden she'd admired so much in Montreal. Emotion had clogged her throat. It was the perfect reminder of that perfect day in Montreal.

Then had come time spent together last night holding hands, kissing, cuddling, sharing about the moments of the past few weeks. As Holly had shared, Brent's attention absorbing her in like she uttered diamonds, she'd known an increasing certainty: there was nowhere else she'd rather be, nobody's hand she'd rather hold. Her heart had swelled, seemed to shift a degree closer to certainty regarding the future should he ever speak the words.

They'd attended the Christmas service this morning, filled with joy and hope as they sang side by side about the birth of their Savior. She sighed happily. Was there any better time of year than Christmas?

Brent turned from where he and Mike had been discussing the best snowboarding options for Ben when he visited B.C. next month. "You doing okay?" he whispered, his fingers tangling with hers under the table.

She nodded. His eyes, fringed by those gorgeous black lashes, were slate blue today, like his shirt. His grin held such warmth and tenderness she couldn't help but smile back. Whatever happened with the Games, she knew a confidence deep within that God was sorting her future. "Everything's perfect."

He squeezed her hand under the table.

"Perfect, huh?" Mike eyed Brent, brow lifting. "Things would be a little more perfect if you knew for sure about Canada's team selections, eh, Brent?"

"I'm trying not to think about it," Brent confessed.

"Only five days to go," Bree said in a sing-song voice. "Five days to go, and then you'll know…"

Brent rolled his eyes, and Holly squeezed his hand again. "I'm sure you'll make it. And help Canada win."

Mike's chuckle filled the room. "Can you imagine the devastation if we don't?"

The table quietened as every male Canadian bowed his head slightly, as if praying God would spare them from such a fate.

"Amen." Bree laughed and turned to Holly's parents. "So, are you looking forward to seeing Detroit?"

Holly settled back in her seat, listening as Brent filled them in on the glorious plan he'd mentioned to her weeks ago. Even though Brent had to leave soon for his flight home, this parting didn't hold the usual ache. She smiled. In five days, she'd be in Detroit too.

His phone buzzed a message. Brent tugged it out of his pocket, smiled at the sender's name, and excused himself from the Ritz-Carlton function room the Wings had secured for the latest round of video game challenge loosely disguised as team building purposes. He found a seat in a small alcove and tapped open the full message.

Hi Brent. Sorry about the loss tonight—great game by you though! Just want you to know I'm thinking of you and praying for you. God has good plans for you—whatever happens tomorrow morning!
I love you heaps, Holly

Brent smiled. He'd received quite a few encouraging texts and emails over the past days as the upcoming Canadian team announcement drew closer. He tapped out a reply.

Her reply flashed up a minute later.

Sweet dreams? He'd dream about Holly tonight for sure—if the nerves boiling in his stomach let him sleep at all. He stood and slowly made his way up to his room.

Early morning clamor. Doug mumbled from the bed opposite. "That'll be for you." Blinking in the darkness, Brent fumbled for his phone. "Hello?"

"Brent Karlsson?"

"Yeah." He rubbed sleep from his eyes as his heartbeat picked up pace.

"Brent, this is the assistant manager of the Canadian hockey team."

Doug had turned on his light. Brent's heart began galloping. *Lord, help me cope—*

"Brent, congratulations. You're in the team."

"Really?" He sat up. "You're sure?" He winced. Duh. How dumb did he sound?

A chuckle. "You're not the first to ask. But yes, we're sure."

"Thanks, that's awesome!"

Doug sat on the edge of his bed and fist pumped the air, a

wide grin on his face that probably matched the silly one Brent could feel on his own.

They discussed a few more details, then, "Brent, people will be in touch. Have a good day."

"You too. Thanks again."

He slowly placed his phone back on the bedside table, his heart dancing to some crazy rhythm. *Thank You, God! Thank You—*

"Dude, that's totally awesome!" Doug leapt off the bed to give him a bear hug. "Karlsson's going to Vancouver, baby! Hooyah!"

It was a good thing this hotel went to so much trouble to soundproof their rooms, the way Doug was carrying on. "Okay, okay. I gotta make some calls."

The rest of the day was a buzz of conversations as he spoke with his folks, Holly, Bree and Mike, and a host of others who'd done so much to support him and his career. Excitement pulsed through his body as he soon found out who else from the Wings was going to B.C. in February: their captain Erik was the other Canadian member, there was a Swedish representative, and a couple of guys who'd play for Slovakia. He watched the announcement on TV and found out who else had made the team. Seriously? It was such an honor to even be mentioned in the same breath as these guys, let alone play with them and represent his country.

That afternoon, when they arrived back in Detroit, the Vancouver-bound players were given a big welcome from some waiting fans. Autographs, photos, media interviews, some business at the club, then he was finally free to head home and tumble into bed. But the excitement continued to hum through his body. He was going to compete at the Winter Games! And tomorrow, Holly and her family were coming to watch the game against Colorado and attend the Wings' New Year's Eve party. He rolled over to his side and closed his eyes. And smiled.

CHAPTER 25

Detroit, Michigan
New Year's Eve

"Hey, beautiful." Brent gave Holly a slightly less exuberant hug and kiss than he would have had her parents and brother not been watching. He led them inside his house, down the hall to the kitchen, made coffees and teas, and asked about their past few days. "How was the drive down?"

"Niagara Falls was spectacular. So much snow and ice, the frozen trees. Nothing like what we'd see back home this time of year."

"We might not have Aussie-type beaches, but there are some cool things nearby. There are lots of lakes in Michigan."

"How many with waves?" Holly raised her eyebrows.

"Yeah, nothing Wollongong-worthy. Might need to go back to Hawaii one day."

Her eyes widened, her cheeks pink as she quickly glanced at her parents. He smiled.

This wasn't exactly the time to talk futures, but at Christmas he'd felt something click into place. And the sight of Holly now, sitting inside his house, relaxed, holding a cup of tea, dared the whispers of his heart to speak a little louder.

He showed them through his house, pointing out the features he'd renovated—the modern kitchen and bathrooms, the multi-paned glass, the refinished floors. He hurried through the upstairs bedrooms, but not before he saw Holly sneak a longer look at the main. His heart double-thumped.

"I love the yard," Holly said as they overlooked the stone patio, sheltered by snow-capped trees.

"The colors are spectacular in fall."

His hand found hers and gave a squeeze. Would she consider living here one day? He glanced at her parents, suddenly glad he didn't have the mansion-style house some of his teammates preferred. John's gaze met his. He gave a small nod, and Brent's chest eased. Maybe this would have a way of working out.

After a late lunch together, he gave the Traverses some tourist tips for an afternoon downtown after they checked in to their hotel while he disappeared to prepare for the game.

Several hours later, he met Holly at Little Caesar's Arena in the room reserved for players' families and friends. He gave her a hug. "You got your seats okay?"

She nodded, eyes wide. "They're fantastic, right down near the glass. Thanks."

Holly was in the middle of sharing about their afternoon when Doug appeared. "Holly, how's it going? Nice to see you again."

"You too. It's good to finally be here to see a game."

"Brent's been pining." Doug smirked. "Every night we're away it's 'Holly this' or 'Holly that.' He goes to sleep crying." He shook his head. "It's getting sad, man."

Brent punched Doug—hard—on the arm. "Get lost."

Holly laughed. "Well, while that's good to know, I should

probably let you two go do your male bonding thing." She leaned forward and kissed Brent lightly on the lips. "Play well!"

"Do I get one too?"

She rolled her eyes, smiled a *bye, Doug*, and disappeared.

"Wow." Doug exhaled. "Hate to see you go, love to watch you leave."

Brent punched Doug again—harder—but yeah, wow. Holly looked way too good in her jeans, boots, and new red jersey with #25 on the back, all topped off by that amazing smile.

He exhaled. "Come on. We've got a game to play."

Holly grinned at her mother, who was covering her ears with her hands. "C'mon, Mum, it's supposed to be fun."

Ben looked around the packed arena with a huge grin. "There must be thousands here."

Holly nodded, her gaze on the ceiling, where numerous banners hung proclaiming the Wings' storied history. "Brent says they can get over twenty thousand people if you include standing room."

He shook his head. "Amazing."

Holly's heart increased its pace to match the quickened music tempo. It was amazing all right. It was amazing to actually be here, having only seen games in Detroit on TV or via her computer. It was amazing that she was here as Brent's girlfriend. Earlier, he'd introduced her to some of the other girlfriends and wives, some of whom looked like Barbie wannabes even if they had proven nice and polite. She looked down at her outfit. Was she supposed to dress up more? At lunch, Brent had given them all jerseys with *Karlsson* on the back, assuring them he didn't mind if they didn't wear them. They all had—proudly. But did Brent want her to dress more...sophisticated?

The crowd's roar increased as the team skated onto the ice.

"There he is!" Her father stood cheering as Holly smiled. Even her dad was excited?

The Detroit players skated warm-up maneuvers, then the national anthem was sung and the game started. Shouts, whistles, penalties, bodies slamming into boards, grunts, more penalties, horns, pucks over glass. It was a rollercoaster of a first period, the fans as well as the game proving to be entertaining.

During the first break between periods, the announcer and camera crew focused on some guests in the audience. A famous baseball player in attendance chatted briefly with one of the mobile television crews. Wedged between her parents and Ben, Holly watched the interview on the Jumbotron, enjoying the atmosphere. Then the announcer began again.

"And now, we know some ladies will be disappointed, but we're excited to hear one of our Wings favorites has found himself a lovely girl, and they're both competing at Vancouver next year. So, good luck at the Games to Brent Karlsson and Aussie World Cup short track winner, Holly Travers!"

A spotlight settled on her, and a camera zoomed in close. She hadn't paid much attention until she'd heard Brent's name and seen his image on the big screen. Now the whole stadium was looking at her, pointing her out, clapping and cheering. She glanced up at the Jumbotron again. How embarrassing. Until her tests came back clear, there weren't any guarantees. Cheeks heating, she gave a weak smile and little wave and prayed for the attention to soon switch to someone else.

The entertainment wound up, the players returned to the ice, and two more periods of adrenaline-pumping entertainment followed. Brent's skills floored her—the fastest man on the ice and so strong as he shrugged off attackers or barged them away from the puck. To see him in his element, to see this side, so different to the joker she knew, was a little awe-inducing. She could totally understand why the selectors had chosen him. He was an all-round player, his line the best, lifting their teammates' performances as he and Doug scored a goal apiece.

He'd promised to meet them in the ballroom of their fancy downtown hotel after the game, the site of a New Year's Eve party tonight. They returned, and Holly changed into one of the dresses Bree had bought for her. This dark blue number made the most of her waist and legs, and paired with heels, she thought she might even reach Brent's chin.

He texted, and within five minutes, she was putting her theory to the test.

His eyes widened. He grabbed her hand and whistled as she did a slow spin. "Holly, honey, it's not right that you look so good," he murmured, kissing her neck. "I don't know if I can take it."

"You'll just have to manage somehow," she said, laughing as his lips slid to her cheek in a far more tame kiss as her family joined her.

Her pulse accelerated. The way he got on with Mum, Dad, and Ben boded so well for the future—whatever that future might be. She shivered.

"Are you cold?"

Brent was so solicitous. "I'm okay. Let's go."

Holly held onto Brent's hand, her brother and parents close behind as Brent led the way to the function room booked for the Wings' New Year's Eve celebration. They made their way inside, and Brent was soon shaking hands with the team owner and other VIPs, introducing Holly and her family. Holly had a chance to thank the team manager and assure him she was improving. By the time his coach was being introduced, Holly's hands were getting sweaty and her quota of small talk had almost run out.

"Holly. We've heard a lot about you. Nice to meet you at last."

"Good to meet you too." Coach Reynolds seemed like an older, more grizzled version of her uncle Richard.

"And you're a skater." He nodded. "Your tips seem to be paying off for Brent here."

"I'm glad."

"Good to see you're recovered now. Are you set for competing in Vancouver?"

"I have tests in two days when I return to Calgary. I'm praying they go well."

He clapped Brent on the back. "You'll be good for each other, I wager." He turned to Ben. "Are you into sports too?"

Over the next few minutes, Coach Reynolds found out about Ben's rugby career, and they started discussing the finer points of the game, the coach's son playing it at college. Making their excuses, Brent led Holly away, and they spent the next half hour enjoying some food whilst Holly attempted to remember names as they chatted with his teammates and their partners.

Doug came over, and light conversation resumed until Holly noticed a blonde woman in a distinctive red dress. Brent was talking to someone when the woman sidled up to him, catching him unawares as she planted a big kiss on his cheek. "Brent! How are you? It's been so long. You were amazing tonight."

She flicked a look at Holly, who was suddenly uncomfortably aware of how plainly she'd dressed in comparison. The dress and heels she wore might be another one of Bree's special outfits, practical for Detroit's freezing temperatures, but right now it just seemed kind of boring. The woman giggled, then tried to rub the red lipstick mark off Brent's face. "Oops, sorry!"

Brent stepped away and drew closer to Holly, snaking an arm around her waist and giving her a kiss. "Holly, this is Larissa, Alex's sister. Larissa, this is Holly, my girlfriend."

"Nice to meet you, Larissa." Holly didn't need to be insecure. Not with Brent's lips imprinted on hers.

"Oh." Larissa's smile slipped a little. "I didn't know you'd be here."

"Surprise."

The red lips pushed into a pout.

Brent picked up Holly's hand and gave it a kiss. "Holly's an amazing skater…"

As Brent started going on and on about Holly's accomplishments, Larissa's eyes glazed over. It wasn't long before she made her excuses and left.

"Seems you made quite an impression there," Holly said wryly.

"What can I say? I'm just an impressive kind of guy."

"Yeah, but where I'm from, the really impressive guys don't talk about how impressive they are."

Brent laughed before encircling her with both arms. "You know, Holly, the only person I really want to impress is right in front of me."

When he looked at her like that, the intensity of his gaze made her feel all quivery inside. Or was that just his magic aftershave at work again? Her smile felt wobbly. "Okay then. Keep trying."

He laughed again, shaking his head. "You're such a hard taskmaster."

Holly smiled into his eyes. "But you love me anyway."

"Yes, I do." He kissed her again. "Now, do you want some more hors d'oeuvres?" His eyes grew big. "I think I just saw some with prawns. Or was it scallops?"

"Are you making fun of me?"

He grinned. "No, I'm having fun *with* you."

The hotel ballroom was filled with Detroit players, management, sponsors, and other supporters. A local television station was doing interviews with various team members, asking about their New Year's Eve resolutions. The pretty brunette hosting the show zeroed in on Brent and Holly. With the camera rolling, she asked, "Hi, Brent, how are you? Is this Holly, your girlfriend?"

"Yes." He gripped Holly's hand tighter.

"Holly, tell us, what did you think of Brent's performance tonight?"

"I was very impressed. He was great!" She threw him a smile and squeezed his hand.

The woman thrust the microphone closer. "So, Holly, I heard a rumor you're going to compete at the upcoming Games in Vancouver."

Holly nodded. "It's not a rumor, it's true." *Please, God.*

The interviewer blinked. "Uh…"

"I'm competing in short track speed skating."

"Wow." The interviewer looked faintly impressed. "And is that a British accent I hear?"

"No. I'm Australian."

"Australia. Wow. I guess there's not much hockey there." She gave a big smile.

The interviewer didn't need to sound so patronizing. "No, there's an ice hockey league, but it's not very big. Australia's pretty good at field hockey though."

"Right." The brunette's eyes slid past her. "Well, thanks, Holly. I'm sure there are plenty of female fans who'd love to be in your shoes." As the interviewer dismissed her, Holly worked to keep the smile from slipping. "Now, Brent, what are your New Year's resolutions? I'm guessing going to the gym more or quitting smoking is not amongst them?"

"You're right. I'm not much for New Year's resolutions. I'd rather try to make good choices each day."

"Wow, that's deep. Okay, well, I know there's a lot of disappointed ladies out there, Brent." The interviewer turned back to the camera. "Yes, that's right, ladies, you heard it here, Brent Karlsson is off the market. Now, back to you at the desk."

THANK God for the end of media interviews. Brent took Holly's hand and led her to a window alcove overlooking the river. "Sorry about that. I didn't realize that would take so long."

"You're obviously popular. Sounds like you've got lots of fans interested in you."

"Maybe, but it'd be nice if they weren't quite so interested. Know what I mean?"

"No, can't say that I do, Brent. I've never had fans—apart from you, of course."

He nuzzled her neck. "Of course."

She laughed. "But I guess it can't be easy." Her smile faded. "Larissa was a little obvious."

Was Holly jealous? He tugged her closer. "Nah, she's harmless."

Holly leaned back in his arms and raised her eyebrows. "Will there really be lots of disappointed women?"

He could feel his cheeks heat. "I've done nothing to encourage it. Well, not for the past few years anyway. You've got nothing to worry about. You know that, don't you?"

Her gaze was steady, sure. "I do. I trust you."

Only a kiss could suffice in reply. He took his time to kiss her thoroughly, then held her close, her back to his chest, as they studied the twinkling lights on the river.

Tension drained away. He closed his eyes. Tilted his face to inhale the fragrance of her hair. His senses sharpened, his pulse increased. He loved this girl. Loved so many things about her. Loved feeling like he could relax and be completely himself with her. Loved knowing that she felt the same. The time was right. He opened his mouth to say—

"Holly? Oh, there you are."

He turned as Holly slipped from his arms to face her parents. Parents. His mouth dried. Should probably talk to—

"We're a little tired and thought we might head up to our room." Beth smiled at him. "I don't know if we'll see you at the airport tomorrow, Brent, so we thought we'd thank you again for a wonderful time."

"You're very welcome."

She glanced at Holly, rubbing her daughter's shoulder gently. "It was truly a blessing to come when Holly wasn't well. Now she's doing so much better."

"I'm so glad." He exchanged warm smiles with her, then turned to John, offering his hand. "Thank you for coming, sir."

John looked at him seriously. "Thank you for doing all you've done to help my daughter."

This might be the last time he'd get the chance to say what was needed. As Holly and her mother exchanged hugs, he angled Holly's father to one side and dropped his voice. "I love Holly. And I promise I'll do all I can for the rest of my days to demonstrate that."

A beat. Startled eyes. "I didn't realize—"

"I'm very serious, John."

"What are you so serious about?" Holly grinned up at him, her arm twining around his waist.

He could get lost in the smoky depths of her eyes. "You."

Her breath caught. "Well, you are a flatterer, aren't you?"

"Nope. Not tonight. Not any time when it comes to you. I really think you're amazing."

Her cheeks pinked, and she gave an embarrassed-sounding chuckle. "If I didn't know any better, I'd think you've been drinking some new year's cheer."

"You're all the cheer I need."

Conscious John was still regarding him, he turned. "I hope, sir, that you'll give consideration to what I said."

He nodded. "Considered. And approved."

Fireworks exploded in his heart. "Thank you, sir."

"What's been approved?" Holly glanced between them. "What are you two up to?"

"Nothing you need to worry about, hon." Her father patted her back. "Don't stay up too late. Your flight to Calgary leaves soon after ours."

"We won't be too much longer," Brent promised.

"Take care of her, Brent." A look, deep in meaning, passed between them.

"Always. Thank you, sir."

Another handshake, a kiss on the cheek for Beth, then they left.

"That seemed a little intense."

Brent gave an exaggerated sigh. "Your dad is a little scary, babe."

"He has to be, to deal with all those miners in his work." She studied Brent curiously. "You're not going to tell me what that was about, are you?"

"Nope."

"Are you sure you don't want to?" She moved closer, up onto tiptoes, pressed a kiss to his jaw.

His pulse scampered. He exhaled heavily. "Holly, honey…"

Her hand trailed along his cheek, to his chin, down his throat, igniting heat.

He swallowed. "Sweetheart—"

"Holly." Ben appeared, glanced between them. "Whoa. Didn't mean to interrupt." He frowned at his sister. "Have you seen the folks?"

"They've gone upstairs."

"Are you coming soon?"

"In a bit. There's a countdown to stay for."

"Right. Sure." He raised an eyebrow at Brent. "Bring her up soon."

"Will do." He shook Ben's hand, wished him safe travels. Ben would travel with Holly to Calgary tomorrow before heading to B.C. to snowboard.

"Soon, yeah?" Ben said again.

Brent nodded. Exhaled. It didn't matter how protective-older-brother Ben wanted to be. Holly's dad had given his blessing, and that was all that was needed.

With Ben's departure, Brent took Holly closer to the window. Maybe over here they could finally get some privacy and he could say what his heart longed to say. This setting was romantic enough, surely.

She sighed. "It's a gorgeous night. Doesn't the river look beautiful?"

"Beautiful is the right word for it." He wrapped his arms around her and drew her close, kissed her cheek, drew in her scent. "Beautiful."

"Flatterer."

"Teller of truth."

She chuckled, snuggling against his chest as his chin rested on her head, then looking out at the reflected lights on the inky water.

"Holly." Suddenly the words weren't there. How could he step off this precipice? He was fumbling for how best to introduce this subject when she sighed.

Concern creased his heart. "What's wrong?"

"I'm trying to live in the moment, but I can't help but wonder how the specialist assessment will go the day after next."

The magic in the air dissipated. "You're feeling better, aren't you?"

"I managed some basic skating back in Toronto, and things felt okay."

"Don't worry. Whatever the outcome, God's plans for you are good."

"You're right." Her shoulders lost some stiffness. "I'm so good at worrying."

"Hey, we all can be."

She tugged his arms more firmly around her. "I wish we could do this forever. But I suppose if everything goes okay, it'll only be six weeks until I'll see you again."

Six weeks was just so long. The more time he spent with her, the more he longed to be with her, a powerful kind of craving within. Their kisses had only fueled this aching need. "We arrive February fourteen."

"Valentine's Day." She exhaled. "Hopefully we can spend that day together."

Maybe that would provide a better opportunity for him to say what had to be said. "I'll make sure of it," he promised. And he'd make it a day she'd never forget.

From the main function room, the countdown began, the shouts getting louder until "...three...two...one....Happy New Year!"

Brent gazed deeply into her beautiful, clear green eyes. "I love you, Holly Travers."

She smiled her delicious smile that made his heart dance. "I love you, Brent Karlsson."

He leaned closer and claimed her lips with his.

And the new year began, filled with promise.

CHAPTER 26

Hi Brent,
I hope your flight to Phoenix went well and you're not too tired
from NYE. I had such a lovely time. Thank you for inviting us
all to see your house, to watch your game, and meet your team-
mates at the party. My flight went well, no concussion symp-
toms at all, thank You, Jesus! Ben's here with me for another
week until he heads into snowboarding country before visiting
Dean. (Your brother is kindly hosting him until the Games.
How nice is that?) Mum and Dad are now back in Oz, recov-
ering after their crazy long flights and heading back to work
tomorrow. Off to the specialist soon. Please pray all goes well.
Love you, Holly

Hey Holly,
You're always in my heart and in my prayers. I believe you'll
be just fine, but remember—whatever happens, stay up. God is
good. He loves you, and so do I.
Brent xx

∾

Hi all!
Forgive the group email, but I'm so excited—I passed my tests!
The doctors cleared me in each category, so I've now returned
to training. Although my head and knee feel really good, I
know there's a lot to make up for (can't believe it's nearly two
months since Marquette), but my coaches tell me that muscle
memory goes a long way to helping once my fitness returns.
Here's praying that's true!
Appreciate your prayers.
Holly

∾

Sweetheart,
So sorry I missed your invite to talk. We were flying to
Anaheim. I might've just let out a giant cheer when I read your
news. So happy for you. I can't wait to see you in B.C. Maybe
we can video call tomorrow? It's hard to remember. This road
trip is crazy—Phoenix, Anaheim, LA, San Jose, then we're in
New York. Who makes up these schedules? I saw Beau, so that
was good, but if I'm a little dazed and confused when I see you,
forgive me ;) I love you.
Brent.

∾

Dear Brent,
Coach Mathieson has stepped up training another level and
now has extra support: Coach Chan is here in Calgary with
Jess and the Aussie men's relay team. It's nice to have some
friends around, although Coach C. is still going on and on
about distractions. I got some good tips from some Games

veterans, and practicing with them makes me try harder. The other day one of them said about the Games, "Enjoy it, but remember—ultimately it's only another competition." Only another competition? Yeah, right! I've never had to do much in the way of media, but in the past week I've had five newspaper and two television interviews. The Aussie sports reporters were pretty good—they're focused on my skating at least—but the North American reporters always manage to bring you into conversation. Not that I mind talking about you (don't worry: I'm getting good at "no commenting" with a smile!), but it's a little disconcerting when I've spent so many years working toward this and all they want to talk about is my love life!
Love you, my oh-so-clever Brent,
H.

~

Hey Holly,
Was so nice to chat with you briefly last night. Ever feel these times apart get harder, not easier? I ask myself how people managed separations years ago and thank God that at least these days we have so many more options for connecting rather than just letters or a telegram.
I miss you. I miss your smile, your scent, your laugh, your kiss. Can't wait to see you again.
Love you so hard. B

~

Dear Brent,
I tried to call today but had to leave a message, which was basically this: I love you.
Even seeing you interviewed after a game gives me a partial Brent fix. I can't wait until I can see you every day for two

entire weeks! Can you believe we've never done that? That's just crazy. I feel like you are now such a part of my world that if you weren't in it I'd be incomplete.
I love you. H

~

Hey Holl,
I caught up with Ben and Dean at church in San Jose this morning. Nice to get a day off to get some perspective—especially after a loss like that (ouch!). Was so nice of them to surprise me by flying down. Ben seems to have enjoyed his snowboarding so much that Dean's tagging along next weekend.
Love you so much I can't sleep, thinking about you, dreaming...
Brent

~

Hi everyone,
Only two weeks to go until competition starts, and one week until we fly to B.C. I'm so relieved I'm skating much better now. Still not perfect (hey, was it ever?), but at least I feel more like I won't be a laughingstock once I get to Vancouver. It's kind of weird, but I'm actually having more fun now. I really feel that with people knowing about my accident, the pressure is off. That might sound like a cop out, but it's not. I just feel more relaxed. Looking forward to seeing some family and friends there—thanks, as always, for your prayers.
Holly

~

Hey Super girl,

~

Hi all,
We've arrived in Vancouver! The past few days involved regis-
tration and getting settled into my fabulous apartment, shared
with Coach Chan and my friend Jess, who qualified in the
1500. Our apartment looks out across the harbour—SO pretty,
with the mountains behind. Collecting my uniform was fun—
almost two bags' worth! Formal wear (no, not a ballgown,
Bree), training gear, team tracksuit, and that yellow podium
jacket that everyone hopes to get the chance to wear. My skin
suit looks awesome: dark green with pale yellow stripes like a
skeleton pattern. I've already had a few training sessions, and
I'm feeling (and looking!) good.
Last night was the official reception for the Australian
competitors. Mr. Pearson from the Winter Sports Institute was
there and talked me up. I still pinch myself to be here,
surrounded by so many high calibre athletes. The flag raising
ceremony was a little rainy, but then we went inside, where all
of us were presented with plaques for making the team. It was a
fun night—a nice break from the intensity of training and a
terrific way to connect with my teammates.
The athletes' dining hall is immense! A huge variety of cuisines
for all the athletes and staff—even different types of rice, to
keep the Japanese, Chinese, and Korean taste buds satisfied.
(There's an onsite McDonalds too—what the?) The energy in
the room is amazing. So many people with such different back-
grounds, but all with one goal—to win! Some of us checked out
the athletes' lounge. It has a movie theatre, pool tables, and Wii

games so we can relax after training and competition. I'll definitely have to come back (after my competition). Tonight's the opening ceremony, and my heats start tomorrow—please pray!
Love,
Holly

~

Hi Holly,
Just finished Bible study. The guys wish you well, but not as much as I do. Can I say how much I miss you? It's like the Grand Canyon lives in my heart, and only seeing you will fill these spaces again. Not long to go now.
Brent

~

Hi all,
Just got back from my 1000m heat. I'm through! Second in my heat—yay! I was so nervous. The Pacific Coliseum is huge, but the crowd was super supportive for everyone. There seems to be a healthy contingent of Aussies here, too! My friend Jess crashed out in the 1500, which is disappointing for her, but at least she can enjoy the rest of the Games stress free. I'm now free for a few days—time to catch up with Mum, Dad, and Ben, who are all here (and say hi!)—until the 1000 finals on Wednesday.
Last night was the opening ceremony. We were all dressed up in our glamorous green and gold, and our bus wouldn't start! Everyone was worried because we're one of the first countries to enter, but fortunately we made it just in time. The cheer we got when we entered was amazing!!! So many spectators! Watching the music and cultural performances and the lighting of the cauldron made it a very special night.

~

*H*olly's stomach rumbled, protesting its lengthy wait since her last proper refueling. She smiled apologetically at the Latvian girl in front of her and collected a chicken salad and some fruit and yoghurt for dessert. It was hard to stay on the strict training diet when there were so many delectable cuisines on offer. She sat with Jess and other Australian teammates and inhaled her food. Racing always made her hungry.

As they encouraged each other about their results, Holly finally relaxed, the stress from earlier ebbing away. It was a tough physical challenge at times, balancing the adrenaline demands of this frenetic sport with relaxation in order to conserve energy.

Jess turned to Holly. "Want to come see what movie is on?"

Maybe she should. Brent had a game and wasn't due in until the small hours of the morning. But the movie could scarcely hold her attention, her thoughts on Brent, his game against Ottawa, his schedule once he arrived. It seemed they'd have a lot of clashes when their competitions were on. Disappointment spiked. Why was it always this way? At least they'd find some time tomorrow. *Please, God.*

A GENTLE KNOCK woke Holly later than normal. The emotions and physical intensity of the previous day had left her pretty tired, and with only a few scheduled training sessions, it was great to have a few days to live at a more relaxed pace before Wednesday's thousand finals. She yawned a "hello" and the door opened. Jess popped around the side. "Holly, there's something you have to come see."

Huh? Holly stumbled from bed and took a moment in the bathroom for the world's quickest brush of teeth—brushing her hair could wait—then made her way to the open front door. Several athletes from the adjoining apartment were standing in the hallway, smiling. Holly shoved a hand through bedhead hair before noticing an enormous bouquet of red and pink roses being held by—

"Brent!"

He laughed and held his arms wide—flowers out of harm's way—as she leapt at him, arms around his neck, legs around his waist.

"I could get used to this." He held her and nuzzled her neck, his scent, his arms shooting electricity to every nerve ending as he backed her into her apartment.

"I'll take these," Jess said, winking at Holly as she moved the roses away.

But Holly barely noticed, so fixated was she on his beloved features. Brent's eyes darkened before he swooped in to kiss her again.

His lips held a kind of tender ferocity, as if he wanted to show the depths of his love by never letting go. A fresh wave of longing swept through Holly, tensing low in her stomach, and she clung more ardently as he moved to seat her on the kitchenette counter.

Here, entwined in his strong arms, she was the perfect height, he the perfect haven from the world. His kisses deepened, his lips teasing hers apart, and soon her head was swimming.

"Six weeks is too long," she breathed against his mouth.

"Way too long," he murmured. "Don't want to do it again."

She drew back—oh, lightheaded!—and breathed unsteady breaths. Convinced swollen lips to lift. "Hi."

He chuckled. Stole another kiss. "Best hello I've ever had."

She laughed, then shifted forward to hug him again. Then realized, as his hands touched the bare skin of her waist, "I'm still wearing my PJs!"

"And your bed hair," Jess said from the door. "Not that lover boy seems to mind."

"Hi, Jess," he said, eyes crinkling as his gaze stayed fixed on Holly. "Nope, this man doesn't mind." He smoothed her hair.

"Gotta say, that was a swoon-worthy kiss, like something from a movie," Jess continued. "Well done, Holly. Didn't know you had it in you."

"I didn't either," Holly confessed. From this position, she could see the shifting green-blue-gray depths of his eyes and the faint shadows underlining them. He must've come here after what little sleep he'd managed since getting in super late last night—or early this morning.

"What time did you get in?" She caressed his cheeks, her fingertips savoring the bristled touch. "You must be exhausted."

"It was early, but I couldn't miss a second of Valentine's Day with my girl."

"Happy Valentine's Day," she said, moving in for another kiss. She sank back into bliss. "Oh, I could do this forever."

He drew back, tilted his forehead on hers, eyes intense. "About that—"

"Holly! What you doing?"

Holly flinched. Eased away. "Good morning, Coach Chan."

"You." Her scowl shifted from Holly to Brent. "How long you been here?"

"Good morning, Coach Chan. It's nice to see you again."

"Hmph." Her frown swung back to Holly. "Very disappointed in you. You know no guests in rooms."

"What? Brent only just arrived. And you should know I'd never invite a man to my room."

"Not what it looks like here."

Oh. Dear. Had it looked that bad? Holly glanced down. Folded her arms. These PJs weren't as thick as some. Had Brent noticed *everything* in their hug?

"Coach Chan, I let Brent in not even twenty minutes ago," Jess said. "You should know Holly would never do something like that."

"He distraction," Coach Chan said, pointing at him. "He need to leave. You need to put more clothes on."

"I'd better scram," Brent said, hands heating Holly's waist as he helped her down from the counter. "I have a team meeting this morning, but it should be finished by two. Catch you then?"

"I have an ice session booked until three. I can get my workouts done this morning and be free later."

"Sounds good." He swiftly kissed her again. "Love you, sweetheart."

"Love you too."

Light filled his features as he turned, grinned at Jess, saluted Coach Chan, then exited, closing the door firmly behind him.

"OMG," Jess breathed. "He is…" She fanned herself.

Yes. Yes, he was.

"Look, he's written a card, too."

Holly gently touched the roses, then opened the envelope and read the inscription on the card inside: "For Holly, my best friend, my sweetheart, my future-to-be. Happy Valentine's Day. I love you, Brent."

Her heart expanded into warm sunshine. Brent could be mushy! This was beyond sweet. She buried her nose in the fragrant blooms.

"What do you think he means by 'future-to-be'?" Jess asked.

Holly shivered, her insides tightening again. Did he truly mean to suggest—?

"Holly." The stern note in her coach's voice bade Holly to face her. "He distraction. You work so hard so long, and now you throw it away?"

"I'm not throwing anything away," Holly said, meeting her coach's black eyes evenly. "He helps me. He never hinders."

"You need to stay focused on competition. What we've all worked for so long."

"I *am* focused, Coach Chan. But I also know that short track isn't forever. One day I'll be too old for this, but I don't want to be too old and miss my chance with Brent."

"He not wait for you?"

"He's not proposed, if that's what you mean."

Although, judging from the *future-to-be* comment, perhaps that wasn't too much to hope for, one day soon.

"You can't have both."

"I think I can," Holly said with quiet determination. "Coach Chan, I love Brent, and he *is* part of my future," Holly continued. "So is short track. And I can assure you that I won't jeopardize my skating goals by caring about him too."

"But, Holly—"

"I will do my absolute best." Holly squared her shoulders. "Just watch me."

～

"You saw your girl?"

Brent nodded to Erik, his roommate for the tourney. Oh yeah. He'd seen Holly, held her, kissed her in a way that'd make it hard to sleep tonight. Not that he'd complain. Seeing her was oxygen for his soul.

"Welcome." The assistant coach for the team nodded to Brent and the others who'd arrived last night—no, today. "Hope you got something to eat. Today's gonna be a long day."

He turned back to the others, crowded around a couple of tables in a room just off the dining hall, and explained the schedule for the next few days. Brent nodded. They had to bond quickly to establish the trust and connections that would enable good play as a team.

The coach eyed them all carefully. "I know you only played together intermittently at the August camp, but we based your selection in this team on how you've been performing and what strengths you can bring—whether you'll contribute to lots of goals. Now's the time to prove we were right to include you."

Brent drew in a deep breath as the coach drilled him with his eyes. Okay, so maybe Brent's inclusion hadn't been unanimous. The knowledge fired grit within—he'd give them all he had and then some.

They spent the rest of the morning discussing strategy, then it was time for lunch, further planning, and finally they headed to the rink.

They waited as the Russian team completed their practice and trooped off the ice. Other national teams were in the same position, their pro hockey players practicing as a team rarely, so each team highly valued their ice time.

Brent skated onto the ice, following each instruction to the letter, practicing passing, shooting, skating, finding his rhythm and flow with the other guys, getting a feel for the ice. It helped to have Erik, whose moves he could anticipate. Their allotted hour up, they skated off, and Coach Reynolds gave their assignment for the next afternoon: Canada against Norway. Should be a straightforward result, but nothing in life was certain. Although, judging from Holly's greeting this morning, perhaps he could be a little more certain about a future with her.

"THIS ISN'T EXACTLY how I imagined our first Valentine's dinner," Brent said, looking up from his plate of chow mein.

"The fact I'm having dinner with you at all is amazing to me." Holly carefully layered her fork with salad. "Most years I have World Cup events at this time of year, so this is really special."

He held her hand. Special it was all right. Even if it wasn't the most romantic place to be, surrounded as they were by the chatter of athletes from around the world.

They'd caught up after her training and risked the rain to walk along the stone-walled harbor, but his mood didn't need any boost from the happy buzz around them. It was enough to be with her, to have her tucked beside him as they walked and laughed and shared about their days and the past weeks apart—and avoided returning too quickly to face Coach Chan's wrath.

Their meal soon finished, they exited to a quiet corner in the lounge where they could chat more privately. Was this the time to share what was on his heart? Had his actions—his Valentine's card—fueled expectations now? Perhaps he should wait and see...

"So, your first game tomorrow. Are you excited?"

"Yeah." He yawned.

"That's so convincing."

He smiled. "How about you? What's on your agenda tomorrow?"

"I've got training and some gym work in the morning, then I meet up with my family."

"How are you feeling about Wednesday?"

"For once, I'm actually excited. I feel pretty good, my legs feel great, training's been good." Her head tilted. "It's amazing how good I feel, all things considered."

"You'll do great."

Holly sighed. He motioned for her to lift her legs and place them on his lap, then began massaging her calves. "That better?"

She closed her eyes and leaned back on the cushions. "You need to stop."

He paused. "Does that hurt? Sorry, I—"

"No," she groaned. "It's just too nice. You're too nice. And I'm wondering how I'll manage when I have to go back to real life."

"Live in the moment, Holl."

She nodded, opened her eyes with a heavy-lidded gaze. "Thank you for my roses this morning. You always give the right sort of flowers. Reds and pinks."

"The reds are because I love you, and the pinks are because you're my best friend. That's what Granny Violet told me they meant, anyway."

"You asked your grandmother?" He nodded and her face softened more. "That's so sweet." She reached up and gave him a kiss, an arm around his neck. He took a deep draught of her perfume. Beautiful.

"I've never had a Valentine's gift before."

"I find that hard to believe. Other men must be blind."

She smirked. "Don't they say love is blind?"

"Hope that means you're blind too."

"Oh, you know I am. So blind." She pulled a small envelope from her pocket and handed it to him. "I know it's not much, but I wasn't sure what time would be best to give this to you. So, anyway, happy Valentine's Day, Brent." She leaned forward in another impressive abdominal crunch and kissed him. "I love you."

He slowly opened the envelope to find a tiny heart-shaped homemade card. He traced the outside. "It's really pretty, like the one for Granny V's birthday. Did you make this too?" At her nod, he opened it.

Dear Brent,
You have my heart, always and forever.
I love you.
Holly

Tenderness washed across his heart. He reread it, tracing the neat writing. "You do?" He leaned down, gazing into her beautiful eyes. Green jewels surrounded by amethysts, with a golden heart.

"I do."

Her eyes widened as if catching the implications of that phrase.

Maybe this was the time. But would such a question steal her focus from her events? He didn't want to distract her, but...

Impatience spurted—he'd waited long enough. She had to know. And today was Valentine's Day, after all. Heart hammering, he opened his mouth—

"There you are." Erik and three other Canadian teammates claimed the nearby free lounges and, after introductions, talked about tomorrow's game, the athletes' village atmosphere, their respective home teams' Conference standings.

Brent slouched back against the cushions, barely taking in their words, vacillating between regret at the interruption and the loss of opportunity to speak about what really mattered, and trying to get his fill of watching Holly's animated beauty, holding her hand, thinking about kissing—

Holly stifled a yawn, shifted her legs, and stood. "Well, it was really nice to meet you, but I need to go to bed. Good luck tomorrow."

"You too."

"Thanks." She glanced at him uncertainly. "You coming, or do you want to stay here some more?"

How was that even a question? "I'll walk you back, then be back here shortly." He didn't want any misunderstandings with his teammates like Holly's coach had thought.

They walked slowly to her apartment, the moon's reflection sparkling on the harbor.

"So, do you think your coach has forgiven me?"

She pressed closer, arcing tingles down his side. "I made it clear that short track can't last forever. Eventually, we all age out and have to transition to something new."

He swung around to face her, pools of light illuminating her features. "So, am I your something new?"

A beat. "You're something all right."

He laughed and wrapped her closer as they walked the last steps to her building.

"So, this is you," Brent said, looking up at the apartment block the Aussies shared with the Finnish and French teams, "right next to me." He glanced at the Canadian block next door.

"Very convenient."

He pulled her close and murmured into her ear, "For once."

She snuggled into the bulky warmth of his jacket. "Call me when you get a moment." She hugged him for a long, long moment, then reached up and kissed him lightly on the lips, then stepped away. "Sleep well."

"You too." He smiled at her. "Goodnight, Holly."

"Good night."

CHAPTER 27

*H*olly arrived at the Pacific Coliseum around 4:00 p.m. Her thousand meter quarterfinal was the second for the night, which meant she would be on around 5:10 p.m. She stretched, warming up. Her parents and brother were in the stands, but she didn't have time to look for them. Now was all about visualizing the race, trying to get her head back into competition mode. Nerves bit. A chuckle washed them away. So what if her first real competition since her concussion just so happened to be the pinnacle of athletic endeavor. Anyway, she'd done okay in the heats, even if they seemed ages ago now, the schedule here different to the usual World Cup program which was completed in four days.

"Ladies, you're on."

Holly removed her guards and headed to center ice. She shook out her legs as the race was announced and the competitors introduced. She waved, then skated forward to the starting position.

Her name was called, and she moved to the outside position, knowing she needed to make a strong start. She was up against Min Weng, Kelsey Hendry, a Bulgarian, and a Canadian girl with the crowd's support, judging from the roar as she was introduced.

"Ready." Holly sucked in a breath. *Lord, help me keep You first.*

BANG!

Skate, skate, skate, skate. She pounded down the straight, then curved sharply to gain second position behind Min. Holly breathed slowly, working to keep her legs steady and her leans exactly right. The strategy had to differ from the five hundred meters. While the shorter race was about pace and maneuvers, the thousand meters demanded more in the way of stamina and control. And with nine laps, it didn't hurt to have someone else break the air currents and establish a slipstream to race in.

But as she skated, Holly realized this was fun. The joyous sensation of flying, the sounds and smell of the ice, seemed to trump the old desperate panic to win. She didn't need to prove herself. The fact she had qualified meant she could enjoy this moment of doing what her body had been created and honed to do.

Min's red skinsuit and gold blades flashed in front as they powered through the bends, maintaining position. Two laps down. The crowd was mere background noise, Holly focused on the scrape and hiss of blades on ice. Three laps. Four. She felt okay, her muscle memory kicking in just as Coach Mathieson had said it would. Five laps done. Six. Her senses seemed as sharp as ever too, noting every move of those nearby. Seven laps, eight. The bell rang. One lap to go. As they rounded the bend, Min seemed to hesitate and Holly had to go wide to avoid crashing into her. No! She watched as Kelsey's blue and red suit flashed past her, taking advantage of Holly's misstep and loss of speed. Holly hurried to regain position, but it was too late. Min crossed first, Kelsey second. Holly was out.

She skated the cool-down, hands on her hips, blinking to keep the disappointment from leaking out of her eyes as she fought for self-control. She'd worked so hard and for so long, and for what?

No. She lifted her head. She was trusting God's purposes now.

Kelsey skated up and flashed a smile that Holly returned. "Good job, Kels."

"You would've had me if Min…" The blonde shook her head.

"But that's short track, right?"

Kelsey nodded to where the coaches and officials were engaged in very animated discussions. "Looks like this race isn't over yet."

Holly watched as Coach Chan shook her finger in somebody's face, like a terrier barking at a Great Dane. She bit her lip. Hopefully they wouldn't be receiving any fines for poor sportsmanship. But the way Coach Chan was nodding sparked hope in Holly's heart. Maybe justice would be served. *Please, God…*

She tried to relax as she watched the scoreboard that kept flashing *Decision pending*. Finally, the chief steward grabbed a microphone and stood in the middle of the ice. "The Chinese competitor has been disqualified for impeding another skater. The competitor from the United States is the winner, and the competitor from Australia has also qualified for the semifinal."

Yes! Kelsey gave Holly a high five, and together they skated off the ice. Holly tried not to look as Min stood shaking her head while the head Chinese coach continued protesting, then turned on Min and said something that made the former champion go white.

That was tough to witness. She'd never complain about Coach Chan again. *Lord, please help Min.*

"Holly, you through!" Coach Chan gave one of her rare smiles. "That Bob"—she nodded to the chief steward—"he no mess with me."

Relief surged through Holly, escaping in a giggle. Nobody in his right mind would ever want to mess with Coach Chan.

She skated off the ice, collecting her guards before consulting with her coach as she cycled to reduce the buildup of lactic acid in her legs. She watched the men's five thousand meter relay heats, cheering on the Aussies who progressed to quarterfinals.

"Women's semifinals."

Holly adjusted her goggles, then took a deep breath and slowly exhaled, glancing at her fellow competitors. Erika from the Netherlands, England's Katie Brummell, and Hira Ito from her Montreal World Cup quarterfinal.

"Quiet, please." The announcer's voice boomed across the arena. The crowd hushed. "Ready."

She touched her knee. *Lord...*

BANG!

Holly propelled herself into second behind Erika, Hira close behind. She needed to stay focused, stay up, and finish top two to progress to the medal round.

One lap down. She kept pace steadily, the English and Japanese girls behind her. Two laps down, three, four. She felt good today. Despite the Brent distraction, her training hadn't been as affected as Coach Chan had feared. Holly smiled slightly. Five laps down.

She pressed on with smooth, fluid movements, scanning the ice to find the grooves that would enable better flow. Three laps to go. Hira crept closer. Holly picked up the pace. Two laps to go. From the corner of her eye she noticed a slight commotion. Rounding the bend she saw the English girl had slipped and slid to the padded boards. *Don't lose focus. Keep going.* The bell sounded. Sprint time. Legs and arms pumping, she raced Hira around the final bend...only to see Hira slip through on the inside and cross the line second after Erika.

Disappointment swelled. But she'd made final B, the classification round, and she could be proud of her achievement. And hey, there was always the five hundred still to come.

Hands on her knees, Holly rounded the curve on the cool-down lap, spying an Australian flag near the top of the bleachers. She smiled, waving at her family, who waved and gave her the thumbs-up. *Thank You, Lord.*

~

Hey Doug,
Couldn't sleep tonight—Erik snores, plus there's too much
going on in my head. After crushing Norway 8 zip, we couldn't
believe we had to go to shootout against Switzerland. At least
we won that. It's unbelievable just how much pressure there is
to win. EVERYONE expects it (well, maybe not you guys).
Our game against USA will be a good challenge. I still pinch
myself that it's me who's here and feel like I've got even more
to prove, with so many great guys not selected. Caught up with
my folks, who are here to see a few games, which is great. Been
nice to see Holly a lot more too. She made it to the semis for
1000m, came 7th overall, which is pretty awesome considering
she was in hospital just a few months ago. One of those mira-
cles, maybe? But she's really set on the 500. Her heats are on
today while we have training, but I plan to watch her next
week in the finals. Hoping we're in the finals too, but you
never know with these things. Learning to never take things
for granted. So if you feel like being daring, pray for me and
Holly (and yes, I will try to get you a Team USA jersey—XL,
right?)
Brent

~

CANADA HOCKEY PLACE was alive with loud energy. Holly leaned forward in her seat, watching for Canada's number twenty-five to enter the ice. "There he is!"

Brent's parents and Mike stood, peering down onto the ice. Rob Karlsson rubbed his hands. "This is going to be a great game."

Mike nodded. "USA might be young, but they're confident. We've got our work cut out, for sure."

Mike was a prophet: within the first minute, the US signaled their intentions with a goal.

"Whoa." The enthusiasm level of the crowd dropped markedly. Brent skated onto the ice for his first shift. He grabbed the puck, skated down toward USA's blue line, and was tripped.

"Refs!" The crowd booed as the refs overlooked it and play continued.

"Is he okay?" Holly and Pam shared a worried look, but Brent was already up and into the thick of the action again.

The following few minutes saw two penalties called amidst a flurry of shots before the puck finally went in for Canada. The crowd erupted but soon sobered when the US scored the following minute. More intense play, then the first period was over.

The Karlssons chatted with Mike, and Holly sat back in her seat, able to breathe again. How did Brent do this? This intensity was incredible.

The second period began. Holly watched as Brent intercepted a pass from the American goal, neatly sending it to a fellow forward who tucked it into goal. She leapt to her feet, cheering. It was now two all. The chant *go Canada go* reverberated around the arena. Each time Brent skated on, she held her breath. *Lord, keep him safe!* The Canadians were doing a good job staying in the US end, but the USA scored again to the crowd's disgust. The second period closed with the score 3-2, USA.

Holly took another slurp from her water bottle. "This is insane." She shook her head at Mike. "I don't know how you can sit and watch it so calmly. I'm going to need to sleep for a week to recover."

"If it's any comfort, Brent said something pretty similar when he watched you race."

"Oh." She let that thought settle for a moment. "It's different when you're involved."

"For sure."

The teams trooped back, ready for period three. "C'mon, Brent!" She turned to Mike. "Do you think we're going to win?"

He shrugged. "Never say never, but USA is pretty fast tonight."

The break must have included a rallying pep talk, because the renewed intensity was fierce. More shots on goal, more penalties called for high sticking and slashing. Every time one of those sticks connected with a player, Holly winced. The bruises these guys must end up with!

A penalty against Canada resulted in the Americans scoring again. 4-2.

"Oh no." Holly groaned. Two goals down was becoming a psychological hurdle. It was much easier to believe you could still win when the difference was only one.

The crowd's chanting picked up in fervency as they willed their home team to score. Brent continued to be in the thick of play, scrambling to retrieve the puck from his opponents, making some shots on goal but to no avail. Finally, with less than five minutes to go, one of Canada's superstar centers shot and scored.

"Yes!" The crowd's cheering almost made her copy poor Pam, who sat with her hands over her ears, a smile on her face.

But despite the Canadians' best efforts, the Americans still remained in the lead. Then in the final minute, the Canadian goalkeeper came off, and the US scored with forty-five seconds left on the clock.

The atmosphere was desperate, the fans unbelieving. How wrong—this was not how the fairytale was supposed to be written! When the final siren blew, the few American fans in the crowd cheered, but a little less overtly, surrounded as they were by a shocked, devastated crowd. Holly watched for the number twenty-five as Brent and his teammates skated off the ice. *Lord, help him.*

THE LOCKER ROOM was very quiet. Some sat with their heads in their hands, others stared off into nothing. Several guys had come in swearing, kicking at the detritus of the room. Everyone took bad news differently. Brent just felt numb.

Unbelievable. How could they have lost? He shook his head and focused on breathing past the disappointment.

Coach Reynolds stood in the center of the room, waiting, allowing time to breathe. He sighed, then nodded. "Okay. Not what we wanted. Here's what we need to do."

Brent listened carefully as his coach, in characteristic fashion, began to analyze and encourage. He described some of their poor decisions, highlighting some penalties that had resulted in powerplays for the opposition. "And goal shooting. We need to be more accurate." As the coach outlined the strategy for the next few days before their game against Germany, Brent felt the weight of expectation settle on his shoulders. The only good thing was that they wouldn't be complacent again. This loss had only fueled their desire to win.

When Holly eventually saw him later that night, she gave him a consolatory hug. "You okay?"

"Yeah. It's not the end of the world."

"I've heard some people say it's only a game…" She raised her eyebrows.

He pulled out a reluctant smile. "Don't let the other guys hear you say that. They'd think it blasphemous."

HE SPENT some time in the following days replying to the many messages from family, friends, and the Bible study guys, some of whom—okay, Jai and Beau—seemed to have enjoyed ribbing him about the US victory a little too much. He answered Doug's latest email as well.

Hey Doug,
What a difference two days make. We needed the win, and even though it was Germany, we're not underestimating anyone anymore. It was nice to get clicking, nicer still to score & feel like I'm contributing. The relief when we won! Through to the quarterfinals tomorrow night: against the Russians, who are way more competitive. Pray for us.
Brent

AFTER A FOCUSED DAY with gym sessions, strategy meetings with the coaches, and a brief nap in the afternoon, Brent felt ready.

Two minutes in: goal for Canada. Five minutes later: penalty kill. Another three minutes: powerplay, then a powerplay goal. Another goal. 3-0 Canada. The Russians scored, Canada replied, and it was 4-1 at first period's close.

Second period. Brent skated on, grabbing the puck when a Russian suddenly loomed to check him. Brent twisted hard just in time, his shoulder taking most of the impact. He still managed to protect the puck, sending it along the boards to a waiting defenseman at point. He shot and scored. 5-1. Yes! Brent skated off, got his shoulder checked over by the trainer, who pronounced him fine. He arrived back to find goals scored by each team. 6-2.

Brent waited for his next shift. Got the tap on the shoulder.

He narrowed his eyes, skating hard. Today was all about showing the current world champion team who really was boss, not allowing them room to skate or score. The puck slid his way, and he fed it to his line mate, who skated closer to the goal. Brent raced hard, received the pass, and tipped it in. Goal! 7-2. Finally, he was showing his position on the team was justified. After the celebratory fist bump down the bench, he sat for a quick breather, sucking down water, watching without emotion as the Russians scored again.

Third period. The momentum see-sawed, the aggression real with plenty of penalties: interference, tripping, high sticking, and more. Tough opponents called for tough tactics.

The crowd started chanting "We want Slovakia! We want Slovakia!" They'd done this yesterday against Germany, demanding the team play well enough to win and progress to the next round. Slovakia would be their semifinal opponents. Bring it on.

Less than three minutes later, the final whistle blew to the insane roar of the crowd. Brent made his way through to the locker room and sat down, exhaling as the physical and emotional intensity slowly ebbed away. *Thanks, God.* He blinked and looked up at the wall clock. *And thanks that I get to see Holly soon.*

CHAPTER 28

Holly breathed in the atmosphere. Excitement, anticipation, hope, dreams, and fears mixed and mingled and made a potent concoction, for the spectators as well as the athletes they'd come to support. Her family and Brent were seated out there somewhere, no doubt holding that huge flag they'd threatened to bring last night.

The nerves loosened their grip as she smiled. Catching up with her parents and brother yesterday had been good, although clearing the security had been a nightmare. Walking through the buzzy streets of Vancouver, alive with color and excitement, had been fun. She'd worn her Aussie uniform and had a few tourists recognize her and request photos. It had been fun, but it made her appreciate the haven that the athletes' village was, away from media and fans.

She stretched, trying to keep her legs warm. It was so good Brent had a night off and could be here tonight. He'd rung after last night's game where Canada had crushed Russia, an incredibly encouraging result for the home team. Brent had mentioned the enormous weight of expectation he and his teammates were under from his country and media. Nothing less than a gold medal would suffice. Holly's lips tilted. That was one of the nice things about being here. She could fly pretty much under the radar. Nobody—apart from Coach Chan—was placing any gold medal pressure on her.

Holly had warmed up earlier, and the men's five thousand meter relay quarterfinals were now on. The Aussie team was out there somewhere. Training hadn't been so straightforward for them. Coach Chan had even seemed a little stressed when she and Holly had talked strategy this morning. They'd been halfway through outlining her main rivals and their strengths and weaknesses when Coach Chan had received a text, frowned, and sworn. "Sean and Chris are sick." She shook her head. "Need to man up!"

Holly had stifled amusement. Coach Chan could only have heard that expression from Jess.

"I'm sure they'll be right tonight. They haven't come all this way not to compete. And it is easy for sniffles to spread, with everyone living as close as we are."

Coach Chan's brow had still been dark as they finished their prep and she disappeared to check on the boys. They'd obviously received a pep talk and a half, because all four had shown up, ready to race for their lives.

The noise from the main arena ramped up. Holly ducked past the officials and caught the final minute of the race. The boys completed their lap to push the next competitor around the track. Korea won, USA was next, followed by Germany and Great Britain.

The next race had her compatriots. She frowned. Even from this distance she could see that Chris didn't look fully fit. He seemed stiff, his body not as limber as usual. The race began. Holly joined the other skaters on the sidelines to cheer on their teammates.

"Come on, Chris!" She yelled harder. "C'mon, Aussies!"

Around, around, around they circled, pushing each other on.

Each time one of them passed near her, Holly yelled again. Encouraging others was an effective way of keeping the nerves at bay, even if the Aussies were fighting Italy for third. Third to fourth to third again.

Sean finished his lap and came in to push Chris. Chris made it around the bend before slipping, crashing out to the side. The crowd gave a collective gasp, then a cheer as Chris quickly clambered back up to rejoin the race. But even though that's what they'd all been told to do, it was more for pride and possible points. There was no way they'd come third now. Holly winced. That was a tough way to lose.

She cheered anyway as they finally crossed the line, their expressions dejected. She had to hurry back to prepare for her race. *God, please help them not be too upset and to see the positives...*

She stripped off her warm up jacket, collected her gloves, helmet, and goggles, and went to the marshalling area, taking deep breaths to stop the nerves from stealing her concentration. *God, thanks for today and this opportunity. Help me to honor You.*

The first quarterfinal held a previous world champion and girls who had beaten her times before. Holly swallowed the dryness in her mouth. This competition was such high caliber. She glanced at the other girls in her quarterfinal, the second in the program. Ilse from Germany, Canada's Stacey, and Hira from Japan. She mentally ticked off their strengths: start, pace, and finish. Holly sucked in another breath, suddenly not caring about who won this first quarterfinal—she had her own race to win. She pulled her ponytail tighter, adjusted her goggles, and entered the zone.

Visualize the turns. Feel God's presence and peace. Whatever happened, she was loved.

It was time. She shook out her legs and moved onto the track, briefly waving at the crowd as her name was called. There was no time to search the crowd for family and friends. She'd drawn the first position, closest to the inside. She needed to capitalize on it, go out really strong.

"Go to the start." The crowd quietened.

She skated to the pale blue line and anchored her foot, waiting.

"Ready…"

Her stomach clenched.

BANG!

Skate, skate, skate, skate, skate! With maximum energy, Holly propelled her body forward, surging into the first bend. Carefully maneuvering her body, she kept her eyes forward, her peripheral vision scanning for other competitors as she straightened up to push through the straight. So far, so good. She leaned into the next curve, hand outstretched. The roar of the crowd dimmed. Blood pulsed in her ears, blades scraped, breath exhaled. Round the next curve, then the next, she powered on. Her legs were feeling really good today, her knee really strong. The bell for the final lap; the end was in sight. Steady, maintain speed and balance. She rounded the last bend, sprinted to the end, crossing the line—first!

Yes! *Thanks, God.* As she skated slowly around the track, heart still beating frantically, Holly looked up and scanned the crowd. An Australian flag was waving high up in the stands, held by some familiar faces. She smiled and waved, relaxing further. Her mum blew her a kiss, and Holly responded in kind. Brent sat with her parents and brother and gave her the thumbs-up. And surprise, surprise—next to him were Bree and Mike! Holly's smile stretched wider.

"Clear the ice."

Holly gave a final wave, then collected her guards and went to prepare for the semifinals. Coach Chan gave her a hug and further instructions regarding her fellow competitors. Holly cycled slowly on the stationary bike, taking mental notes as she kept her muscles warm. It was one of those rare times when her legs felt like they'd "arrived" and could take whatever came today. Sometimes her legs just felt heavy or unresponsive, so to feel like this today was excellent. *Thanks, God.* The rest of the women's five hundred quarters finished, followed by the men's thousand heats. There was a quick break while they resurfaced the ice, then they were back on.

Holly's nerves bit. Irina, the Russian she'd been warned about earlier, was in this race, as were Korea's Su Kim and an Italian competitor—World Cup top ten, each of them.

"Go to the start." They moved from the secondary line to the starting line. She assumed position, hoping the shake in her legs wouldn't prevent a strong start. She tensed and relaxed.

"Ready." Her leg felt twitchy from anticipation. She moved.

BANG BANG!

"False start."

Faint mutters of disgust from the other girls. No-one liked false starts. They exacerbated the stress and tension. The nervous energy filling the Pacific Coliseum ramped up another gear.

Holly exhaled and skated back with the others to prepare again. She was allowed one false start; the next meant disqualification. She moved back into position. *God, help me not break again. Fill me with Your peace.*

"Ready." She anchored her foot, waiting, waiting…

BANG!

Skate, skate, skate, skate. Irina exploded into the lead, Holly scooting in behind. Coach Chan had said Irina's strong starts made her almost invincible, so Holly would have to take her soon or settle for second. Holly attempted to maneuver around her on the first corner, going slightly wide. She gritted her teeth. She'd lost some precious momentum. Now to make up for it. She increased her pace, arms pumping before the next bend loomed. Round she slid, still second. Now Su Kim was trying to make a move and came in close to Holly. Two laps completed, it was still Russia, Australia, Korea, and Italy. Then, in an attempt to move past, Su Kim seemed to slip before recovering, just as the Italian girl stumbled and went careening off to the boards.

Stay up. Holly sucked in another breath. She only needed to cross in the first two to be in the final. Three laps down. The intensity of the evening was starting to wear on her, and she concentrated on her breathing, on staying smooth. Her body knew what to do; it just needed to keep doing it. The bell sounded. One lap to go. Two bends. There appeared no way to get round Irina, so Holly decided to wait. There was no point crashing out and missing the final. The last bend, then the scramble as they crossed the finish line. She glanced up at the scoreboard and sighed in relief. Second, but she'd qualified for final A, and that was all that mattered.

Final A! The Games final! Her dream was so close. *Thank You, God.*

Breathing hard, she searched out her supporters, who continued to wave the Aussie flag high. She waved again before skating off to find Coach Chan and prepare for the final. With less than an hour to go, she really needed to focus now. In her race, she was up against Irina, Min Weng, and Kelsey from America. The Chinese girl was the favorite and current world champ, Kelsey had won at Turin four years ago, Irina was a World Cup powerhouse, and then there was Holly.

Holly closed her eyes as she stretched and concentrated on her breathing, fighting to keep the nerves at bay. *Help me focus on You, God.* Slowly, verses from Philippians seeped into her memory. She exhaled. Instead of being anxious, she needed to pray, to thank God, which brought the peace that would guard her heart and mind. The truth of this hit her again. *Thank You, God, for this opportunity. Thanks for Your goodness and grace. Thank You for Brent, my family and friends, for Coach Chan, and all the others who have helped me get here.*

Her heart began to relax. She stretched some more, visualizing the race ahead. Final B was held first, with the competitors who'd come third and fourth in the semis racing to determine their standings. She didn't really pay attention, only noticing a Canadian girl had won it. That much was obvious from the intense cheering from the stands. Then it was her turn.

She skated onto the ice. Waved when her name was called.

"Go to the start."

She lined up in fourth position. The others had all skated faster than she in the semis, so she needed an amazing start to be in it at all. *God, use me for Your purposes. Have Your way today.*

"Ready."

She breathed in, then out slowly, waiting, waiting. Her thudding heartbeat seemed to break the silence of the arena.

BANG!

Like an arrow, she skated hard and fast, straight into second position behind Min, Holly's lightning quick reflexes taking Irina by surprise. They rounded the second bend. Arm outstretched, Holly maintained her balance. Then push, push, push, she skated hard before slowing minimally for the next curve. Min was handling the lead really well, not allowing a spare millimeter for someone to move past.

Holly heard Irina right on her tail, Kelsey a second off the lead. But Min was so strong. Holly looked for a way to move past, but any extra movement out wide would take precious milliseconds she didn't have. Completing the second lap, she concentrated on her speed, inching closer. One foot carefully positioned in front of the other, a slide round the bend, then it was another stride and another before the third lap was complete. Kelsey was now out of it unless something disastrous happened. Irina was angling, looking for the smallest chink in Holly's defenses. The bell rang. They completed the penultimate turn.

Skate, skate, skate, skate. The final bend. Min flashed round a fraction wider than on her previous turns. Now!

Holly's body instinctively leapt into the tiny space and she completed the turn on the inside, just missing the marker, her momentum and the shorter turn taking her to the lead. From the corner of her eye she could see the red skinsuit desperately lunging, and Holly pushed forward, skate out, crossing the line in a blur with Min. The deafening roar of the crowd assured her it was one of the most spectacular finishes they'd seen that night. And hey, wherever she'd come, she'd done her best…

Holly put her hands on her knees, sucking in air, her mouth tasting of metal and blood. She coasted, waiting for the scoreboard to light up while vaguely noticing some Aussie flags being waved madly and Coach Chan jumping up and down.

And there it was: she'd won.

Holly was the champion!

She clapped a hand over her mouth, checked the scoreboard again, and skated slowly to the side. Coach Chan was screaming. "You did it, Holly! You win! You win!"

Holly needed more oxygen. This felt unreal. But as Coach Chan hugged her tight, then wrapped an Australian flag around her shoulders, and her fellow competitors congratulated her amidst the crowd's continuing cheers, certainty settled in her heart. She *was* the champion. *Thank You, God!*

Delight bubbled up into laughter, escaping in happy tears as the biggest smile of her life threatened to split her face. She skated a final lap, past a beaming Coach Mathieson and the cheering Canadian squad members she'd trained with, past the screaming crowds, waving at the Australian flags in the stands. This was surreal. Waving a final time, she left the ice, collecting her blade guards, then made her way backstage where, after congratulating the other girls, she finally sat down. *Wow, God. Is this for real?*

But the congratulations continued, the attendants

applauding her even as she removed her gloves, neck guard, and skates, and changed into her team tracksuit. She gulped a bottle of water.

"Holly! You were so awesome!"

Holly smiled up at where Tori was waving from the sidelines. "It feels like a dream."

She noticed Min's tight expression, and wondered if she felt it more like a nightmare.

"Ladies, we have the flower ceremony now. Please come this way."

Holly stood and followed the attendant back onto the ice, which now held a strip of red carpet and a dais. The medals would be awarded the following night at B.C. Place in front of a huge crowd, but for now, tonight's accomplishment would be acknowledged by the people whose roars swelled around her. This was so amazing, so humbling. She waved and smiled at the audience applauding their achievements. Several TV cameras were in front of them, and the officials guided them to their respective positions.

The announcer began, *"Mesdames et Messieurs…"* then introduced Irina, who'd placed third. Standing on the dais, she received her small bouquet of flowers, then was followed by Min. Now it was Holly's turn.

"Ladies and gentlemen, the champion for the ladies five hundred meter short track, representing Australia, is Holly Travers."

She climbed to the highest position, euphoria filling every cell in her body, and waved both arms as the crowd responded in kind. Maybe they liked to see an underdog win. Only one other Australian had received a gold medal in short track, back in Salt Lake City in 2002 when Stephen Bradbury, the last man standing after a spectacular crash, had crossed the line first.

First.

Tears blurred. *Lord, thank You, thank You, thank You.*

She took a moment to breathe it in before encouraging the others to join her on the top step for a photo. She looked out at the crowd, searching desperately for Brent and her family...

"Come on. This way." An official motioned them to the side, so Holly waved to the crowd one last time, posed for another photo, then made her way off the ice for the final time that night.

"Hey, Holly!" Looking up, she saw her parents, flanked by Brent and Ben, leaning over the railing. Oh... Her eyes filled again. "Congratulations!"

"Thanks, Dad!" She stood on tiptoe and grabbed their hands.

"Holly, you're amazing!" Brent's eyes held her as warmly as a hug. "So proud of you, sweetheart."

"I can't believe it!" She laughed. "I can't believe this is happening."

"We'll catch up with you later."

She nodded before being ushered away by officials, then sighed as warm contentment filled her being. That proud look on their faces made all of this worthwhile.

"I'm shocked! I still can't believe it. The other skaters are just so good, so to be the one sitting here talking to you all is just amazing."

Brent settled back with a grin, loving the animated way Holly talked to the reporters in the media room. The room was crammed with TV, print, and radio journalists, and Holly's obvious joy and delight in her unexpected win seemed to be winning them over.

She'd been so awesome. At times it had seemed hard to believe the woman skimming across the ice in that dark green skinsuit was his Holly. The composure and grace she'd displayed on the ice was still evident now as she answered questions from the disappointed Chinese media, who'd apparently expected a gold medal to crown their World Cup aspirations.

Holly nodded gently. "Min is an absolutely outstanding competitor. I feel very privileged and honored to even be in a final with her."

Warmth flowed through Brent's chest. Holly's humility had this crowd eating out of her hand. Had she really studied health science? She could probably lecture on media relations the way she was going.

"Miss Travers," another person began, "your result today seems almost miraculous after your terrible accident in November. How do you account for this amazing turnaround?"

Holly nodded, then leaned closer to the microphone. "I do consider it a miracle. My accident in Marquette was really challenging. I'd just had my first World Cup win, then to be injured like that—to be honest, I truly doubted whether I'd ever make it here. But in some ways, I think that time off proved a necessary reminder that I am more than just my sport. For way too long I've measured my worth based on my results, which led to a sense of near constant agitation where my circumstances dictated my emotional wellbeing."

She cleared her throat, took a sip of water. "Time off helped me see I'm more than my performance, and my family, friends, coaches, and faith really helped me to relax and realize that whatever happened, I would still be okay. I think that helped me to overcome my fear of not performing well so I could have peace and just have fun today." Joy lit up her face. "I never dreamed I'd be having this much fun."

Laughter rippled around the room.

Another hand waved. She smiled. "Hi, Ken."

Brent leaned forward to catch a dark-haired man in his fifties grinning broadly. "Holly, congratulations from everyone in Australia! You must feel on top of the world."

"From Down Under to top of the world, huh?" She laughed.

"It's been such a long road, and there've been many times when I've needed reminding to 'stay up,' so yes, it's nice to win."

She didn't know Brent was here, did she? That comment about staying up… Brent glanced at Drew, his reporter friend who'd smuggled him in, but Drew was as transfixed as everyone else, watching Holly shine in her moment in the sun.

Another hand. "Can you tell us what was going through your mind just before the final?"

Holly nodded. "I was trying to relax, trying not to worry—I'm way too good at that. I prayed and committed the race to God, and then just focused on trying to get the best possible start." She smiled. "I knew I needed a good start to be in it at all."

"So are you saying God helped you win?"

Brent frowned at the reporter's sneering tone.

Holly remained composed. "I'm saying God helped me stay calm and focused and able to do my best. But you know, I don't think He's too concerned about whether or not I win. He's more concerned about the state of my heart. And I'm so thankful that I've found that peace so I could have fun and skate freely, using the skills I've learned from my awesome coaches, and do my best today. I just love skating, you know?"

Brent could've stood and cheered. She was disarming even the hardest nosed journalist.

"Holly, we understand you have a few Canadian connections?"

Holly took another swig of water. "I was an exchange student in Toronto years ago, I learned to skate there, I've spent some time in the past year training in Calgary, and I have a number of very good Canadian friends, so yes, I'm a big fan of this country."

Drew threw him a sly look and stood. Uh oh. "Rumors suggest one of them is a very, very good friend."

She blushed. "Yes, there is a very special friend, yes, he's

Canadian, and no, I don't want to talk about it anymore tonight." She patted her stomach. "I'm really hungry."

There was laughter before another voice asked, "Will you talk more about it tomorrow?"

Holly laughed. "Maybe."

The official sitting at the table conferred briefly with Holly and nodded. "As Miss Travers has pointed out, she needs food, and we still have some other business to take care of, so we will resume things again tomorrow."

Holly smiled again. "Thanks, everyone."

Brent thought he heard a few murmured *you're welcome*s from the media nearby before people finished scribbling notes and collecting their recording devices and headed to the door. He pulled his baseball cap tighter, slouching deeper in his seat as various reporters he knew walked past. Tonight was supposed to be about Holly's success, not anything else.

Drew leaned over. "Happy now?"

"I owe you one."

"Exclusive interview with you two?"

"I don't owe you that much."

Drew laughed, gathered his coat, and stood.

Brent's attention switched back to the front, where Holly was standing near the exit. He had to catch her.

He rose and moved swiftly past the press of bodies, not caring anymore if he was recognized. He reached her just as the official swung the door open. "Hey, Holls."

Holly turned, her long ponytail swinging, eyes wide with surprise. "Brent! How long have you been here for?"

"Long enough to see a media star being born." He drew near, wrapped his arms around her, felt her shoulders relax. "You were so awesome tonight, Holly."

She pulled back to gaze at him, her eyes soft with that happy contentment he loved to see. He leaned down and kissed her. This felt so right...

A photographer's flash filled the room. Brent pulled back with a sigh and turned.

"Brent! Can you tell us about you and Holly?"

With a brief glance at Holly, Brent shook his head. "I'm sorry, that's personal. Let's concentrate on Holly's achievements tonight."

Drew stepped closer, grinning. "Any truth to the rumor that you taught Holly to skate?"

"Maybe, but everything you've seen tonight is due to Holly's hard work."

"And my coaches," Holly chimed in. Brent wrapped his arm around her.

The other reporter shoved his microphone closer. "How do you feel about Holly's victory tonight?"

"She's done fantastically well. To achieve what she has after all she's faced shows her guts, grit, and grace. I'm incredibly proud of Holly, and so, so pleased to see her rewarded." He turned to her. "Holly is an inspiration to me and to many."

Holly's features grew soft, her gaze melding with his in a deep look that really made him wish he could tell her, show her, the depths of his admiration. He ushered her to a corner where he could grab a moment's privacy amid the media storm. "How are you feeling?"

"I'm a little tired, but okay. This is just crazy." She glanced around with a smile. "Good crazy though." She shook her head. "I still can't believe it."

"You earned it. You deserve it." He kissed her. "I'm so proud of you, Holly. I wish I could come celebrate with you tonight."

Holly bit her lip and looked down. "Yeah, me too. But I suppose you gotta sleep. Maybe I can catch you after the game tomorrow night?"

"Holly, we need to go." The official looked weary.

Brent reluctantly released her. "You mean after your gold medal ceremony?"

"Oh! Yeah." Holly opened her eyes wider. "Wow." She quickly kissed him before turning to the official, who seemed anxious now. "Okay, I'm ready."

"I love you, Wonder Woman," he called as she was ushered away.

Holly glanced back a final time, her smile pure joy. "I love you too!"

The doors swung closed, and she was lost from sight.

As Brent traveled back to the athletes' village, his emotions tumbled and turned. Thrilled Holly had won, it was hard to swallow his disappointment at missing her celebrations. Sure, she had family and friends and teammates to party with, but he wanted to be there too, soaking in her joyful presence, watching her face light up, hearing her voice, that gurgly laughter he loved. Still, he was here at these Games with a job to do. He swallowed. He just hoped his team could emulate Holly's success.

olly yawned. Three hours' sleep wasn't nearly enough but was all she'd been able to manage before the interviews had started again super early this morning. Several North American east coast breakfast shows had interviewed her already. This was number four.

"Holly, would you like a coffee?"

How about more sleep? She managed a smile and nodded as the CBC reporter ran over a few questions Holly could expect from the Toronto broadcasters. Thank God this wasn't her normal. Much more would drive her insane.

The coffee arrived, and she sipped it carefully, the heat radiating through her. Vancouver had finally decided to get cold overnight, and every bit of warmth was welcome.

"Okay, and we're live in five, four, three..." The reporter pointed, and Holly smiled at the camera like she'd been instructed. *Smile. Keep calm and carry on.*

Ten minutes later, the reporter was collecting her earpiece but still shaking her head. "So you really are the girlfriend of Brent Karlsson? I can't believe it."

Neither could anyone else, apparently. The identity of her

"special friend" had surprised people as much as her winning gold had done. She sighed. More of what Brent had warned her about. It had been such a lovely surprise to see him last night—to see that proud look in his eyes, to feel his arms around her, a protective cloak from the insanity surrounding her. For a few seconds she'd been able to relax, to have some sense of normalcy.

After the drug testing and the media circus, it had been nice to celebrate with her family and friends and some teammates at her parents' hotel. But as other Aussie tourists and media found out, the night had stretched on far longer than she'd wanted. The interviews kept going—apparently she was ripe fodder for the current affairs shows back home. Her phone kept beeping new congratulatory messages. Then, when she arrived back at her apartment, she'd discovered another hundred emails demanding attention, including one from the Prime Minister's office.

She yawned again. Today's top priority would have to be taking a moment to read her Bible and get her heart connected with God. Even though this craziness was what she'd hoped and dreamed and prayed about for so many years, she needed to stay grounded in what really mattered, in the One who had made her paths straight. She smiled. *Thanks, God.*

A GOLD MEDAL.

Gold.

Not silver or bronze, but *gold*.

Holly stood behind the giant curtain at B.C. Place, excitement coursing through her body. She wanted to sing or shout—maybe even dance. She, Holly Travers, from humble, hard-working Wollongong, Australia, was getting a gold medal tonight. Dressed in her bright yellow podium jacket and dark green pants, Holly listened to the music from the province being showcased tonight. It was Prince Edward Island's turn, and they'd even included a song from the *Anne of Green Gables* musical. She grinned. How amazing that of all the provinces showcased, tonight's was the one place she'd dreamed about visiting for years. Maybe she and Brent could go one day.

Brent. She bit her lip. She'd tried to watch some of his game but couldn't watch for long—only enough to know this game wasn't going as easily as others had. *Lord, keep him safe, help him play well...*

"Ladies, it's time."

The officials guided them to their places, then she watched as the Mounties took the flags out before finally entering the stadium to cheers and cowbells. From where Holly stood behind the podium, the atmosphere was amazing. Somewhere out there were her family, coach, and teammates.

Irina was presented with her bronze medal and flowers to loud cheers from the crowd. Holly clapped hard as the music swelled. Then the silver medal was given to Min to similar applause. Holly clapped, still amazed that she'd beaten the favorite.

Then the announcer spoke in French before repeating it in English: "Ladies and gentlemen, the champion and gold medalist, representing Australia, Holly Travers."

Holly stepped up to the highest point of the podium to deafening cheers. The official came forward, Holly bent down, and they placed the large gold medal around her neck.

"Congratulations."

"Thank you." This smile was never coming off. She was handed her bunch of flowers, and she waved once again to the crowd. The announcer introduced Australia's national anthem, and as the opening strains began, Holly felt the tears prickle. *Thank You, God. Thank You!*

She lustily sang the words of "Advance Australia Fair," watching as the Australian flag lifted to the highest place in the room. When it was done, she raised her arms up high for a final wave at the crowd as confetti shot everywhere. Holly and her fellow medal winners posed for photos, then the officials led the way off stage to a special reserved section, where she found her parents and brother and they could watch the rest of the ceremony. Medalists from other sports were awarded, including live crosses to the Whistler medal ceremonies, where various snowboarding medalists were honored. The announcer's deep voice boomed. "And now, it's time to party with Hedley!"

Ben squeezed her shoulders as pop music filled the arena. "You having fun?"

"This is just amazing. I even feel like dancing!"

He laughed. "Come on, then, let's see you boogie."

After the concert, Mr. Pearson and some other Australian team officials came up to shake Holly's hand. "Holly, we have a special team party arranged. Are you ready to go?"

"Oh!" She shot a quick glance at her parents. "Um, sure, I guess."

He frowned slightly. "Is there a problem?"

"No, no. I have some friends downtown who are waiting for me."

He nodded and patted her arm. "Then let's go so you can see them before midnight."

Midnight? "Okay."

The team party was fun. Various teammates, officials, team sponsors, and media filled the Sheraton's function room. She had more interviews and photos and then was finally released to head a few blocks across town to her parents' hotel. The streets were filled with excited tourists, athletes, and spectators, the buildings alive with Games-themed signage and displays. By the time she arrived, word had obviously passed around that Australia's newest gold medal winner was here, because the hotel was swarming with green and gold and Aussie flags. An Australian news crew was there, their reporter rushing up with a big microphone and camera in place. "And here's Australia's newest golden girl, Holly Travers! Tell us, Holly, how do you feel?"

After answering some questions and promising a more extensive interview soon, Holly was finally freed to enter the function room. It was déjà vu.

"Here she is!" Bree's shriek of excitement caused all heads to turn their way, and suddenly Holly was in the midst of a heavy mass of adulation. "Holly!" Bree hurried to give her a big squeeze. "You did it! Well done. We always knew you could."

"I still can't believe it." Holly's cheeks were getting sore from all the smiling.

"Believe it, Holl. It's hanging around your neck." Mike grinned. "Hey, look who's here."

Brent made his way to her side, and she gave him a hug. "How'd your game go?"

Brent sighed. "We won. Just. But let's not think about that right now—let's see Wonder Woman's gold medal."

She passed the medal around for inspection.

"It's pretty big." Bree fingered the wavy design.

"So, do you think you'll get your face on a postage stamp now?" her dad asked. "That's what Australia Post does for its gold medal winners."

She felt dazed. Was this really happening? "I don't know. Maybe."

"And doesn't Australia's Games Committee give money to its medal winners?" Ben laughed. "Maybe you'll finally get another sponsor. Who knows, you might even get rich, Holl."

"Ha! Not rich. Just able to finally start paying Mum and Dad back."

"Let's hope you get a medal too," Bree said to her brother.

Brent groaned. "No pressure, is there?"

"None at all." Mike slapped him on the back.

Holly posed for photos, signed autographs, and listened as

the cheers of *Aussie, Aussie, Aussie! Oi! Oi! Oi!* filled the room before she finally got the chance to sit and relax. Food was ordered, and a bottle of champagne was brought over to their table. Holly had a small sip as toasts were made. Several Australian team members and other officials also made their presence felt. Holly grinned. There was nothing like a gold medal to help you feel the love.

As the night progressed, Holly felt her energy levels drop rapidly, so after making plans for the next day, then their farewells, she and Brent caught another taxi back to the athletes' village. Once there, she could breathe a little easier, although the medal round her neck still drew plenty of attention. Brent walked her back to her room, giving her a lingering kiss good-bye. "I love you, my superstar. I'm so proud of you."

"And I love you." She stayed by the open door, watching as he descended the stairs out of view. Sighing happily, she closed the door, chatting briefly with Jess and Coach Chan before heading to her room. She sat on the bed, took the medal off, and looked at it with awe. *God, I know it's You who made all this possible.* Tears welled. *Thanks so much for all the support I've been given. Mum and Dad, Ben, Brent, Bree, my coaches...They've all done so much—and I'm the one who gets this.*

After a hot shower, she put on her pajamas, and moved to her laptop.

Hi all,

Well, just in case you haven't seen the news by now—I won! Who said miracles can't happen? I've attached a photo of the medal so you have proof. It felt truly surreal to be standing on top of the podium, green and gold among a sea of red and white, but amid all the celebrations, I hope you know it's you and your support and encouragement and prayers that have helped this dream come true. I can't wait to talk with you personally one day soon and let you hold this hunk of gold (it's

really heavy!), but first I have World Championships in Bulgaria, where I hope to crack the top ten. I wanted you to know how much I appreciate you, and that I'm only too aware of how good and gracious God is and how this medal really is ours. Please pray for Brent (my boyfriend, who is playing for Canada in ice hockey). He plays for the gold on Sunday. The pressure on them is unreal!
Going to bed now—love you all. God bless you, Holly

Group email finally written, she clambered into bed and drifted off to sleep.

AFTER THE INTENSITY of the past days, to have a day when they could just be—just relax and hold each other, stare at the snow-capped mountains from the lounge while they drank coffee and ate McDonalds—was simply perfect. Brent had another session on the ice later, but this time together, lying on a couch with Holly in his arms, was what he'd longed for. Would be what he missed when, after the Games, their competitions took them opposite directions once more.

Holly squeezed his arm. "Tell me where you play after all this."

"We go to Minnesota, then Chicago, then we're back home for a while."

"And when are you next in Calgary?" She yawned.

"Middle of March, I think. Can't wait to see you then."

"It'll be a little longer, I'm afraid. I'm in Bulgaria for the World Championships around then."

He sighed. Would this conflict of schedules never end?

"But I'll be finished after that, so maybe I could come visit you in Detroit again."

"Did you enjoy your time there?"

She snuggled closer. "It's not exactly Wollongong, but it had some pluses."

"Oh yeah?" He twirled a strand of her hair around his finger. "Such as?"

"Well, the last time I was there I visited this cute Tudor house."

"Did you now?"

"Uh huh. Someone's done some great renovations, but it still needs a little decorating."

"Maybe some paintings on the wall. Maybe a painting of a Japanese garden."

Her breath hitched. She tipped her head to look at him. "Brent, don't say things like that. Not unless you mean them."

"Holly, honey. Didn't you read my card?"

She nodded.

"Future-to-be? That's you. At least, I hope it's you. I mean, I hope *you* think it's you." Why did this not sound as smooth as when he'd practiced it in his head? "I guess what I'm trying to say is, Holly, can you see a future with me?"

Her eyes widened. She licked her bottom lip.

Why was she hesitating?

"Coach Chan is worried I'd have trained all this time for nothing," she said slowly. "I know I can't compete forever, but I wouldn't want to give it up just yet."

"No one is asking you to."

"Then what *are* you asking?"

Her gaze, so direct, pushed inside him and stole his words. How could he explain the magnitude of his admiration and wonder for this woman? But he still sensed the moment wasn't right—and he didn't want her coach interrupting halfway through. Best he pull back, talk generalities.

"I'm saying one day I want us to live in the same city, live in the same house, share the same last name."

"Really?"

He nodded. "I know it can't be soon—you have your training in Calgary, and I'm based in Detroit—but surely God hasn't brought us this far for us to say it's too hard."

"He's big enough to make a way."

"And loves us enough to help us find it."

She nodded, settling in as she lay back against his chest. They stayed in their little cocoon of calm, peace easing around them like a warm blanket.

After some time, Holly stirred again. "Do you want kids?"

He blinked. Wow. "One day. Not any time soon." He felt her shoulders relax and smiled. "Bree has taken the heat off me there."

"God bless Bree," she said with a sleepy-sounding chuckle.

Yes, God bless his twin, whose persistence had granted him the woman of his dreams.

CHAPTER 30

Brent's nerves made their presence felt from the moment he opened his eyes. Throughout his morning jog, breakfast, and warm-ups, the pulsing excitement thrummed. Some polls had suggested that as long as Canada won the gold medal, it would satisfy the nation—that a hockey gold counted for more than the total gold medal haul. While that really diminished the massive achievements of the many Canadian athletes here, he couldn't escape the fact that as ice hockey's originator, Canada believed they were the gold's rightful recipients—and that there'd be hell to pay should they lose.

He finished taping his stick, taking a moment to reread the verses he'd scrawled on the end. Romans 5:3-4. *We rejoice in our sufferings, knowing that suffering produces endurance, and endurance produces character, and character produces hope.* He nodded, allowing the words to sink into his soul. Maybe he was naturally more of a sunny side up kinda guy, but today he'd need to remember this all the more. This was a joy. Whatever happened, he'd rejoice. Win or lose, whatever trial might come, he'd rejoice. Because God was with him, helping him endure so he'd be mature in God and lack nothing.

The game began at 12:15 p.m. Even here in the locker room they could hear the crowd's screams of *go Canada go*. Brent concentrated on the final instructions before the guys high-fived and made their way down the tunnel to the ice.

The stands roared, a shaking mass of red and white. Brent breathed deep, glancing down at the maple leaf on his uniform.

The opening face-off went to Canada. Brent watched from the bench as the players' hits and grit instantly showed no one was going to score easily today. Today was a grudge match, as the shots on goal proved, both goalkeepers making great saves.

"Twenty-five!"

Brent clambered over the side, glad to be in the rush. He chased the puck to the USA blueline, scooped it up, and passed to Erik. He neatly swooped around the goal in his classic smooth move before someone knocked the puck from him. Brent raced over and checked the American into the boards, seized the puck and shot toward goal. The goalie deflected it but didn't hold on, allowing Erik another chance. He stretched out and tipped it in. Score!

One goal up.

"Man, you were beasting it out there," Erik shouted as the crowd went crazy. They skated off to fist-bump down the bench before taking a seat. Brent glanced up at the Jumbotron showing a replay. Sweet. Twelve minutes in and they were in the lead.

A penalty a couple of minutes later, more big hits and big shots, then it was the end of the first period. The locker room filled with restrained anticipation and wise words from the coaching staff. "Remember to breathe, take it one play at a time, and above all, think positive."

Recharged, regrouped, they headed back out.

The second period began. Applying the pressure, the Canadians made numerous shots on goal, but the defense proved too strong. Brent's shifts were hard, physical, but no slip in concentration was permissible. Nobody would knock the puck from his stick. Today was the day to win.

His shift done, he skated back, sucking down a Gatorade, watching as they called yet another penalty. Desperation made skaters careless. Nobody wanted to be sitting in the penalty box watching the opposition score on a man advantage. Fortunately, they killed that penalty and normal play resumed. Moments later, the horn blared. Another goal to Canada. As the crowd leapt to its feet, Brent watched the replay. Very cool. The successful line skated in for their kudos. "Awesome!" He fist bumped the three forwards and two of Jai's Blackhawk teammates who'd been on that shift. "Great job."

The crowd's enthusiasm level dropped markedly a couple of minutes later when USA scored. And despite the strong, consistent pressure, Canada couldn't capitalize, and the second period ended with the score 2-1.

~

"How are you doing, Holly?"

Holly attempted a smile for Tori. "I feel like throwing up. This game is so intense."

"It's pretty awesome, eh?"

"It's amazing." Holly glanced around the vast crowd of athletes watching on the big screen in the athletes' village. Each time Brent's name or number was mentioned, she felt eyes in the crowd seeking her reaction, but as the commentary team pointed out, he was doing a great job, giving it his all. *Lord, keep him safe...*

~

Nervous energy radiated around the room. Coach Reynolds spoke calmly, encouraging them, then it was time for the third period. The US applied further pressure on the Canadian goalie, but he was Superman. Brent tried a slapshot but was blocked. Everyone was playing cleanly, with no room for error. They were going to win. He could feel it. The stadium could feel it. This was Canada's gold. There was only a minute left. Brent watched from the bench as the US took out their goaltender for an extra attacker. Thirty seconds left. An American forward grabbed the puck, shot toward goal, where it was deflected and punched in for another goal.

No!

Siren. End of third period. Score: 2-2

The crowd fell silent. Now they'd need overtime.

Brent followed his teammates back to the locker room, passing his stick to the crew before sitting in front of his stall as the coach and captain gave encouragement. "Come on. We know someone will score for us. Don't give up."

The nerves of the day washed away. Stay up. Rejoice. Brent felt peace steal into his soul, and he joined the chorus of encouragement filling the room. "Let's do it."

Back on the ice, the tension was chainsaw-worthy thick. It was do or die.

In these games, overtime lasted twenty minutes, and if no one scored, it would go to a shoot-out. Canada, then the USA tried to score, but between goalies blocking and shots going wide, no result was forthcoming. Brent completed his shift, then skated back to sit down. He glanced up at the stadium pulsating with patriotism. "Go, Canada, go! Go, Canada, go!"

Seven minutes down. Brent sat on the edge of his seat, heart hammering as he watched his teammates scrabble the puck loose from the boards. A shot, rebound, another shot, save. Their goalie was amazing, leaping and diving to protect the net.

Another scuffle along the boards. A desperate yell, and the puck was shot to their center, who shot—

And scored! The horn blared.

Canada had won!

Brent jumped over the boards, joining the rest of his teammates in a wild scrum in the corner. He flung himself on the pile of bodies, exhausted, exuberant, elated.

The crowd went ballistic, banging on the plexiglass, screaming their approval.

Brent hugged and hollered and let off the energy, glad the weight of expectation was finally off their shoulders. He gazed up into the massive crowd, recalling a similar frenzy surrounding last year's Cup win.

The handshake line was tough. Each American face wore bitter disappointment, and it was hard to contain his own joy and make his *good game* sound genuine.

The next hour was a blur. Red carpet rolled out. The medal ceremony began. Each Canadian team member had his name read aloud to huge cheers. Brent ducked his head for a medal and some flowers. He picked up the medal and looked at it. Yep. Big, wavy, and gold, just like Holly's. His heart swelled with joy and pride.

The medals and bouquets were handed out, then it was time for the national anthem. The crowd rose, and the strains of "O Canada" filled the stadium. Brent sang his heart out, standing on home soil, having helped win a gold medal for his country, watching as the maple leaf flag was raised highest. *Thank You, God, for my home, for my family, for this opportunity, for Your goodness, for Holly.* The anthem finished, a show of fireworks loudly screamed through the arena, then the official ceremony concluded.

Back in the dressing room, the Canadian Prime Minister came in and congratulated them, yet another memory to store up and think about later. It was a real honor to meet him and shake his hand, even if Brent felt a little smelly and sweaty. Most of the guys were leaving soon to find family and friends before they had to head back for their NHL commitments, but they took time once more to congratulate each other, thank the coaches and team staff. The hard work and sacrifice had been thoroughly worth it.

∼

B.C. Place held thousands of excited spectators awaiting the closing ceremony. Holly waited to enter, dressed in her Australian team uniform, her gold medal prominently displayed, camera at the ready. The past hour had been a rush of excited congratulations as she and her teammates watched the final moments of the hockey game before racing over here to be ready to enter with the rest of the Australian contingent.

"You okay, Holly?" Holly nodded at Coach Chan, who frowned slightly. "Make sure you rest later, yes?"

Holly nodded again. She'd rest later, but there was plenty of celebrating to do before that would happen.

They ushered the Australian team through the tunnel, then out into the enclosed stadium. Holly lingered near the entrance as the crowd roared and hundreds of cameras flashed. The closing ceremony was far more relaxed than its opening twin. There were none of the rigid rules about the athletes entering in national groups. Tonight was showing everyone how sport could unite the world. Athletes from different countries hugged, took photos, high-fived the volunteers who stood patiently on the sidelines, directing the flow of pedestrians. Holly kept her eyes peeled, looking for Brent.

∼

AFTER RUSHED GOODBYES to his teammates, Brent sped over to B.C. Place, determined not to miss the closing ceremony. Some of the other guys couldn't get away, but as this might be his only Games, and having already missed the opening ceremony, he wasn't gonna miss this one. Even before he entered the arena, the roar from the crowd was amazing.

With his new gold medal swinging from his neck, he received congratulations from lots of people, but he really only had eyes for one person: the woman dressed in green with a gold medal, waiting for him.

"Hey, Holly."

Her face lit. "Congratulations! I'm so proud of you!" She placed her hands on either side of his face and kissed him thoroughly. After a huge hug, they entered the arena hand in hand, to the spectators' cheers and applause.

He took a moment to soak in his country's celebration, snapped a few photos of the crowd and of himself and Holly, grins in place, gold medals in hand.

They found their seats, and she snuggled next to him, his hand in both of hers. "That was a totally amazing game. I was so nervous—I don't know how you kept it together. How are you feeling?"

"Pretty fantastic right now." He leaned closer, touching her medal. "I bet this is how you felt a little while ago."

There it was, that glorious smile. "It's pretty special."

"Not as special as this." He took his time kissing her, enjoying the fact she was enjoying him too. She eventually pulled back with a slight gasp. Yeah, he knew how that felt. He gave her another quick kiss on the nose. "You're very special."

She grinned before leaning in to have a closer look at his official uniform jacket. "Ooh. Cute moose. I like your hat, too."

"We're going to have to teach you the lingo."

"It's okay." She smirked. "I know you really call it a beanie."

He snickered at her word for his toque and held her hand as they watched the official speeches and performers. Out came the floats—the blow-up beaver and Mounties, even hockey player performers, which made Holly laugh. "This reminds me of the Sydney Games, where they brought out all our national stereotypes. We had a blow-up koala, a giant thong—"

"A giant what?"

She glanced up at him. "Oh! I forgot. I mean a giant flip flop, jandal, sandal?" She laughed again. "I don't know what you guys call it." Her cheeks heated. "But not *that*."

He chuckled and tucked her closer as they watched more of the performances, dances, music, speeches. "You want to go soon?" He kissed the back of her hand. "It looks like the party will keep going for a while, but our families are probably waiting."

She nodded. "Let's go."

A short time later, they were in a taxi, watching as the shimmer of fireworks bounced through the night air. "Beautiful." Holly craned her neck to get a better look. "I love fireworks, but not when they're too close—they're too noisy."

"Speaking of close…" He wrapped an arm around her, pulling her nearer. "While I've got you all to myself…" He pulled her in for a kiss, one that soon ignited heat. Fortunately, the taxi driver was too busy to notice as he worked to avoid exuberant revelers who still filled the streets.

Holly pulled away with a sigh as the taxi halted again to let more red-and-white-clad people cross the street. "This is unbelievable! So many people." Holly squeezed his hand. "You're like a national hero."

"Not me. Our last goal scorer, he'll be the hero. Which is good, because I just want to be with my girl." He studied her again. The glowing heart motto displayed everywhere at the Games? He could totally relate.

Revelers surrounded the taxi, so many they'd be here for a while. Their families were waiting. He'd be leaving tomorrow—wouldn't see her for another month.

He blinked. Maybe this was the right time after all.

He drew her closer, shifted so the taxi driver couldn't see. "Holly?"

"Yes?" Her smile was so sweet.

"Do you remember what you said to me after Bree's wedding?"

A small frown furrowed her brow. "No. That seems like ages ago now."

"We were talking about Bree and Mike getting married, and I said something about them needing to be best friends."

Her eyes widened. "Oh."

"In fact, I asked you a certain question."

"You really have an amazing memory." Her lips lifted on one side.

"I asked if you wanted to get married. Remember?"

She shivered and nodded.

He angled closer still. "I remember, because you asked me if that was an offer." He whispered into her ear, "I should've said yes."

Holly released a gasp.

His palms were getting sweaty with what he had to say. He took a deep breath. "I said something about wanting to get married at the right time, to the right girl…"

Her eyes were huge.

"I've found the right girl, and Holly, I think it's the right time." He touched her cheek. "You know I love you."

"Yes."

"And I dare to believe that you love me too."

"You know I do," she whispered.

"Holly, would you marry me?"

"Truly?"

"For better or worse, richer or poorer, in sickness and in health, I'm yours. Please say you'll be mine," he added hoarsely.

"Oh, Brent." Her fingers traced his cheek, her eyes holding tenderness and truth. "Of course I will."

He lowered his mouth to hers, and their lips met in a sacred promise, a moment of utter sweetness he'd never forget. His heart wanted to sing, to dance, to burst, but he settled for exploring the softness of her mouth, relishing her taste, her scent, her tiny sighs that thrilled him and made him wonder just how soon they could make a wedding work.

A cough came from the front seat, drawing him away. "Excuse me, sir. We're almost there," the taxi driver interrupted with a grin. "And you might want to put your medal away for a moment. It might get a little crazy otherwise." He asked for an autograph, and Brent obliged.

Brent turned to Holly. "You up for running the gauntlet?" She nodded, and he pushed open the door, sliding across the vinyl seat to help Holly out. He held her hand and kept his head low, and they walked fast through the crush, entering the hotel unscathed. A quick check with the wide-eyed receptionist, then they were directed to a small function room where their families awaited.

THE CRUSH of humanity outside was almost matched by the number of people in here. Holly's heart was full as she hugged her special secret to herself, even as she searched and found face after familiar face.

"They're here!" At Bree's shout, they were swamped with hugs, kisses, and handshakes.

"Congrats, man." Mike bear-hugged Brent. "You did us proud."

"Mate, great game." Ben slapped Brent on the shoulder.

"You two! I'm so proud of you." Bree hugged them both. She guided them to their large round table, reserved for their extended families.

The next hour was filled with love, laughter, and food! Delicious food, and Holly didn't worry once about the calories. She finished her dessert and licked her spoon. Yum. This chocolate gateau should be outlawed, it was so good. Would anyone notice if she licked the plate?

"Babe." She glanced up to see Brent's grin as he shook his head.

"I'm enjoying myself." She smiled, put the plate down reluctantly, and sat back in her chair, looking around the table. It was the first time all members of their immediate families were together, and it was lovely to watch the interaction between everyone.

Ben and Dean were sharing stories about their recent snowboarding adventures. Laura, Bree, and Pam Karlsson discussed babies, while Holly's mother played peekaboo with Dean and Laura's toddler, Ronan, probably picturing when she'd finally be a grandma. The patriarchs of each family were having an animated discussion with Mike and Brent about the game, Brent reliving each moment and the others sharing their perspectives from the crowd.

Holly sighed happily. This was how family should be. She sipped her tea. How wonderful that they all got on so well—another of God's blessings.

Brent leaned over, a smile in his blue-green eyes. "How are you doing?"

"I'm fine. I'm more than fine. This is just so good."

"Yeah, it is, isn't it?" He gazed around at the happy people, then turned back to Holly. "You let me know when you want to go, okay? I don't want you too tired, otherwise I'll have to carry you all the way home."

She laughed. "Worried your muscles can't take it?" He grinned, and her heart fluttered again. "Aren't you tired yet? It's been such a big day."

"I'm good. I can sleep on the plane tomorrow. We can't do this then."

They shared a smile that blocked the world out. There was only Brent, his eyes full of laughter, his heart full of love, his lips full of—

"Holly, Brent." Rob Karlsson's voice stole their attention as he stood and cleared his throat. "I think I speak on behalf of everyone here when I say how proud we are of you both. Holly, your win this week was nothing short of phenomenal. When I think back to the young girl who came and stayed with us all those years ago, someone who first learned to ice skate when staying with us…"

He paused and cleared his throat again. Holly blinked against tears. How sweet.

"And now," Rob continued, "look at you, the gold medal champion. Congratulations, Holly. Let's raise our glasses, to Holly."

Holly's cheeks grew hot as she looked around at her well-wishers. "Thank you."

"Now, Brent. Today was a remarkable accomplishment—for you, your team, and for Canada. We're all so proud of you. Bravo. To Brent!"

Holly lifted her glass, caught Brent's gaze, and smiled. Her heart was full.

"Ah, you two are just so sweet. Anything you want to say, brother dear?" Bree asked.

Brent shot Holly a glance, squeezed her fingers. "Shall we tell them?" he murmured.

"I don't think we'll have a better chance."

He nodded and turned to Bree. "Thank you, everyone, for all your support over the years. I know it hasn't always been easy, but I know I speak for Holly as well when I say we appreciate you from the bottom of our hearts. And I'd also like to give a special shout out to dearest Breanna, for encouraging me to pursue Holly—"

"Ha! You can tell me I was right."

"—and yes, you were right. I've finally found the woman I wish to make my wife. And wonder of wonders, she's agreed."

"What?"

Holly laughed at the expressions around the table. Mum and Pam's delight, Dad's nod of satisfaction, Mike and Ben's shared smirks, Bree's open-mouthed astonishment.

"When? When did this happen? I can't *believe* you kept this from me, Holly Travers."

"It's still rather new."

"How new?"

Holly shot Brent a smile. "Like, in-the-taxi-coming-here new."

"Are you serious?" Bree's face held horror as she looked at her brother. "You proposed in a taxi?"

Brent lifted Holly's hand and kissed it. "Holly once told me she's not into clichés, so I had to avoid fancy restaurants, beaches, and romantic fireside scenes. It was tough, so taxi it was."

"And Holly, you truly don't mind?" Bree seemed genuinely concerned.

"Bree, I care about the man, not about how he proposes."

Holly turned to study Brent, this patient, godly, strong, and handsome man, who truly had pursued her, even when she'd pushed him away. "I want to marry you. The sooner the better."

His eyes lit. "After the World Championships?"

She laughed. "Next month might be a little too soon."

"Oh, how wonderful!" Bree clapped her hands. "Looks like we've got another wedding to plan."

Holly turned to Brent, her smile the faintest expression of

the joy overflowing from her heart. This man, this wonderful
unexpected gift of a man, proof of God's most miraculous
blessings.

EPILOGUE

Four months later

The soft, warm breeze caressed her face and danced with strands of hair. Holly took a deep breath of the salty sea air and exhaled. *Lord, You are so amazing. Thanks so much for all this beauty. Thanks for Your love. Thanks for Your goodness. Thanks for blessing me so much. Thank You, thank You, thank You.*

She opened her eyes and watched the billowing clouds ascend the heavens as the sun began its farewell to another day in a swirl of pink and gold. Seagulls called as they swooped in the sky before ducking to the ocean to dance in the foamy breaks of the Pacific Ocean. The sun sank lower, suffusing the scene with rose and amber, a glorious golden masterpiece painted by the ultimate Master.

Peace.

"It's just so lovely." Holly took a deep breath and sighed in contentment. "I think it gets better every day."

An arm snaked around her waist, and she felt warm lips on her ear, then kisses trailing heat down her neck to her shoulder. "I agree about the lovely…and the getting better."

Brent's fingers slid to her bikini strap. Breath caught as shivers melded with internal fire. She leaned back, tilting her head up so she could see her husband's face. Her husband! He smiled down at her, that sexy, joy-filled smile that made her insides wobble.

What a whirlwind these past four months had been. World Championships: she'd placed fifth for the five hundred—what a miraculous season she'd been gifted! Then a flight home to Wollongong for some time with family before packing up and travelling to Toronto for the christening of Bree and Mike's gorgeous son. And then the wedding Pam and Bree had planned. Brent's playoff run had finished in May, permitting a mid-June wedding attended by all their family, friends, and teammates and a late-June honeymoon before they'd travel back to Detroit and start their respective training. Her plan was to rejoin the Calgary crew, but she was open to change. Coach Mathieson had mentioned the possibility of training in Montreal or in Milwaukee. She and Brent would figure it out, and in the meantime, they'd enjoy the thrill of reconnecting whenever possible.

She shivered.

"You okay?"

"More than okay."

He smiled, leaned down and kissed her. "So, a honeymoon on a tropical island isn't too clichéd for you?"

She laughed. "Let's see. A handsome husband, gorgeous weather, waves so I can boogie board, delicious seafood, and a private beach and villa like this?" She waved at the sumptuous grounds. "I've really struggled these past few days, Brent. Really struggled."

He grinned and turned her around, hooking his hands

behind her back. "I've noticed how difficult things have been for you, and honey, I consider it my husbandly duty to try and improve matters as much as possible."

His eyes darkened and his lips were on hers, sweetly possessive. He took his time, kissing her thoroughly in that way they'd discovered now they no longer needed to keep their passion restrained. One hand pulled her closer while the other slid under her hair as the glorious sunset faded into insignificance.

She drew back in order to breathe, placing her hand on his lean, hard, muscular chest. "Wow."

He looked as dazed as she. "You certainly know how to kiss, Holly Karlsson." He gave a sly smile. "And do other things…"

As he raised his eyebrows, she felt her cheeks heat. "You're so bad."

"Not bad. Actually, now we're married I believe our pastors would say it's all good."

"Oh, it's definitely all good."

He chuckled, then bent to kiss her throat. "I love being here with you."

She leaned back and traced the five interlocked rings tattooed over his heart, five rings that matched those now decorating her right ankle. "Come on, admit it. You love seeing me wear whatever new thing comes out of that purple bag Bree packed for each night, don't you?"

"I love what you wear"—his smile curled higher—"but I love *you* even more."

She wrapped her arms around his neck. "I really love you too."

She stared into his eyes. They seemed intensely blue today. "You have amazing eyes. They seem to change color." She blinked to try and draw herself out of her dreamy state.

He chuckled. "Sweetheart, you're just amazing."

She pressed her body closer to his and kissed his jaw, smiling at his intake of breath. "But Brent, I'm a little worried…"

His brow furrowed. "What?"

"I'm afraid…" She pressed closer and leaned up on tiptoes and whispered in his ear. "I've got nothing new left to wear."

He made a low noise in his throat and swung her up into his arms, his eyes darkening. "I think I'll manage."

She laughed as he carried her back to their villa. "I'm sure you will." She smiled. "Babe."

THE END

Check out Checked Impressions, the next book in the Original Six contemporary romance series

A NOTE FROM THE AUTHOR

Thank you for reading *Love on Ice*, the second book in my new contemporary romance series, which combines my love of ice hockey with appreciation for the cities that comprised the NHL's original six teams. This story began way back in 2010 when I saw an Australian female athlete walk into the closing ceremony of the Vancouver Winter Olympics holding hands with a North American male athlete, and I wondered how two elite athletes from opposite sides of the world could meet, let alone sustain a relationship. Despite my best efforts, I couldn't find out, so *Love on Ice* became 'their' story. I hoped you've enjoyed!

Please make sure you check out the other books in the Original Six hockey romance series, a sweet & swoony, slightly sporty Christian contemporary romance series.

The Breakup Project
Checked Impressions
Hearts and Goals
Big Apple Atonement

Reviews help other readers find new-to-them authors, so if you can spare a moment to write a quick review at Goodreads / your place of purchase, I'd be very grateful.

I'd love for you to check out my other books and to sign up for my newsletter at www.carolynmillerauthor.com where you can be the first to learn all my book and contest news, and discover more behind-the-book details and photos.

A huge thank you to the following people for their encouragement and eagle eyes: Iola Goulton (who helped shape my original *Love on Ice* into something readable!), Ros, Sylvia, Jacqueline, Caitlin, Abby, Rebekah, Nancy, Brittany, Susan, Kaye, Bea & Becky - I appreciate you all so much! Big thanks to the ladies in my Facebook group, Carolyn's Books & Friends, for all your support in helping promote my books.

Please turn the page for a peek at *Checked Impressions*, the next in the Original Six hockey romance series.

CHECKED IMPRESSIONS

"And now, may I draw your attention to what I consider the room's finest work if you, like me, are someone who appreciates that first impressions need not last forever."

Allison Davis smiled at her silly pun and moved to the opposite wall, the museum's visitors shifting their stance to follow like sunflowers following the light. Sure, some might prefer Monet and his haystacks or waterlilies or Renoir and his ballerinas, but Georges Seurat's *A Sunday Afternoon on the Island of La Grande Jatte* was one of her very favorite pieces in all of the Institute's hundreds of thousands of artworks. Something about the light and optical effects called to her, inspiring her with her own work.

"At first glance it may seem easy to dismiss this painting as simply a collection of tiny dots. But this is one of the most iconic paintings of the Post-Impressionism period and demonstrates pointillism at its best. Here we see many figures that represent different walks of life as they gather on the banks of the Seine river on a Sunday afternoon. The use of color makes the artwork seem very alive, yet there is a stillness, with everyone bar a handful of figures facing the Seine on the left. There are things to ponder here: Why is the boater seated on the left so much larger compared to the couple sitting next to him? Why is the girl in white facing the viewer? And why did Seurat paint this?"

She watched as the museum's visitors paused, their faces melding into expressions of what she hoped was interest and not simply a desire to know how many more minutes remained of her tour on this sticky, stifling late-August day.

"Pointillism is a technique of painting in tiny dots, often in complementary colors. Avant-garde artists in the late nineteenth century would consider complementary colors of the color wheel and how to use them to create effect. Complementary colors include yellow and purple, blue and orange, and red and green. When placed next to each other, they have a flickering quality, the pigments almost having a shimmer to them. Pointillism was a completely different approach to painting."

She talked more about the significance of the shadows, Seurat's process, and related works by Seurat, including how this piece perfectly complemented his previous painting, *Bathers at Asnières*, which hung in the National Gallery of London. "Because of Seurat's technique and subject matter, this is one of those paintings that we can return to again and again and not grow tired, because there is always something else to find that is unusual, that makes you think differently about what you thought you knew. To my mind, this is the sign of a great painting, and it's one of the reasons I love the Impressionist movement so much."

She turned to the small group of art enthusiasts signed up for this free tour. "And that concludes our tour of the highlights of the Art Institute. I trust you have enjoyed our time today and will take the opportunity to visit the other galleries, filled with many other treasures. I'm happy to answer any questions you may have, but once again, thank you for your visit, and we hope you will enjoy your time in the Windy City."

No questions—save for directions to the nearest restrooms —and after a couple of murmured thanks, she was released to slowly wander back to the staffroom. Some days she still pinched herself to think she got to work here. She truly had one of the best jobs in the world.

She paused to look at Renoir's dancers, taking a moment to let the colors and shapes infuse her senses, then, conscious that Dave, the security guard, was looking at her with his usual tilted-head expression of concern, she smiled and moved on. How people could not stop and linger at every painting amazed her, and while most people who worked here were art enthusiasts, some, she knew, viewed this as merely a way to make a living.

Wryness tweaked her lips. Few artists made much of a living from their work, as she well knew. Oh, to be successful…

She pushed open the staffroom door and was greeted by the scent of stale coffee and perspiration.

Selina Wemble looked up and waved her hands in a fanning motion. "It's so hot today."

Allie nodded, swiping a strand of damp dark-blonde hair behind her ears. Selina had always made her tongue-tied, ever since that first encounter years ago when the polished, pretty art student had met her as they waited for a job interview, casting a look over Allie's Target ensemble with a raised brow and curled lip. Of course, Allie's lack of chattiness hadn't helped matters either and had possibly been construed as unfriendly. In reality, it stemmed more from a case of literally not having the words to say. Allie's lips curved to one side. It seemed some first impressions could last.

She moved to the fridge to collect her now-chilled eco-bottle of water, briefly resting it against her forehead. These late-summer days in Chicago often reached a point of heated heaviness that even the building's stone walls did little to alleviate. Thank goodness her two shifts of tour guiding were done for the day and she could now relax into the administrivia of her role as part of the Public Relations and Learning team. Pity whoever had to run the kids' talk this afternoon with the intern. Given this late stage of school vacation, that was bound to be lots of fun.

"How was the highlights tour?" Selina asked.

"G-good."

Selina glanced at her and shrugged. Surely she was used to Allie's lack of detailed replies by now. "Did you see the roster changes?"

"No."

Trepidation slowed Allie's progress to the whiteboard, where a glance at the roster changes evoked an inward groan. Kids' talk. Again. On hot days like today, the air-conditioned Art Institute was a favorite place to take kids who were *really* ready to finish vacation and go back to school. She loved kids, and as the favorite aunt to two nephews, kids seemed to like her in return, but seriously. Again? A protest formed in her brain, then faltered. Was there any point in complaint? She released a sigh instead.

"Hey, it'll be better than last time, I'm sure."

Allie hitched an eyebrow. If Selina was so sure, then why hadn't she volunteered?

"Don't look at me like that. I would've volunteered, but I'm working on the wording for the new promotion, and—"

Allie's chest grew tight, thumping sense from the rest of the words. That was supposed to be hers! Myra Fordley had as good as *promised* that promotion to her. "Since when?" she said carefully.

"Oh." Selina's face instantly melded into contrition. "Myra just wanted someone who could articulate things very quickly, and, well, we all know that's not exactly your forte, so I volunteered."

Volunteered? Or snatched it from her? She didn't buy Selina's innocent act for a second.

She glanced at Myra's office door. Shut. Which meant she was either busy or not in.

"Myra's out, if that's what you're wondering."

As per Myra's usual policy on sticky summer days, when she managed to either be elsewhere or what she liked to call "developing strategic partnerships with other museums," which Allie strongly suspected was code for visiting the nearby Holborne Museum—more specifically, its director of programming, Neil Blanchard.

Tension gnarled knots in her stomach. Her scruples protested Myra's frequent visits to a very married man and made her vacillate between wanting to tell Neil's wife and praying that God would reveal it another way. As he wasn't on staff here, it wasn't something that broke protocol as far as the museum's policies, but the morality of it had sunk her opinion of Myra very low. And the knowledge that Myra *knew* that Allie knew, due to an unintended and most unfortunate glimpse of their encounter in a supplies closet, and that Myra was so far unwilling to say anything, had led to a strange standoff between them in which Allie was reluctant to make the first move. This news was just the latest in a series of events that showed the power games some people liked to play. Selina had learned from the best.

"Look, I'm sorry, Allie. I did try to tell her you were the best for the job—"

Sure she had.

"—but I'm afraid it can't be changed now. And those kids will be here soon, and Taylah really needs someone to keep her in line so she doesn't spend the whole time on her phone."

Anger rose in Allie's chest. Taylah, the summer intern who

had impressed Myra so much in the interview, then done virtually nothing since. Allie couldn't help but be glad that Taylah's time with them was nearing its close and she wouldn't have to work with her again.

"And it makes sense that the person with the most patience is the one who deals with the kids now," Selina continued.

And the one least likely to complain.

"I'm sorry, Allie." Selina shrugged. "I wish I could help."

Swap then, Allie longed to say. But the words stayed stubbornly locked inside, refusing to spill from her mouth.

The phone rang, and Selina snatched it up. "Hello, Public Relations and Learning, this is Selina speaking."

The door opened, and Taylah entered in her usual sliding manner that denoted the level of enthusiasm she seemed to hold for her role, the bouncy gait of those first few days most definitely gone. No point trying to impress Myra now.

Taylah glanced at the whiteboard and made a face. "Kids? Again?"

Looked like Allie would have to dredge up enthusiasm for the two of them. She forced a smile. "I'm sure it will go really well."

There. Why could she talk so smoothly in moments when it didn't matter, but other times she might as well have her piano on her chest?

"At least it's with you," Taylah muttered, casting a glance at Selina, who was still talking animatedly on the phone, waving a hand and flashing a grin like she was a celebrity filmed for a TV telethon event. "I think Selina thinks I'm an idiot."

Selina likely thought the same about Allie. Shaking off the thought, she motioned to the cupboard where the kids' activities were stored. "We'd better go and get things set up."

"It's still half an hour until we're due to start."

"By now, you know what some parents are like—that they like to get there early."

"Yeah. They're happy for some free babysitting."

Which Allie didn't mind—not if it meant their children were being encouraged to explore their God-given creativity and dream larger than their immediate worlds. Unless, of course, their kids were bratty. Then it was a problem when the parents weren't there.

She moved to the cupboard and began withdrawing the papers she'd printed off last week along with the stencils and pencils in their respective baskets. Best not to think about the injustices but on the positives. She was blessed with this job. Blessed to work so close to home. Blessed with family, friends, and a great church nearby.

Allie pushed her hair behind her ears, slid her glasses up her nose, and internally braced for the next hour. This would go well. God was still on the throne, even if it felt He'd dropped the ball on a few things lately. He'd straighten her paths. Eventually. She could do this, just like she'd done it a hundred times before.

Beckoning for Taylah to follow, she moved to the creative learning space and began setting up. Sure enough, families soon started gathering, waiting for the magic moment when the rope enclosing the creative learning space would drop and the children were welcomed in.

Twenty minutes later, given the space was heaving with kids already, Allie signaled for Taylah to place the *Sorry, we're at full capacity* placard on the easel nearby and judged it best to begin. She drew in a deep breath.

"Good afternoon, boys and girls, moms, dads, and caregivers. We're so glad you've decided to join us today for the Summer Art Spaces series here at the Institute. My name is Allie"—so much easier for the kids to say than Allison—"and this is my colleague, Taylah"—Taylah grinned and gave a wave—"and we hope you'll enjoy yourself this afternoon as we learn about the wonderful French artist Claude Monet."

She glanced around at the faces lifted expectantly to her—

apart from one man, glasses and baseball cap on, looking at his phone already. Indignation rose in her chest. "I would like to take this opportunity to encourage parents and caregivers to explore the world of art with their children, to be in *this* moment right now."

Did that sound too sharp? Taylah's raised brow suggested yes. Allie softened her tone. The man still hadn't looked up. Oh well.

She went on to explain the usual procedures, then began the brief slideshow of some of the Institute's more famous treasures, some of which she'd also covered in the painting tour this morning. But kids liked the treasure hunting aspect, and after this, they would be released to go and explore with their families using the special kid-friendly "treasure maps" of the Institute, a concept she'd designed and implemented two years ago, for which Myra had taken the credit.

Speaking of being in the moment, she needed to forget the injustices of the past and focus on right now. She completed her spiel and outlined instructions for the activity, unable to ignore the baseball cap man who *still* hadn't looked up.

"Are there any questions?" She glanced around, saw a small boy put up his hand. "Yes?"

"Yeah, I want to know something."

From the edge of her vision, she noticed the man finally lift his gaze to pay attention. "Yes, what is it?"

"Why do you talk so weird?"

She blinked, all thought of further talk draining away in a special two-for-one deal of frustration and mortification. For that man looked exactly like none other than her favorite hockey player of all time, the one whom she'd had a crush on since she'd first learned of his existence: the left wing for Chicago's top line, the fastest man on ice.

Jai Mullins.

Guilt shoved Jai's phone into his back pocket as a titter raced around the room. He became aware that the woman who'd been speaking—a classy looking, glasses-wearing blonde with a mesmerizing, musical voice—had stopped and was staring at him.

Then he heard that other voice again. "You talk funny."

Air pushed past his gritted teeth. Kyle. Why on earth had he agreed to help Kat out today by looking after her son? "I'm sorry," he muttered, pushing forward. He sure hoped nobody here recognized him. He squatted until he could eye his nephew. "You are being rude. You need to apologize to the nice lady."

"Don't want to."

And this was why he'd agreed to help Kat out. Imagine having to put up with this disrespect every day. "Now, or we're leaving."

Kyle crossed his arms, his bottom lip projecting.

Jai sighed, glanced up with an apologetic smile for the museum employee. "Sorry."

She shook her head, her gaze not meeting his, her cheeks bright pink. The knife in his gut twisted harder. He placed a firm hand on Kyle's shoulder and gently squeezed.

"Sorry," Kyle muttered.

Jai wasn't sure if the museum employee had heard, but he'd take it as apology enough. It might be the first time Kyle had apologized this week. Or was it this month?

A glance up showed the woman had retreated to the farthest corner, as if determined to get away from both Mullins men, and her college-aged associate was now leading things.

Man. Now he *really* needed to apologize. He glanced at Kyle, who had started coloring a picture Jai thought might have been a haystack. Maybe the kid could manage a minute of scribbling unsupervised while Jai made up for Kyle's rudeness.

A glance around the room revealed that nobody here had recognized him—he'd put that down to the cap and glasses—so he shifted through the groups of chatting parents to where the art guide talked with a round-cheeked, redheaded woman. He listened and was once again caught by the musical cadences of the art guide's voice. Then she pivoted and caught his gaze, and her mouth fell open as her words stumbled to a halt.

"Hey, I'm sorry for interrupting. Please continue." He made a small gesture to reinforce his words.

"Oh, it's nothing," the plump redhead said before giving him a quick scan and a smile that rippled uncertainty within. She moved on, leaving him standing awkwardly with the lady his nephew had embarrassed. His glance drifted down past her tiny cross necklace to her name badge: Allie.

She cleared her throat, and his gaze snapped up to her now-narrowed eyes as he suddenly realized how his gaze might be construed. No. No, no. "Allie, uh, I mean, Miss, I wasn't, um, checking you out—"

Her jaw dropped.

Kill me now. Could he insult her any further? "I mean, not that you're not pretty, because you are, and I, well, it's obvious that"—he shared his nephew's gift for rudeness. He took a breath and tried again. "I'm really—"

"E-excuse me," she murmured, then hurried away.

Whoa. He'd really outdone himself there.

"Uncle Jai?"

He spun to hurry to his nephew. It'd be better for all concerned if the people here didn't know his identity. It wouldn't help the team PR if they knew their left wing was prone to random spurts of obnoxiousness. "Hey, buddy. What have you got there?"

"It's a farm."

"Uh huh." Looked more like a squiggled mess, but okay. Good to have the clarification.

He snuck another glance at Allie, whose gaze instantly shifted away before she removed her glasses and wiped them. That was hardly surprising, seeing it was so hot in here, the collection of smaller and larger bodies contributing to a heat that probably rivaled outside, like the building's air-conditioning had given up.

The noise level seemed to ramp up, echoing off the hard interiors, and another sneaked peek revealed a wash of what looked like fatigue on Allie's face as her smile dropped and dimmed and her fingers clutched the back of a chair.

He gestured to the other girl—her name tag read Taylah—and murmured, "Is your boss okay?"

"She's not my boss, but"—her gaze flicked to Allie—"she doesn't look great, does she?"

No. Allie was wiping her forehead. "Is there something you can do to help?" he suggested, eyebrows raised.

"Oh. Maybe. I dunno."

He figured Allie wouldn't necessarily appreciate any more of his verbal vomitings, so any further approach from him might need to be avoided. "How much longer is the session supposed to go for?"

"Um, I dunno. Maybe ten minutes?"

"We started early, so we're probably close to being finished anyway. Maybe you could start cleaning up. That might help people get the idea that it's time to go."

"Oh. Yeah. Okay." Her eyes lit. "Then we all could go, right?"

Good to see that her desire to finish didn't stem from self-interest at all. "Right."

"It's so hot, isn't it?" she said, waving a hand to fan herself.

He nodded. "Should I help you start clearing up?"

"Aren't you nice?"

Or maybe still feeling a little guilty. He shrugged. "Maybe you should make an announcement that you're ending soon."

"Oh, yeah. Good idea." She batted her eyelashes.

He stepped back, turned to help Kyle clean up. Please. As if he needed to encourage some clueless college girl to start flirting with him. "Kyle, it's time to go. Let's clean up now."

"But Uncle Jai—"

"Now."

Kyle's bottom lip protruded, but Jai was made of stronger stuff than his sister and ignored it. He grew aware of Allie moving closer, asking Taylah what she was doing.

"Oh, it's so hot we thought it might be best to finish up."

A beat, then, "I beg your pardon?"

Jai glanced at her. Smiled. "This has been great!" He clapped Kyle on the shoulder. "You've enjoyed yourself, haven't you, buddy?"

"Yeah."

Okay, so that disconsolate tone wasn't exactly selling enthusiasm. Judging from the twitch of her lips, Allie might even agree. He needed to try harder. "I'm sure the other parents here would agree. You do a great job of helping kids learn more about art."

Her lips pressed together, and she nodded, her eyes still not meeting his. What had he said now?

She murmured something to Taylah, then shifted to the middle of the room and clapped her hands. "Thank you, everyone," she said in that slow and gracious way she had. "We trust you enjoyed yourselves today. If you can assist us by helping to put the pencils and crayons back in their baskets, that would be most appreciated. And if you would like to explore more of the treasures of the Art Institute, then you may wish to obtain a special treasure map from Taylah near the exit."

"Treasure?" Kyle exclaimed at the top of his lungs. "I want some treasure."

"They don't mean real treasure, buddy," Jai said in a voice he thought was for his nephew's ears only. Apparently, it was heard by Allie, even above the sounds of rushing and exiting by people who seemed to have ignored her request for help to clean up in their haste to leave.

"This *is* real t-treasure," she said, her brown-eyed gaze finally meeting his before dropping to his nephew. "But I'm afraid it's only for looking at, not for keeping. Unless, of course, you want to buy a postcard at the gift shop."

"Aww," Kyle complained in that high-pitched whiney sound that always got Jai's goat.

"Perhaps it's t-time for you to take your son home," she said, thrusting a paper at him, then hurrying away with a murmured, "He seems very t-tired."

His son?

Kyle glanced up at him, then back at Allie. "Hey, lady, Uncle Jai is my *uncle*, not my dad. Are you stupid or something?"

God, help me. Jai hoisted Kyle to his feet and hurried after the woman, whose look of shock mirrored the sensation stealing across his chest. Yeah, he couldn't believe Kyle's rudeness either. "I'm so sorry. He's not, well, he's just—"

How to explain his nephew had neither the smarts nor the filtering wherewithal to understand let alone practice good manners. Or that his sister seemed to have long given up her understanding of what parenting actually was.

Allie shook her head, and he thought he glimpsed tears before she turned away and began stacking chairs.

Man. What a fail this had been. He blew out a breath, crouched to Kyle's eye level, and muttered, "You have been very rude to this poor lady. You need to say sorry."

"Why?"

He had a feeling that reasoning with an eight-year-old was not going to succeed. He'd never been one for giving up though. "Because you've hurt her feelings and made her cry."

"Are you crying?" Kyle said in his too-loud voice.

She paused in her chair-stacking endeavor, facing away from him as the noise that had dropped at Kyle's comment picked up into whispers again.

As much as Jai wanted to help with stacking chairs, knew a desire to help her any way he could, he figured the best way he could help her was probably to leave with big-mouth Kyle as quickly as he could. And ensure that neither of them ever visited this art museum again.

Purchase your copy of Checked Impressions today.

ABOUT THE AUTHOR

Carolyn Miller lives in the beautiful Southern Highlands of New South Wales, Australia, with her husband and four children. A long-time lover of romance, especially that of Jane Austen, Georgette Heyer and LM Montgomery, Carolyn loves to write contemporary and historical romance that draws readers into fictional worlds that show the truth of God's grace in our lives.

To find out more about Carolyn's books, and to subscribe to her newsletter, please visit www.carolynmillerauthor.com

You can also connect with her at

Winning Miss Winthrop

Miss Serena's Secret

The Making of Mrs Hale

<u>Regency Brides: Daughters of Aynsley</u>

A Hero for Miss Hatherleigh

Underestimating Miss Cecilia

Misleading Miss Verity

'Heaven and Nature Sing' from the Joy to the World Christmas
novella collection